I0718481

CARNIVAL
HILL

THE HARLEQUIN CREW SERIES

CAROLINE PECKHAM
&
SUSANNE VALENTI

This book is dedicated to Mutt.

He knows when shit is up and he knows how to pee on a motherfucker when they're down.

We love your rage and your furious, unforgiving nature all wrapped up in a tiny little fluffball package.

We love that you pee in Fox's plant pots daily, and that you will never, ever forgive him for shouting at you because HOW. DARE. HE?

And we love that, unbeknownst to Fox, you've been using his pillow to scratch your ass whenever you get the chance.

So we salute you Mutt!

CHAPTER ONE

My eyes were closed and my head was full of the sound of Otis Redding singing Sittin' On the Dock of the Bay as I imagined the feeling of the sun on my skin and my toes in the water alongside the taste of freedom on my lips.

Heaven had always been that simple for me. Laughter in the air and warm bodies close to mine while we drank stolen beers and let the tide take our troubles away with it.

So that was where I was. Out in the sun with my boys, not stuck inside this metal coffin. There wasn't dust clogging my throat and my limbs weren't screaming at me to move from being stuck here for so fucking long.

I wasn't slumped with my knees half bent and my feet screaming in pain from the stilettos I couldn't reach to unbuckle. There was no agony in my heart as fear for my boys ripped me apart and I kept replaying the last moments where I'd seen Chase before the building came down in my head.

None of that was real. It couldn't be real.

Because Otis Redding was singing the chorus and my heart felt light as I laughed.

"I dare you, little one," Chase encouraged and I groaned, throwing an

arm over my eyes as I flopped back onto the hot wooden boards of the little jetty dramatically.

"You guys pick on me because I'm the only girl," I accused, one eye cracking open as I found JJ grinning at me while he swigged on his beer.

"Not true," he said. "We pick on you because you're the bravest. Chase didn't dare anyone else because he knew we wouldn't do it."

I smirked at the idea of that and pushed up onto my elbows as I kicked my toes back and forth in the cool water.

"Really?"

"No," Maverick denied. "I'm not scared to do it."

I snorted because of course he wasn't. Rick wasn't scared to do anything.

Fox's eyes were fixed on me and he glanced around towards his house before shaking his head.

"I'll do it," he said. "I won't get in as much trouble if I get caught."

"Boo," I complained. "Then it's no fun."

I sank the last of my beer, enjoying the fuzziness it left in my head as I sprang up and looked towards Harlequin House too. Stealing the keys might be the simplest way, but as I looked back towards the fancy speedboat which Luther had just bought, I found I didn't want to go with easy. Besides, creeping into that house while Fox's scary ass daddy was home did not appeal.

"I can do it without the keys," I decided, preferring that idea to the chance of Luther catching me in the house.

"It was just a joke, pretty girl." JJ caught my hand to stop me as I set my gaze on the boat, but I just rolled my eyes.

"If I can boost a car, I can boost a boat, JJ. Besides, Luther will never even know we took it. Don't tell me you're all going to go chicken shit on me now?"

There was a clamour of protests at that suggestion and I grinned as I unbuckled my shorts and dropped them before tossing my shirt down too.

"Don't laugh," I snapped as they all stared at my stupid lilac bikini which didn't fit right anymore. "My dumb boobs keep growing and I already know it doesn't fit properly. But I tried to steal a new one from that kiosk up on Tide Street the other day and the bitch working there spotted me, so I had to run for it."

"Yeah, I was just thinking how dumb your boobs are. You look fucking terrible, beautiful," Maverick snorted and Fox punched him in the arm.

"Yeah, well it would piss you off if your dick just kept growing and growing all the damn time and you had no boxers that fit anymore," I snarked at him.

"I think JJ's having that problem right now," Chase joked and JJ cursed him out, pouncing on him and punching as they rolled across the jetty.

"Fuck you guys," I grouched, turning my attention back to the speedboat before diving into the sea and disappearing beneath the waves.

The water kissed my sun heated skin as I slipped beneath it, swimming for the boat and surfacing on the far side of it before heaving myself up and into it.

I ducked down low just in case any of Luther's men looked out and spotted me, then popped open the panel beside the wheel and started work on hot wiring this thing.

I grinned widely as the engine snarled to life and the boys all whooped in triumph as they raced to get onboard too, throwing more beers and snacks to me as Fox untethered the vessel and we were soon racing out towards the horizon with laughter colouring the air.

I stayed there on that boat with my boys laughing and the sun kissing my flesh.

I wasn't trapped here.

I wasn't finding it hard to breathe.

I wasn't going to die all alone in the dark.

I was drinking in the sunshine with a smile on my face and Otis Redding was singing again, and that's where I'd stay for as long as I could. In fact, I'd stay there forever if I had a choice in it. Because nothing good ever came of stepping out of that sunshine and back into the shadows of my reality. So I'd stay and stay and there would be love in my heart and laughter on my lips and reality couldn't catch me because our speedboat was too fast and we were gonna chase the horizon forever.

CHAPTER TWO

"**R**ogue!" I roared, clawing at the rubble, throwing lumps of huge stone away from me as I fought to dig into the depths of the destroyed Dollhouse. "Call out to me, beautiful, show me where you are."

The morning sun was beating down on my back, my shirt discarded and sweat clung to me as I gasped for water. But I wouldn't stop. I'd worked like a madman through the night trying to get to her, and I wasn't going to give up until she was back in my arms. I'd barely gotten out of the fucking place when the roof had fallen down, but by some miracle I'd made it to the balcony and dove off of it into the pool. And alright, fucking Fox and JJ had made it too. Not that I gave a shit about that.

A small, desperate voice in the back of my head kept whispering to me that Chase was in the depths of this rubble as well as my girl, and I may have hated that asshole, but somehow him dying here like this didn't seem right. He was meant to die at *my* hands, dammit.

"Here." Luther appeared, thrusting a bottle of water at me.

He was shirtless too, a mess of dust lining his tattooed chest as he worked alongside us. The whole of the Harlequin Crew were here digging and I just ignored them, keeping my distance from Fox and JJ who were working on the other side of the building along with half of the town who'd shown up to help. The fire department, police and goddamn sea rescue were here too, everyone battling to get the survivors out as soon as possible. Every time someone was pulled from the wreckage, a cry went up and my eyes went to their hair, my hopes rising only to be dashed to pieces all over again.

Where the fuck is she?

I knocked Luther's hand away from my face with the bottle in it and he grabbed hold of my arm, shoving the water into my grip. I growled, not looking at him, but chugged the water all the same, drinking every last drop and figuring it was best I didn't drop dead from thirst and heat exhaustion before I found her.

"That'll need looking at." He pointed at the wound on my arm which was clogged up with dust and dirt but I just returned to digging, throwing the water bottle back at him so it bounced off his abs.

"We'll find her, son," Luther promised and the little white and brown dog at his heels yipped like it agreed.

Luther had turned up with the mutt around half an hour after the building had gone down and it had been running back and forth between him, JJ and Fox all night, yapping and sniffing like he was as desperate as the rest of us to find Rogue. She had mentioned she'd taken in a little stray, and I wondered if this was it. The dog didn't seem to know what to make of me, but sometimes it crept closer to sniff at my heels.

Luther had been in a rage after Fox had told him Jolene had betrayed him, sold him out to fucking Shawn. His eyes had become steely and murderous, but when Fox had told him she was dead, he'd nodded and the darkness had lifted a little from his gaze. I only knew one bastard savage enough to nod satisfactorily to hear his own flesh and blood had fallen to their death alongside their husband. And that was him. She might have betrayed him, but fuck me he was coldblooded. Not that that was news to me. He hadn't even blinked when their bodies had been hauled out of the rubble around dawn. He'd just stared at the broken body of his sister for several long seconds then spat at the ground beside her and gone back to digging.

"You don't know that," I snarled at Luther, throwing a huge lump of rock behind me.

There were men working to clear anything we tossed aside so the piles never got too big, but they stood pretty far back from me because it was a fucking hazard zone.

"She's strong," Luther said firmly. "And she's smart too. She'll have found a way to-"

"Don't," I snapped at him. "Stop wasting your energy, old man, and get digging."

He nodded, moving closer to me and helping me shift the rubble. I didn't tell him to fuck off because I needed the manpower and so long as he was silent, I could tolerate him for now. For Rogue.

We worked like dogs, our hands bloody and blistered, the hours slipping by and making worry burn a hole in my chest.

Where is she?

She can't be gone.

My girl has to be here somewhere.

I'd spent too long living in a world without Rogue Easton in it and I didn't want to go back to it.

Panic was desperately trying to set in, but if I fell apart I'd be no good to her. I just wished my body was even stronger, wished I could work faster. It reminded me of the helplessness I'd felt in prison and the darkness in my soul spilled out, infecting me everywhere until my mind was nothing but a cage of my worst memories.

I focused on her, bringing her to the forefront of my mind and tearing my way back through the past until I was riding my motorcycle through town with her on the back, her arms wrapped around me and her chin on my shoulder.

"Hold on, beautiful," I called to her, taking a left turn down the street and loosing the throttle.

She whooped as I drove right over the sidewalk onto the beach and I smirked as I kicked sand all over a couple of lotioned-up lovebirds sucking each other's faces off. They yelled at us as I drove away and Rogue laughed wildly as I raced towards the vacant end of the beach where Sinners' Playground's shadow was cast across the water.

"Faster!" she cried.

I gave her what she wanted, flying along the beach and she suddenly let go of me.

"Rogue," I growled in alarm, turning my head and finding her with her arms stretched wide and her head tipped back. Her dark hair tumbled around her in the breeze and I was so captivated by her that I lost control of the damn bike.

We hit a bump and I cursed, slowing us down as much as possible as the wheels skidded out and the bike tilted sideways.

I twisted around, grabbing hold of her and pulling her off onto the sand before my motorcycle slammed down to the ground ahead of us with an angry crunch that said something had just broken.

I didn't give a shit about that though, I rolled towards Rogue in fear of her being injured, but found her laughing her damn head off, making a snow angel in the sand.

"Fucking hell," I chuckled, pushing my hand into my hair as relief swept through me.

"Is your bike okay?" She asked as she propped herself up on her elbows, looking over at it in concern.

"It'll live," I said with a shrug, reaching out to her knee which was reddening with a bruise. I rubbed my thumb over it, a pang going through me at putting her at risk. "Sorry, beautiful."

"You'll have to kiss it better," she said teasingly and I surprised her as I leaned down and pressed my mouth to it, making her suck in a small breath. She tasted like coconut and motor oil and as I leaned back and my cock started swelling, I guessed that had just become my new favourite scent.

She twirled a lock of hair around her finger, her eyes darting from me to the sea as a blush lined her cheeks. Did I cause that?

She drew the hair over her upper lip to make a moustache and pulled a face at me. "Would I make a sexy man, Rick? You could call me Roger."

I snorted a laugh, shoving her arm. Stupid ass girl. I was pretty sure I'd still want her if she was a guy though, which was saying something as I had a real fondness for tits.

I gripped the sides of my chest, pushing my pecs together to try and make some cleavage and put on the most girlish voice I could pull off. "Do I make a sexy girl, Roger baby?"

She giggled, kicking sand at me. "Yeah, I'd bang you."

I grinned darkly at that but then a shout drew my attention down the beach and I let go of my fake tits.

"Stop right there!" some busy body cop shouted and I swore, dragging Rogue to her feet.

"Oh shit," she breathed, running with me toward my bike.

I picked it up, hoping the thing wouldn't let me down as I swung my leg over the seat and Rogue jumped on the back. I turned the key in the ignition and it growled in protest, making my heart beat harder.

"Hey!" the cop shouted as I tried the ignition again.

The engine rumbled to life and I grinned, shooting away down the beach with my girl at my back and her laughter in my ear. I'd always find a way out of trouble, especially when she was involved. I was her ride or die, and today we were gonna ride, ride, ride.

"Here - here!" a fireman yelled fifty yards away and people swarmed over to help him dig. I ran with Luther at my side, my heart beating a hundred miles an hour as everyone worked together to move the bricks.

A girl's muffled shout came from somewhere in the rubble and it was too distorted for me to tell if it was Rogue's.

Fox and JJ arrived, digging furiously, working in perfect synchronisation with each other as they battled to get the girl out. They were covered in dust and dirt and blood, JJ's shirt half torn from his body while Fox's was gone completely.

A hand appeared, reaching through the bricks and a second later, a fireman lifted the girl out of a safe space which looked like it had been forged between two fallen pillars. A spill of blonde hair and a bright blue dress made my heart fall and Rosie Morgan wailed as she held onto the fireman.

"I'm alive!" she cried dramatically. "I'm aliiiive!"

"Great," I gritted out. "Put her back in," I snarled then strode off back to where I'd been working.

The little dog followed me, trotting along with determination in his stride and I glanced down at it with a frown.

"Can you smell her, boy? Where is she?"

He released a low whine, looking up at me then running away across the rubble, back and forth, back and forth before finally sitting down on a flat lump of rock and yapping loudly.

My heart beat harder and though it might have just been random, my gut told me to dig where that little pup was. The area was newly cleared, a place where the police department had been working but there was still a long way to go. I moved in front of the dog and started digging while he barked in encouragement and my hope was marginally restored.

Fox and JJ appeared, followed by Luther and I gritted my teeth as they started helping me, my brow furrowing as I set my gaze on my work and ignored them. My mind hooked on the moment I'd hauled Fox to safety after he'd nearly fallen to his death inside The Dollhouse. I wasn't even entirely sure how I'd made the decision. One second I'd been ten feet away, the next I'd been flat on my stomach dragging him outa that hole and knowing I wasn't gonna let him fall. Seemed like a mindfuck I wasn't gonna explore though.

"That's it, boys," Luther encouraged. "Just keep working together."

"Shut your mouth," I snarled. "If you're gonna talk, do it elsewhere."

"Rogue!" JJ called out as we lifted a large door between us and threw it aside. Okay so maybe it was one percent easier working with them, but that didn't mean I was any less inclined to shoot them when I was done here.

"Can you hear me, baby?!" Fox yelled. "I'm coming, just hold on."

"You know Chase is down there too, right?" I muttered. "Though I guess you don't give a shit about him anymore now he's not your little bro."

"Chase?" JJ breathed in horror as Fox stared at me like he was trying to work out if I was just messing with them.

"Me and him came here together." I shrugged.

"You did?" Luther asked in surprise.

"Yeah, we had some common business to take care of that's all."

"Chase!" JJ bellowed in alarm as he put his back into the work. "Rogue!"

"Fuck." Fox scraped a palm down his face, his terror clear as he continued digging and I clenched my jaw as I helped.

The dog yapped furiously and that was all the encouragement I needed to produce fuel for my muscles. I was either gonna find my girl somewhere here or we were digging our way into a food store which the dog wanted to raid.

I guessed I was going to find out soon enough, because I wasn't going to stop until I reached the very bottom of the devastation and found my lost girl in its depths.

CHAPTER THREE

I coughed as the dust and darkness swirled around me, my mouth unbearably dry and making my tongue swell as every piece of my body ached from the position I was stuck in.

Trapped. Alone. Unable to move and pinned beneath tons and tons of rubble while the sounds of it groaning and shifting above me filled me with fear that it might all come crashing down again.

My breaths came faster, harsher and I started to cough more as the dust lodged in my lungs and panic tried to take hold of me. I was going to die down here alone. Stuck. After I'd sworn to myself I'd never let myself become trapped in any situation ever again, here I was, literally confined to a box smaller than a coffin with no way out.

"We're going out, sugarpie. Clean yourself up. I won't have my girl looking like some freshly fucked slut for all the world to see."

Shawn yanked his dick out of me with a smirk, slapping the side of my thigh as he enjoyed the view from his knees and tugged the condom off.

I just watched him, the fuzziness in my head closing in as I turned his words around in my brain and tried to feel something about them. I was a freshly fucked slut though, wasn't I? His freshly fucked slut. That was exactly how he liked me and yet he hated it too. It was kinda hard to win in that situation.

I rolled off the bed and headed into the bathroom, turning the water on in the shower and waiting for it to heat up as I looked at myself in the mirror. Steam began to cloud my reflection, so I reached out with my finger and painted an X over each of my eyes.

My mind trailed away for a moment as I considered running. I considered running a lot. But where would I run to? I couldn't take anything with me if I ran or Shawn would hunt me down and gut me for stealing from him. So I'd be penniless and friendless and I remembered what sleeping rough tasted like.

It was a constant state of fear, the desperate need to close your eyes and the worry of what might happen when I did. It was hunger and shivering and being even more alone than I was here. Because at least here I had Shawn. And for all his faults, he kept me safe, warm and fed. Out there was a jungle built of concrete and broken dreams where desperation made monsters out of everyone and fear was a way of life.

This was better than that. I had food and running water and a man who wanted me.

This was better than that. I reminded myself of that every time I considered running and I soon forgot the idea.

I stepped into the shower and sucked in a breath between my teeth as the water burned me, but I didn't make a move to turn the dial. I wanted to burn. I needed to feel it on the outside as well as the inside. And I needed to scrub my skin clean of who I was. Or who I wasn't.

I picked up a loofa and did just that. I scrubbed and scrubbed as my skin burned and steam billowed all around the room, but I couldn't get clean. I'd never get clean.

I felt almost as hot as I had in that shower as beads of sweat trailed down my back and plastered my rainbow coloured hair to my neck.

Was the sun shining up there? Or was the sky as dark as it was down here? The lack of light was pressing in on my eyes so hard that I couldn't remember if they were open or closed anymore.

I was going to die down here.

All alone.

Poor little dead girl. I guessed fate had finally caught up to me at last.

I tried to bend my leg and reach for the straps on my stilettos for the millionth time, but my knee hit the door of the safe which had been pushed almost fully closed by the falling rubble and I couldn't raise my foot any higher.

I was all alone in the dark. Fuck, why was that so terrifying now when I'd been living that way for so long before this moment? Alone and forgotten were my standard settings. They had been for so long. But they weren't once.

"I saw her stealing from the cafe down in town," Rosie's nasally voice called to me and I rolled over in my stupid bunk bed and frowned as Mary Beth replied.

"When was this?" she demanded in a tone which told me I'd be punished if she found me.

"Earlier today," Rosie said and I slipped out of bed on silent feet, creeping to the door. I'd been about to go to sleep, but there was no fucking way I was hanging around here to get in trouble thanks to Rosie's big fat mouth. Gah, I hated that stupid twat. "I didn't want to have to tell you, but-"

I didn't have time to waste so I pulled a pair of shorts on, kicked on my combat boots, grabbed my battered skateboard and pocketed my cell, but the stupid thing had died on me and I hadn't gotten the chance to charge it yet. I only paused for two seconds to toss a glass of water onto the centre of Rosie's bed beneath her comforter. My other two roommates averted their eyes, knowing it was best to keep out of any drama around here and I was out the door and down the hall by the time Mary Beth's booming voice called for me to get my ass downstairs.

That would be a fuck no.

I shoved open the door to the boys' room and Clive cursed as he fought to cover up his pasty body with his hands. He had boxers on so I didn't know why the hell he even gave a shit, but I also had no time for that.

"Jellybeans?" I asked Jake, confirming the price this freedom would cost me as he shifted upright in his bed and shoved his window open for me.

"Always. And if you can grab me a can of Dr Pepper I'll even convince Rosie to tell Mary Beth she got confused and it wasn't you who stole anything after all."

"Fuck yes," I agreed, not wanting the details on how he'd manage that

because I was pretty sure it had something to do with him making out with her and the idea of that was too gross for words. "But in the meantime, I'm getting the hell outa here." I hopped out of the window, ignoring Clive the clinger as he called out for me to wait while he got dressed so that he could tag along. I was gonna have to punch his stupid face again soon if he didn't stop with that shit. He kept lurking around outside the bathroom whenever any of the girls were showering too and I was getting seriously sick of his crap. We weren't friends. Never had been, never would be.

I scrambled along the narrow sliver of roof outside the window then made my way to the ground, dropped my skateboard, and kicked off the asphalt at speed.

The sun was setting and I glanced up at the sky, kicking hard to move faster as I approached the house at the end of the street where Axel lived. The Harlequin gangbanger gave me the fucking creeps and I worked hard to avoid him whenever I could, but my heart sank as I spotted him out front by his car, a few other tatted up gangsters lurking around as they looked beneath the hood.

"Lookin' good, sweet thing," Axel hollered as I sped by and I called some vague greeting as a shudder slipped down my spine. That guy had 'run away' stamped all over him, but I also couldn't just tell him to go get fucked like I wanted to thanks to his Harlequin status. So I maintained the smallest amount of politeness I could get away with around him and mostly just tried to avoid him whenever I could.

With my cell dead and the night closing in, I quickly turned left at the end of the street and decided that JJ was my best bet. His house was closest, and his mom was pretty sweet when she wasn't too busy entertaining clients.

I raced down the familiar streets to his house, but just as I arrived, a guy strode up to the front door, swaggering like he thought he was the man even though he clearly had to pay for pussy if he wanted any.

I hung back as I watched JJ's mom answer the door and let him in, then I hurried 'round back and found a few pebbles to toss up at his window.

I had to throw eight of the fuckers before he finally appeared, looking bleary eyed in his boxers as he shoved the window open to look down at me.

"What are you doing here, pretty girl?" JJ called.

"Rosie told on me, so I'm on the run. I'm here for a sleepover," I said *with a grin.*

JJ cleared his throat, looking over his shoulder for a moment and the sound of his mom's moans coloured the air, letting me know why he was hesitating.

"Come on, J. You know I don't give a fuck about some sex noises, and it's not like I can go to any of the others' places."

Harlequin House was always out of the question unless Luther happened to be away which was approximately never, so I couldn't go to Fox and Maverick's and Chase would have a heart attack if I got within ten miles of his dickhead dad.

"Oh, so that's why you picked me?" JJ asked, half teasing, half frowning.

"No. I picked you because you're my favourite."

JJ grinned at that then nodded and I tossed my skateboard up for him to catch before grabbing hold of the drainpipe and scrambling up to his window.

He caught my hand and helped heave me inside and I grinned as I looked around his room. It wasn't exactly spotless, but JJ liked to keep the place clean, so the mess was more of the comic books and stolen hair products variety than there being any dirty clothes tossed about the place.

"Oh, baby, use me like you own me!" JJ's mom screamed from the room next door as the mystery man grunted like a pig.

JJ winced but I didn't give a shit. People did all kinds of things to survive in Sunset Cove.

"I was listening to some music to drown it out," JJ said, pointing to his bed where a set of headphones were plugged into an old school ghetto blaster.

I grinned at him and kicked off my boots before jumping onto his bed and patting the mattress beside me invitingly.

JJ pulled on a pair of shorts then grabbed a chair and wedged it beneath the door handle before joining me. The single bed wasn't really big enough for two, so our shoulders were jammed together and I was half crushed against the wall, but I didn't mind.

JJ offered me an earbud and I put one in while he claimed the other, the sound of Love the Way You Lie by Eminem and Rihanna reaching me and mixing with his mom's continued screams of, "You're so big, tear me apart, big boy, rip me open."

"Wow, she makes sex sound painful," I joked and JJ snorted, though his cheeks were pinking.

"I think she's stroking his ego. She told me once that all men love hearing how big their dicks are, especially if they're actually not at all. So..."

"So. Fucking. Big," his mom moaned and I giggled.

"You think he's actually got a tiny pecker then?" I whispered.

"I generally try really hard not to think about that at all."

I laughed and rearranged myself so that I was lying on my side as I tried to get more comfortable.

"Okay, so why don't we play a game?" I suggested.

"Like what?"

"Let's think up all the best ways for me to get revenge on Rosie fucking Morgan."

"You could pour water on her bed and start up those rumours about her peeing herself again."

"Already did it." I grinned and wriggled some more, still not finding enough room to get comfy. "I was thinking I could add the juice from a can of tuna to her shampoo."

"Or put dog shit inside her shoes?" JJ suggested.

"Eww, where am I getting the dog shit from?"

"I could help you find some. But it's on you to pick it up."

I shoved him as I laughed and he cursed as he fell out of the bed. My laughter filled the air just as his mom yelled, "I'm gonna come so hard all over your monster cock, big boy. Make me moan for you! Take me to the moon!"

JJ cursed while I laughed louder and he grabbed me as he got back in the bed, wrapping his arm around me and tugging me close so that my head fell against his chest as he slapped a hand down over my mouth.

"If he hears you laughing, you'll put him off his game," he hissed, looking both amused and disgusted by those words. "Or worse, he'll come in here all pissed off, looking for someone to blame for his cock failure."

I peeled his fingers from my lips and sniggered. "Will you rescue me from the pencil dick, JJ?" I asked, wrapping my leg over his waist too as we finally settled down into a comfortable position.

"Yeah, pretty girl, I'll rescue you," he promised, slowly tucking a lock

of my brunette hair behind my ear as the loud climactic sounds of his mom finishing her job rocked the damn wall. When it finally went silent, I sighed, my eyes closing as I listened to the sold thump of JJ's heart beneath my ear. "I'll always rescue you, Rogue."

I swear his voice followed me out of my memories and into the dark and a sob escaped me as reality heaved me back into its embrace.

The pain and the dark all rushed in on me as I found myself still trapped in that fucking safe. Wondering if I was destined to die down here or if anyone might really want to rescue me for once. The sound of JJ saying my name still echoed in my ears, but it couldn't be real. It was just my imagination, making me hear what I was aching for.

"Rogue!"

I sucked in a breath that made me cough but I tilted my head back all the same, because as faint and distant as that had sounded, I could have sworn it was no figment of my imagination.

"JJ?" I yelled. But it wasn't really a yell, more a croak and a cough and a sob all mixed together.

But just as I was beginning to think I had imagined it, I swear I heard someone else calling my name too and my heart began to race with the thought of it.

Could it be real? Had they come for me?

A bark pierced the air, distant but oh so familiar and I sobbed again as I tried to yell once more, but I was coughing before I even began and my voice was betraying me.

My heart thundered with the thought of them moving away without ever even knowing I was here and I started scrambling around, thumping my fists against the metal sides of the safe before finding a lump of masonry that was wedged in the almost closed door.

I grabbed it and tugged, my fingernails cracking and splitting as my whole body screamed with pain, but I refused to give up.

I yanked even harder and suddenly the piece came free, a rough scream escaping me as the movement dislodged more of the rubble and everything groaned and shifted around me, smacking against the safe and making my skull rattle from the noise.

But I kept hold of the lump of rock and as soon as I was certain I wasn't going to be crushed in here, I started banging it against the wall of the safe.

The noise made my head pound and skull throb with pain, but I wouldn't stop. I struck the metal again and again and again.

I wasn't going to die down here without putting up one hell of a fight. And if the way my heart was racing was any indication, then I was starting to believe my saviour was coming for me like he'd always promised he would.

I may have told him I didn't want rescuing but right now, I needed a white night or a dark saviour or even just a deal with a devil. Because I wasn't done with this life no matter how shitty it had been to me. And I was ready to emerge from the dark at last.

CHAPTER FOUR

The midday sun beat down on my back, baking me through until all I could feel was blinding heat, the pain in my hands and ache in my spine. I worked tirelessly with Fox, Maverick and Luther, all of us falling into this desperate, endless rhythm as we just dug through the rubble in silence. But the silence wasn't in my head. In my mind, there was a roar of noise, of fears, regrets and panic.

I should have gotten to her sooner.

I should have held onto her tighter.

We never should have come here at all.

A paramedic appeared, offering out water and checking to see if anyone needed help. Fox's right hand was fucked up, the strip of his shirt he'd wrapped around it bloody and caked in dust, but I knew he wouldn't let anyone tend to it until Rogue was back in his arms.

I'm so sorry pretty girl. I won't abandon you again. I'm coming. Just hang on, please hang on.

Luther thrust a bottle of water into each of our hands when none of us paid any attention to the paramedic's offerings. Mutt yipped and after I guzzled down half the bottle, I moved over to him and held it to his mouth.

He lapped at the water thirstily and I gave him as much as he wanted before pouring the rest over his back to keep him cool.

Fox's face was fixed in a mask of determination as I re-joined his side and kept digging. I could see the war in his eyes which he was fighting to win, because if he gave in to the fog of panic that hung around us, he'd lose it. I was battling that same war and all I could do was focus on one brick at a time as we clawed our way deeper into the devastation.

A team of Harlequins worked around us, clearing the rubble we shifted aside so it never piled up too high and I'd never been so glad to have the Crew at my back.

I thought of Chase down in the shattered building too, my friend, my fucking brother. He had no one in this world but us and I hated thinking of him dying alone, made an outcast from his family, believing none of us loved him anymore. But I did. What he'd done was terrible, but I knew where it came from with him. I knew he was just trying to hold on to the one thing life had gifted him. And that was us. Me and Fox. But he'd gone and shot himself in the foot, lost us in his stupid attempt to keep us. Now none of that mattered to me. I just needed to get him out, needed to see he was okay.

The panic was welling and I started to lose my grip as it reared up and surrounded me.

Rogue…Chase. Oh god.

Please be alive, please.

"Fox," I rasped, feeling myself slipping as I rested a hand on his arm.

"Don't JJ, just keep digging," he demanded, clearly sensing where my head was at.

"But Fox," I croaked.

"Keep fucking digging," he barked and I did.

I hadn't ever been going to stop anyway, I just had to fight back the doubts creeping in, refuse to let them take over.

I took in a few ragged breaths and met Maverick's gaze from where he stood across from me. He gave me a stiff nod of encouragement and I continued, the pain in my body starting to recede into a numbness that I wished would seep into my heart so I didn't have to face the agony of doubt clawing at it.

We worked on and on until Mutt jumped forward as we made it through a section of shattered tiles, his little nose twitching as he sniffed. Then he barked loudly again and again, wagging his tail and I shared a look with the others before we all grabbed more of the debris and started tearing through it at a furious pace.

"Rogue!" Fox bellowed.

"I'm coming for you!" Maverick roared.

"Rogue – Chase!?" I yelled and my heart all but stopped as a repetitive banging sound reached us.

"Rogue," Maverick gasped. "Dig!"

We all fell into a frenzy, shifting more and more of the debris in our determination to get beneath it. To see her, find her safe. *It has to be her. It has to be or I'll die.*

"Rogue!" I bellowed and a muffled voice called back to me.

We all froze in the same moment, listening to see if we really had heard anything or if we were all just losing our minds to the desperation of hope.

"I'm here!" Rogue shouted from somewhere beneath us and the crushing sensation in my chest lifted.

"Holy fuck, dig faster," Luther commanded.

"I'm coming, hummingbird!" Fox called, digging ferociously through the rubble.

We were all forced closer together as Rogue continued to call out to us and we were soon focusing on one small area, our shoulders knocking against each other's as we tossed tiles and bricks and mortar away from us. I clenched my teeth, my mind set on this one task and the furious intent in my muscles to pull her from the wreckage.

I'm coming, pretty girl, I'm coming.

We reached the top of an iron safe and Maverick kicked away a wooden beam resting over it as her hand reached up to us from the slightly open door at the front of it. I grabbed her fingers, squeezing tight as a flood of relief washed over me and her hands wrapped around mine, a relieved sob escaping her.

Maverick forced himself down into a gap we'd created just in front of the safe and we all worked to move the debris in front of the door before he wrenched it wide.

"I got you," he said, drawing her out of the safe into his arms and holding her against him as she sobbed in relief, her fingers curling around the back of his neck as she clung to him.

Fox and I reached for her as Mutt barked happily, wagging his tail so fast I was surprised he didn't take off like a helicopter.

"Pass her up," I begged, holding my hands out for her as Luther pulled some pipes away from them which were sliding down the rubble.

Maverick reluctantly lifted her towards us and I got hold of her, dragging her against me and feeling the soft warmth of her flesh as she trembled in my arms and buried her face against my neck. I fell back onto my ass, wrapping her in my hold and kissing her hair again and again as my heart beat powerfully against hers.

"I'm here, pretty girl," I panted. "You're okay."

"JJ," she croaked. "Swear you're here. Swear I'm out."

"I swear it," I vowed.

"Give her to me," Fox commanded, his hands snaring her but I held on tight, not wanting to let go. "JJ!" he barked and I reluctantly released her, my heart tugging as Fox pulled her against his chest, kneeling down and resting his forehead to hers.

"Are you hurt?" he asked, looking her over as she clung to his neck for support.

"I'm okay, I think," she said but she didn't really look it. Her skin was pale and it seemed like the only thing holding her up was Fox. "But Chase. Where's Chase?"

"We'll find him," I promised, moving closer and checking her over for injuries, finding a sizeable gash on one leg that clearly needed attendance.

"Please take my fucking shoes off," she half sobbed and I reached for them, unbuckling the stupid things and throwing them away. She tipped her head back against Fox's shoulder with a heavy sigh of relief. "Thank you."

Maverick climbed out of the gap, refusing Luther's offer of help before he scrambled his way over to us and tried to yank Rogue from Fox's arms. He didn't let her go though, a low growl leaving him as Mutt jumped up at her, licking her arms and she released another sob as she petted him.

"Ow," she moaned, clutching her hand back against her chest and I moved closer to her, gently examining it.

"I think you've broken some fingers, pretty girl," I said softly, cupping her cheek in my palm, needing to just see those ocean blue eyes shining with life.

"I had to keep banging. I needed you to find me," she breathed, staring at me like I was the rising sun, but then she gave that same look to Fox and Maverick as they continued to fight over her.

"Stop," she begged as Luther hurried forward with some water. Fox snatched it from his hand, holding it to her lips and she drank greedily, finishing the whole lot.

"She needs to go to the hospital," Maverick insisted. The paramedics were circling but they seemed to be well aware of who we were and how dangerous it would be to force their presence on us uninvited. "Stop kneeling there with her and take her to a fucking ambulance." He shoved Fox who got to his feet, clutching her tighter against him.

We all moved after him and I picked Mutt up, rubbing his head and whispering a thank you in his ear for finding her. He whined as he stared at her, looking as desperate as I felt to be closer.

We got down to the ambulances and paramedics hurried together, laying Rogue on a stretcher as Di, Lyla and Bella came running over from where they'd been digging.

"Holy shit, bitch!" Lyla cried, tears rolling down her cheeks. "We were so worried."

"Just a little house on my head, no big deal," Rogue said through a hiccup of laughter then winced as one of the paramedics started cleaning the wound on her leg. Her gaze found mine and darkness swirled in her eyes as tears gathered there. I stepped closer, placing Mutt on top of her and he snuggled down on her stomach, licking her arm.

"Find Chase," she ordered me. "Please, JJ. You have to find him."

Di, Bella and Lyla all piled into the ambulance and I expected Fox to go too, but he just squeezed her ankle and stepped back.

"We'll find him, hummingbird," Fox promised, his brows knitting together as the doors were pulled closed and the ambulance drove away. We stood there for several long seconds and I was surprised when Maverick strode straight back up onto the wreckage and started digging again.

I shared a look with Fox and we strode after him while Luther headed off to speak with some of the Crew. The three of us fell back into a rhythm as we dug for our brother and my heart started to crack again as I feared the worst.

"If you hadn't kicked him out of the Crew, he would have been with us. He would have gotten out," I bit at Fox, fear cleaving my chest apart.

"Don't," Fox warned, his jaw ticking as he threw a huge piece of marble over his shoulder.

"He's all alone down there, and what if he died thinking we hate him?" I demanded, my throat sore from inhaling the dust and making my voice hoarse.

"Stop it, JJ," Fox growled, digging more furiously, his muscles bunching and flexing as he refused to look at me.

"He was sorry," I croaked. "Things could have been different. We could have worked something out."

"I said stop it!" he snapped, looking up at me with a snarl on his lips. "Just dig."

"You didn't have to do what you did," I pressed, my heart like a wild animal in my chest as emotion tore me apart. "You didn't have to banish him."

"I should have killed him," he hissed, glaring at me with his upper lip curled back. "Don't you get that? He should already be dead, Johnny James, but I let him go. He got off lightly for what he did. He betrayed us. He betrayed Rogue."

"He didn't mean it," I rasped.

"You're only soft on him because it's Chase," he spat. "If it was anyone else you would have cheered me on to put him in the ground."

"That's the point though, isn't it?" I demanded, stepping closer to him as fury pounded through me. "You know Chase. You know who he is, and he's not some traitor."

"That's exactly what he is," he growled, staring me down, a warning in his eyes.

The whole Crew was here, if I challenged Fox he was going to put me in my place, but right now maybe I'd relish the violence.

Maverick was watching us curiously, but he kept his opinions to himself, if he even had any.

"You didn't give him a chance," I snarled, getting up in his face.

"Back. Down," he said through his teeth.

"You don't get to be the king when it comes to the five of us," I snapped. "I should have had a say in what happened to him. So should Rogue. It wasn't Crew business."

"Everything is Crew business." He shoved me back a step but I came at him again, just an inch away from his face as my muscles tightened with the need for a fight. "We don't get the luxury of being a democracy anymore, JJ. We're not kids. This is real life. And he fucked us over. I had to send him away."

"No you didn't!" I threw my shoulder into his chest, knocking him backwards, his foot slipping on the rubble and sending us crashing to the ground.

I got in two punches before Fox flipped us over, shoving me down against the rocks and locking his hands around my throat.

"Enough!" he boomed, but I didn't stop, breaking his choke hold on me and throwing my fist into his side.

I forced us over once more and we wrestled on the shattered bricks, my exhausted body somehow summoning the strength to fight. I didn't mind being bossed around by Fox when it came to the Crew, in fact, I preferred it, but when it came to my family, he didn't have a right not to listen to me. He didn't have a right to take one of my brothers away or lay a claim on a girl who was a part of our lives long before we took a vow into the Harlequins.

Maverick's booming laughter filled the air as Fox punched me hard enough to wind me, then crushed me down onto the bricks with his whole body, not letting me move.

"Stop," he growled in my face, but the fight was already going out of me. Everything hurt and I knew this wasn't helping to bring Chase back. I needed to keep digging for him, keep fighting for him.

"He may have done bad shit, but he was sorry. And he didn't deserve *this*," I hissed at Fox.

"I didn't bring the house down, JJ," he said, his eyes two furious pools of jade.

"You did," I said. "Just not this one." I shoved him back and he got off of me, stalking away across the rubble to start digging in another spot.

Maverick appeared, standing in front of me and blocking the sun. He had a bottle of water in his hand and he causally tipped it up pouring it all over my head and I cursed.

"Why are you still here?" I demanded in irritation.

"I want a front row seat to watch you pick pieces of Chase out of the rubble." He smirked cruelly as I got to my feet. "Nice to know Foxy's always got your back by the way. Or did he just make an example of you in front of his Crew like a good boy while his Daddy's watching?"

"You're full of shit, Maverick," I snapped, straightening my spine as I squared up to him.

"How so?" he asked coolly.

"Because if you wanted us all dead so bad you could pull a gun any second. I reckon you could shoot at least me and Fox before anyone managed to return fire. Maybe Luther too."

Maverick clucked his tongue, his eyes darkening as he stepped closer to me. "What you fail to understand, Johnny James, is that I don't just want your deaths. I wanna stand in hell with you and watch you burn first." He gestured to the wreckage around us. "So I'm gonna be right here for the show when Chase Cohen's head is dragged out of the debris to see your little heart imploding."

I opened my arms wide, glaring at him, my body bloody and coated in dust. "Well I hope you're enjoying the show, Maverick. I hope our brother's death makes you very fucking happy."

His jaw tightened and I turned my back on him, marching away to work alone and search for Chase in peace. If he was under this endless pile of stones, I'd find him. Everyone else may have given up on him in this life, but not me. He was my best friend and I knew he'd be right here searching for me if the tables were turned. It didn't matter if he was a Harlequin or not, he shared a soul with me and I was sure I'd know if he was dead.

Hang in there, Ace, I won't give up on you.

CHAPTER FIVE

There were whispers in the corners of my mind. Voices that crept in past my closed eyes and aching soul and caressed some long dormant part of me. They wound their way around my heart and slipped past the walls I'd been working so hard to keep in place as they beckoned me home.

And it was such sweet torture to listen to them. Such beautiful agony to live in the dreams they promised.

But life had never gone that easy on me. I wasn't suited for happily ever afters. Though I was tempted to grab a happy for now and cling onto it as hard as I could.

"Are the drugs keeping her asleep?" a familiar voice asked.

"No," a woman replied. "She's just sleeping. Her body has been through a trauma and she needs a lot of rest to regain her strength, but all in all she's in pretty good shape for someone who had a building collapse on top of her. She'll wake when she's ready."

"Not good enough," Fox growled. "I need to be sure she's okay. And I can't do that until I can look into her eyes and hear her say the words."

"Well you'll likely have to wait until tomorrow for that. She needs rest more than she needs to soothe your concerns," the woman bustled and a door closed a moment later.

"Does that bitch know who the fuck I am?" Fox snarled.

"Everyone knows exactly who you are," JJ snapped, his tone harsher than I was used to. "A ruthless son of a bitch who will rip the world apart just so long as you get whatever the fuck you want."

"JJ," Fox gritted out. "You know that in my position, I have to-"

"Shhh," I mumbled, lifting a bandaged hand and waving it in the direction of their voices to silence their noise.

The sound of a chair scraping across linoleum was instantly followed by the feeling of a set of hands clasping my good one and someone else running their fingers down the side of my face.

"Rogue?" Fox asked, his voice cracking on my name.

"It's us, pretty girl," JJ said softly.

I groaned a little then forced my eyes to part, finding Fox right in my breathing space, his eyes hunting mine as his fingers pushed into my hair.

"Are you alright, baby? Do you know where you are?" Fox asked.

"Being suffocated by a badger," I mumbled, my fingers flexing around JJ's as I felt his lips press to the back of my hand and a choked noise escaped him.

"Fuck, I never thought I'd be glad to hear you call me that," Fox breathed a laugh, but the pain in his green eyes didn't falter and I frowned as it drew me in.

"What's wrong?" I asked him, trying to see past him to JJ but he was devouring the space around me and trapping me in those emerald eyes.

Fox kissed me and I stilled, my throat closing up as my fingers tightened on JJ's and I didn't even know if I should kiss him back or shove him off or just close my eyes and fall back into the dark. My skin came alive for him though, my treacherous heart racing as he branded his name onto my lips and tried to drive it all the way down to my soul.

"Get the fuck off of her and let her breathe," JJ snarled and Fox actually did as he'd asked, pulling away and sighing, his head dropping as he swiped a hand down his face and allowed JJ to move forward.

"Hey, pretty girl," Johnny James murmured as he looked down at me, a smile playing around his lips which seemed full of relief, though it fell away again so fast that I couldn't be certain. "Are you feeling alright?"

"I could use a water," I replied, licking my lips and tasting blood from a split in one of them.

A cup appeared with a straw jammed in the top of it and JJ guided it between my lips, holding it in place as I drank down the lot and sighed.

"You can sit up if you want to," JJ said, handing me a little control thingy for the bed and I played with it until I was mostly upright.

I glanced down at my bandaged hand, feeling a dull ache in my left leg too as I tried to piece together what had happened, but the hours I'd spent stuck down in that safe had merged into one long nightmare and I wasn't totally sure how much my memories of it reflected reality and how many were figments of my imagination.

"You have a bitch of a cut on your leg," JJ explained softly, lifting the covers to show me the dressing taped to my left calf. "It's been cleaned up and glued shut though, so it'll be all good within a few weeks. And they said your fingers are just badly bruised and swollen – no breaks."

He gave me a reassuring smile as he tucked the covers back over me and I sighed as I leaned back against the pillows, plucking at my hospital gown with my good hand.

"Who knew having a building collapse on you could be so anticlimactic," I muttered as I took that in. I was clearly dehydrated and a little bashed up, but I had to think that it was something close to miraculous that these few injuries were all I'd ended up with after surviving that carnage.

I took in the lavish hospital room I'd been set up in. Lavender walls surrounded me, and a tall vase of flowers sat in a wide windowsill.

"Shit," I muttered, glancing at the needle threaded into the back of my hand and the bag of fluids attached to it. "We should get the fuck out of here before they come asking how I'm going to be paying for this place."

"It's taken care of," Fox said firmly. "The Harlequins look after their own."

"Are you saying my gang membership comes with a health care plan?" I teased but when neither of them laughed, my amusement fell into a frown. "What aren't you telling me?"

"You should get some more rest," JJ said softly, tugging on my blankets to tuck me in better.

"Just spit it out," I demanded as he avoided my eye and Fox sighed, dropping into a chair beside my bed and giving me an intent look.

"They called off the search, hummingbird. They've stopped looking for survivors in the rubble," he explained slowly.

"So?" I demanded. I might have been out of it a lot, but I'd had enough lucid moments to understand that it must have been days since they'd pulled me out of that building.

"So...Chase didn't make it out," Fox breathed, his face written with pain as those words passed his lips.

I heard them. I understood them. But they didn't make it beyond that part of my brain. I interpreted the words, and I knew what they meant but I rejected them as fast as I computed them.

"No," I said simply.

I'd been away from my boys before. I'd been far away and aching for them and hurting over all they'd done, but deep down inside me I'd still felt them there. Sometimes it felt like a splinter of glass driving into my heart and other times like a kiss whispered across my lips while I slept, but either way, I felt them. I felt them then and now and always and I still felt him.

"No," I repeated more firmly.

"Pretty girl," JJ croaked, his hand finding mine again and his honey brown eyes filling with tears as he looked up at me with more hurt in his heart than I'd ever thought possible. "We stayed out there for days. We didn't sleep, hardly ate...all we did was dig and dig, but it's been too long. The rubble is too dense. The authorities called off the search for survivors and-"

"No!" I yelled at him, snatching my hand out of his and slapping him when he fought to take it again.

JJ jerked back at the feeling of my palm striking his cheek, the pain in his eyes cutting into me like razor blades, but I didn't care. Because it shouldn't have been there at all. There was no need for it.

"I feel him," I snarled, jabbing my chest above my heart so hard that it hurt. "He's still here, which means he's still out there. So stop looking at me like that and let's go and find him."

I grabbed the line attaching the needle to my hand and yanked it out, cursing at the pain of it but throwing the blankets off of me without even looking to see how much I was bleeding.

I just needed to get out there. I could find him. This hurt in my heart was tethered to him and it would draw me to him. All I had to do was get back out there and I knew I'd figure it out. He was waiting for us to save him. I could feel it. And I wasn't going to let him down no matter what other shit had passed between us.

Fox and JJ grabbed me, trying to wrestle me back into the bed but I smacked their hands and knocked them away, ignoring the things they were saying to me as I focused on the only thing that mattered.

Chase was out there somewhere, and he needed me.

That was all I cared about.

I shoved out of the bed, but a cry escaped me as I tried to stand and my legs gave way, leaving me to crash to the floor.

Pain radiated through my feet and legs, clearly the result of the hours I'd spent trapped in that hell in those fucking shoes, unable to do anything other than stand in them and slump against the walls in agony.

Strong arms banded around me and I was hoisted back off of the ground just as the door swung open and several nurses and a doctor hurried in.

"Let me go," I demanded, fighting against Fox as he shoved me down onto the bed, ignoring the way my fingernails were slicing into the skin of his arms as I thrashed and tried to force him to release me.

I was vaguely aware of JJ informing the nurse about what was happening and people rushing all around me as Fox shoved me down against the mattress and used his weight on my shoulders to keep me there.

"We'll give her a sedative," the doctor said between my yells and I started cursing.

"Let me go!" I screamed. "I'm warning you, Fox, I'll never forgive you for this if you don't take me out there! He needs us! Chase *needs* us!"

Fox shushed me, his eyes brimming with emotion as the sharp scratch of a needle drove into my arm.

"You need to rest, hummingbird," he said, his grip on me only loosening when the drugs began to steal the strength from my limbs and all I could do was glare at him as I slumped back against the bed.

"I'm so sorry, pretty girl," JJ choked out, wrapping his fingers between mine as a long blink slipped across my vision.

I turned my gaze to him as a tear finally slipped free of my control and tracked a path down my cheek.

"He saved me," I breathed, my voice so low that even I couldn't hear it and JJ's brow furrowed as he leaned in, trying to catch the words.

I blinked once more and this time, I couldn't open my eyes again after. My fingers fell slack in JJ's grip and the only thing I was left with in the dark was pain.

Memories of the boy I'd lost welled up in my heart and I slipped away from consciousness with them destroying me, two bright blue eyes staring back into my soul from that corner of my heart which would always belong to Chase Cohen.

He saved me.

And now he was gone.

CHAPTER SIX

The weeks slipped by and I felt like my chest was in a vice, the metal closing over my heart tighter and tighter day by day. JJ was still angry with me, and Rogue seemed so broken that I didn't know what to do. I was trying to juggle the running of the Crew and the attacks across town from Shawn's gang while starting to rebuild something normal in my home. It was impossibly hard and left me exhausted, every moment of every day another trial I had to weather.

JJ spent a lot time out of the house and when he was here, he headed off into Chase's room with Rogue where they'd talk about old times and I'd find myself listening at the door, wishing I belonged in that room with them. But I didn't. I was an outsider to this grief, unwelcome to it because of the actions I'd taken against Chase. I knew deep down JJ just needed someone to punish, to blame, but weeks of his anger and rejection were taking its toll on me. So today I wanted to try and fix it.

I headed upstairs with a plate of nachos, walking to Chase's room with my heart ripping down the middle. JJ's anger had only burned a deeper hole of guilt in my chest over Chase than I'd already been subjected to. But I couldn't regret what I'd done. I couldn't have known things would end up this way, and it wasn't my fault that he'd been at The Dollhouse the night Shawn had brought it down.

The fact that he'd saved Rogue left my head spinning and placed an ache in me which I tried not to examine. I couldn't grieve in a normal way, not when I'd put Chase on his knees outside this house and pressed a gun to his head. I'd been so close to pulling that trigger, and I'd wondered afterwards if I should have. Because traitors didn't get second chances in this Crew and he hadn't just betrayed me and JJ, he'd betrayed Rogue. He'd *hurt* Rogue. And that was unforgiveable, no matter what way I looked at it.

I knocked on the door and Rogue and JJ's voices fell quiet.

"Can I come in?" I asked when neither of them said anything.

"No," JJ said just as Rogue said, "Yes."

I opened the door and found them lying close to one another on Chase's bed, a fact that set a line of jealousy scoring through my heart. But I didn't say anything. JJ wouldn't lay his hands on her, he knew better than that. And I knew they needed each other to get through this grief, I just wished I could be a part of it.

Rogue was wearing one of Chase's black band t-shirts with knee high socks. Her eyes were puffy as she sat up and JJ looked pointedly at the ceiling, ignoring me. Mutt was laid out on the end of the bed on one of Chase's blankets, upside down and sniffing the air as I brought the nachos closer. He didn't ever spend any time with me anymore, even my chicken treats not enough to buy his love. He started vomiting up his chicken in the mornings sometimes too and I swear he looked me in the eye while he did like he was punishing me. He'd never gotten over me shouting at him when I'd almost shot Chase and I swear he was going to hold it against me until the end of time.

"I got you something to eat," I said, offering the food to them.

Rogue took it with a sad smile of thanks and my gaze moved to JJ.

"Can I talk to you, brother?" I asked.

"Is it Crew business?" he asked.

"No."

"Then no," he said simply, placing a hand behind his head as his eyes slid onto me, full of iciness. I'd never really experienced being on the end of JJ's wrath, and I didn't much like it.

"Just talk to me," I commanded.

"I said no," he gritted out.

"JJ," Rogue tried gently, but he only shook his head.

Mutt jumped up, moving to try and snag a nacho as Rogue placed them down on the nightstand. My gaze snagged on a photo sat there of the three of us – me, Chase and JJ on a night out a few years back. We were all laughing, our arms slung around each other and in that shot you could hardly even see the emptiness in my soul where Rogue should have been. We looked happy, like a family, unbreakable. My jaw tightened and my heart crushed to dust. I turned my head away, needing to look anywhere else and my gaze settled on JJ once more. If he wouldn't talk to me in private, then I'd just have to say my piece right here.

"I know you're angry with me," I started.

"Wow, you should have been a private investigator, brother," he said dryly.

"Can you at least fucking look at me?" I growled, unable to contain my frustration.

"Yes, boss," he said, his eyes moving onto me as he sneered. Great, this was fucking worse.

"You have to know everything I do is to protect us, I never wanted any of this," I said earnestly. "I have a duty to our family, it wasn't easy to banish him."

"I get why you did it, Fox," JJ said in an empty sort of voice. "But maybe I'm getting tired of you doing things in our best interest without consulting us first."

I bit back my immediate snippy response and tried to hear him out, looking to Rogue as she nodded her agreement.

Give me fucking patience.

"Go on then," I growled, folding my arms as I gazed at them both. "Give me hell, tell me what an asshole I am."

They shared a look, seeming intrigued by that idea and Rogue started it off.

"You're an overbearing, bossy dick," she said and I nodded, figuring that was fair.

"You're controlling and domineering, and you don't listen to anything we fucking say," JJ snarled next.

"You think just because you're the Harlequin prince, you can treat us like you treat all the rest of your men," Rogue said with pursed lips.

"And you call us family, but when it comes down to it, you won't listen to our opinions because you think the great Fox Harlequin knows best. Always. Even when you fucking don't," JJ snapped, venom in his eyes.

"I'm just trying to protect you," I said heavily, feeling the sting of their words.

"Your way of protecting us is sometimes suffocating," Rogue said, though her tone softened a little as she gazed at me.

"Don't spare his feelings, pretty girl, it's *always* suffocating," JJ said with a glare.

"Alright," I growled. "I'll try to be less…controlling. Is that what you wanna hear?"

JJ shoved to his feet, stalking toward me and for a moment I thought he was gonna start another fight with me. "No, Fox. Because it's too late. Chase is gone. Maverick's gone. And this house is starting to feel real empty."

"And that's my fault?" I snarled.

"Maybe it is. And maybe you're gonna wake up alone in this big old house and wonder why one day, because you just can't see it, can you?" he hissed then shoulder barged past me and headed out the door, his footsteps pounding off downstairs as my heart jerked.

I looked to Rogue, heat rising up the back of my neck. I turned to leave but she called out to me, "Wait. Stay."

Those two words meant more to me right then than she would ever know. Between gang meetings and handling the attacks on our hometown, plus wrestling with the cloying grief and guilt that plagued me over Chase, I barely slept and spent way too much time alone.

I was trying so hard to hold myself together so I could keep the last of my family safe, that I had barely spent any time with Rogue, unsure if she even wanted me around.

She patted the bed beside her and I moved into the spot JJ had vacated. She slid closer, wrapping her arm around me and resting her head on my chest.

The cold clutch of grief on my heart eased a little as the scent of coconut slid under my nose and I just closed my eyes and held her, wishing I could take her pain away, trap it in a jar, weigh it down with rocks and throw it into the ocean.

"I'm sorry," I breathed, meaning that on so many levels. "Don't hate me."

"I don't hate you, Fox," she sighed. "It's not your fault. JJ just needs someone to be angry at right now."

"I know," I admitted. "And I'll be his punching bag if that's what helps him through this."

Silence fell between us and I listened to Rogue's soft breaths as I held her close, so fucking tired I wished I could fall asleep. But I had a hundred things to do today, responsibilities I couldn't escape, but I so badly wanted to. For now, I'd steal a little peace with my girl as our grief spilled between us and bound us together in a new way that I'd never wanted.

"I don't think I can bear it, Fox," she whispered. "It doesn't seem real. I can still feel him right here." She moved a hand to her heart and I took hold of her fingers, moving them onto my own heart.

"I feel him too," I said gently.

The last human remains had been pulled from the ruins of The Dollhouse last week, but there was nothing identifiable among them. The bodies had been so badly damaged in the collapse that the police were going to be using dental records and DNA to try and identify the final missing people. But when it came down to it, they'd all been declared dead and that was that. Either way, we had no body to bury, no grave to give us closure. He was just…gone. And maybe that was why we were all so lost in this house, we were waiting for a call that wasn't going to come. Holding onto the futile hope that he might just walk back in the front door one day, because it didn't seem possible that he wasn't a part of this world anymore.

Hot tears ran over my chest and I held Rogue tighter as she came apart.

"He saved me," she choked out. "That was the last thing he did, and I know he hurt me before and that he was a raging asshole sometimes but…" She didn't have words to finish that sentence and I just soaked in the weight of that final thing he'd done, wishing I could thank him for it.

A crash sounded and Rogue lifted her head as we wheeled around, finding Mutt had knocked the nachos onto the floor and he dove down after them with a yip of celebration before he tucked into his meal.

A low laugh escaped me, breaking the tension in my body and Rogue chuckled too, her watery eyes lighting up a little.

She looked back at me and traced her thumb over the corner of my lips where the smallest of smiles sat.

"Go talk to JJ," she urged. "I'm gonna take a shower."

"Okay," I agreed. "Though I don't think it'll do much good."

"It will," she said firmly. "Just don't be an asshole."

"Impossible," I said with something of a smirk and she returned it.

"I have faith in you, Badger." She got off the bed, heading into Chase's en suite and leaving Mutt to his meal.

I headed out of the room and shut the door, walking downstairs to find my brother. I didn't really know what I could say to fix things between us, but I had to try even if he didn't wanna hear it.

I found him sitting with his feet in the pool on the patio, smoking Chase's cigarettes and staring at the water like it held the key to curing his misery. The sky was dark today, the air heavy with the promise of rain and the humidity made my skin prickle. I noticed he was wearing one of Chase's wife beaters and I guessed he and Rogue were just trying to surround themselves with him for as long as they could before they had to let go. It wasn't like I wanted to move on, but maybe it was time we tried to say goodbye. Though the mere thought of that sent a sharp pain daggering through my chest.

I moved to sit beside him, swiping a cigarette from the box and lighting it up with the green lighter inside it which was covered in palm trees. I decided talking probably wasn't my best form of action as I only seemed to piss him off when I tried that, so I just sat there, hoping he'd bridge the silence between us and the chasm of anger he felt for me.

"He'd have hated this," JJ said eventually. "Us all sitting around moping. He always said he wanted us to throw a party if he died."

I released a soft breath of amusement. "Yeah, and he said we needed to leave a glass of rum out for him night after night so his ghost could get drunk."

JJ chuckled, but the sound quickly died in his throat and he hung his head, his hair falling forward into his eyes. He looked so broken and I felt a crevice opening in my own soul for Chase, for JJ, Rogue.

"You're not really to blame," JJ croaked. "I'm sorry I've been such an asshole."

"That's okay," I said, knocking my shoulder against his. "It makes a change from me being one."

He released a cracked laugh and I rested a hand on his back, taking a long toke on my cigarette. It tasted like acid and loss, but I swallowed it down, owning what I'd done. I couldn't regret it. My decisions had to be made with full confidence because if I waivered on them at all, I'd weaken my authority in the Crew. There were rules for a reason and though I'd never wanted to become my father, I knew why he'd made some of the decisions he had when we were kids. Some things were worth being hated for. And there was no reality that existed where I could have pardoned Chase for his crimes. A traitor was a traitor, brother or otherwise. I'd spared his life and fate had taken it anyway. I had no choice but to live with that.

"I keep thinking he's gonna call or show up somewhere in town," JJ said, shaking his head at himself as he flicked his cigarette butt away and lit up another one. "It's stupid."

"It's not stupid," I said gently. "I feel like that too."

"Except if he saw you, he'd run for the hills," JJ pointed out and I snorted.

"He'll probably start haunting my ass now," I said and JJ laughed.

"Yeah you're screwed, man, you can't banish a ghost."

I smiled at the thought of Chase still being close, but the pressure in my chest didn't lessen. He may have been a traitor, but I still loved that fucking boy even after everything. And losing him was unbearable.

A clang in the kitchen made me turn and I found Rogue there washing up the nacho plate. She glanced over her shoulder, giving us an apologetic look as she tried to slip out of the room again but I jerked my head to beckon her.

"Get out here," I called just as the first splashes of rain fell against my cheeks.

"Come on, pretty girl," JJ encouraged. "And bring the rum."

She stepped outside barefooted in one of Chase's white shirts, her hair hanging wet around her shoulders. Me and JJ shifted apart so she could sit between us and I rested my hand on her knee as she offered me the bottle of rum. I took a long drink of it, letting it burn away the ache in my chest a little before watching as she and JJ sank two large measures.

Rogue kicked her feet back and forth in the pool, resting her head on JJ's shoulder while her fingers interlocked with mine.

I bathed in the comfort of their company, not wanting to be anywhere else in the world right then and mentally deciding to put off all Crew responsibilities for today. I just needed to be around my family and cling to their presence, facing the huge cavity in my chest where Chase belonged. The five of us were never going to sit together again and though that had been fairly obvious where Maverick was concerned, now it made that reality permanent. And it just plain fucking hurt. I thought of Maverick saving me at The Dollhouse, chewing over the meaning of that once again. I'd probably never understand his motivations, but I knew for sure it hadn't been because he cared about me. Maverick had stopped feeling anything for me years ago, the gunshot scar on my neck was proof of that.

"I don't want to say goodbye," Rogue said, her voice unsteady as she took a cigarette from the box.

"Maybe we don't have to," JJ said. "Maybe it's better to keep thinking he's going to show up again, maybe I don't wanna stop feeling like he's right round the corner or in the next room or down at Raiders Gym."

"Yeah," Rogue agreed and I guessed that wasn't the worst idea in the world, though I didn't want that to mean their pain went on longer than necessary.

Then again, if I was being really honest, I knew saying goodbye wouldn't erase our pain anyway. Chase wasn't just going to be forgotten or moved on from, he was too integral to us. When Maverick had cut us off, I'd at least known he was out there, hating us maybe, but not gone. There'd been a small sort of comfort in that, even though it hurt like a bitch.

Wherever Chase was now, I knew he was still as attached to us as he always was, just as my adopted brother was too. The five of us couldn't escape each other, even in death. It was something intangible I couldn't really explain but which lived in us like our souls were tethered together by unbreakable chains. And wherever it was that he'd gone in death, I knew one day we'd follow Chase there, because our souls would hunt for their counterparts to the ends of the universe. And I was fairly sure they wouldn't find true peace until they were together once more.

I woke with my arms wrapped around Rogue and the rough brush of a man's fingers on my arm. My eyes cracked open and I inhaled the scent of Chase, Rogue and JJ. We were in his room again, the three of us taken to sleeping here together – well four of us if you counted Mutt. He was currently wedged in between my head and Rogue's, curled up in a tiny ball with his little paw over his nose. His butt was pointed towards me of course, but I had hope that him being willing to sleep so close to me meant he might start coming around to me again one of these days.

None of us commented on the strange sleeping arrangement we'd come to, we just all seemed to end up here night after night, watching Chase's collection of horror movies on his TV and falling asleep way after midnight as we reminisced about the good times in our childhood. It was nostalgic, peaceful, but I knew I was hiding from reality. Every day I was avoiding too many of my tasks, putting off my duties so I could just be at home with Rogue and JJ. Luther was hounding my ass for a meeting, but I wanted a little longer. *Just a few more days.*

I shut my eyes, holding Rogue tighter and letting the weight of sleep fall back over me so that I didn't have to face the truth again. Because every day when I woke up, I remembered that Chase was dead. And that truth never seemed to get any easier to face.

A door slammed downstairs and I bolted upright, making Rogue roll into my spot and JJ roll with her so he faceplanted her tits.

Gah. I shoved him off of her and he flopped onto his back with a groan. Mutt growled as I disturbed him too and I slipped out of bed as footsteps thumped up the stairs. I reached for my gun on the nightstand, but I'd know the sound of those furious footfalls anywhere. Just in case he fancied murdering us, I kept the gun in my grip as I stood up and the door flew open.

Luther took a sweeping look through the room as JJ sat up, bleary eyed and with a pistol in his hand. He was shirtless, in bed with my girl and I was only in my boxers too, so this all looked very fucking strange, but I didn't need to explain myself to my father.

Luther's eyes widened and he seemed lost for words for a moment before he regained his composure.

"It's nearly eleven am," he barked, his glare flicking onto me. "You missed the Crew meeting at the clubhouse, why the fuck was your phone off?"

I looked around for it, spotting it on the floor where it had died. "Err…" I rubbed a hand over my face, the taste of rum still lingering in the back of my throat from last night.

"Sorry, boss," JJ tried, stepping out of bed and pulling some sweatpants on while Rogue continued to sleep like the dead. Mutt bounded across the mattress, jumping at Luther with blind faith and he caught him out the air in surprise.

"Get up. All of you," Luther commanded, scratching Mutt's ears while the little dog licked him and threw me a side eyed glare. "We need to talk."

He strode out of the room and I shared a look with JJ where we silently questioned our sanity about sleeping in this bed together. It was what we needed right now though and I guessed it was how we were coping with losing Chase, but if I really analysed it I could possibly come to the conclusion that this was actually a way to hold onto him and never let go.

"Come on, pretty girl. Time to wake up." JJ shook Rogue, but that didn't work so I moved over to her other side and patted her cheek.

"Hummingbird," I tried, patting her cheek a little harder. "Baby?"

She reached out in her sleep, her hand landing right on my cock and squeezing.

"Jesus," I grunted, pushing her hand away as my dick got overexcited. "Wake up." I scooped her into my arms and her eyes finally fluttered open.

"Where are we going?" she murmured. "I'm hungry. Was that a footlong sub I just felt? Gimme it. Put it in my mouth."

"Tempting, baby, but Luther's here," I said and she woke up a little more sharply.

She wriggled out of my arms, grabbing a pair of Chase's sweatpants from his drawer and pulling them on, tying the cord so they yanked tight around her waist. I frowned at her, seeing the stubbornness in her eyes to keep a part of him with her like she feared if she stopped surrounding herself with him, he'd disappear forever. I knew she was conflicted over him, we all were, but none of us had wanted to see him dead and I didn't wanna let go yet either.

We headed down to the office along the hall and I was reminded of being disciplined in here by my father as a kid. It was my domain now, but as I stepped into the room and found him behind the desk, I didn't feel much ownership of it. The three of us stood shoulder to shoulder and he regarded us with a pitying look on his face, but quickly schooled it into a hard mask.

"Shut the door," he ordered even though there was no one else in the house and JJ moved to obey. "I know you're all grieving," he said with a frown as his gaze travelled across us. "But it's time to move on. Our Crew is at war, and I have intelligence that says Shawn is going to make another move against us tonight."

"Where?" I demanded as Rogue's spine straightened.

My jaw clenched at that single movement, because I knew my father owned her now and I didn't have the power to keep her from trying to attack Shawn if that was what he wanted. JJ had been teaching her to shoot while I stubbornly refused to acknowledge the fact that she would ever need to use a gun against Shawn. I hadn't stopped him all the same though, she needed to be able to protect herself, so I turned a blind eye to it and tried not to think about her going anywhere near the front line in a fight against The Dead Dogs.

"He's going to strike at The Oasis. One of my men caught a Dead Dog early this morning and squeezed Shawn's plans outa him. I guess one of Shawn's little spies heard about our annual summer party there tonight," Luther said, resting his hands on the desk as his eyes darkened. I'd forgotten all about that, the days having merged together. "And you will all be there when he does."

"Rogue stays out of it," I demanded.

"No," she said simply. "I get to kill Shawn, that's the reason I've got an ugly ass tattoo on the back of my thigh."

"Which one?" I gritted out and she threw me a death glare.

"She's not your solider, she's mine," my dad growled, pulling fucking rank on me. "And Shawn's gonna be there tonight, so the wildcat gets her shot at him. That was our deal."

"And what was the other part of that deal, Dad?" I demanded, still having had no more information on that from Rogue.

"That's between me and her," he said. "Now bite your tongue and listen to me."

I did as he said, but there were still a thousand thoughts going through my head about how I could prevent Rogue from taking part in this fight today without directly ordering it.

"Word is, Shawn's going in hard tonight. He's bringing a lot of men and a lot ammo. He wants this war won which means he's going to be gunning to take me and you out, kid."

"So what's the plan?" JJ asked, sounding ready to go in to battle.

"I've got scouts trying to track down his location so we can get the jump on him, but his men never seem to take the same roads in and outa town. As you know, Shawn rarely shows his face when his men strike, but I guarantee he'll show up tonight if he thinks he'll get a chance to kill us."

"Well there's only two roads that lead to the clubhouse," I said thoughtfully, trying to compartmentalise my concerns over Rogue as I focused on making a plan. "We could try to ambush him before he makes it to The Oasis."

"Exactly my thinking," Luther said with a smirk. "But he'll be cautious, he'll send scouts ahead to make sure we're all definitely at the clubhouse before he risks his own neck."

"So we let them through?" I guessed and Luther nodded, scratching at the ink on his neck.

"Which means you and me will need to show our faces there long enough for the word to get back to Shawn. Rogue too."

"I don't want Rogue involved in this," I said in a growl, my hands balling into fists.

"That's not really up to you, is it Badge?" she said and anger built in my chest.

"She's right, and Shawn's made it clear he's after the girl, so I want her front and centre, dangling there like a nice juicy apple," my dad said and anger flashed through me.

"No," I snapped.

"Yes," Luther hissed back. "This is happening, son, so get used to it."

"I'll make sure I'm the juiciest apple ever, then I'll poison his ass when he takes a bite," Rogue said passionately.

My heart beat frantically and I looked from her to my father to JJ whose brows were knitted together. I could see I had no choice in this which meant I needed to take control of it in another way.

"She doesn't leave my sight and if she kills Shawn, it'll be because he's been handed to her on his knees with his wrists bound," I snapped.

"You're so ridiculous," Rogue sighed.

I swung around, glaring down at her. "You think it's ridiculous to protect you? To stop you from going off half-cocked and untrained to kill the most dangerous enemy we've ever faced?" I snapped and she rolled her eyes like I was being dramatic.

"You'll stay with Fox," Luther agreed and some of my panic eased, but not nearly enough.

"Great, and by the way I'm not untrained, JJ has been teaching me to shoot," she said, raising her chin.

"You think shooting at a few glass bottles in the woods can prepare you for facing a man twice your size with years of practice hunting his victims? You don't know what it's like to fight for your life in that situation, Rogue."

"Well I beat a rapist to death with an iron poker when I was sixteen despite him being three times the size of me so I think I can figure it out, Badge, but thanks for your concern."

I opened my mouth to retort, but Luther raised a hand to halt me. "That's enough. You're giving me a headache. I've delivered my orders, now don't question me on them or I'll consider making you stay home, Fox."

For fuck's sake.

I sealed my lips tight, just knowing he'd do it.

"Good," Luther said with a satisfied smile. "Now grab some chairs and sit down. We're gonna make a plan to catch Shawn Mackenzie and skin him alive."

CHAPTER SEVEN

The Oasis had always been this taboo place from my childhood. Pretty much the one and only place in the whole of Sunset Cove where the five of us didn't fuck around or pull stunts, break into, or generally use to our advantage. It was the heart of the Harlequin Crew, therefore none of us had wanted a thing to do with it. So strolling in through the front door on the arm of their prince with their king right beside us was something of a mindfuck to say the least.

Every gang member in attendance cheered as they spotted us and I fought a blush at the attention, not least because I was the only woman in the entire place, so I was getting more than my fair share of curious looks.

Since Luther had sworn me in, I hadn't exactly spent much time among the rest of the gang and if I was being totally honest, the amount of men in attendance here had my head spinning. Fuck, there were a lot of them. And I had no goddamn idea what they must have been thinking about me. But then I remembered that I didn't give a shit and the whole thing seemed a lot less intimidating.

It was hot today, summer was in full swing and we were officially into the second week of a heatwave, so I'd chosen to wear a playsuit instead of a dress. It was pale blue with little pink flowers embroidered onto it and my ass wasn't entirely contained within the shorts, but I was cool with that. The top half of it was strappy and the material thin and despite Fox's protests, I wasn't wearing a Kevlar. There was no fucking way I could have gotten away with wearing it unnoticed and if Shawn was sending scouts ahead of him, then seeing me decked out in a bullet proof vest would be a pretty obvious giveaway to let them know we were on to them.

And lucky for me, Luther agreed, so I was currently on the arm of one angry badger as standard, but I looked freaking cute in my outfit, so I gave no shits. I'd paired the bodysuit with some white tennis shoes, forgoing heels. I was almost certain I'd never wear high heels again after being trapped in them for hours inside that fucking safe, and I definitely wasn't going to risk wearing some when there was a chance Shawn might start chasing me again. Nope, this time I'd be ready to run or dick kick or do whatever the hell I needed to so far as footwear went.

The guys were dressed up in their best jeans and smart shirt combos which was about as fancy as the dudes around here ever got and I was not so secretly eye fucking my two old friends. Fox's ink seemed gilded on his muscular arms tonight, the deep brown shirt he was wearing doing his tan all kinds of favours. And JJ had opted for white which coupled with his ink black hair and the devilish look in his eyes made me want to lick him. I mean, I always kinda wanted to lick him, but right now I was up for doing it slowly and repeatedly and in all the best ways.

Harlequins flocked around Luther and Fox, wanting their face time with the bosses and I quickly slipped away from them, taking JJ's arm as he led me to the bar at the back of the open room.

There was aircon pumping in here, but amongst the press of bodies it was still hot, so I was more than glad to escape for a drink.

The Oasis wasn't as terrifying as my imagination had conjured. The place was huge and built with white wood, the downstairs dedicated to this communal bar area, with tables dotted around and a few pool tables off to the right of the bar. A balcony ran over the bar with a guard blocking off the stairs from anyone wanting to head up there aside from the heads of this criminal organisation. Luther had an office upstairs somewhere as well as a suite where he stayed when he was in town, and I knew Fox had his own office here too. I guessed running a gang included a bunch of paperwork, though I couldn't imagine what.

"What are you drinking, pretty girl?" JJ asked me as we moved to stand by the bar and I shrugged.

"A shot of something that hits hard," I said and he grinned at me before making an order with the Harlequin acting as bartender.

I knocked back the disgustingly strong shot of liquor and smacked my lips through the wince it brought to my face as it burned all the way down. That was what I needed to take the edge off and I sighed as I leaned my elbows back against the bar and looked out over the crowd.

"How does it feel being here?" JJ asked me.

"Like I'm a fish in a conga line," I said. "I know all the right moves, but I'm never really gonna seem like I'm in the right place."

JJ offered me half a smile which was the most I could get out of him since we'd lost Chase and I tried not to let the thoughts of him creep in. Not tonight. I needed to stay sharp and focus on finishing the asshole responsible for all of my pain.

If I'd thought I hated Shawn Mackenzie before he'd brought The Dollhouse down and killed one of the few people I'd ever truly loved in my life then I'd known nothing of the venomous hatred I was capable of feeling for him now.

Before I'd ached for his demise, but now I hungered for his death with every single beat of my heart. I dreamed of spilling his blood and hearing his screams and making him beg at my fucking feet for a mercy that would never come.

My shiny new cell phone buzzed in my back pocket and I straightened my spine. Luther had gotten it for me, promising that there was no chance Fox was monitoring it in any way and even swearing that he wasn't either. I wasn't totally certain I believed him on the second part of that promise, but as he was onboard with me and Maverick being in contact, it didn't matter so much.

"I'm gonna use the bathroom," I said to JJ, taking the phone from my pocket and killing the call. Rick knew to wait for me to call him back when I did that. Sometimes I could dial him back right away, other times it would be hours or even the next day, but for the most part we'd been able to keep in touch. It wasn't the same as actually seeing him though, and I longed for his company with an ache in my soul which I knew wouldn't be healed until I was in his arms again.

JJ glanced at my phone and I knew he knew. But he hadn't confronted me about it yet. In fact, he hadn't said a word to me about Rick since the night the asshole had found us in that train car in the woods and we'd all entered into what was arguably some of the hottest sex of my life. We probably needed to talk about it. But we really hadn't done a lot of talking about anything other than the old days and missing Chase since we'd lost him.

"Come on. Luther said you can use the bathroom in his suite while we're here rather than having to use the men's room." JJ jerked his chin towards the stairs that led to the balcony and I fell in at his side as we headed past the guard and upstairs.

We passed a few closed doors before JJ led me down a short corridor and into a modest suite with a large bed in the centre of it and a small living area looking out onto the balcony that ringed the front of the building with a distant view of the sea beyond.

"You can go through to the bathroom if you want," JJ said, pointing to a door in the back of the room. "Or you can call him back with me here. Presuming you trust me."

I rolled my eyes at him and dropped onto one of the armchairs before dialling Rick.

He answered before the first ring even finished and I swallowed a lump in my throat at the sound of his rough voice.

"What are you wearing, beautiful?"

"Hang on and I'll show you." I moved the phone away from myself and took a selfie while miming sucking a dick before forwarding it on to him. JJ raised an eyebrow as he dropped onto the chair opposite me and watched with interest.

"Sometimes I think you snark me because you want me to punish you, baby girl," Maverick growled. "Is that what you're hoping for? That I'll get on a boat and come spank your ass raw?"

"Maybe," I hedged, wondering if JJ could make out Maverick's words or not because his face gave nothing away. "But not today. I have something on."

"Oh?"

"Yeah. I'm gonna put a bullet in Shawn Mackenzie's fucking skull at last."

"Shit, baby, you really know how to get me hard. Can you do it close range so I can fuck you while you're still splattered with his blood?"

I snorted a laugh then bit my lip, unsure if he was joking or if that turned me on. Or if I was just losing the plot altogether and I had no fucking idea what to think of anything anymore.

"I'll call you if I do," I promised.

"Fuck that, I'm gonna come to watch the show firsthand. I can't imagine anything hotter than watching you blow that asshole away, beautiful."

"You don't know where I am. And even if you did, you wouldn't be welcome here," I pointed out.

"Ah, ah, ah. Don't make silly assumptions. I could be watching you right now and you'd never even know it."

"Bullshit."

"See you soon, baby." Rick cut the call and I just stared at the phone for a minute before shaking my head and pocketing it.

"I take it he has no objections to you killing Shawn then?" JJ asked, leaning towards me and resting his elbows on his knees.

"Apparently watching me kill the motherfucker would be a turn on," I said. "He likes the idea of me painted in the blood of my enemies or some shit."

I expected JJ to scoff or make some joke about Maverick being a psychopath, but he just ran his gaze over me slowly, licking his lips like he was giving that mental image some thought too.

"Man has good taste, I'll give him that," he said eventually and I bit my lip.

Johnny James, being the asshole he was, knew exactly where my mind had just gone and he leaned back again, jerking his chin at me in a silent command.

I should have told him to get fucked. But I got to my feet instead and slowly closed the distance between us. I'd blame that move on my vagina – I might have been a strong, take no shit kind of girl, but she was a submissive little hussy who loved following the orders of men with huge dicks. It was a constant struggle of our wills, but she definitely won whenever it came to Johnny James.

JJ placed his arms over the back of the large chair he sat in and waited for me to make my move.

We'd been together a few times since Chase had...gone, but it had always been a merging of our grief. A slow, cathartic giving and taking of our pain mixed with love and the comfort we found in each other's arms. But the look he was giving me now was all heated. The gangster who usually hid beneath the surface of his skin looking up at me with dark promises in his honey brown eyes.

I moved to place my knees on the cushions either side of his muscular thighs, reaching for his chest before he caught my wrists in his grasp and placed them down on the armrests either side of us instead.

"Hold your weight up," he commanded gripping my ass and lifting it from his knees so that I was kneeling over him instead of balancing on top of him. "Now tell me how worked up you are about today. Tell me how much you've been thinking about killing that piece of shit who laid his fucking hands on you."

"I need to do it, JJ," I growled, my skin tingling with the intensity of the hatred I felt towards Shawn. "And I want to look him in the fucking eyes as I do. I want him to look at me the same way I did him when his hands were wrapped tight around my throat."

JJ moved his hand between my thighs and I sucked my lower lip into my mouth as he tugged the material of my playsuit aside before pausing.

"No panties?"

"You could see them through the playsuit," I reasoned as he slicked a single finger through my wetness and my chest heaved.

"Fuck," he growled, using his other hand to adjust his swelling cock, but as I reached out to try and touch him, he caught my wrist and placed my hand back on the armrest with a shake of his head.

"Keep talking about what you wanna do to that motherfucker, pretty girl. I'm gonna help you lose some of the tension you're holding over doing it. I promise you'll aim straighter once I loosen you up."

I was going to tell him to stop. That I wasn't some bloodthirsty creature who wanted to get off on the idea of murdering someone, but that wasn't what came out of my mouth, so I was clearly just lying to myself in my own mind.

"I want him to look at me and know I'm his death," I breathed, moaning as JJ sank two fingers into me and rocking my hips as he began to pump his hand.

"He'll be fucking terrified of you," he growled, watching me with the same desire for Shawn's death in his eyes as I felt burning through my soul.

"I want him to beg," I gasped as JJ moved his fingers faster, driving in deeper before dropping his thumb against my clit and making me moan so loud that my gaze flicked to the door in fear of being caught.

"Keep talking," JJ demanded and I nodded as I fought for the words I needed.

"I want him to grovel, apologise, plead, say everything he can think of to try and make me change my mind and know it's no use," I panted, my fingernails biting into the arms of the chair as my legs began to tremble with the oncoming storm which was building in my flesh.

"How will you end him?" JJ asked, his cock straining against his fly so hard that it had to hurt. I wanted to touch him so badly, but I knew that wasn't what this was about, and I had to admit that I was a fan of this darker, more dominant side of my smiling sex god.

"A gun," I breathed because as much as I wished I could choke the life out of Shawn the way he'd tried to kill me for poetic justice, the call of a powerful weapon kissing his forehead while a single stroke of my finger blew him away had me daydreaming about it all the goddamn time.

JJ took a pistol from his belt and showed it to me. "Like this one?"

"Yes," I panted, watching as he shifted it onto my inner thigh and began to run it up the inside of my leg.

A moan escaped me. Too loud again, but fuck, I was so turned on. This was the darkest part of me brought to life, the vengeful, hungry, aching part which was brutal and fearless and craved chaos.

JJ drew his fingers out of my soaking pussy while keeping his thumb firmly circling my clit.

"It makes you so hot, doesn't it?" he growled. "The thought of taking this gun and blowing his fucking brains out." The cold metal pressed against my core and I gasped as JJ pushed the end of it inside me, just a little, just enough to make sure I could feel the ice cold kiss of it so my muscles clamped down hard around it.

"Yes," I moaned, sinking down and taking the decision away from him as the cold barrel of the gun slid inside me.

"You're going to tear him from this world," JJ swore to me as he began to fuck me with the lethal weapon and I moaned as my hips bucked against it and my heart raced. That thing had to be loaded. He wouldn't have it on him if it wasn't and as fucking crazy as that made this, it only turned me on more.

"I'm going to watch every second of it," I panted. "And I'm going to bathe in his blood."

JJ groaned as he watched me, my hips flexing as he fucked me with his gun and I loved every goddamn, exhilarating second of it. It was so cold, so deadly, so twisted and so fucking good all at once.

"Think of your finger on that trigger," JJ commanded, his thumb more forceful against my clit as he drove the gun into me harder, faster. I bit down on my lip to contain the noises escaping me as I did what he said, my pussy clenching tight as my climax rolled up on me and I visualised what he was telling me to do. "Now pull it, pretty girl. Fucking pull it and claim what you need."

My mind filled with the image of me doing that, of Shawn's blood splattering my skin and the last ties he held on me breaking apart like they'd never been there in the first place. My fingers clenched the arm rests and I cried out as pleasure exploded through my body, my pussy squeezing tight around the barrel of the gun and a lust filled moan escaping me as I came so hard my head spun.

JJ drew the gun back out of me slowly, holstering it again as I collapsed onto his chest and tried to come down from that high. JJ found my aching nipple through my playsuit and tugged hard, making my pussy clench again as an aftershock of pleasure shivered through me.

"Your damage is so beautiful, pretty girl," he breathed. "And your vengeance is so fucking hot." He stood in a fluid motion, lifting me in his arms before driving me back against the wall beside the door and kissing me hard.

I felt my shields crumbling apart in that kiss, feeling how much he hungered for me in it, how much he enjoyed worshipping me, how much he wanted to, needed to. Now more than ever our time together felt precious, stolen and also like claiming back something we were owed.

"Rogue?" Fox called, his footsteps approaching from outside and JJ dropped me to my feet suddenly with a curse.

"There's lipstick on your mouth," I hissed at him and he swore, sprinting away from me and throwing the bathroom door closed behind him a second before Fox entered the room.

I'd managed to whip my phone out and opened up some dumb game app half a blink before the badger was looming over me.

"The scouts have been seen," Fox growled. "What are the two of you doing up here anyway?"

"I needed a wee. Then JJ decided he wanted to take a shit in Luther's bathroom," I said with a shrug, keeping my eyes on my phone as I tried to get my rampant heartbeat back under control.

JJ clearly heard me and promptly flushed the toilet before opening the bathroom door and striding out.

"Dude, did you even wash your hands?" Fox asked in disgust.

"Oh shit, I must have forgot." JJ started backing up again, but as Fox looked away from him, he pushed the two fingers he'd had inside me into his mouth and sucked them in a way that was so sexual that my greedy pussy throbbed in response.

I quickly averted my gaze and shoved my phone away as JJ made a song and dance about washing his hands then Fox led us out of the suite and down the corridor until we were all stepping onto the balcony which fronted the clubhouse.

Luther was already out there, talking and laughing with a few of his men like he didn't have a care in the fucking world.

"What now?" I breathed, letting Fox take my hand as he guided me towards the railing and he grabbed a few beers from a helpful little sausage who I was guessing was a new recruit.

The look he gave me said he knew that I was only just sworn in too and I smirked at him over my beer, not giving a single shit about getting preferential treatment. I was fucking owed it after Luther stole ten years of my life. In fact, I was owed a lot more than that.

"Now we wait," Fox said, leaning close to me and pushing my hair back over my shoulder. My skin heated at his touch, my hard nipples driving against the fabric of my playsuit as my gaze fell to his mouth. God he looked good tonight and I couldn't help but fantasise a little as I looked at him, imagining him pinning me down and showing me what it was like to be dominated by the prince of the Harlequins. "And you stay by my side until it's all over."

I nodded my agreement as I tore my gaze from eye fucking the life out of him and glanced towards the road, wondering if we were being watched right now. If Shawn was already drawing close. And as my gaze dropped to the pistol hanging from JJ's belt, I couldn't help but agree that his tactic had worked. I felt calm and collected, focused and ready.

I was going to put a bullet in Shawn Mackenzie's skull today.

And maybe after that, I could start figuring out what kind of life I had left to live.

CHAPTER EIGHT

I pulled on a black hoody and a ski mask as I snuck out the back of the clubhouse and moved into the trees. Rogue was still spinning in my mind and my heart was pounding to a manic tune that wouldn't settle after having stolen that filthy, perfect moment with her. But I was growing tired of stealing moments. I wanted her on my arm in broad daylight, I wanted to stop hiding, but most of all I wanted Fox to accept that we were together. And that was the most hopeless want of all.

I stayed under the cover of dark with a handgun in my grip as I moved towards the eastern road to meet my team. It was about a quarter of a mile through the trees before I made it to the bank where some of the Harlequins were gathered. I could hardly see them in the dark, five of them spread out on this side of the road and another five on the other. I headed to one end of the group, getting in to place against a boulder and peering down at the road beyond it as I melded into the shadows.

I slowed my breathing as the leaves rustled in the wind and waited for something to happen. And waited.

Nothing.

Everything was painfully quiet and I took a moment to text the team who were covering the west road, but they hadn't seen anything either. So I guessed it was just a waiting game now.

Someone moved closer to me and I looked up to find one of the Harlequins there dressed in black with a ski mask covering his face.

"Hey, get back in position," I hissed, pointing further down along the tree line.

"This *is* my position," he said and my neck prickled at the sound of Maverick's deep voice.

"What the fuck are you doing?" I demanded in a frantic whisper, glancing over at the others but they were too far away to hear us.

"Rogue invited me."

"No she didn't," I hissed.

He moved against the boulder, raising a revolver and gazing down at the road. "Sure she did. So when's the special guest arriving?"

"You can't be here," I pressed.

"I can actually, because here I am. But if you don't *want* me here Johnny James that's a whole different kettle of fish and I don't really give a fuck about boiling it."

I leaned against the boulder, our arms pressed tight up against each other's as I glared at him. "How did you know where to find us?" I asked in dismay.

"It's cute that you don't think I have eyes among your people, JJ," he snorted in amusement and my pulse thumped unevenly. *Jesus*. Fox was gonna freak out when he heard that nugget of shit.

I took my phone from my pocket, figuring it would be best to give him a heads up, but Maverick snatched it from my grip, smoothly tucking it into his own pocket.

"I'll give that back when the fun's over," he said quietly. "You're such a little snitch these days. But I bet you didn't tell Foxy boy about what we did with Rogue in the train car."

"Fuck off," I muttered.

"When are we doing that again, by the way? I've been waiting in that train car every night like Juliet waiting for her Romeo to show up, but you never do. You really know how to keep a man's balls blue, JJ."

"Shut up," I snarled. "We're not doing it again."

He laughed low in his throat. "Chicken shit."

"I'm not afraid of you," I hissed.

"Maybe not, but you *are* afraid of the big, bad Fox," he taunted. "Do you think he'd show you the same courtesy as he did Chase? Or is fucking his girl a worse crime than trying to get rid of her?" He tutted under his breath and my chest knotted. "He might really pull the trigger this time."

"Fuck. You," I snarled.

"Is that an offer? I don't have any cash on me right now, but I'll owe you a blowjob after you've made me come, deal?"

It took every ounce of restraint I had not to attack him as I forced my gaze onto the road and tried to concentrate.

"Out of interest, how much do you charge per hour?" he asked and I tried to tune him out. "I just need to know so I can save up my pennies for next time. Or do you charge per sexual act? Do you do special offers? Buy two hand jobs get one free? Can I give the free one to a friend?"

"Shut up, Maverick," I snarled, failing at ignoring him as he talked continuously in my ear.

"Rogue's really clocking up the hours, huh? She must owe you a fortune," he said and I knew he was baiting me but I couldn't rise to it right now. Shawn could show up at any second and I couldn't be busy beating Maverick's head in when he did. "I suppose her pussy is payment enough though. It's so fucking tight, isn't it? Do you think we could both fit inside her at the same time?"

"Maverick," I snapped in as quiet a voice as I could manage. "If you don't shut your mouth, I'll shut it permanently."

"Like with a needle and thread? That'd take some time. Shawn might show up by then, and you wouldn't wanna be distracted." He chuckled and my hand tightened on my gun.

"If I'm distracted and Shawn manages to get past us because of it, that's on you. And Rogue is at the clubhouse, so if you care about her at all then stop talking," I demanded and he fell quiet. At least he did for two seconds, then he started talking again.

"I just need a date and time for the next fuck fest, I have a busy schedule so you might wanna book me in," he whispered.

I said nothing so he took out my phone and started adding his contact information under the name Tyrannosaurus Cock. Then he flicked the camera on, wrapped an arm around my shoulders and tugged up his ski mask as he snapped a photo of us using the night vision. I lunged for the phone, but he held it away as he sent the photo to Fox with the caption *Me and Rick are getting frisky in the woods. Wanna join? P.S. Bring the unicorn.*

He passed my phone back to me and I sighed as it started blowing up with anxious messages from Fox. I sent him one back to say I had the situation under control then pocketed it, figuring there was nothing more I could do to calm him down right now. Fox hadn't spoken about Maverick since we'd all worked to dig at The Dollhouse wreckage for day after day, hunting for Chase. Eventually, the police had forced us to leave and Maverick had looked as broken as I felt about that before getting on his motorbike and driving away. Fox and I had loaded Chase's bike into his truck and driven it home; it had felt like carrying a coffin back to the house and I couldn't bear seeing it every time I went down to the garage, but I hadn't covered it up. The pain was a reminder of him, and I didn't wanna forget him, so I just let it hurt.

Silence fell at last and we waited there in the dark as an owl hooted somewhere out in the trees and I listened intently for sounds of an approaching car.

"Would you rather be a dog with no legs or a bird with no wings?" Maverick whispered and it caught me so off guard I almost cracked a smile. But not quite.

I forced my lips to remain flat and didn't answer, so he elbowed me and for a moment I was reminded of playing this game with him when we were kids. It was a favourite of all of ours and we'd try to come up with the most ludicrous 'would you rather' questions that we could to make each other laugh. I'd often played it with Chase whenever we'd been out on a job together and the memories of that had my heart tugging sharp enough to make it bleed.

"A bird with no wings," I murmured. "A legless dog can't go anywhere."

"It can if you throw it hard enough," he whispered and my head snapped around at those words as a surprised laugh escaped me.

He didn't look at me, but I could see the smirk in his eyes. It was something of a catchphrase for us when playing this game, and whenever one of us had the chance to say it we'd always cracked up like it was the funniest thing in the world.

"Your turn," he muttered and I wondered why he was trying to play this game with me right now. The familiarity of it was too enticing to ignore though and it wasn't like I couldn't watch the road at the same time.

"Would you rather be invisible or be able to fly?"

"Invisible," he said instantly. "Then I could walk into Harlequin House and kill you all in your sleep. Bang, bang, bang," he mimed firing his gun and my heart sank as I stared at the road with a scowl, fully reminded that we were enemies and this little ceasefire we had right now was entirely to do with Rogue. Without her, he'd be turning that gun on me and making sure my brains decorated the trees.

"Don't pout about it, J," Maverick growled. "That's what this'll all come to in the end."

"I'm not sure what I ever did to you to make you wanna kill me, Maverick."

He remained quiet for a few beats before he answered. "You didn't fight for Rogue while I was gone. You may have continued writing to me in prison and I'm sure you cried to Luther about trying to get me out, but that all pales to nothing when I think about you abandoning her."

"You don't know anything," I bit at him. "I tried every chance I got to find her, we all did. But Luther was…" I trailed off, unsure what the point even was of trying to explain this to him. He didn't care, he wasn't going to hear it. He'd made his mind up about me and my boys a long time ago.

"What?" he grunted.

"It doesn't matter," I murmured. "It won't change anything."

"How do you know unless you say it, Johnny James?" he pushed and I rolled my eyes.

"After we initiated, Luther had eyes on us constantly," I said. "He expected us to go looking for her, so he had his men surrounding us. He got Chase and I to move into Harlequin House with Fox and we couldn't even take a shit without Luther knowing about it. By the time he let us breathe a little, Rogue was already gone. She ran away from Fox's aunt's house and buried herself so we'd never find her. We spent the last ten years hunting for her, Fox even put out photos online with paid goddamn advertising to try and find her. But she didn't want to be found, Maverick, she hated us. I think a part of her will always hate us."

Maverick thought on those words for a long moment. "I would have found her," he said assuredly.

"Keep telling yourself that," I gritted out. "You don't know shit. You think we didn't try everything? You think you really could have done anything more than we already did?"

"Yeah, I do," he said stubbornly and I just shook my head at him.

"Look I'm sorry for whatever happened to you in prison, I'm sorry if you feel like we abandoned you, but I'm not sorry for not trying harder to find Rogue. Because there isn't a single thing more we could have done, and eventually we had to accept that she didn't want to be found or else she would have come home. And while you were suffering in prison, we were suffering out here in our own version of it."

"You were a free man," he said icily.

"Since when?" I scoffed. "I'm a Harlequin, Rick, I'm not free. But that's life. You pick your chains and in the end, those are the ones I chose. Because I may have to do things that tarnish my soul sometimes, but I also have a home, I have Fox and Ch-" I cut myself off, grief tearing down the centre of me as I missed my brother so fiercely that it cut me to shreds.

I turned away from Maverick, not wanting him to see any of the pain in my eyes. I slid my finger onto the trigger of my gun, wishing Shawn would show his face so I could start shattering bones. That motherfucker was responsible for Chase's death, so it was going to take everything I had not to kill him on sight. Rogue deserved that kill and I wanted to watch as she planted a bullet between his eyes, but there was no rule that said I couldn't rip off a few of his limbs first.

Maverick remained quiet but his arm pressed to mine and for a moment it felt like we were sharing in the agony of our lost brother, but I wasn't sure that was true. Maverick may have cared for Rogue, but I'd seen his hatred for the rest of us as clear as day. Still, he'd stayed to dig in the ruins after Rogue had been found, so maybe some piece of him had wanted to find Chase alive. I hoped so. Because the idea that Maverick was lost forever had always haunted me. He still felt this bond to us on some level, but I didn't know how deep it ran anymore or if it would make any difference in the end. Maybe one day I really would end up bloody at his feet. But he'd saved Fox's life while the building was collapsing too – not that either of them seemed inclined to acknowledge that in any way. I'd seen it with my own two eyes though and it meant something. I just wasn't sure what yet.

A scream spiralled into the air from somewhere to the west and my breath snagged in my throat. I snatched my phone out of my pocket, calling the other team and a beat later Santiago answered, breathing heavily. "Under…attack," he said, sounding in pain.

"Hang on," I gasped. "We're coming." I whistled to my team and they hurried toward us.

"No – no please!" Santiago wailed but the sound turned to gargles and he fell quiet as more screams sounded in the background.

My stomach knotted as a deep voice spoke down the line. "Well hello, sunshine," Shawn purred. "Your men are in an itty bitty situation over here, are you coming to the rescue?"

"Fuck you," I snarled. "You're dead tonight."

"I hardly think so," he laughed. "I'm alive and kicking and your king and his son's blood is gonna rain from the sky by the time I'm done. Tell me, Johnny James, do you think you can reach the clubhouse before I do, so you have a chance to say goodbye?"

I cut the call, already running as I dialled Fox's number, my pulse thundering in my head.

"JJ?" Fox answered. "What's happening? Is Maverick still with-"

"Shawn's attacked the western team," I blurted. "He's heading for the clubhouse, keep Rogue safe and prepare the men."

"Fuck," he cursed. "Get back here. Now."

"On it." I hung up, tearing along as Maverick caught up with me, powering his arms back and forth like he was trying to outpace me, but there was no chance of that.

My family were in trouble and I was going to be right there when our enemies arrived, ready to fight to the death to protect them. I wasn't going to lose any more of them to Shawn Mackenzie.

Tonight, we ended this and got vengeance for our boy.

CHAPTER NINE

The clubhouse was dark, all lights switched off to make sure the Dead Dogs couldn't see any of us inside as every Harlequin in the place took cover around the windows and held weapons ready to fire.

I stood with Fox, my pulse racing as we sheltered behind a thick beam which ran to the right of the largest window in the place. His left hand pressed to the wall beside my head as he boxed me in against it, my spine flush with the bricks and his chest brushing mine.

He held a Glock in his other hand and had another gun hanging from his belt.

"I don't like this," some guy murmured from his position crouched beneath the window frame as we all waited.

Luther was to our left, his gaze fixed on the view beyond the open doors as he held his own gun ready.

"Here, wildcat," he murmured, drawing my attention from the window and I bit my bottom lip as I accepted the pistol he was holding out for me.

The weight was familiar now and after practicing with JJ every day for the last month, I was confident in my aim. Shawn wouldn't get away from me this time.

Fox growled like a fucking dog as he shifted his weight, penning me in against the wall even tighter.

"She won't need that until the end when he's trussed up at her feet and waiting for her to finish him," he hissed.

"So you'd leave her unarmed and unprotected until then?" Luther asked, arching a brow at his son.

"I'm right here. She has more protection than anyone else in this place. And I won't let a single thing happen to her. But with a weapon of her own she's unpredictable. She'll probably try and run off and pull some crazy stunt like last time."

I choked down the desire to snap at him, to remind him that I was a fully capable woman and that my crazy stunts had equalled my survival up until this date. Then I reached out to touch his arm instead, feeling the tension in his posture as my fingers ran over the solid muscle of his flexed bicep.

"I'm not going anywhere, Fox," I promised him. "So long as you don't try to cut me out of this, I promise I'll stand by you. I won't leave your side for a single second. Kay?"

Fox dropped his gaze to meet mine, blowing out a slow breath as he nodded and eased back a little to give me some room to breathe.

"I can't lose you too, hummingbird," he murmured, the pain we all felt over Chase creeping into the space between us and I nodded, squeezing his arm a little where I held it.

The sound of a gunshot broke through the silence and suddenly the whole place was carnage.

Glass shattered, men yelled and bullets tore through the sky in every direction.

I tried to peek out the window and take a shot of my own, but Fox flattened me against the wall, a snarl on his face as he leaned out and returned fire.

Luther started bellowing orders for his men to focus on Shawn and there was a flurry of movement as someone shouted back saying they'd just seen him approaching from the west road and that everyone who had been positioned that way was dead.

"JJ," I gasped, trying to shove my way past Fox as the gun in my hand weighed me down with thoughts of what I needed to do with it.

"He was to the east," Fox growled. "He's fine."

I knew that made sense on some level, but he was still out there and Shawn was so close. Within reach. And that dark, angry, raging part of me hungered for the blood he owed me more furiously than I could have imagined. "Come on."

I managed to scramble towards the door, but I lurched back with a scream as a bullet tore through the wood.

A Harlequin roared in pain as he was hit in the shoulder and two of the other gang members grabbed him and started hauling him away from the doorway.

Luther stepped out of cover with a manic smile lighting his face as he stood his ground and fired with two pistols at once, emptying them before jumping back away from the door just as return fire ripped through the wood.

Fox grabbed my arm and hauled me back towards him, boxing me in against the wall again as he continued to shoot out of the broken window into the darkness beyond.

His gun rang empty and I snatched a magazine from his belt, reloading it for him as he ejected the empty one to the floor.

Fox caught my eye with half a smile which quickly dissolved into a frown as he returned his attention to shooting outside again. His muscles were bulging with tension and heat poured from his body into mine as he shielded me. It would have been insanely hot if it wasn't for our current situation - or maybe that was what was making it even hotter.

"Hold your fire!" Shawn's voice bellowed above the clamour of gunshots and I sucked in a sharp breath as my grip on my pistol tightened. "Or your pretty boy here gets a whole lot less pretty."

It seemed like every Harlequin in the clubhouse was holding their breath and fear twisted my heart, shredding it to ribbons in my chest even before I managed to lean far enough over to see who he held as his hostage.

Blood pissed down the side of JJ's face, soaking into his white shirt and making the most horrifying sense of inevitability wash through my skin. Shawn stood at his back, a gun pressed firmly to his temple and a grin on his face which said he knew how valuable the piece he was holding was.

"What do you want?!" Fox roared, his entire body seeming to radiate fury as he pressed his chest to mine and flattened me against the wall like he thought I might just run out there at any moment. And maybe I would.

"What a question. There are just so many answers to it, too," Shawn said, shoving the gun against JJ's temple even harder. "I mean, how far back are we going here? 'Cause I coulda done with a few more warm hugs from my pa. And if I'm being totally honest with ya - I'm kinda hungry right now, so a burger wouldn't go amiss. I'd also like a pretty little beachside town with some lovely warehouses to store all kinds of merchandise for me and my business associates. I'd love a boat. Nothing practical - one of those fancy things that rich people have for shits and giggles. A nice hat wouldn't be a bad shout either. But most of all...I'd say I'd like to feel the wash of this asshole's brains splattering all over my face as I pull the trigger and break your little Harlequin heart all over again."

"Stop!" I screamed, lurching towards the window as Shawn took a step back and smacked the barrel of his pistol against the back of JJ's skull. "Shawn, don't - he's-"

Fox roared something unintelligible as he leapt on me, taking me out and sending the two of us rolling across the glass covered floor just as gunshots rang in my ears and bullets tore through the space where I'd just been standing.

"Hold your fucking fire!" Shawn bellowed outside and the gunfire came to an abrupt end as I found myself pinned beneath Fox with slivers of glass digging into my skin and so much fear in my heart that I was certain I was going to be torn apart by it. "I just thought of something I want more than all of that. I want my girl back. I want that tight ass and those perky tits and that pouty fucking mouth which was just made to take my cock. I want her on her knees and begging for my forgiveness. And in return, I'll up and leave. Pack up my shit and get outa town. We can have peace, your boy here can have life, and I can have my little woman back warming my bed where she belongs. How 'bout that?"

Fear bit into my soul at his words, at the thought of doing what he was suggesting, of going back to the girl I'd been when I was with him. Surely he was full of shit. Surely he didn't want me now for any reason other than to punish and destroy me - finish me the way he'd meant to the first time around.

I didn't believe for one second that he'd give up this war for the sake of getting me back. But maybe he would give up JJ.

"Don't even fucking think about it," Fox snarled, keeping me in place beneath him as my heart pattered with terror over what I was considering.

"It's JJ," I breathed, because he had to understand that. This wasn't about me. It was about my boy. The man I'd hated then lusted for and had never stopped loving throughout it all.

"And you're *you*," Fox growled, his features pinching with distress.

"Don't you even consider it, pretty girl!" JJ yelled from outside and the sound of a gun firing made me scream in utter fear.

Fox and I scrambled back towards the window and a sob of relief escaped me as I peeked out and found Shawn with his gun aimed towards the sky while JJ still stood tall and bloody before him.

"How about I give you a countdown, sugarpie? And if your sweet ass isn't out here by the time I reach zero, I'll blow this one's brains out and we can all get back to trying to kill each other as planned."

"Shawn, don't!" I yelled, my voice cracking with panic but he just smirked cruelly as he began his countdown.

"Ten...nine..."

CHAPTER TEN

I'd gotten separated from JJ the moment we reached the woods at the edge of the clubhouse when a bunch of Dead Dogs ambushed us. JJ had fought like a goddamn hero to try and make it back inside to reach Rogue and Fox, but the problem with heroes was that they always did stupid shit. That was why I preferred the villain lifestyle. So I'd hung back, gutted as many men as I could and now look? JJ had been caught and I was as free as a bird.

I crept through the trees as Shawn paused his countdown to continue boasting about his win and I rolled my eyes at the motherfucker. His monologues were his damn downfall, but I for one was happy to be the one to shut him up.

"-and that was the first time I gutted a man with a steak knife," Shawn said theatrically. "Such a rich red colour his blood was, I swear it's never shone so bright in any other corpse I've seen since, but maybe this boy's blood will be as pretty as his face, huh? Now where was I? Oh yeah, six…five…four – Oh Fox, did I ever tell you about the time I bent Rogue over a table and fucked her sweet pussy in front of a mirror? She touched herself the whole time, just looking at me railing that tight hole o' hers."

"Shut your fucking mouth!" Fox bellowed from the clubhouse as my skin itched over Shawn's words.

Keep talking, dead man.

One of Shawn's men was just ahead of me in the woods and I moved up silently behind him, my knife in my grip. I lunged forward, slamming my hand down over his mouth and driving my blade up hard between his ribs, stifling his scream as he died. I was making a mental tally of my victims that I'd be sure to ink onto my body later tonight. If I survived that long.

I lowered him into the shadows and stepped over his body, moving closer to my target as I wiped my knife off on my jeans, placing it back in its holster before taking out my gun.

"Speaking of holes, I'd best get on with putting one in your boy Johnny James, unless you wanna come out here, sugarpie?" Shawn called.

"Let him go, you can have me instead," Fox offered and Luther instantly shouted out in refusal of that.

"No!" Rogue screamed, terror coating her voice.

"I don't want you, Fox, I want your girl," Shawn chuckled. "And you're down to three seconds now to send my little whore out here. Three – two-"

I raised my gun, lining Shawn up in my sights and aiming for his back. I was tempted for the kill shot, but I'd promised that to my little unicorn. I'd make sure he was maimed good though.

"One and three quarters – one and a half-"

"JJ!" Rogue screamed. "I'm coming, I'm-" Her voice cut off and I had the feeling Fox was responsible.

"One and a quarter," Shawn went on.

Shut your goddamn mouth.

Shawn aimed his gun at JJ, ready to take another one of my brothers from the world, and yeah I was pissed about Chase. Because that death should have been mine. Fuck if it meant more to me than that. And fuck if it still hurt me every goddamn day.

My upper lip peeled back as hatred and rage ebbed under my skin and I pulled the trigger.

The bang split the air and Shawn was thrown to the ground from the blast, knocking JJ down with him. A cacophony of noise rang out as Fox and his men started firing and Shawn's gang returned it, war descending in an instant.

JJ crawled away, scrambling to his feet and I ran towards him, firing at an asshole Dead Dog coming up behind him and dropping him to the ground like a fly. I pulled JJ backwards towards the trees for cover, shoving him into the woods before turning back to get hold of Shawn.

The motherfucker was already on his feet and through his torn shirt, I saw a fucking Kevlar vest covering his body.

"No," I spat as he sprinted away into the throng of his men and called a retreat as the Harlequins spilled out of the clubhouse.

The Dead Dogs tore away into the woodland and I lost sight of Shawn, a snarl ripping from my throat as I stepped forward to go after him. JJ caught my arm, dragging me back into the trees and I cursed as I tried to shove him away.

"Get off of me," I snapped, but he didn't let go, digging his heels in.

"He's gone," he insisted. "And if you run into that war, you'll end up dead. The Harlequins will shoot you if The Dead Dogs don't."

I'd taken my ski mask off and tossed it somewhere and I cursed myself out for it as the bloodlust pumped through my chest. In that instant, I didn't give a fuck if I put myself at risk, I just wanted Shawn bloody and on his knees for Rogue. I didn't give a damn what it cost me. He'd hurt her, he'd killed Chase, he'd-

"Maverick," JJ barked, shoving me against a tree so hard that my skull impacted with the bark. "You need to get out of here."

Gunfire filled the night and the Harlequins were swarming the whole area. I shoved his hands off of me, determined to finish what I'd come here for, but JJ got in my way, his chest slamming against mine.

"If you die, you'll break her heart. She can't take it, not after losing Chase," JJ hissed, grabbing my face in his hand to make me look at him and I saw the grief in his eyes, hating how it mirrored some jagged piece of my soul.

I shoved him back with a growl, but was forced to acknowledge the desperation in his gaze and I frowned as I wondered if JJ actually gave a shit about me. Did he really give a damn if I died today?

"JJ!" Rogue ran into the trees, colliding with him and knocking him back a step from me as she held onto him.

He hugged her tight, kissing her head as she clutched him like the sky would fall if he left this world then she turned to me, fisting her hand in my shirt and tugging me closer. Her lips met mine and I knotted my fingers in her hair, crushing my mouth harder to hers as she continued to hold onto us both and keep us close. Despite failing her tonight, she tasted like victory, like I was stepping onto my homeland for the first time after years in battle.

"Thank you," she said breathlessly. "You saved him."

"It wasn't a rescue mission, beautiful," I said dismissively. "I was just trying to cut down Shawn."

I ignored JJ's probing look and stole another kiss from Rogue, tugging her fully away from him and gripping her ass as I pressed my tongue into her mouth. God it had been too fucking long since I'd tasted her.

"JJ?!" Fox called anxiously, heading this way and Rogue tried to wriggle free of my arms, but I didn't let her go, kissing her more fiercely, possessively, showing her who she belonged to. And it certainly wasn't the asshole running toward us.

"What the- get the fuck away from her!" Fox barked and I finally let Rogue break the kiss but kept her tight against my body.

I found myself staring down the barrel of Foxy boy's gun and arched a brow at him in boredom.

"Fox, calm down," Rogue gasped, raising her hand to try and knock the gun away, but he didn't move it.

"Yeah, calm down, Foxy," I taunted as his upper lip peeled back and his right eye practically twitched with fury. "She's right where she wants to be, aren't you baby girl?"

"Stop being an asshole," she demanded. But that sure as fuck wasn't a denial.

JJ looked between us with concern lining his brow and Fox stepped closer, his finger tightening around the trigger of his gun as he pressed it to my forehead.

"Let. Her. Go," he commanded in his bossiest voice and I yawned provocatively.

"Rick," Rogue hissed, still trying to get free of my arms. "I don't think he's fucking around."

"I'm not," Fox warned. "You've got five seconds to get your hands off of her."

"Are you really gonna kill me, Foxy?" I asked curiously. "Are you sure you can watch me die?"

"I can watch with my eyes wide open," he said in a deathly calm voice. "You're down to three seconds."

"This is a long five seconds," I pointed out. "Five, four, three, two, one. See? I should be dead by now. You're as bad as fucking Shawn."

"Let her go!" he snarled and JJ took hold of Fox's arm, trying to tug the gun down.

"Fox," JJ growled, trying to make him look at him. "Stop."

"Aww, even your bestie thinks you're an asshole. Must be a sad life you lead these days, Foxy," I taunted.

"Fox, put the gun down," Rogue ordered, still trying to escape the cage of my arms, but I knew as soon as I let go she was gonna be taken from me again and I didn't know when I'd see her next. Sure, the other option was having my brains blown out, but I was one helluva stubborn asshole, so I might just take that option over being cowed down by Fox Harlequin.

"Put the gun down, son," Luther's booming voice reached me and I gave my ex adopted father a dry look as he appeared.

"Well isn't this the fun family reunion?" I deadpanned.

"Fox, that was an order," Luther said sharply and Fox growled in frustration before lowering the gun.

JJ's shoulders relaxed and he reached for Rogue's hand. "Come on, pretty girl."

I pulled her tighter against me, dragging her backwards through the trees and wondering if I could make it to my motorcycle with her over my shoulder and these three assholes chasing me.

"Rick, stop it," she said, pushing at my arms.

"Nah, I'm good, beautiful. I think I'm in the mood to kidnap you and take you back to my lair." I dropped my mouth to her ear, tugging it between my teeth and Fox looked like he was about to blow a blood vessel as I stared him dead in the eye. Which was all the more reason to keep doing it.

"Rick, that's enough. Let her go. She needs to go home, it's not safe out here," Luther said firmly.

"I think I know how to keep her safe, thanks *Dad*," I mocked.

"How about you let her make her own decision?" JJ pushed.

"Nope," I said.

"Rick," she snapped. "Stop being a prick and let me go."

I sighed in frustration as she shoved my arms again and I finally released her. She took a step away and I felt the distance between us growing like an uncrossable sea.

"Come home, Rogue, we need to make plans against Shawn," Luther urged and I glared at the motherfucker, reaching for the gun at my hip. Maybe I'd just shoot them all to shit now and get rid of all my problems at once.

She took another step towards them and I lunged for Rogue, planning to take her after all, but she was already moving away to join them and the second she got close enough, Fox closed an arm around her shoulders, sneering at me in a clear warning.

"I need to go, Rick," she said to me with a frown. "I'll see you soon."

"Not if I have anything to do with it," Fox said through his teeth.

"Well she's not your property, Foxy, she can do what she likes," I said, a threat in my tone.

"Stop alpha dogging." Rogue tried to escape Fox's hold, but it was clearly as tight as mine had been and JJ moved to flank her other side, turning and taking her away as Luther remained there in the shadows. She glanced back at me in goodbye and what remained of my heart went with her, frustration flashing through me.

"There's a bed for you at that house too," my crazy ass adopted father offered.

"Thanks, but I think I'd rather enjoy some equally fun activity tonight, like skinning myself alive." I turned my back on him, stalking off into the trees as I headed for my motorbike with my mood descending into a black pit.

By the time I arrived at the dock, I was tempted to tie myself to the saddle of my bike and drive myself right off the end of it. Instead, I boarded the boat I'd used to get here and started heading across the water towards Dead Man's Isle, my soul a little more blackened and alone than usual.

Mia was at the compound today and she'd be asking about how my treatment was going. Because yeah, I now had to pretend I had dick rot so I didn't have to stick it in her – an idea I'd gotten from Rogue after she'd told me JJ had been using the excuse to avoid his escorts.

My special sauce to that idea was not telling Mia specifically what I had because I was 'too embarrassed' to talk about it. Whatever it was apparently lasted weeks and was highly contagious though, so it was doing the damn trick. But her patience was wearing thinner and thinner and she was starting to question my bullshit lies a little more than I was comfortable with. I had to somehow keep her sweet a while longer though because Kaiser Rosewood's next poker night was approaching and I was pretty sure he was gonna extend the invite to me this time. So long as Mia didn't dump my ass before then, I might finally get a chance to head onto the Rosewood estate and check out the crypt where all of our downfalls lay.

And after that alpha cunt display tonight from Fox, I was hungrier than ever to get on with my plan to destroy him. When it was done, I'd ride off into the sunset with Rogue and enjoy our honeymoon period until she used up all the good left in me and I drowned in the sea of bad waiting to reclaim me. Then my revolver would offer me peace at last and my short, torturous life on earth would finally be done.

CHAPTER ELEVEN

I sat across the table from Fox as he aggressively ate cereal at me and I yawned around my slice of toast.

"Spit it out, Badge, or you're gonna give yourself constipation."

Fox's eyes narrowed and he tossed his bowl down onto the table, dropping the spoon into it with a clatter which I was guessing was designed to make me flinch.

"I've had meaner assholes than you try to intimidate me, Fox. So if you get your kicks out of scaring people then you'll have to work harder with me," I commented, taking a bite of my toast.

It was early. Too goddamn early. But I'd been woken by the feeling of a pissy animal hanging around in my space and had found Fox sitting in a chair at the foot of my bed watching me sleep like a psycho. And I knew it wasn't the first time. So I'd yelled at him and called him crazy and he'd stormed out of the room again, slamming the door so fucking hard the walls had rattled.

I'd had a shower, gotten dressed into one of Chase's shirts and a pair of shorts and now I was sitting here at the asshole of dawn having a face off with a gang leader. I was getting too goddamn old for this shit.

"Well excuse me if I can't figure out what the fuck it is you like," Fox snapped. "Because if I'm judging by your psycho ex-boyfriend who tried to murder us all last night and the motherfucker who had his tongue in your mouth when I found you and JJ in the woods, I can only assume asshole behaviour turns you on."

A million snarky responses sprung to my lips and I was about to start hurling them in his face but something about the look in his eyes made me pause.

"I like you, Fox," I sighed. "But you just don't like me."

"Bullshit. I like everything about you," he replied instantly.

"So you like thinking about what me and Rick got up to on Dead Man's Isle?" I shot back.

"That's not the same as not liking you," he ground out.

"Fine. Forget about my sex life then. Do you like thinking about me and Shawn spending so much time together when I was with him? Do you like imagining the way I was with him? How he found me broken and bleeding inside and that was what drew him to me? Do you ever think about why I was with him for so long? Or about how shitty my life must have been for me to have preferred being his toy over the alternative of a life out there on the forgotten streets? Or do you just get so angry when you think about me fucking him that it doesn't even occur to you to wonder about any of the rest of my life outside of who I gave access to my pussy?"

"How am I supposed to think about any of that when you won't tell me about it?" Fox asked.

"Fine. Ask."

Fox's eyes flashed with some emotion I couldn't place and he leaned forward, resting his forearms on the table which divided us.

"Did he hit you?" he asked me.

"No. Not before the night he tried to kill me," I replied. "I told you before that I had rules. I wouldn't stand for cheating or hitting. If a guy wanted me exclusively, he'd do me the same favour and I refused to be anyone's punching bag."

"So that's it as far as your standards went? Who cares if they were assholes so long as they didn't smack you or let their dick wander?"

"Pot, kettle, Fox. If you want me to take objection to dating assholes, then I don't see the two of us having much chance at getting together."

The corner of Fox's lips lifted into the ghost of a smile and I sighed, finishing the last bite of my toast and climbing up onto the table. I shifted across it and pushed his empty bowl aside so that I could sit in front of him and rest my feet in his lap.

Fox instantly curled his fingers around my ankles and the heat of his skin against mine was like a balm to the ache which lived in me.

"Tell me," he murmured as I reached out to push my fingers into his messy blonde hair and he closed his eyes for a moment like he was relishing that touch.

I didn't like talking about this. Hell, I didn't even like thinking about it, but I was beginning to see that I was going to have to tell him if we were going to figure out a way past it, so I took a deep breath and prepared to do just that.

"I didn't notice it at first," I breathed, my skin prickling as memories of the girl I'd been for Shawn tickled at my subconscious. "But after a couple of months of us hooking up on and off, seeing him at parties and him turning up at the apartment I was sharing with a few other guys when he was horny, he told me he didn't want me where he couldn't find me all the time anymore. He said that if I was his girl he'd take care of me, and I wouldn't have to worry about assholes hanging around me, trying to take something that was his."

Fox growled at that word, his grip on my ankles tightening like the idea of Shawn ever having any kind of claim on me burned him up inside.

"So what? He moved you in with him?"

I shook my head. "He had some properties here and there, nothing fancy, but he said they were safe houses for if anything ever went to shit and he needed somewhere to run to." Fox nodded and I was sure that was something him and his crew had all over town too. "So he put me up in a little apartment not too far from his place and for a while, that all seemed great. I'd never really had any space to myself, and I paid him a couple hundred bucks a month in rent which he always laughed at, but he took my money all the same, saying I could be an independent woman if I wanted to be."

"Where were you getting that money?"

I shrugged. "The usual. Running jobs, boosting cars. There was a chop shop not too far from my apartment and I could steal whatever I needed."

"Right, so you were somewhat *independent*," Fox said the word like he hated it and I snorted.

"Of course I wasn't. But I didn't see that, I guess. If I'm honest, I don't think I wanted to. Life was easy. So fucking easy. I didn't have to sleep with one eye open or worry about the next person waiting to fuck me over. And after eight years of that shit, I was just so fucking tired. Shawn offered me a reprieve and I took it because I was so sick of fighting against the tide every goddamn day just to survive."

"I'm never going to be able say I'm sorry enough over those years," Fox said, his hands shifting up the backs of my calves as he leaned into me. "I've never wanted anything so badly as I wish for a do-over with you. To go back to that night when you killed Axel and do it all differently. Maybe we could have called my dad. Or maybe we should have just run right there and then and never looked back."

I swallowed a lump in my throat and shook my head. "The past is already written," I muttered. "And the future is out of our hands. All we have is right now."

"Well right now, all I want is to hold you in my arms and never let go," Fox growled, trying to tug me down into his lap, but I drew back.

"That's the problem though, Fox," I said, moving my right hand from his hair down to skim the line of his strong jaw as he looked up at me with those deep green eyes of his. "I can't be someone's captive again. The girl I was when I was with Shawn..."

I trailed off and looked away from him, but he caught my jaw and made me meet his gaze again.

"Tell me," he commanded, holding me there.

"I'm not even sure when it started," I said slowly, trying to explain it. "It happened so slowly, bit by bit, like this wall being built around me one brick at a time. I never noticed any of the bricks as they were laid, but one day I found myself trapped inside a wall which I couldn't remember how to scale anymore."

The confusion in Fox's eyes coupled with the pain I could see there over him not understanding this pushed me to go on, and I blew out a breath as I continued.

"Sometimes he'd call and tell me to dress up nice for him and come over, so I would. But then he'd give me this look when I arrived like...I dunno really, but I'd know I'd fucked up. He'd say something like, 'did my men think my girl was coming over to see me or did they assume I hired myself a hooker?' So the next time he'd tell me to come I'd wear something that covered me up more, and now that I look back on it I can't even understand why I did that. Why I was so fixed on pleasing him or meeting this impossible standard he set, but...I did. So anyway, then he'd look at me and say something like, 'holy shit you look like crap, sweet cheeks. What the fuck did I do to deserve this shit show of an outfit?' It made me feel like...like I was always missing the bar he set and I kinda hated that, but I was kinda numb to it too. It was still the best I'd had it since I'd left here. And then he'd laugh and slap my ass and tell me not to look so fucking pouty unless I was hoping to suck his dick. He'd switch on the charm again or start up one of his bullshit stories and I'd forget about it. Mostly."

"Rogue," Fox growled, but I placed my fingers on his lips because I needed to get this out so that I didn't have to keep picking at this scab.

"After a while, he started to make more suggestions for me to follow. He didn't like me going to parties. He didn't want me near his men either - sometimes he'd say they were too rough around the edges and that I was too good for the likes of them. Other times he'd tell me I had the look of a whore about me, and he didn't need his men thinking his girl was for sale. I didn't have that many friends, but the few I did have before I became his all disappeared and I feel like he warned them away, but I don't know for sure. He liked to call me names when he fucked me. But then he'd make it seem like I was being touchy or silly if I said anything about it or frowned at it. He'd ask me if I loved cock like he loved the idea of that then call me a whore if I said I did. He pushed harder the longer we were together but for some reason I just kept going back for more. I didn't feel the sting of those words like I knew I should have. I didn't have it in me to care about them. I was just this vacant body for him to use, trying to care about something enough for it to matter. Sex was an escape to me even if I had to get myself off. I could feel that. So sometimes he'd tell me I looked like a slut and I'd just drop to my knees and start sucking his dick because then it wasn't an insult anymore. Then he was groaning and fisting my hair and calling me a good slut, *his slut* but not like he liked that, more like he was half disgusted with me for it, and I guess in hindsight that wasn't okay but at the time it seemed like it was. And it was better than the alternative anyway. Because if I left him then I had nothing and no one all over again and I was just so fucking tired of being alone. I was better off warming his bed and being his good little whore than I would have been out there."

"I'll fucking destroy him before I kill him," Fox snarled and I could see how much my words were hurting him but he needed to understand them if he was going to understand me.

"It wasn't all like that. He'd buy me flowers and call me beautiful sometimes. He'd bring me to see his mom and show me off the whole time, telling her how in love we were and how he'd be giving her grand babies soon. I didn't want that and he didn't either but it was a pretty lie whenever we went over to her place. But every day I spent with him, more bricks were added to that wall. I was his and I was alone aside from him. And now you want to lock me up in this house and I...I just can't go back to being like-"

Fox stood up suddenly and pulled me into his arms, squeezing me so tight that I felt like my bones might crack though I never wanted him to stop either. I just wanted to stay here, safe in his arms like I'd wished I could so many times in the deepest depths of my heart.

"I would never make you a prisoner like that," he swore, his muscles trembling with barely contained rage as he fought to stay there with me instead of charging out of here in pursuit of fucking Shawn. "I just want you to be safe. I want you to be here. I want to look after you and provide for you and-"

"You threw me away," I choked out, pushing against him until he was forced to release me and I stood there staring up at him with tears in my eyes. "You shoved me down in the mud and told me to never come back, Fox. And I get it. I understand that none of you really wanted that and I know that Luther forced your hand. Maybe I can even forgive you for it. But it doesn't change it. It doesn't change what that set in motion. The only place that I was ever truly safe was here and then I wasn't here anymore, and I was just a fucking kid. So I did what I had to and I don't like the person it made me into, or the things it forced me to do, but somehow I found my way back here and I'm really trying to reclaim the pieces of me that once lived here. I don't want to be this jaded, broken mess of a girl anymore, Fox. But more than that, I don't want to be a man's plaything ever again. I can't be your prisoner even if the walls you'd build around me were made from love. I need to breathe. I need to make my own choices and fuck up in my own ways and I can't here. Not like this."

"You can't expect me to just stop wanting to protect you," he said desperately, taking a step forward as I stepped back. "I don't want to clip your wings, hummingbird. I just want you safe."

I nodded because I got that. But it couldn't go on like this. "Your version of safe is going to break us," I whispered, hating the way my words hit him but needing to say them anyway. "I've been waiting ten years to claim a life for myself and now you're the thing standing between me and it. I want my freedom to include you, Fox. But I can't be a prisoner anymore."

Fox opened his mouth then swiped a hand down his face before turning and striding away from me. I watched in confusion as he headed into the kitchen and pulled open a drawer. He rummaged in the back of it and returned with a set of keys for me, taking my hand and placing them in my palm alongside a heavy flick knife.

"I want you to keep this knife on you at all times. Please don't use these things to do anything insane. I only want to keep you here because I need you to be safe. But I heard you and it fucking guts me to think of you living like that with that fucking monster. You need to know your worth, hummingbird, and I promise you, you're priceless. That asshole saw it too and he wanted to cage you to keep you to himself, but I won't be that to you again. I don't want you to be here because I'm keeping the door locked. I want you to be here because it's where you belong. And I trust you to come to that decision when you're ready to give me your heart, no matter how broken it might be."

Fox leaned down and pressed a kiss against my forehead then turned and headed for the exit, ready to set out on his morning run. He tried to tickle Mutt's ears as he passed him by, but my little pup turned his ass towards him and marched in the opposite direction where he curled up on the floor right beside the fancy ass bed Fox had bought for him. Not in it. I was pretty sure that dog was gonna hold a grudge against Fox for yelling at him until the end of time.

Fox left me there and I twisted the set of keys through my fingers before sighing and leaving them down on the worktop. I inspected the knife a little more closely, frowning as I read Maverick's name on it and remembering it from when we were kids. Luther had given the two of them a blade each but had accidentally handed over the wrong name to each of them. They'd decided to keep the ones with each other's names on and had carried them everywhere with them ever since. I set the blade down, wondering if I really was being granted my freedom as I started cleaning up after breakfast.

JJ emerged as I finished washing up and I frowned at him as he slumped down in a chair at the breakfast table, looking dejected.

"What's up?" I asked curiously, tossing some toast on for him and pouring him a pity coffee.

"My cut is due in two days and I just got off the phone to Estelle at the club and I haven't got enough to give Luther."

"Is that normal?" I asked curiously, realising that I didn't have any cash to give Luther either. But then again, I'd never made any promises to give him shit beyond his family being reunited and Shawn's head in a sack, so I wasn't fussed.

"I used to have more than enough every month. But recently it's been a bit harder to pull the money together."

"Why?" I asked.

JJ cleared his throat and looked away from me. "Don't worry about it, pretty girl, I'll figure it out."

I frowned at that statement, wondering why he didn't want to tell me before figuring it out for myself.

"It's because you stopped escorting when we started hooking up," I said, knowing that was the answer without needing to phrase it as a question.

JJ winced a little then nodded. "It's my own fault really. Once I got into the swing of the escort game, I just kinda saw it as easy cash. I mean, sure, I had to blank off my emotions and play up to all kinds of bullshit, but I was raking in the dollars. I guess Luther got used to me being able to pull that kind of money in on the regular and now he expects it. I know Fox would have my back if I told him I wanted out of that side of the game, but he'd also wanna know why..."

I pursed my lips and leaned forward over the kitchen island. "Maybe it's time we told him the truth then," I suggested. "What's the worst that can happen?"

"Are you fucking kidding me? You saw the worst that could happen when he found out Chase had betrayed him. And he hadn't even gone against a direct order. In fact, fuck that - you didn't see the worst that could happen because he banished Chase instead of shooting him right there on the beach."

"Fox wouldn't have-"

"There's a whole lot you don't know about Fox these days, Rogue," JJ growled. "He's not just Luther's number two because he's his kid. He's a fucking animal when he has to be. Brutal, ruthless, and as cutthroat as they come. I've seen what he does to men who betray him and as much as I might like to think that him being my brother means something to him which might save me from that wrath, I've had more than enough evidence to prove it won't. I fucking hate lying to him and I swear I wouldn't about anything else, but..."

The look he gave me melted my heart into a puddle in my chest and I found myself walking around the kitchen island to him before my mind even caught up to what my body needed.

JJ turned on his stool and I stepped between his thighs, running my hands up his chest until they were clasped at the back of his neck and I was looking right into his honey brown eyes.

"I'm not giving this up for anything, J," I promised him, pushing my fingers into his hair and breathing him in. "You're my sunshine when I'm caught in the dark. You make me feel alive even when I'm struggling to hold myself together. You make me feel like I'm worth something even when it's hard for me to see it. You're my rock, Johnny James. I think I need you more than I need the Green Power Ranger."

A breath of laughter escaped him and I stole the smile on his lips by pressing mine to it and drinking it in. His hands came around my waist and he dragged me closer, groaning as I pushed my tongue into his mouth and wound my arms right around him.

"Don't ever let me go, pretty girl," JJ breathed, his eyes flashing with vulnerability which cut me to the quick.

"Never," I growled, surprised by how much I meant that. I didn't let myself indulge in fantasies of the future because I'd learned my lesson on that years ago, but I knew in my heart that no matter what it looked like, I wanted this man right here with me in it.

JJ lifted me suddenly and I squealed as my ass hit the kitchen island, but as tempted as I was to take advantage of Fox being out for the next hour, there was something more important that we needed to deal with, so I pressed him back.

"No sex until we sort out our little problem," I said firmly and JJ groaned.

"The only problem I've got right now is that all the blood in my body has rushed to my-"

"We need to run a job to get you the money you need to pay Luther," I said firmly. "There's no fucking way I'm allowing you to come up short and face that asshole's wrath, let alone the fact that it would bring up some questions for Fox which we don't have an easy answer to right now. So you and me are gonna go run a job and once you've got the money you need, I'll consider letting you between my thighs - but until then your balls are officially on ice."

"Rogue," JJ huffed in protest, trying to push forward, but I leaned back on my elbows and placed my bare foot against his chest to hold him off as I raised a finger to tell him to shh.

I grabbed my cell phone from my pocket then quickly dialled my fancy pants new friend.

"Hey, Rogue, where the hell have you been?" Tatum asked as she answered the call and I smiled as I filled her in on the last week while JJ stayed exactly where he was, his gaze roaming over me while he pouted over being cock blocked. I'd chatted to Tatum a fair bit over the last few weeks, my lockdown status in Fox's house meaning I could only keep in contact with my friends by phone or text recently.

"I was actually hoping you might have some rich asshole you wanna pick to be a mark for me. We need to be able to take shit that we can sell on easily though - nothing too hot-"

"How about cash?" Tatum asked temptingly and I grinned.

"That would be a hell yes."

"A neighbour of ours is a total sleaze, and he also loves flashing his cash about like it's going out of fashion. He's actually been pissing Saint off recently because he parks wonky or some shit and-"

"He parks his car at an obnoxious angle purely to infuriate me," her boyfriend's voice came from the background of the call. "I have informed him of his less than civilised standards and the very next day he had yet again parked across a white line. I am working on a plan to-"

"So yeah," Tatum cut in again. "Saint would fucking love it if you knocked him down a peg or two and the asshole always brags that he carries like ten grand in cash wherever he goes, so it'll be an easy payday for you."

"Sounds good. So should we just hit him at his house, or-"

"He has a morning tennis match today which he will return from between ten thirteen and ten twenty seven," Saint interrupted. "I apologise for not being able to be more accurate than that, but his schedules are not adhered to as strictly as I would prefer. He will be driving a ghastly red Audi and will be taking Cool Springs Street back home. I suggest you divert him on the road and if you wish to take his vehicle and destroy it, I will personally give you a further five thousand."

"Errr, fuck yes," I said, glancing up at the time. We needed to get on the road now if we were gonna catch the dude post tennis club but that sounded like a payday which was more than worth it to me. "I'll shoot you a pic of the car once we've finished fucking it up."

"Have fun," Tatum laughed and I cut the call.

"Come on, Johnny James. We've got a job to pull."

The sun beat down on my back as I stood leaning over the open hood of my Jeep with my short shorts on and my ass hanging out the bottom of them. I'd ditched my shirt and now wore a blue string bikini top and I was currently sporting an ebony wig cut into a sharp bob coupled with a pair of big black sunglasses which covered half my face.

JJ was smirking at me from his position crouched down out of sight on the road, enjoying the view as I pretended to fiddle with the engine of my car which was currently blocking the road exactly where we expected our mark to show up at any moment.

And right on cue, the roar of an expensive engine approaching brought a smile to my face. I cocked my hip out as I continued to play mechanic for our unsuspecting mark.

The engine noise fell to a low rumble as I heard the car pull up beside me, but I didn't look around until I heard him call out to me.

"Hey, err, miss, you're blocking the road."

"Could you help me?" I called, going all helpless maiden on him as I waved a hand at the engine and bit my lip. "The water cap fell off down there and I can't reach it no matter how far I bend." I leaned right over to give him an example and a show and smirked at JJ as the sound of the guy's car door swinging open followed.

JJ crept out of sight around my car as the dude left his engine idling and strode up to me. He had slicked back blonde hair and a fancy chinos and shirt combo going on which screamed rich asshole for all the world to see.

"I have a man I can call to come give you a tow?" he offered and I could feel his eyes crawling all over my flesh as he did so. "My place is only a little further along the road so you could come and wait there if you like?"

I glanced up and looked over his shoulder, flashing him a smile as I saw JJ slip behind the wheel of the dude's fancy car. "Oh I don't think that will be necessary," I said sweetly. "If you can just reach it for me, I should be fine. Though I wouldn't say no to a drink between new friends."

The guy smirked at me then stepped forward as I backed up, easily snagging the cap and placing it back where it belonged.

By the time he'd dropped the hood of my car back down and was grinning in triumph, I'd already hopped behind the wheel and snatched the pistol from my door pocket. Mutt perked up on the passenger seat, cocking his head as he watched the show like he was in on the con too.

I started the car up and squealed excitedly as the dude moved around to my window.

"Thank you so much," I gushed as he folded his arms on the top of my open window and leaned in to look at me.

"My pleasure."

"Could you do one more, itty, bitty thing for me?" I asked sweetly and he nodded.

"Sure. Anything."

"Hand over your wallet and that pretty watch you're wearing then, big boy." I lifted the gun and pointed it at his face and the poor fucker actually shrieked in alarm, his eyes going all round and terrified. "Hurry up, dude. I don't have all day and my finger's getting twitchy."

The guy sprang into action and quickly ripped his watch from his wrist, tossing it at me before following up with his wallet which was thick with green, green cash.

I grinned at him, threw my car into drive and sped away with JJ on my ass in his stolen red Audi.

Laughter spilled from my lips as the rich fucker screamed in horror, realising he was losing his car too, but we were long gone before he could even think about doing anything to try and stop us.

JJ hit the gas, his fancy ass sports car giving my sexy little Jeep a run for her money as we tore up the empty roads towards the far side of town where the docks were.

I yanked the wig off and tossed it in the footwell, grinning as my rainbow hair tumbled down around my shoulders and Mutt yipped in triumph.

My phone started ringing just as JJ overtook me like an asshole and I laughed while flipping him off then answered it through the sweet speaker hook up situation I had going in this thing.

"Hey, beautiful," Rick growled, making my toes curl with nothing but those two words.

"I thought you were still pissed at me," I said because the bastard had been refusing my calls ever since I'd chosen to head back with the Harlequins the night of the attack at the clubhouse.

"Yeah, well, I thought you could come make it up to me."

"How tempting," I teased.

"Don't go pretending you're gonna refuse me. I know you've been aching for a taste of my cock since the last time you had it."

"Don't you go pretending that's not a two way street. And while you've been making do with the clam vag, I've had some premium D to keep me satisfied nicely."

"The clam vag doesn't interest me. But if you're so into Johnny James's cock then bring him too. I'm all for pushing your boundaries, beautiful and I've been jerking off to thoughts of you sucking his cock while taking mine ever since the last time."

"You're filthy," I snorted.

"Says the girl who loved every second of it."

I scoffed but damn him, I was more than a little tempted. "Where are you then?"

"Where do you think, baby girl? I'm on the Isle."

"JJ won't just hop in a boat and head over to your little island fortress."

"Not even if I promise to be a good boy?"

"How about you tell all of your men to fuck off for the day and we can call it a peace treaty?" I suggested.

"How about you stop fucking me around and find a way to get your ass in my lap within the next hour or I'll have to come punish you for defying me," Rick growled.

I opened my mouth to tell him to stop bossing me about, but he fucking hung up on me.

JJ pulled in at the bait shop and parked in the centre of the lot. I drove along to a spot in the shade and by the time me and Mutt had jumped out of the Jeep, he was already standing on the hood of the stolen car.

"Who here wants to help the Harlequins send a message to the owner of this car?" he called. "The asshole who owns it can't park for shit, so I say we show him how easily a car like this can get dinged up when you park it in the wrong place!"

The crowd of people at the bait shop all howled their agreement and came running over as JJ jumped down. They started kicking punching and beating the car with anything they could find and the air was soon littered with the sounds of the alarm going off while glass smashed and the hooligans had the time of their damn lives.

I took a quick video and forwarded it on to Tatum with a grin. That was the easiest five grand I'd ever earned for sure.

I laughed, grabbing JJ's hand and dragging him back over to my car before slapping the stolen watch and cash into his hand with a wide smile.

"Looks like we made enough to cover Luther's cut," I said enticingly, my blood still humming with adrenaline as JJ bit down on his bottom lip.

"Shit, pretty girl. That's a lot of fucking money."

"Is it enough to buy me a few hours of your time?" I teased.

"Don't even joke about that," he said softly, placing an arm on the roof bars of my car as he leaned over me. "You can always have as much of my time as you desire, and it still won't be enough for me."

My smile softened and I sighed at not being able to kiss him with so many witnesses around. It was bullshit. We needed to get the fuck out of here, but Fox would be back at the house by now and my trailer was too damn hot during the day. But I had just received an invitation which was playing on my mind…

"Do you trust me, JJ?" I asked.

"You know I do. Why?"

"Does one of the pretty boats docked here happen to belong to the Harlequins? Or shall we steal one?"

"There are more than a few that come under Harlequin rule," he agreed.

"Let's go then. Lead the way."

JJ looked like he was seriously tempted to ask me where we were going, but he gave in to the game and quickly led me down to the dock where a bunch of Harlequin thugs were hanging out and guarding their vessels. We chose a small speedboat and Mutt leapt in with an excited bark as one of the gang bangers offered up a key.

JJ tried to take the helm but I hip checked him, knocking him aside and taking over.

"Sit down, JJ, and enjoy the ride."

He rolled his eyes then did as I said, leaning back against the seats and spreading his arms along the backs of them as he closed his eyes and sunned himself.

I smirked as I drove us out onto the water, wondering if I'd lost my damn mind. But something told me I hadn't. Maverick might still be harping on about wanting to kill the Harlequins and all that shit, but he'd had more than a few chances to do it recently and I knew he wasn't just teasing me over JJ. He was into it. And I was definitely into it. So that was all I really needed to know to make this decision.

If Rick wanted to call my bluff and see if I really would show up with another man in tow, then he was going to find out that I was still the same girl he'd grown up with and I never backed out of a challenge.

So bring it on, Big Bad Wolf, because this little rainbow riding hood didn't know when to back down.

Me and JJ chatted shit while he stayed in his position sunning himself for most of the journey across the water and he only opened his eyes when the angry bark of a man drew his attention.

"This is private property!"

"I have an invite," I called back and Mutt yipped.

"Holy shit, pretty girl," JJ gasped, lurching to his feet and grabbing my arm as he realised where I'd brought him. His other hand went to the pistol at his waist but I caught his wrist and gave him a serious look.

"It'll be fine, Johnny James. Trust me."

"It's not you I have a problem trusting," he gritted out, his eyes on Dead Man's Isle as I directed the boat towards the jetty in front of the huge hotel that Maverick had claimed for his own. "I have a seriously bad feeling about this."

The men on the beach were rushing about, pointing guns and calling more people to them but I just kept my chin raised and guided the boat forward.

"Oh hey, Rupert!" I called, recognising the dude and he narrowed his eyes at me.

"My name is Dave."

"That's basically the same," I reasoned and Mutt barked in agreement.

"Turn back, Rogue," JJ hissed.

"Too late for that now," I pointed out. There were at least six guns aimed our way and the welcoming committee looked all kinds of pissy.

As we drew closer to the dock, Maverick appeared. He was shirtless, his ink gleaming in the sunlight and a black baseball cap was placed backwards on his head. *Jesus*. What was it about a man in a backwards cap and shorts that was so freaking hot? He might as well have had his cock out and be priming it with lube for a fuck fest. Not that he'd have much need of any lube with me, because apparently I was a damn pussy tap for these boys. Drenching panties at the drop of a backwards baseball cap. Although I was pulling off a 'casually disinterested' thing at all times, so at least they had no goddamn idea about that.

"Close your mouth, baby doll, you're drooling," Rick called as he strode towards us and I narrowed my eyes into a scowl at him. *For fuck's sake.*

"You can't boss me about while you don't have any shoes on, Rick. It's impossible to be intimidating while bare foot," I replied scathingly.

JJ was rigid beside me, his eyes skipping between all the guns aimed our way and the man in charge.

"Cute," Rick commented. "But you'll be eating those words soon enough." He glanced around at his men and barked an order at them. "Disarm the Harlequin trash and bring him inside for me to play with."

Two of the guys moved forward and hopped down into the boat, roughly grabbing JJ and taking his pistol from him.

One of them slammed a fist into JJ's gut as he started shoving him towards the dock.

"Hey!" I snapped, lurching forward and trying to grab the asshole as he took another swing for JJ, but he threw his elbow backwards to ward me off and I caught it in the chin.

I was knocked down by the blow, falling to my ass in the middle of the boat with a curse.

A gunshot cracked through the air and blood splattered my bare skin as the Damned Man started screaming to high heaven.

"No one lays a fucking hand on her!" Rick roared, his revolver in his hand and more fury in his eyes than I'd ever seen there before. "The next bullet will go between your fucking eyes. I won't offer this warning out twice."

Mutt whimpered, moving close to lick my cheek and I scrambled upright as the dude who had elbow-clocked me sobbed and clutched at the bleeding hole in his leg.

"Shit, you should get a Band-Aid for that," I told him, holding my hand out to Rick who still looked ready to murder someone.

That fire in his gaze dimmed a little as he turned his eyes on me and he reached out to take my hand, yanking me up and out of the boat so fast that I stumbled and bumped into his chest.

I blinked at him in surprise and he leaned down like he might kiss me, a savage smile lighting his face as he spoke against my lips instead.

"Look who likes following orders after all."

"Fuck you," I tossed at him, stepping back and flicking my rainbow hair, but of course he wouldn't just let me go and his grip on my hand tightened.

"Bring the Harlequin to the freezer," Rick growled at his men before starting off along the jetty and tugging me with him.

Mutt fell into step by our feet as I let Rick guide me along. My little pooch seemed unsure of Maverick but not outwardly hostile.

"Boo. I thought you were gonna be fun today. But you're just gonna play the evil brother role, aren't you? Toss him in the freezer, do your scary mumbo jumbo, threaten to take over the world-"

"I've got the world right here beside me," Rick said, jerking me to a halt as we stepped onto the sand and looking at me like he really meant those words. "What else do I need?"

"Family," I replied instantly and I didn't miss the wince he tried to hide at that word.

"The only person I ever gave a fuck about is looking right at me, beautiful. I don't need no one else."

"I thought the great Maverick Stone wasn't afraid of anything," I taunted.

"I'm not."

"So send the goons away and spend the day with me and Johnny James. I already know you aren't going to kill him, and the freezer is gross and cold. It's a beautiful day and I wanna lose myself in this heat."

Rick considered me for a long moment, turning his gaze back towards JJ who was being held between two of his men while another couple helped the asshole who had been shot get out of the boat.

"P.S. You need to get my boat cleaned," I whisper shouted and Maverick barked a laugh.

"Fine. Fuck it. If you're so desperate to prove something with this little stunt, then come on. Let's see you prove it." Maverick started walking again, leading the way across the sand towards the hotel before striding onto the tiles which surrounded the huge pool.

His men followed until he stopped abruptly by a table and chairs and pointed the guys holding JJ towards it. They shoved him down and I moved to JJ's side, brushing my fingers along his jaw briefly as he gave me a look that said I was seriously pushing his trust in me right now.

"All of you fuck off to the mainland for the rest of the day," Maverick barked. "I've got some unfinished business to deal with here and I don't wanna see a single one of you fuckers hanging around while I do it."

His men hesitated for a few beats then they all took off at once, some hurrying inside and calling out to others while a few just headed straight back to the jetty.

Rick and JJ entered into some kind of scary dude stare off, so I slipped away towards the bar beyond the pool, hunting out something refreshing.

Mutt scurried along beside me, peeing on things he wanted to claim for his own and sniffing everything before trotting into the hotel to investigate further.

I found a bottle of whiskey and grabbed it. It wasn't really my first choice, but booze was booze, so I cracked it open and took a long swig.

The Damned Men were still making a meal out of fucking all the way off, so I located the music system and hooked my phone up to it, playing Kiss Me More by Doja Cat and SZA as I started dancing.

JJ and Rick were trading insults or having a dick measuring contest or some shit, so I was happy doing me while they got over it.

I tipped my head back, swigged my whiskey and just danced with the feeling of the sun on my skin. I'd once heard the phrase 'dance like nobody is watching' when I was a kid and I'd made that my nindo (my ninja way). Life was short and happiness was fleeting so I grabbed everything by the balls and just ran with it. It may have been messy, but it meant I had a smile on my face more often than I didn't.

"Tell me why you came here, baby girl," Maverick called when I was about eight songs in and feeling the buzz of the whiskey. "Because I was pretty certain it wasn't meant to be about dancing."

I opened my eyes and gave him a coy smile, shrugging one shoulder as I looked between him and JJ who were now both sitting at the table together apparently just watching me.

There was no signed of any Damned Men anywhere, so I was guessing they'd taken Rick's command seriously and we were all alone now.

"Would you rather be trapped on a desert island with your best friends forever, or have an enormous mansion all to yourself for the rest of time?" I asked, moving towards them slowly while their eyes remained riveted on me.

"Do you count as my friend?" Rick asked. "Because I feel like we crossed through the friends barrier when I taught you how to take my cock like a good girl."

"Oh please." I rolled my eyes. "I haven't been good a day in my life."

JJ snorted and reached out for the whiskey in my hand so I stepped closer to him, holding the bottle to his lips and giving him a taste. His fingers brushed the back of my knee, trailing higher as he swallowed and I drew the bottle back.

"All the best friends fuck, Maverick. Haven't you figured that out yet?" JJ taunted and I smiled at him as the feeling of his fingers on my flesh sent shivers of pleasure through my body.

"Makes sense," Maverick replied. "Because I both hate you and have no desire to stick my cock into you. So we must not be friends. In which case, as the only friend I have is you, beautiful, I'll take that desert island and spend my forever searching for buried treasure between your thighs."

"So we're just hanging out now, are we?" JJ asked, arching an eyebrow at me as I shrugged innocently.

Rick's men had disarmed him and Maverick still casually aimed his revolver at him across the table, but aside from that it did kinda feel like we were just chilling like we used to.

"I'm just deciding on which way I'd most enjoy gutting you, pretty boy," Maverick said with a sneer. "Don't go thinking I'm getting soft."

"Yeah, I'm not buying your bullshit anymore, Rick," JJ said casually, his eyes fixed on me as I stroked my fingers down the side of his cheek. "Because I've seen you now. I watched you save Fox in The Dollhouse and I was there right by your side as we hunted that rubble for Chase and-"

"I was hunting for Rogue," Rick snarled, ignoring the comment about Fox but I searched his face for reaction to that. JJ had told me about it, and it made me think Luther might not be quite as delusional as he seemed when it came to reuniting his sons. Crazy as a coot, for sure, but maybe not a bandicoot.

"Well you stayed long after we pulled her out of the rubble. And if you wanna keep spouting that bullshit about hoping to see his mangled corpse, you can. But I know you. I know you even though you wish I didn't, and the man I saw while we were out there digging through the remains of The Dollhouse was the same one I grew up with. The same one I loved like a-"

Rick leapt to his feet, tossed his revolver aside and hurled the table to the ground with a bellow of rage before diving onto JJ and slamming his fist into his jaw.

I barely managed to scramble away from them as they went crashing to the ground and the two of them started swearing and snarling insults at each other while fighting like a couple of feral dogs.

I tutted at them, taking one more swig of my drink as I turned away and placed it down on the edge of the pool.

I unbuttoned my shorts and dropped them to the floor, glancing over my shoulder just as JJ managed to roll the two of them over and pin Rick beneath him with one knee while throwing a fist into his face.

Maverick reared forward and bit his arm and JJ cursed as he lurched away, giving Maverick the opportunity to throw him down on his back again.

I caught the string of my bikini top and tugged, pulling the whole thing off and tossing it aside before rolling the bottoms off too.

"When you assholes are done with that, you can come and play Marco Polo with me," I called, looking back over my shoulder at them and they both paused in their alpha dog bullshit long enough to glance at me.

I smirked as they fell still, their eyes raking over my naked ass before I turned away again and dove into the pool.

Boys were so dumb sometimes.

The water engulfed me and I released a sigh as the feeling of it wrapping around my skin made me feel at home again.

This was where I belonged. I really should have been born a mermaid. Plus the lack of vag would probably halve my problems. I swear my vagina got me into at least fifty percent of the messes I found myself in. She was a law unto herself and the fact that I was skinny dipping right now in an attempt to lure some bad men after me, only proved my point on that.

I swam all the way to the far side of the pool and smirked as I surfaced and found the two of them standing on the edge of the water watching me like a pair of hungry hounds.

"You're it," I called as my toes scraped the bottom and I bobbed in the water, keeping my nipples below the surface.

"Get your ass back over here before I have to come get it," Maverick demanded.

"That's not the game," I called. "Don't tell me you can't remember the rules."

"What does the winner get?" JJ asked, dropping his shorts and standing there half erect with his muscle flexing and zero fucking shame about showing off his body. Which I was more than on board with.

"Bragging rights," I offered.

"Fuck that," Maverick replied, licking his bottom lip. "Winner gets to take control for what comes next."

"And what's that?" I asked innocently.

"You can't pull off the sweet girl act, beautiful. So stop pretending you're only wet because of the pool and just say what you want from us," Maverick demanded.

The corner of JJ's lips pulled up into a smirk as I batted my eyelashes at them. I knew the answer to that question and the thought of it alone made my stomach knot, but I refused to back down so I forced the words past my lips. "Honestly? I want you both. And if that were to happen at once then I'd want that even more."

"Your wish is my command, pretty girl." JJ dropped into the water and dutifully closed his eyes while Maverick just stood there watching us.

I arched my eyebrow at the moody gangster but he just folded his tattooed arms, so I shrugged and quickly swam to the other side of the pool.

"Marco," JJ called.

"Polo," I replied, biting my lip as he kept his eyes closed and began to swim through the water to find me.

I bit down a laugh and started swimming away from him, clinging to the edge of the pool as he surfaced and called out Marco again.

JJ kept chasing me around the pool and my pulse thumped to a heady rhythm as I both worked to escape him and fantasised about him catching me.

I crept around the edge and as I surfaced again, a deep voice spoke in my ear, making me jump.

"Marco," Maverick growled and I tried to jerk away from him, but he caught my wrist and tugged me against his chest, my hard nipples brushing his slick skin.

"Polo," I muttered, looking up at him as he gave me a dark look which promised me all the right kinds of punishment.

Maverick spun me in his arms, pressing my back to his chest and holding me there as JJ swum towards us beneath the water.

He surfaced right in front of me, his dark eyes sparkling with the reflections of the water as he reached out to take my hand in his, lifting my knuckles to his mouth and biting down.

"Come on then, Rick," JJ said, seeming completely unfazed by seeing me in the arms of his enemy. "You won – even if you clearly cheated. So take control like you're desperate to then. Tell me all about the fantasies you've been having about me and our girl."

"Ours?" Maverick scoffed. "Would you agree with that assessment of your ownership, beautiful? Do you belong to both of us, or are you mine like you told me?"

"Can't I be both?" I asked, knowing that should have sounded crazier than it did, but in a way it had always been true. I'd always loved them all the same. I'd never had a favourite. So why did sex make any difference? "We always used to do everything together anyway. Seems to me like growing up just made the games more interesting."

Maverick laughed then bit down on my neck, making me gasp and arch my spine against his hold. "Let's put that to the test then, shall we? I'm gonna watch my old *friend* fuck my girl. And we'll see if I can resist the urge to put a bullet in his skull for it or not."

JJ scoffed like he wasn't the least bit afraid of Maverick then moved forward and kissed me, pinning me between the two of them and making my whole body come alive with this forbidden contact.

I wrapped my legs around JJ's waist, the solid length of his cock dragging across my opening and making me moan with need as our kiss deepened.

Maverick shifted a hand to my nipple, roughly tugging on it as he ran his mouth down my neck.

"What the fuck are you waiting for?" Rick growled as JJ kept kissing me, his cock staying painfully absent from my body.

"I need a condom, asshole," JJ snapped before drawing away from me and moving to go and retrieve one from the pocket of his shorts which he'd discarded beside the pool.

Maverick snorted in amusement before sinking two fingers into me and making me gasp his name.

"I wouldn't want a barrier between my cock and this sweet pussy, would I baby girl?"

"That's because you're a dickhead," I moaned, trying to move away from him but he just wrapped his other hand around my throat and squeezed to keep me in place.

My pussy clenched around him as he held me like that, completely at his mercy while he slowly drove his fingers in and out of me.

"I'm gonna watch you come all over his cock, beautiful," he growled in my ear. "I'm gonna watch him please you and make you scream so that I have enough reasons not to kill him. You know that's why I haven't ended him yet, don't you? Because you want him, and I want you. And I don't wanna make you cry."

"You're a fucking psychopath," I panted as he continued to fuck me with his hand and his grip on my throat tightened.

Maverick lifted my chin, making me look at JJ as he sat on the edge of the pool and slowly rolled a condom over his throbbing cock. The sight was enough to make my mouth water and as JJ fisted his length and began to work himself to the sight of us, Maverick squeezed tighter and I came hard.

My pussy locked around Rick's inked fingers and he chuckled in my ear as he ground his hard cock against my ass through the fabric of his shorts, still choking me while I rode out the waves of pleasure unfolding through my skin.

I sucked in a sharp breath as he released his hold, panting in his arms as he withdrew his fingers then gave me a little shove towards JJ.

"Go to the shallow end and fuck her like you own her, Johnny James. I want to see how much this hurts."

I turned back to look at Rick, arching an eyebrow at him in question, wondering why he'd want that.

"Maverick, if you don't want to-"

"Keep your lips sealed and do as I said, beautiful. If you can't manage that, I'll give you something to choke on to make you stay quiet."

I flashed him a dangerous look as I considered my options on that one then decided to play his game. I couldn't say I hated him taking control of me and I was happy to play sub for him when he wanted me to.

I dove beneath the water and swam for the shallow end, finding JJ waiting for me as I surfaced. I put some swing into my hips as I emerged from the water and started up the slope which led out of the pool, the water running down my curves and revealing my body inch by inch as I went. I looked like a freaking Bond girl, all wet and sexy and shit - or at least I did until I stepped on a sharp bit of tile, leapt onto one foot and cursed like a sailor as I fell on my ass in the foot high water.

JJ laughed as he moved to help me, but instead of pulling me upright, he dropped down over my body, kissing me hard and pushing me down beneath him.

My legs parted as his weight fell over me and I moaned into his mouth as he shifted onto his knees between my thighs.

JJ grabbed my hips, tugging my ass up into his lap as my back fell flat against the tiles and the shallow water lapped around me. He groaned as he looked down at me, hooking one of my ankles over his shoulder and my other knee over his elbow as his cock drove against my entrance.

"Eyes on him, pretty girl," JJ growled, drinking in the sight of me laid out for him. "Let's give the asshole the show he's looking for."

My nipples hardened and I groaned as all of my muscles clenched deliciously at the thought of what we were about to do. I wasn't shy about sex, but I couldn't say I'd ever had an audience before and the thought of Maverick's eyes drinking in the sight of me laid out for another man like this had my flesh heating.

I turned my head as commanded and the moment my eyes met Rick's, JJ drove the thick length of his cock into me and made me curse so loudly I was sure the dolphins in the sea were blushing.

JJ started fucking me hard, his thrusts brutal and making me moan loudly with every strike of his cock deep inside me.

Maverick's gaze darkened as he watched us and I moaned even loader as I pawed at my breasts, tugging my nipples and begging for more.

The water lapped around us, washing up and over my body in time with JJ's thrusts and I lost myself to the feeling of him destroying me.

"I want her on top," Maverick snapped suddenly and JJ, pro sex god that he was, flipped us over before I'd even processed those words.

My knees bit into the rough texture of the tiles as I began to ride him instead, his cock sinking deeper with this new angle and making me moan louder as I dug my fingernails into his chest to keep my balance.

JJ placed his feet flat on the floor behind me, bending his knees before pushing me back to lean against his thighs and grabbing my hips to take control of our movements. He slammed his cock up into me with the kind of talent that had earned him his reputation and I forgot about Rick watching us as I panted JJ's name, riding him as we fought for control of the movement and chased down as much pleasure as we could take from one another.

"Lean forward again, baby girl," Maverick growled in my ear and I gasped as I turned my head to find him right behind me, his gaze a mixture of furious jealousy and dangerous lust.

JJ tugged me down into a kiss, laying his legs out flat behind me again as Rick moved to kneel at my spine.

"Look at her, Johnny James," Maverick said roughly as he slid one hand around my throat and moved another down to toy with my clit. "Have you ever seen such a captivating woman?"

"There are no other women who compare to her," JJ panted, his fingers digging into my ass as the combination of his cock and Rick's fingers on my clit made it impossible for me to say a single thing.

"She's the one, isn't she?" Rick said, his hand shifting lower and I gasped as he brushed his fingers down to my opening alongside JJ's dick. "The only fucking one."

"There's only ever been her," JJ agreed and my heart twisted at his words because they were so fucking honest. I could see it in his eyes, and I felt the same about them.

"There's only ever been you for me too," I gasped.

"You mean that in the plural sense," Rick growled and I nodded because yeah, I did. It was me and my boys. Even when I hated them, even when it was fucked up and even when I was having sex apparently too. "Such a filthy, filthy, girl," Rick growled and a moan unlike anything I'd ever heard escaped me as he pushed his fingers into me alongside JJ's dick.

Fuck. I was stretched so tight that my body locked up, but as JJ pushed up onto his elbows and kissed me, I let him guide me back into a rhythm again and my head spun with how fucking good it felt.

Rick bit down on my neck as he pumped his fingers in and out slowly, purposefully falling out of rhythm with JJ's thrusts so that I never got a moment to breathe between one of them owning me.

They kept that up, working me over until I was falling, crashing, spinning and screaming, my entire body exploding in ecstasy that just went on and on and on.

Rick took his fingers back out of me but of course JJ wasn't done and he fisted a hand in my hair as he dragged me down over him and kissed me hard.

A cry escaped me as Rick pushed the fingers he'd just had inside my slick pussy into my ass and I broke the kiss with JJ as I looked around at him, my eyes widening.

"Please tell me that doe eyed look means no one has ever fucked this sweet ass of yours, beautiful," Rick growled and I shook my head at him as my muscles all clenched at that suggestion, trapping his fingers inside me as he began to rotate them.

"I never really thought I'd like it," I murmured as JJ slowed his pace and I could feel his eyes on me too.

"Oh, I know you'll like it," Rick replied cockily, shoving his shorts down to reveal his thick, inked cock. "Besides, you owe me a first, baby girl."

I bit my lip, glancing back at JJ who was smirking at me like he was enjoying seeing me falter too.

"Stop looking at me like that," I snapped and he laughed.

"Stop acting like some blushing virgin then," JJ teased.

"Get your cock out of the way, Johnny James, I need some lube for this, she's as tight as fuck back here," Rick growled and yeah I was definitely blushing now, but as Rick lifted me off of JJ's cock and positioned me on my hands and knees above him, I found the desire in my body was enough to help me push through it.

Rick was brutal as always as he slammed his cock into my soaked pussy and he groaned loudly, muttering something about that being the best feeling in the fucking world as he took a few minutes to fuck me like that. JJ fisted his cock as he lay beneath us watching the show, the sight of his fist pumping up and down making my mouth water with the urge to suck him like a lollipop.

I was about to suggest that solution to our two dick issue instead of the ass thing, but Maverick pulled his cock out of me and shifted it further back, my own wetness giving him all the lubrication he'd wanted as he teased my ass.

"Tell me you want to feel me owning your ass, baby girl," he growled, pressing forward enough to make my muscles tighten as I gasped and panted, unsure if I wanted to say no to this or if I was fucking desperate for it.

"Relax, pretty girl," JJ said, his hand moving to my clit and making me moan again as he began to massage it in slow circles. "Don't fight it."

I licked my lips, making the decision before I could back out of it and closing my eyes as I tried to force my body to obey JJ's commands.

"I want to feel it, Rick," I panted. "Remind me who owns me."

Maverick chuckled like an asshole then slapped my ass so hard I knew he must have left a handprint. I yelped, but before I'd even gotten over the sting of that, he pressed his cock into my ass and all of my words dried up in my throat.

My fingernails bit into JJ's chest and a whimper escaped me as Rick stretched me out, the almost-pain making me want to tell him to stop until suddenly he'd finished pushing in and a growl of satisfaction escaped his lips which had me trembling.

It felt strange and my pussy was aching with the emptiness of being left out, but as Maverick slowly began to move inside me, I couldn't help but moan for him. I still didn't know if I-

"Fuck," I gasped my muscles clenching as the discomfort fell away and I started to get used to the strange sensation. No. I wasn't getting used to it – I was starting to really freaking like it. "Fuck, fuck, fuck...*more*."

"Fucking filthy," Rick laughed, slapping my ass again and I didn't care if I was filthy. I wanted him owning me and I fucking loved it too.

JJ tugged me down and Rick moved with me and my pulse scattered, but I was done hesitating now. I wanted this. I wanted both of them at once. And I was more than ready to take them.

My breath was stolen all over again as JJ's cock filled my pussy and all of my dirtiest daydreams about the two of them came true at once.

They started moving, slowly at first then gaining speed as my moans encouraged them, my body owning theirs and theirs owning mine.

We were loud and sweating and the water kept washing over us as we moved together. Every single thought in my mind just fell away as I was lost to them, these two savage men, working as one to bring me to ruin for them. These nightmares of mine who had owned me through all of my hatred and heartache were showing me where I belonged and who I belonged with and in that moment, I knew it was true. I was done fighting it. Fighting them. I was home and I was here to stay even if it would never be whole without Chase amongst us, and as the three of us fell apart in each other's arms with moans and curses and so much fucking pleasure that I could hardly take it, I knew what I had to do.

I had to find a way to do what Luther had asked of me. I needed to try and fix what was left of our family. Because I knew in my soul that I would never have another home aside from this place and these men. And even if the broken parts of what remained of us would never fit together right now that Chase was gone, I knew they'd be better off together than apart. So I was just going to have to figure it the fuck out.

CHAPTER TWELVE

*T*he rowboat rocked beneath me as I gazed up at the night sky, the side knocking against the dock as I bobbed on the waves. There were so many stars. There had to be endless worlds out there. I wonder if there's a boy like me on some other planet, but he's rich and strong and his dad loves him. I wonder if he has a girl like Rogue.

Nah no one's like Rogue.

Four shadows fell over me up on the dock, blocking out the light of the full moon. I hadn't called them, and yet they'd found me anyway.

"You can't sleep there, bro," Fox said, jumping down into the boat with me and I pushed myself up with a shrug.

"How'd you even find me?" I asked with a frown, glad of the darkness to hide my fresh bruises.

"One of the Harlequins saw you sneak down here," Fox said. "Dad told me if I didn't come and move you, one of his men would."

"Luther's a killjoy," I muttered with a frown as Rogue jumped down into the boat too and wrapped her arms around me. She practically nuzzled me and I snorted at her affection, hooking an arm around her waist and keeping her tight against me.

"We can all sleep at the Rosewood summerhouse," Maverick suggested. "I've got a bottle of rum."

"Where'd you get that?" I asked, getting to my feet and Rogue continued to cling to me like a limpet. I liked that. And I especially liked the way her fingers sought out the bruises along my chest, like she was drawn to my pain, wanting to soothe it away. Her presence alone did that. I was sure I could heal from a gunshot to the head so long as she was there to nurse me better.

"Stole it out of Dad's liquor cabinet," Maverick said with a smirk.

"I swear he makes it way too easy to get in there," Fox said as they shared a grin.

"Nah I'm just the best lock picker in the Cove," Maverick said with a smug expression.

"Bullshit, Luther's definitely letting you get in there lately," Rogue said. "He probably wants to lure you into a sense of false security, then one day he'll catch you with your hand in the cookie jar and make you pay him back for all the free booze by having to cut off his enemies' heads or some shit."

I barked a laugh as JJ turned a little pale.

"Shit if it's a head per bottle, beautiful, I'm gonna be bloody by the time I'm done paying off our debt," Maverick laughed.

"We'll be bloody you mean," Fox said with a flicker of darkness in his eyes that reminded me of his dad for a second.

"Yeah all of us, you're not the only one who sank his booze and we're a team anyway, remember?" Rogue said.

"Come on then, let's go rack up our debt with a drinking game," Maverick encouraged.

"I got a new deck of cards," JJ announced, offering me a hand to help me out of the boat. We climbed up onto the dock and Rogue rested her shoulder against mine as I held her close and we walked along the jetty.

"New or stolen?" I asked.

"Can't it be both?" JJ said through a grin.

"We could play strip poker," Maverick suggested.

"That sounds like a dickfest I don't want a ticket to," Rogue said and I laughed, knowing exactly who Maverick wanted to see naked. If we played, us boys would probably all end up with our balls out and Rogue fully clothed *while she raked in the pretend poker chips – which would likely be a bunch of shit that happened to be floating around in our pockets. That girl had the best damn poker face I'd ever seen.*

"We'll give you an advantage, beautiful," Maverick teased. "We'll all start with one item of clothing off. And that makes it an extra advantage because girls have all kinds of extra padding and undergarments going on."

"Undergarments?" Rogue burst out laughing and me and JJ laughed too.

"Drop it, man," Fox bit at him, but their shoulders rubbed as they walked and they were soon smiling again as we made it to Fox's truck parked up on the road.

"I'm just kidding. She's like a dude to me," Maverick said, though the hungry look he gave Rogue said he didn't really think that and it made possessiveness writhe in my chest as I held her tighter.

"I'd never wanna be a stinky dude. I mean, you guys are okay, but most guys are so hairy and sweaty and ew."

"I pray your opinion on that never changes," Fox muttered as Rogue got into his truck so she didn't hear it.

I had to agreed with that. There'd been plenty of guys interested in Rogue in our class, but fuck if any of us let them near her. Fox had followed Peter Dirkin home last week after he'd posted a photo of him and Rogue working together in Math with the caption 'I love math debating with this girl'. The masturbation pun had not been missed, and he'd turned up to school with a bruised face and no more interest in our girl the next day.

We piled into the cab and Rogue sat on my lap, her fingers still trailing over me in a way that made my pulse skip and dance. Everywhere her hands grazed stung and I was addicted to that kind of pain. I hated her seeing me weak, so I never flinched, but I was lost to her caresses and the way her brow pinched as if she could feel each hurt in me.

JJ blasted Billionaire by Travie McCoy and Bruno Mars and we were all soon singing along at the top of our voices, my heart so full I forgot all about my father and the fear of returning to that house where he'd peel away my happiness piece by piece. But I always got it back when I was with my friends. They were the only cure I needed for any wound. I'd do anything for them, and

My head was heavy, throbbing and there was a rattling noise in the back of my skull that wouldn't quit since Shawn's last beating a few days ago. I sat on the floor with my back to the cold stone wall, my bare feet pressed to the equally cold floor as I tried to summon the heat of the sun in my past, sure I was forgetting how it felt already.

The right side of my face was so painful that I couldn't touch it without fire flaring along my flesh. But sometimes I did, trying to work out how damaged it really was now I had a vicious X slashed through my right eye. Every time it even tried to heal, Shawn made sure it didn't so now I was blind on one side and that whole area of my face was swollen and fucking unbearable. I didn't fucking care though. I was a dead man anyway, just waiting for Shawn to grow tired of trying to pull truths out of me which I'd never give up.

I wasn't sure exactly how long I'd been down here, but it must have been weeks and that meant my time was running out. I knew the drill, I'd been on the other side of this game a few times in my life. You gave a man a while to break, but in the end you had to cut your losses and pull the trigger. Mostly, I was left here alone in the cold and dark for days with nothing but a bucket to piss in and a cheese sandwich pushed through the door twice a day. It was a steel door and sometimes I heard a female voice on the other side of it which seemed to call out to me, but I didn't answer it.

I remained in a trance for as long as I could, disappearing into the bliss of my past and trying to soak it all in before this was over. There was one thing to be said for being kept a prisoner and tortured, it sure humbled me. I'd spent too much of my life being an arrogant prick, and that was mostly because deep down I thought nothing of myself, so I'd worked hard to try and prove that I did. But it hadn't worked anyway, so now I'd never get a chance to be anything else in my family's memories. Just a fuck up who got what he deserved.

I knew they were alive. Shawn's big mouth meant I got a play by play of everything he got up to involving my old Crew, including the attack he'd struck against The Oasis Clubhouse.

My heart had shuddered with fear as he told the story, especially when he reached the part about getting hold of JJ. He'd spent a lot of time dangling his death over my head before finally revealing that he was alive. The motherfucker liked to do that. He'd figured out my attachment to the people I loved was one of the best ways to get under my skin, so he taunted me about my boys, about Rogue. And I had to endure it, knowing the only thing I could do was protect them by guarding the knowledge I had in my head and ensuring Shawn never got his hands on it.

I scratched at the rough beard coating my jaw and groaned as the movement sent a wave of pain down my left arm. Shawn had burned away the Harlequin tattoo on my shoulder the other day, stealing the last thing that bound me to my brothers. Now I was just a coconut adrift at sea, bob, bob, bobbing away on the tide.

I spent some time thinking about eating a coconut and drooped against the wall, but that only cause more pain to flash through me from the whip marks which striped my back.

That was one of Shawn's favourite games, he even showed up in a cowboy hat once, his whip in hand as he scarred the inked flesh of my back and cut through the map of Sunset Cove, striking the places he claimed he was gonna own. I cursed him with every word I knew until I grew tired of it and found some numb place to withdraw into. He always got bored after that.

A metallic bang sounded somewhere above me and I drew in a shaky breath as the sound of footfalls came from the basement stairs. *Here we go again.*

The steel door unlocked then pushed open a beat later and Shawn walked in with two men in tow.

"Good morning, sunshine." He smiled like we were old friends before clicking his fingers at his men and they moved forward to haul me to my feet. "On the hook," he commanded and they bound my hands in front of me before dragging me to one side of the room and lifting me up, hanging me from a hook designed for a punching bag.

As I hung there from the rope tethering my wrists, they tied my feet together too and I stared impassively at Shawn as he dismissed his men and walked over to me with swagger in his gait. He causally flexed his fingers, drawing my attention to the chunky gold rings cladding them as his lips lifted in a smirk. My gaze moved to the leather bracelets on his wrist which he'd taken from me, wearing them to taunt me. There were four of them, one for each of my friends, though I'd never told them that. I'd bought them when I was thirteen at the carnival, the man who sold them some mystic who said they were meant to draw your soulmate to you and bind them to you forever. Back then, I'd seen Fox, JJ, Maverick and Rogue as my soulmates, so I'd bought four of them – much to the guy's surprise. Though Fox had pointed out later that day, the apparent mystic was just the hobo who slept in that part of town who everyone called Carnival Bill. He'd wrapped himself in a fishing net and had probably stolen the bracelets off of some unsuspecting carnival-goer. Anyway, eventually I'd gotten so attached to wearing them that even as an old, bitter asshole, I still kept them on to this day. Well, I had until Shawn had taken them.

"I'm feeling good today, boy, wanna know why?" Shawn asked and I said nothing.

He moved in front of me, pushing me in the chest so I swung back and forth towards him. "The polite thing to do would be to say *yes, boss*," he said, his smile flattening. "So let's try again. Do you wanna know why, Chase Cohen?"

I spat in his face and his lips split into a sneer before his first fist came at me, striking my ribs, then the next and the next. The rings he wore made each blow ten times more vicious and I clenched my teeth through the pain as he hammered away at my body, splitting the skin more than once. It didn't matter anyway, I was covered in scars and cuts now, he'd fucked me up good and I was used to this ritual. I'd been trained for it by my father, Shawn was just taking that training to another level.

"You should learn to respect your superiors, pretty eyes," he snarled. "Or should I call you, pretty *eye*?" He roared a laugh at his own joke, stepping back as he admired the mess he'd made of me. "Hmm, you need a pirate name now. Cap'n Chase Cohen does have something of a ring to it. If you give up the goods on Fox Harlequin, I'll be sure to buy you a boat and send you on your merry way." He waited for me to respond, but I didn't. "No? Pity. You're making this real hard on yourself, boy. Harder than it needs to be. Why are you protecting them anyway? They aren't thinking of you, Chase. They've already forgotten all about you."

My chest tugged and I fought against believing those words, but they sliced deep.

"Yeah," he said, grinning as he observed my expression. "They didn't even give you a grave to mourn over, pretty eyes. I thought they might get around to it eventually, but I guess they forgot."

My throat thickened as I gazed at him, seeing the truth in his eyes. He'd been quick to tell me the Harlequins thought I'd died in The Dollhouse, finding that fucking hilarious apparently. I knew I'd been outcasted and Fox, JJ and Rogue didn't have any reason to care about me anymore, but it still hurt more than I liked to know they'd moved on from me already.

"You're a ghost now, I guess," Shawn purred. "I'm the only person in the world who knows you still exist. So maybe you should make more of an effort with me. I can be quite good fun when I want to be."

He headed over to grab the wooden chair on one side of the room, pulling it over so it screeched across the floor then placing it in front of me before he sat down. He took a pack of cigarettes from his pocket that had been among the things he'd taken from me when I'd been kidnapped. He lit one up with my Zippo lighter, puffing on the end of it so the smoke coiled around me and made me pine for a taste of it.

"I coulda been a therapist," he mused. "Always had a way with people." He tipped his head back, blowing smoke rings up towards the ceiling.

"You have a way of fucking annoying people that's for sure," I growled, my shoulders burning from the restriction.

He barked a laugh. "I'm not in the business of being liked, pretty eyes. I'm in the business of fucking the whole world and taking what I can get from it. She's a feisty slut who likes sucking my cock now I've made her my bitch." He smirked at his little analogy and went on. "You know who else is a feisty slut?"

My muscles bunched and I tried not to react, but I'd shown my cards on my feelings over this too many times. He knew how to push my buttons.

"Rogue," he announced like it was a surprise. He grabbed hold of his junk through his jeans, squeezing hard. "I almost had her, pretty eyes. She was one Fox away from coming out and sacrificing herself for Johnny James. Stupid little whore."

"Shut your fucking mouth," I snarled.

He pushed out of his seat, in his element now as he got a rise from me and he walked forward, taking a drag of his cigarette. "I'm gonna get her, Chase. All I need is the right leverage, and I've figured out all of your weaknesses. You, Fox, JJ and her. There's something there, something beautiful, and I'm gonna twist it to my advantage."

"If you touch her, I'll destroy you," I spat.

"Big words for a man strung up like a rack of meat," he laughed. "I think I'll make you watch when I get hold of her. I'll bring her in here, tie her down and fuck her until she cries."

"I'll fucking kill you," I snapped, blood pounding in my head. I knew he was just trying to goad me, but I also knew he'd do it too. And I couldn't fucking stand it.

He moved closer to me and stubbed out his cigarette on my chest, making me hiss through the pain.

Worthless, useless, good for nothing.

My father's voice echoed in the back of my head and I shut my eyes, trying to get out of this inescapable chasm as it swallowed me up. But I was sinking in deep, losing my hold on the inch of control I still had left. I was just a kid again at the mercy of a monster and I felt disgustingly weak. But this time it wasn't me I wanted to save, it was Rogue, my brothers. I'd been captured by this motherfucker and for what?

"Just tell me Fox's routines and the pain will end, pretty eyes," Shawn promised, his breath fanning over my chest where he'd left the burn mark.

I tried to find a good memory in my past to hold onto, but they all seemed to scatter until only the dark ones remained. I saw my father striding towards me while I was huddled in the corner of my bedroom, my knees hugged to my chest while he flexed a belt between his hands. I heard my mother's screams in the room next to mine, I heard their bed hitting the wall over and over and the way she went so quiet. Like she was just…gone. And wherever she'd checked out to, I wanted to go there now too. I needed to find the sun, my friends, but they weren't there anymore, there was just darkness and fear and the feeling of being so small I could be crushed under this man's boots.

My dad's voice filled my head once again, "*I didn't want you, your mother didn't want you. You're a plague on this house, boy."*

Shawn's fists were cracking against my flesh again, but it was my father's hands I felt. And I wished they'd just wrap around my throat and end it, place me into the dark where I could disappear forever. Being nothing would be far easier if I was dead.

Eventually the beating stopped and my flesh hummed with what felt like a thousand fresh bruises. There was barely a place on my body that didn't hurt, but the worst place of all right now was my mind. I was a child in a cold house, facing the wrath of a man who smelled like beer and smoke and seemed so large he consumed everything I could see. His yellow teeth were bared at me and his eyes were flared with malice, hate. I tried to remember what love felt like. Objectively, I knew it was my boys and Rogue on a sandy beach with a thousand careless dreams, but I was finding it harder to grasp them now. They'd forgotten me and I was losing my hold on me too.

I am hated.

I am nothing.

I am no one.

"Finish it," I forced out in a challenge, my mind clearing just enough to hook on this one desperate desire. "I'll never tell you anything, so just kill me already," I ordered in a fierce tone that sounded nothing like that small boy. "Finish it!"

His warm hand rested on my flesh, moving from one wound to another until it flattened over my furiously beating heart.

"Oh no, pretty eyes," he said in a low tone. "I won't be doing that. Not yet. Do you know why?"

I grunted and he took that as a cue to keep talking.

"Because I may carve up your body on the outside, but in here is my goal." He walked his fingers up my neck and to my temple. "And here. I'm gonna crawl into those cracks I see in you and you'll never get me out. I know the taste of pain, Chase Cohen, and it ain't the wounds on your flesh that cut the deepest. It's the ones that creep between your veins and burrow into your skull to mark themselves there forever. I'm your infestation, the rats who've moved into the walls of your home, scratching and chewing and gnawing at the beams which hold your house up. And I'm here to stay." His touch left me and I cracked open my good eye as he walked away, heading to the door and leaving me there on that hook as my shoulders ached and begged for relief.

He kicked the door shut with a bang and headed out of the basement, his footfalls thumping back upstairs.

I tried to get my foot on the chair just in front of me, my toes grazing it, but I couldn't get purchase.

"Come on, you piece of shit," I hissed.

I tried to swing myself toward it, but it hurt so fucking much that I had to stop and I hung my head, my hair falling into my eyes and my breaths coming unevenly.

The door sounded and my head snapped up in confusion as it swung slowly open. Shawn always locked it when he left, but I guessed this time he figured I wasn't going anywhere so he hadn't thought to do it. But as a slim, shadowy figure slipped into the space, my heart juddered and I wondered if I'd lost my mind completely. It looked like there was a room adjoining this one through that door and I caught a glimpse of an old rocking chair and a bed beyond it. Was I not the only prisoner down here?

She moved into the light of the single exposed bulb hanging from the ceiling and my brows pulled together at the wrinkled old woman standing there in a white blouse and navy skirt. Her hair was a shock of white and her skin was almost as pale, but I *knew* her. Her eyes were those of a long, lost friend, one I'd grieved, stood at the grave of.

"Miss Mabel?" I croaked in shock, blinking my working eye as I tried to clear this vision. She'd lived in the Rosewood Manor a long time ago when I'd been a kid. Me and the others had done odd jobs for her on the estate while she turned a blind eye to us sneaking onto her property and using her summerhouse. She'd been the one to give us the keys to the Rosewood crypt. She'd been the only adult in our youth who'd shown us true kindness.

"Chase Cohen," she said in an ancient, croaky voice, her hands shaking as she moved closer and reached out to touch my arm.

"I thought you were dead," I rasped, wondering if my body had given up and I was in the middle of crossing over or some shit, because this was a serious headfuck.

"My nephew has everyone fooled," she said bitterly, then moved to the chair and dragged it closer so I could stand on it. As soon as I did, I lifted my hands off of the hook and sighed my relief as I lowered my arms, wincing as pain radiated through my entire torso.

Mabel started tutting, looking me over with a frown as she untied my hands and I untethered my ankles. "That Shawn boy is an evil fellow."

I stepped down off of the chair and stared at this tiny woman who'd been so important to me once upon a time. "How are you here? And how old are you?" I asked in dismay.

"I'm a hundred and six," she announced. "Death is a good friend of mine, we made a deal me and him." She winked, taking hold of my arm and gesturing for me to sit down. I kinda felt like I should be offering her a seat, but she seemed sturdy on her legs and standing was causing me all kinds of fucking agony since Shawn had burned the soles of my feet with a lighter the other day.

"Can we get out?" I looked to the open door with an echo of hope in my chest, but she was already shaking her head.

"The door at the top of the basement stairs is always locked with many bolts and keys," she sighed and that little flame of hope in me snuffed out as fast as it had ignited.

I lowered onto the chair, breathing through the pain as she moved closer to push my hair out of my face and examine my fucked up right eye.

"Oh that little asshole," she said in a warbling tone, shaking her fist. "I'd give him what for myself if I could."

"How fucked is it?" I asked, unsure if I wanted to know or if it even mattered.

"It's…exceptionally fucked, my dear," she said and I released a breath of amusement at this frail old woman swearing like that.

"How are you here Mabel? I don't understand."

She took my hand, squeezing it tight and the comfort of that gesture was so strong that I clung onto her and didn't want to let go. She was a good piece of my past, something tangible right here in front of me, and it helped to draw the darkness back in my mind and let some light in.

"Kaiser faked my death so he could get his greedy hands on his inheritance. He paid off some dodgy official to forge a death certificate and bury an empty coffin," she snipped. "That little shit locked me down here in the rooms adjoining this storage space."

"I'm in the Rosewood Manor?" I gasped, my head whirling with all that meant. Kaiser Rosewood and Shawn Mackenzie must have been allied.

"But he couldn't get it all, see?" she said with a wild glint in her eyes. "He can't have my diamonds."

"Your…diamonds?" I asked, my head struggling to catch up with what was going. I was still half convinced I was delirious.

"They're hidden," she said with a grin. "And I'll never tell them where they are because that inheritance isn't for him. In fact, none of it is." She gave me a twisted kind of smile which reminded me of the feisty old woman I'd known all those years ago. Her smile fell away and she caressed the good side of my face with her withered hand, the feel of that kind touch meaning so much to me in that moment. "But he's too much of a coward to kill me so I suppose one day I'll die with the secret, because I'll never give it up to the likes of him."

"I'm sorry," I murmured, sad that her fate had been so cruel in the end. Maybe Sunset Cove was cursed for people who wanted to live a better life. Maybe we'd all end up bleeding in the dark one day.

"There's no need for that," she said firmly, her eyes watering as she stared at me. "Poor boy, there's such pain in your soul and something tells me it's not because of your wounds."

I thought of Rogue, my final moments with her and the words that had spilled from her lips. *"I've always fucking loved you and that's the problem, isn't it?"*

Those words often circled through my mind and taunted me. They were a riddle I couldn't solve, because she couldn't love me, that wasn't possible, so why had she said it?

"Do you still see those friends of yours?" she asked hopefully. "Fox, Johnny James, the sweet girl Rogue and Maverick?"

"Yeah," I said heavily. "Sort of."

She frowned. "What's happened?"

"So much, Miss Mabel," I sighed. "They're not my friends anymore."

Her thin white brows pulled together. "That can't be true. You were all attached at the hip."

"I ruined it," I muttered. "And this is the price of that." I gestured to my wounds. "I deserve all of them."

"Goodness," she cursed. "Don't talk like that. No one deserves this."

"I do," I said seriously, feeling those words right down to my core.

"Well I may be old but I've still got good ears, and they've been missing the company of a good story for a long time. Will you tell me yours, Chase? Give an old lady something to think on down here in the gloom."

I slid off the chair with a groan, laying down on my side on the cool concrete and letting it soothe away some of the fire in my skin.

"Only if you sit down," I urged and she moved shakily onto the seat.

"Such a good boy," she said and emotion clawed at the inside of my chest.

"I'm not a good boy," I told her, preparing to tell her exactly why. All of it, from the moment Rogue was forced out of town to the second I pushed her into that safe and stole the most bittersweet kiss of my life. "I'm the Devil in this story. You won't like me by the end of it."

CHAPTER THIRTEEN

I lay in my bed in my trailer with the window wide open, the sea breeze blowing in and making me feel at peace. Mutt was chomping on a Boneo thingy at the foot of the bed and I was trying not to drown in my grief.

It hit me worst when I was alone like this - if having ten armed men hanging around outside could be counted as alone - but in the silence, my pain found me.

It wasn't that I didn't feel it at all times. More that I'd made an art out of putting on a brave face over the last ten years, so I knew how to fake it until it almost felt real.

But when I sat in the quiet like this, it cut me more deeply, carved into my heart even sharper and made me feel all the worst kinds of pain.

"Run," Chase urged, grabbing my hand and damn near yanking me off my feet as we hurtled down the corridor away from our English teacher's classroom.

I threw a glance back over my shoulder just as the fuse burned down to the end and the string of firecrackers started banging loudly as they exploded one after another, the sound seeming like gunshots in the empty hall.

Chase yanked me around the corner just as Mr Parker screamed and a laugh tore from my lips.

We kept running all the way through the school until we were racing across the asphalt out front and tearing down the street.

I swung into an alley that ran down the back of a convenience store and tugged Chase after me so hard that he fell over his feet and crashed into me.

I tumbled back against the huge dumpsters lined up there and he slammed into me, cursing and apologising as I was crushed beneath his bulk.

"Sorry, little one," he half laughed as he tugged me upright again and suddenly we were standing too close to one another, my chest brushing his and my hair falling into my eyes as our laughter fell away.

Chase reached out to push my hair aside and I stilled, blinking up at him as my gaze fell to his mouth for a moment and the insane desire to push up onto my tiptoes and close the distance between our lips consumed my thoughts.

"Rogue," he murmured, his hand lingering on my cheek as whatever words he had for me caught in his throat.

"Yeah, Ace?" I breathed, wanting to hear what he had to say to me so desperately for some reason. My heart was racing and my skin was tingling where he touched me but neither of us seemed to know where we were supposed to go from here.

"I-"

"There you assholes are," Fox called and Chase flinched away from me like he'd been burned. "We finished egging his car, did you guys pull off the firecrackers?"

"Yeah, man," Chase agreed, stepping back and scrubbing a hand through his dark curls as he moved towards Fox and avoided my gaze. "You shoulda heard him scream."

My mind kept running over that day, the answer to what I'd been wanting so clear to me now when it had seemed so unclear back then. I'd been a kid growing into a woman, falling in love with her best friends and unsure how to adjust to that shift in our dynamic. I'd been a mess of hormones and in denial because I hadn't wanted anything to change and yet now, I wished I'd just taken that fucking kiss. I wished I'd seen him smile more often. I wished I could have been the one to save him from the hell of his home life. I wished so many things that could never come to pass now…

"Hummingbird?" Fox's voice made me flinch and I sat up sharply, ignoring the tears which coated my cheeks because it was already too late to hide them from him. And I didn't want to anyway. My grief was his grief even if he still felt conflicted over Chase's betrayal of me on that ferry. But I didn't. Because the more I thought about it, the more I understood. Chase had had so little good in his life. Fox and JJ had literally been the only constant thing he could claim for his own and he'd just been scared that I would ruin that. And he'd been scared far too often and for far too much of his life.

"I miss him too," Fox said softly, taking in the state I was in.

I nodded, patting the bed beside me and shifting along to make room for him. The trailer door had been standing open for Mutt, so it was no surprise he'd just walked on in.

"Did you need something, or..." my question trailed off as my thoughts spun around the boy we'd both lost again.

"Yeah, actually. I'm sorry but the cartel have called a meeting and Luther is insisting you attend with me. Fuck knows why, but he was adamant so here I am."

"Now?" I asked and he nodded.

"Do you want me to tell him to get fucked or-"

"No. It's fine. I don't hurt any less no matter what I'm doing, so I may as well be taking part in gang bullshit." I stood and headed to my closet, choosing to swap out the clothes I'd been wearing on the beach this morning for a fresh crop top and shorts combo, ducking into the shower to rinse off before changing into it.

Fox was waiting for me when I emerged and I reached for his hand, my gut twisting guiltily as he looked down at our woven fingers in surprise.

"You're still my boy, Fox," I told him. "Even if I'm not your girl."

"You're a walking, talking mindfuck, you know that?" he teased.

"You wouldn't want me any other way."

We got into his truck which he'd once again forced down the small walkway which divided my trailer from those surrounding it and he drove us directly to The Oasis where the mysterious cartel contact would be coming for this meeting.

Fuck knew why Luther wanted me here, but I'd shown up - granted I was probably underdressed, but he should have given me a dress code if he'd wanted me looking fancy and Fox didn't appear to be dressed any differently than usual in his board shorts and black tee.

"Don't mouth off with these people," Fox said to me in a low, serious voice. "I'm not kidding here, Rogue. It's best you say as little as possible and believe me I'll be doing the same. We do a bit of business with them, give them an in the country for their drugs and we keep them happy. We don't wanna get any deeper with them than that. And we definitely don't want to piss them off."

"I'm not a fucking idiot, Fox," I replied as we started up the stairs which led into The Oasis Clubhouse. My gaze hooked on the newly repaired windows and the patch jobs that had been done over the various bullet holes in the wood. Once it got a fresh lick of paint that whole night would be as good as forgotten.

"I know, baby, but I can't help but worry. If I had a choice in it, I wouldn't want you anywhere near these people. And I'd rather not deal with them myself either. But the cartel wants in via our town and we aren't dumb enough to think we could stand against them in refusal even if we wanted to. And with the money they pay, Luther didn't want to."

I nodded, my shoulder bumping against his bicep as we walked close to one another and my mind wandered back to that night years ago which had come so close to destroying us all.

"Oh shit," Chase gasped and we all looked around from our laughter and celebrations at the serious tone to his voice. "I just figured out whose boat this is." His face was pale and his hand shook a little where he held the champagne bottle.

"What is it, Ace?" I asked him, moving closer with a frown. We weren't afraid of anything or anyone, so I couldn't figure out why the identity of some rich assholes was making him look like that.

Fox moved up behind me as we looked at what he'd found and a cold, sinking feeling filled my chest as fear crept through my veins like poison.

"Put it back," I breathed, feeling death's fingers clawing their way

closer to me with every passing second.

"We're gonna die," JJ gasped as he saw it too and Chase quickly dropped it, but as I looked around at the fucking mess we'd made of this place, I knew that wasn't going to be good enough.

"Holy fuck," Rick said, snatching my hand and dragging me backwards like he thought he could protect me from this when he knew as well as I did that that was our deaths right there. There was no fucking way we could run from them.

"We'll just tell my dad we didn't know," Fox reasoned. "He'll be able to smooth it over. We didn't know. How could we have known?"

I blinked away the memories, knowing that losing myself in them now would only be more likely to make me fuck up here. But I wasn't stupid. I knew how dangerous the cartel was and I had absolutely no desire to mix it up with them in any way, shape or form. In fact, I hoped they didn't even notice me here because I wanted to stay as far from their radar as possible.

The clubhouse was fairly quiet, but Luther was standing up on the balcony above the bar waiting for us, looking like a tattooed demi-god with all that ink and muscle shining in the sunlight that poured through the window. He jerked his chin in a command and Fox took my hand as he led me up the stairs towards him.

Mutt scampered ahead of us and leapt into Luther's arms, licking his face and wagging his tail like crazy.

"I can't believe that dog prefers my dad to me," Fox grumbled.

"Well, Luther doesn't yell at him," I said.

"That was one fucking time, weeks ago and it was during a pretty intense situation," Fox growled. "I've also spent a small fortune on gourmet dog food and that fancy fucking bed for him and I offer to take him out on my runs with me every morning, but he just pisses in my potted palms and turns his nose up now."

"Mutt doesn't like a try-hard," I teased. "And he won't be bought either. Me and him bonded when I saved him from certain doom by tossing him a couple of fries for his starving tummy even though my own stomach was damn empty too. There is no bond like a life or death bond. You're just the dude who tries to buy him off then yells at him when you're in a mood."

"One fucking time," Fox growled again and I laughed.

"You'll have to do something epic to make it up to him."

Fox huffed irritably as we made it to the top of the stairs and Luther set Mutt down. My little pooch instantly turned and ran over to the suite where Luther was staying while he was in town, nosed the door open then leapt up onto Luther's bed for a snooze which apparently was totally fine with the leader of the Harlequin Crew as he just smiled affectionately.

"No need to look so pale, wildcat," Luther teased as we arrived and I forced a smile for him. Of course he didn't think I had anything to worry about here, but he also had no idea what we'd done eleven years ago. That said, neither did the cartel or we would have all been dead a long damn time ago.

"I ate a dodgy clam," I said.

"I thought you were vegetarian?" Luther questioned and I was surprised that he'd been paying that much attention to me, but I shouldn't have been really. This dude watched everything, knew everything – that was why he was king.

"Well, I looked at it and it smelled gross so same difference," I explained and he nodded like he agreed.

"I need a word with Rogue alone. Our guests will be here in a moment, Fox. Wait for the cartel downstairs and bring them on up to my office once they arrive," Luther ordered.

I could tell Fox didn't like that but I just shrugged, tiptoeing up to press a kiss to his cheek. He half turned towards me in surprise so I caught the corner of his mouth instead and I sucked in a breath, my lips tingling from the contact.

"Go," I urged. "Your dad isn't gonna murder me in his office. No one wants that clean up to deal with in their workspace."

Luther smirked and Fox groaned, shooting his dad a warning look before jogging back downstairs to wait for the cartel.

I followed Luther along a short corridor to a door with two members of the Crew standing guard outside it, fully armed and looking all menacing and shit. *What I wouldn't do for a sharpie to draw fake moustaches on their faces and give one of them a monocle too. He looks like he'd suit monocle life.*

The door clipped shut behind me and I looked around at the fancy office. It was all light and airy, the huge, driftwood desk dominating the space with pale wood bookshelves lining either wall and a long window with a view of the cliffs letting in plenty of light.

Luther sadly blocked off that view by dropping a blind over it before flicking an overhead light on and dropping down behind the desk.

"The cartel don't like us talking near open windows in case the FBI or someone equally irritating may be watching," he explained and I nodded.

Serious law enforcement always seemed so far away from my criminal lifestyle somehow. I knew technically that the things I did to survive weren't legal, but in my reality the cops didn't care about shit like that. I guessed when you were running a multimillion dollar drug ring like the cartel were then you had bigger fish to deal with.

"I was just hoping for an update on the Maverick situation," Luther explained as I headed over to the bookshelves and started looking at the random things he had sitting there aside from books. There were trinkets and nautical accessories, an old compass catching my eye for a moment before I moved on.

"Well he's receptive to spending time with me," I hedged. "Though that has been a little difficult with Fox being so protective that he refuses to let me out of his sight, but now that he's backed off a little, I did manage to go see Rick again."

"And? Is he coming around to the idea of spending some time with the family?"

"Err." I picked up a weird looking rock thing which had orange crystals inside it and turned it over in my hands. "He is still quite resistant."

Luther huffed irritably. "If you're not capable of fixing this mess then maybe I need to rethink our deal."

I placed the rock down with tension prickling along my spine then turned back to face him, raising my chin as I held his gaze. "I didn't say I've made no progress. He let JJ come and visit him on Dead Man's Isle the other day."

"Really?" Luther asked, perking up. "And what did he and Johnny James get up to?"

"It was still pretty tense," I admitted. "But I managed to convince them to find some common ground with me so I would call that progress."

"So they're coming together over you?" Luther asked, looking all smug and shit like his little plan was working out so brilliantly.

"Yep. They definitely came together," I agreed. I didn't need to mention the fact that I meant that literally or that they'd still been pretty hostile towards each other aside from all the fucking, because that didn't seem too relevant.

"Perfect. I'll expect another update from you soon. Make sure you keep doing what you're doing with them and hopefully you can get Fox to join in soon too."

"That would be the dream," I replied, biting my lip and looking away again because fuck yeah, that would be hot as hell. But also, sad times, I just couldn't see Fox being up for it.

There was a low knock on the door and Luther beckoned me over to him so I strode around the desk to stand on his left then tried to figure out if I was supposed to look relaxed or intimidating.

The door swung open before I could figure it out and Fox strode in with a woman right behind him who demanded all of the attention in the room.

She was tall and so well put together that it made me feel like a bug who had rolled through a bag of trash on my way in here. Her cream dress was all sophisticated and shit, hugging her curves and stopping at the neck and knee so that she was at once covered up and sexy. My kind of sexy leaned towards the flesh on show, ass hanging outa my booty shorts style, but this woman looked fucking untouchable. Her dark hair was sleek and twisted into some fancy knot thingy at the base of her neck and her makeup had that whole bare faced perfection thing going for it. My face was actually bare today but hers looked barer. The barest. And yet fucking flawless too. A lot of makeup had gone into her looking so bare. A lot, a lot. I was pretty impressed. So impressed that I was outwardly staring and I didn't even notice that her attention was riveted on me too.

"So it's true then?" she asked, he words lilted with a sexy Mexican accent. Jesus she was the most fuckable yet untouchable woman I'd ever seen. She was like a black widow spider. If anyone dared get close enough to sink their cock into her, I was sure she'd use them up good then feast on their brains when she was done. And they'd love every goddamn second of it.

"It's a pleasure to see you as always, Carmen," Luther greeted her, staying sprawled in his chair while she folded herself into hers opposite him. There were two heavily armed goons at her back, but I didn't pay them any attention as they took up position behind her - they weren't the danger in this room. That was all her. "And yeah, I've finally taken your advice and initiated a woman into my crew."

"Does she talk?" Carmen asked, dark eyes on me.

"She does. And she does tricks," I replied. "I can walk on my hands even after sinking half a bottle of rum."

Fox shot me a look begging me to shut the fuck up, but I was pretty sure Carmen would be interested in my party trick. I was almost certain I could actually pull it off if she wanted me to prove it too.

"Is that so?" Carmen asked, arching a brow at me, but I got the feeling she wasn't after a demonstration sadly.

"Rogue is integral to our hunt for Shawn Mackenzie," Luther cut in. "She has insider knowledge of his habits and routines and has been promised the pleasure of cutting his head from his body once we catch up to him."

"Do you have a fondness for severing heads?" she asked me conversationally.

"I think I will given some practice on Shawn," I agreed. "I'm thinking I'll use a hacksaw."

"I'd suggest an axe for less labour. But of course the hacksaw would take longer if you're aiming to enhance his suffering. However, once he's dead you can always switch back to the axe to finish off."

"Good to know," I said cheerily though that mental image was seriously gross.

"And where did you get that kind of intimate knowledge on Shawn Mackenzie?" Carmen asked me, cutting to the point of it and making me swallow the lump in my throat. But Luther nodded in encouragement and I was pretty sure I could leap out the window and run for the hills if I had to, so I just went with it.

"I used to be his girl. He was a cruel, manipulative motherfucker who screwed with my head and tried to kill me. I woke up in a shallow grave wrapped in a fucking potato sack thanks to him. But his sloppy murder tactics really just served to give me a way out and now I'm gonna pay him back in kind."

Carmen assessed me for a long moment then nodded, her lips curling up at the corner. "There is a certain poetic justice to seeing a man destroyed by a woman he tried to ruin," she said. "I look forward to hearing about your success very soon."

That *very soon* held all kinds of 'otherwise I'll come back here and kill you myself' implications but I just nodded, keeping my mouth shut like I'd promised Fox I would as Carmen and Luther moved on to discussing new drug shipments and money and all kinds of boring shit.

I let my mind glaze over as I thought about Chase. I was always thinking about Chase these days. And I was always hurting over him too. I told him I wished I'd never met him, but that wasn't true. Despite all of the pain he'd caused me and the hurt I'd felt over him, there was a lot of love there too. So much love. He was still my boy even though he wasn't here anymore and I couldn't ever make right what had gone so horribly wrong between us.

Carmen got to her feet and started heading for the door and I snapped out of my depressing thoughts, slapping a stray tear off my cheek, and muttering a goodbye as she assured Luther that she and her men could see themselves out.

The door closed behind them and it felt like the room finally filled with oxygen again.

And I used to think Luther Harlequin was scary. That bitch made him look like a freaking kitten. I was kind of crushing on her though, so what did that say about me?

"That went well," Luther said firmly. "But I'll have a lot of organisation to manage if I want that new shipment to come in without a hitch, especially while Shawn is still hanging around town. The sooner we kill that motherfucker, the better."

"Agreed," Fox growled.

Luther glanced at me with a frown. "Carmen liked you. Which means you're now filed away in her brain as a potential threat. She's the most dangerous woman on the east coast and she'll twist a knife in your back and carve out your spine for good measure if you cross her."

"My kind of girl," I said with a nod.

"No," Luther said in a gruff tone. "She's wolfsbane. Beautiful to look at and deadly poisonous."

"You're only selling her more to me, dude," I said with a shrug and he shook his head in frustration.

"That woman is a prime example of why I know women are the far more lethal sex than men. Every member of her cartel would slit any throat she pointed at, including their own."

"Are you trying to make me question my sexual orientation, Luther? Seems like a weird thing for my mob daddy to do."

"Just stop it," Fox said in irritation, like even picturing me with a woman was too much for his possessive little badgery brain to handle.

"He's the one listing reasons why Carmen's marriage material, maybe Luther's the one with the crush," I tossed at him and Luther just bared his teeth like the idea of that was unthinkable. It made me kinda curious about his sex life – not that I wanted to picture anything like that because he was Fox's dad which made him as sexy as a rock to me, but like, was he celibate? Or did he just hate fuck women then throw them to a great white shark when he was done?

"*Anyway*." Luther gave me a hard look which told me to zip my lip before looking to Fox. I've been invited to a poker night at the Rosewood Manor tonight." He took his phone from his pocket and began typing out a message. "But I need to focus on this, so I'm telling Kaiser that you'll go in my place. Bring Rogue. The two of you could use some fun and I want you gathering information on Kaiser while you're there. He's becoming a big player in our territory and I want to be sure he's not crossing the line with our leniency. He owes me a debt too, so put the pressure on him to fulfil it because I'm getting impatient."

"Got it," Fox added and I smirked at the idea of whooping a bunch of rich assholes at poker. My game was king. I just grinned and laughed my way through it no matter what way the cards fell, and no one could ever figure out what the fuck my hand was looking like.

"You gotta dress up fancy for it. You can take the rest of the day to go buy something to wear and do whatever you kids enjoy doing together," Luther offered like a doting father. The dude gave me whiplash with his multiple personalities.

"Subway," I demanded instantly and Fox groaned.

"You can't be hungry already."

"Err, yes I can, Fox. I am hungry at all times in fact. And right now I want Subway. So I suggest you feed me."

Fox rolled his eyes and held a hand out for me and I grinned as I accepted it and let him lead me outside.

"Come on, Mutt!" I yelled as we went and my little dog raced after us with an enthusiastic yip. "Foot longs are on Fox."

CHAPTER FOURTEEN

"**M**ommy is going to be so excited to meet you," Mia cooed, rubbing my arm as one of my men drove us to the Rosewood Manor. We were sat in the back of the car, my biceps straining against a crisp white shirt, the sleeves folded up to reveal the ink on my arms. I might have needed to make an effort tonight, but you were never gonna see me decked out for a ball. Kaiser was just lucky I wasn't showing up bloody.

"I can't wait," I said, my tone light and rehearsed. She always bought it, this side of me which didn't exist. One that wanted her, was falling for her. It was laughable really. And maybe I'd have given a shit about fucking with her heart if she wasn't so grating. Nah, probably wouldn't though.

"I got you this." She slid a rough blue rock into my palm and I rolled it over with my thumb, eyeing the pointless thing. "It's a wish stone." She leaned closer, the high split in the skirt of her dark green dress spilling open as she spoke breathily in my ear. "Wanna know what I wished for, Rick?"

I really hope it's for a month long trip to anywhere I'm not.

"Tell me," I urged, placing my hand on her bare knee and squeezing in encouragement.

I used to just feel plain numb doing this, now it made me wanna heave my guts up. I had no idea why, unless I counted the fact that Rogue had come back into my life and her pussy had made my cock pledge its allegiance to her kingdom. And I didn't just think about her pussy, I thought about her. The way she felt pressed against me, the way her sharp tongue made me laugh more than I had in years, the way I was able to remember the boy I'd been long before prison had twisted him up into something wicked and black hearted. She made me care what my fucking hair looked like. And that was a long lost memory I hadn't planned on getting back.

How did one girl hold the power to make my heart feel as robust as a snowflake? It wasn't good all of that distraction. I'd made far too many allowances for the Harlequins because of her already, and I needed to stop letting her trap my balls in a vice and go after their blood like I'd always planned. I couldn't even let myself think about the fuck fest I'd had sharing her with JJ. Because then I thought about what it meant, and why I sort of liked having JJ around sometimes, and then I started thinking of the past and our little group. And I especially didn't like thinking of that lately because then I thought of the boy who was no longer around.

Our old family was one down thanks to Shawn. And yet I didn't feel happy about that. No, I felt something far worse brewing in me over Chase. In a deep, deep fucking place somewhere in my festered soul, I wanted vengeance for his death. I'd spent the past weeks hollow and lost and fucking furious and I couldn't shift the ache in me over him. It was stupid, juvenile, linked to some old, forgotten attachment I'd once had to him. But he didn't deserve a scrap of mourning from me, so I didn't acknowledge it. I left those unwanted feelings to rot in a place where I never examined them. They weren't mine. They belonged to a kid who didn't exist anymore. So they could die with him and eventually the pain would stop.

Mia's hand slid onto my dick, caressing to try and coax some life into it, but he was in Rogue's army now, willing to fight battles for her and die on her hill. Not Mia's.

I subtly pushed her hand away then leaned in and kissed her cheek. "Sorry, baby, I'm going through a final course of treatment. It makes everything numb down there."

"Oh dear," she said with a frown. "You can't feel anything at all?"

"Nothing," I said with a sad look. *It feels Rogue's pussy just fine though. Strange that.*

"How much longer?" she asked and I turned away.

"I don't wanna talk about it, Mia," I muttered like I was ashamed and she stroked my arm.

"I'll add more healing crystals to your room," she said. "Are the bedsheets sterilised yet so I can start sleeping with you again?"

"No and there's been a lot of…shedding," I said, making shit up on the spot and she gasped.

"Shedding?" she breathed in horror. "Like a snake skin?"

A laugh hitched in my throat and I swallowed it down, forcing a harsh frown onto my face. "I said I don't want to talk about it."

"Sorry, baby," she said softly, patting my arm. "My cousin is a chiropractor, maybe I could call him for some advice?"

"It's not my back that's the problem, Mia," I bit at her. "It's my cock. And my balls too. My balls are very swollen, they look like two purple turnips. And don't get me started on the smell or the weird diaper I have to wear so that-" I cut myself off, holding a fist to my mouth and closing my eyes like I was horrified by what I'd said.

The guy driving the car glanced at me in the rear mirror with wide eyes and it took everything I had not to crack up laughing. Rogue would have loved this game.

"Oh no," she gasped.

"Yeah," I gritted out. "So can we please stop talking about it?"

"That Rogue girl has a lot to answer for," she growled and I nodded. *Sorry, beautiful, it had to be you who gave it to me.*

We arrived at the huge gates to the Rosewood Manor and my amusement fell away as I sat up straighter. I'd wanted to get in here for so fucking long. I'd put in the time, I'd earned it. And now it was finally going to pay off.

A couple of armed guards opened the gates for us and as we drove inside, I took in the immaculate grounds which had once been overgrown and neglected. I'd preferred it like that, with the grass long and wildflowers everywhere. Kaiser had stamped the character out of it, the lawns perfectly kempt, the old cracking drive repaired and the manor house now gleaming, the porch freshly painted in white and a group of expensive looking rattan garden furniture out on the new decking.

My driver parked us up alongside another vehicle and I scowled out at Fox's truck before exiting the car. I adjusted the gun on my hip as Mia moved to my side and we walked towards the porch where a few guards were standing with machine guns across their bodies. Kaiser wasn't fucking around when it came to security and I had to wonder what he was guarding so fiercely here, or if he was just a nut.

They frisked us then let us inside once they'd taken my gun and we moved through a grand entrance hall with oak flooring and a huge stairway with red carpet that twisted up off towards the next floor. One of the guards led us through the house past opulent rooms that had the scent of fresh paint and new money about them. Kaiser's taste was gross. Everything was bright, mismatching and uncomfortable looking. There was a violently orange rug over a black and white tiled floor and the pictures on the walls looked like something I could have done with a paintbrush clenched between my ass cheeks.

"It's so beautiful here, isn't it?" Mia sighed and I wrinkled my nose. *Of course she fucking likes it.*

We arrived in an enormous room with a large round poker table at the heart of it, the walls decorated with man-sized playing cards, giant guns and a mural of a cartoon version of Kaiser with a gangster hat on and two tommy guns in his hands which fired golden bullets.

What in the fuck is that ugly shit?

Fox was sitting at the table with Rogue beside him in a blood red dress that made her look fucking edible. My gaze dragged over her with intent and my cock woke up like Snow White after being kissed by the prince. She wet her lips as she looked back at me and Fox bristled beside her, his eyes full of a menacing warning which I didn't give two fucks about heeding.

"Mi-Mi!" Kaiser stood from his seat with a wide smile, raising a glass of whiskey to toast our arrival. There were a bunch of other people sat around the table and I recognised Mayor Hardanger with her long red hair and a couple of the local cops among them.

Mia tugged on my arm, pulling me along towards her stepfather who dragged her in for a hug. My gaze moved to a woman as she stood up beside Kaiser, her tits pushed up to the moon in her tight black velvet dress and her upper lip so full of filler it looked like a wet fish had been stapled to her face. Her hair was dark like Mia's, hanging around her shoulders in rippling, silky waves. Her arms were covered in tattoos and one look at them told me who had been in charge of the décor in this place. One sleeve was just a mish-mash of bright, intersecting colours that surrounded a picture of her and Kaiser wrapped around each other naked.

"Come here to Mommy, Maverick, it's so nice to meet you at last. I'm Jasmine," she said in a sultry voice, grabbing me for a hug I didn't consent to and trying to draw my head down to nuzzle her tits. That would be a fuck no.

I vaguely squeezed her back then pulled away, but not before she planted a lipstick kiss on my cheek with those fish lips of hers. It felt like a rhino's asshole stamping to my cheek and they practically popped from the suction as they pulled off of my skin.

"It's great to finally meet you," I said, forcing a smile and Kaiser grabbed me in for a hug next like we were goddamn family.

I felt like I was being molested in front of the whole room, and the fact that Fox was watching this display got my fucking back up. But I had to play along, because this was what I'd been angling towards for a long damn time, it just sucked that he had to be here to witness how low I'd stoop for this shit.

Kaiser clapped my back several times and I nearly choked on his aftershave before he let me go.

"Everyone, this is Maverick Stone, my Mi-Mi's boyfriend," Kaiser announced, then looked to Fox. "Obviously there's a little tension between you and another of my guests so I ask that we keep this civil. Guillermo will be keeping an eye on you all to make sure things remain so." He gestured to his man who was built like a barn and had a machine gun over his chest and an ammunition belt wrapped across his body. "Now please sit and we'll begin the first game of the night."

Mia towed me to our seats which happened to be right next to Rogue and Fox – a fact I had to assume was intentional, but I didn't know what Kaiser's angle was. Maybe he just wanted to figure out how deep our hatred really ran.

Mia tried to take the seat next to Rogue, but I smoothly dropped into it before she could stop me from sitting beside her.

"We won't have any issues, will we Foxy?" I leaned forward to look at him beyond my girl and he gave me a death glare.

"Not unless you cause any," he said icily.

"I never cause trouble, do I baby?" I nudged Mia and she gripped my hand on the table, winding her fingers between mine.

I turned to look at Rogue, examining every inch of her outfit and her gaze narrowed on my hand around Mia's. I could smell coconut on her skin, but it wasn't nearly enough to sate my hunger for her. I wanted to take a vicious bite and leave my mark on her. I also wanted to fuck with her straightened hair and perfect make up, show the world how good she looked roughed up and freshly fucked by me.

"Hello, beautiful," I said in a low tone.

"Hey, Rick," she said with a light, playful smile. *Hmm, she definitely wants my cock.*

A waiter appeared to take our drinks order and another guy cashed in some chips for me and Mia to play the game, so we were soon being dealt our cards and I finally had an excuse to let go of Mia's hand.

I peeked at my cards, glancing at Rogue knowingly. Her poker game was supreme. She could beat our asses as kids ten times over. And I for one was excited to see how hard she could thrash these rich assholes tonight.

Idle chatter broke out around the table as we played and I started to plan how to excuse myself from this shit so I could go and check out the crypt. Rogue had told me she'd gotten onto the property to see it not long after she came back to town, but with the renovation work Mia kept telling me was going on at this manor lately, I'd been worried Kaiser might have done something to it since then. So I needed to see the crypt for myself tonight and make a plan to bust in there ASAP.

"So Foxy, how's Harlequin business?" I asked casually as Mia fell into conversation with the mayor on her other side.

"It'd be great if it wasn't for the two assholes trying to destroy my town. I'm not sure who's more of a threat right now, the piece of shit who hurt Rogue and is now trying to take her and my land, or the family traitor who's also trying to take my girl and thinks he can do whatever he likes without facing the consequences of his actions," Fox said smoothly.

"I'm not your girl," Rogue murmured, but only low enough so we could hear it and I guessed she was playing her role as his tonight for the onlookers.

"Wow, you do have a lot on your plate, brother. It would almost be easier to give up on trying to keep *my* girl from what she really wants," I taunted, looking to rile him.

"I'm not your girl either," she sang, pushing a couple of chips into the game as the play came our way.

I folded, tossing my cards down and giving Rogue and Foxy my full attention.

I dropped my hand onto her thigh under the table, wrapping my fingers around the inside of it and squeezing, making a tiny gasp escape her.

"I beg to disagree, beautiful," I whispered, but Fox caught it and his jaw tightened as he glared at me.

"You're never going to have her," Fox said in a growl and something in his eyes told me he was plotting to make sure those words came true.

"Already have. Been there, done that, came in her, will repeat," I said through a polite smile as Guillermo drifted a little closer and Fox's hand curled into a fist on the table.

"Can you stop bartering over me like I'm a prize cow?" Rogue asked lightly. "I'm not either of yours, never have been, never will be."

Challenge accepted.

Fox painted on a tight smile as my hand slid higher up Rogue's thigh and her legs clamped down on my fingers to stop me going further. I pinched the inside of her leg and she leapt a little in her seat, making her thighs widen enough for me to reach up her skirt and pinch her clit too. She gasped as I tugged my hand away and got to my feet, a smirk dancing around my lips as I ignored her staring up at me in shock.

"What happened?" Fox murmured to her and I sniggered as she shook her head in a refusal to reply.

"Which way to the restroom?" I asked Guillermo and he pointed with his gun towards a door across the room. I nodded, stepping toward Fox and peering over his shoulder as my fingers brushed Rogue's arm and I painted the word *mine* on her flesh.

"A ten and an ace? You've got this in the bag, buddy," I said loudly then slapped Fox's shoulder as he swore under his breath and I walked away to the door, stepping out of it and hurrying down the corridor.

There was a red velvet rope blocking off the end of the hall but no guards around, so that was a good sign. I slipped into the restroom and took out my phone, shooting a text to Rogue.

Rick:

Make your excuses and meet me for a quick fuck.

Rogue:

How about no, dickwad?

Rick:

Fine, meet me for a surprise.

Rogue:

Is the surprise your cock?

Rick:

Maybe.

Rogue:

No thanks! My vag isn't taking requests.

Rick:

How about we go on our adventure then? Operation crypt.

Rogue:

Keep talking...

Rick:

Get your fine ass up and walk it down the hall to me and come play with me out in the dark, dark woods where no one will see me fucking you senseless against the crypt wall.

Rogue:

Moo.

Rick:

??

Rogue:

Cow emoji

Rick:

???

Rogue:

Stop cow buying me.

Rick:

Fine. Sneak out. Creep to the crypt. No fucking.

Rogue:

Deal.

Rick:

Glad you didn't rule out fingering, eating you out, sucking my cock or a cheeky handjob.

She walked through the door swaying her hips. "Kaiser just called an interval. We've got thirty minutes until the game starts again. Fox has been snagged by Kaiser, but he's gonna be on the warpath when he realises I'm gone."

"Luckily I don't give a shit what Fox thinks," I said, grabbing her hand. "But I'd rather he didn't find us sniffing around by the crypt we're gonna use to destroy him."

A small crease formed between her eyes that made me frown, but then it was gone and she towed me out the door. We ran like kids towards the red velvet rope, leaping over it and tearing away down the corridor while stifling our laughter.

A few turns took us to a side door and we pushed through it, finding ourselves in a stone courtyard that led to the gardens. We raced through it, moving faster and faster as we slipped down a pathway and headed for the crypt at the far end of the grounds.

It wasn't long before we made it into the graveyard, finding it carefully tended to unlike the wilderness it had once been ten years ago. The crypt stood tall at the heart of it and my pulse settled as I laid my eyes on it at long last.

We hurried up to the door and I checked that it was all intact then ran my finger over the circular ring of five bronze keyholes with tiny animals beside each one that linked them to our keys. Rogue lay her palm flat to the stone and moved them over the keyholes and I looked down at her as she shut her eyes.

"You okay, beautiful?" I asked and as she opened her eyes, I found them gleaming wetly.

She shook her head and suddenly she threw herself at me, burying her face in my chest and I wrapped my arms around her in surprise.

"What's wrong?" I growled, ready to destroy whoever was the cause of this pain. If Fox had done something, I'd kill him tonight. I'd string him up in front of the whole goddamn party if I had to and take my chances with fucking Guillermo and his machine gun.

"I miss him," she choked out and she didn't have to say who as my chest tightened. I knew instinctively because as soon as she said those words, they opened up a wound in me that I'd been working so hard to ignore.

I cupped her chin, drawing her head up to look at me as tears rolled down her cheeks, making me fucking break.

"You'll be alright," I said, but she shook her head.

"I won't," she said, a crack in her voice. "I won't, Rick, I keep trying to move on, but I can't. Every day is like swimming through tar and one day I'm gonna grow tired and I won't be able to do it anymore. I'll just sink into this grief in me and it's gonna eat me up."

"Don't talk like that," I said firmly. "This will pass."

"It. Won't," she said fiercely, her eyes flaring with pain. "It's over. Any chance I had to be whole is gone. I know it doesn't make sense, I know I'm supposed to hate them all, but I love them too. And now Chase is…is dead," she rasped and my chest crushed like it was under the weight of a ton of iron. "I'm broken for good. I can't recover from this. He's a piece of me which I need in this world, even if he hurt me, even if I hate him more than I love him." She knotted her fingers in my shirt and I pushed her up against the crypt, our end awaiting us inside it.

Through all my plans to destroy the Harlequins, I had never had to factor her into the equation. But I could see she was torn, it was written all over her face. This plan we had to unleash the secrets of this crypt was one I'd been working on for a long time, but if she couldn't handle it, if opening it destroyed her too then how could I go through with it?

"Baby girl," I growled, smearing a tear across her cheek as she looked up at me for an answer I didn't have. "You're stronger than anyone I know. You can recover from this."

"Can *you*?" she breathed, searching my eyes. "Do you really not care he's dead?"

I fell quiet, the answer to that question sitting on my tongue. The truth I didn't want to give. Her fingers dragged along my cheek and I leaned into her touch as my heart beat powerfully for this girl.

"I see him all the time," she whispered. "In every dream, in every waking moment, he's there, feeling so close it's like he's not gone at all. But he is. And the moment I accept that, I'm going to shatter and I won't recover this time, Rick. I don't want to recover."

"Don't say that," I growled, taking hold of her throat in a light grip and pressing her back against the stone door. "I'll hold you together, I'll wrap you up so tight you won't even feel the cracks in your walls."

"You can't," she croaked. "It's too late for all that Rick. Ten years too fucking late. And now he's gone and I…" She closed her eyes and more tears rushed down her cheeks.

I felt frantic, hating that I didn't know what to do or how to heal this pain in her. I couldn't bring Chase back from the dead, and it looked like that was the only thing that could mend this ache.

"I'm sorry, beautiful," I said heavily. "I shouldn't have let him go off alone the night The Dollhouse came down."

"Why were you there with him?" she asked, looking at me once more and I realised we'd never had this conversation.

I swallowed thickly, not wanting to go there, to let this wound split apart. I didn't want to bleed. But Rogue needed me to. I could see how alone she was and I needed to climb down into this pit of despair with her and just let her know I was breaking too. But if she saw that, she'd question everything, *I'd* fucking question everything.

"We caught a Dead Dog," I grunted. "He told us Shawn's plans for The Dollhouse, so we went there together. I don't think he cared if he died that night, he would have given anything to get you and the others out."

"He kissed me," she admitted. "Before he died. I went to see him and we argued and…fuck, if I'd just gone with him or fought harder to make Fox bring him home maybe he wouldn't be dead."

The weight of that news washed over me and I scored my thumb along her chin as I realised something that she'd been trying to tell me all along.

"You never were gonna choose, were you?"

She shook her head. "It's the five of us or nothing. That's how it always was. And I guess things haven't changed. Because it can't be the five of us anymore, Rick, so it's nothing." She said it in a way that told me she felt that nothingness down to her core and I dropped my forehead to hers, despising that, wanting to fill that void but knowing I wasn't enough to do it.

She was right. I'd felt the absence of my brothers like bloody chunks had been carved out of my heart, but I'd been willing to bear that pain in the pursuit of revenge against them too. I was broken a long time ago, a boy hammered and beaten into a shattered illusion of a man. But that had never mattered before because I'd known destroying them would destroy me in turn. I'd been willing to go down with the ship, but now Rogue was involved and she was on this ship too and the water was already coming in.

"Tell me what I can do," I begged. "Tell me there's a way to mend that hurt in you and I'll do it. Whatever it is, baby girl."

I released her throat, dragging my thumb along her collar bone and hooking her necklace into my grasp before running it down to the key. "Is it this? You want the rest of these keys, you want vengeance?"

"I don't know anymore," she breathed, her tears drying up and a horrible numbness filling her gaze instead as she leaned against the door. She looked like she didn't care anymore, and that was the worst thing I'd ever faced. Because Rogue Easton was full to the brim with life, she cared about everything and nothing and brought the sunshine with her wherever she went. But this girl's light was going out and there wasn't enough fire left in me to rekindle her flame.

I went to move away, hating that I was failing her and she caught my collar in her grasp, tugging me toward her. Her lips met mine and she spoke between kisses as my heart thrashed with need for this girl. "If the sun rises tomorrow, we'll watch it together," she said breathily. "And if it doesn't, we'll fall into the dark hand in hand, Maverick Stone. So don't you dare run away from me."

I pushed my tongue into her mouth, pinning her to the crypt and placing my forearm above her head as I kissed her slow and hard, trying to tell her all the words that had abandoned me.

I would be there so long as she needed me, and I'd break with her if that was her fate. But I suddenly feared the path we were walking on, because once we'd cracked this crypt open and let our secrets out into the light, her words were going to come true.

But if Fox and Johnny James fell from grace, both me and Rogue were going to fall with them. And nothing I did could save her.

CHAPTER FIFTEEN

I didn't like Kaiser Rosewood all that much, but I did like his summerhouse, and his basement, and his whiskey, and how easily he swallowed my lies. He thought we were the best of friends, thought his finger was firmly in my pie so that when I took over Sunset Cove I'd be real nice to him, let him keep building the little empire he was on a path to ruling.

But in truth, I was no one's friend. I just liked this house, I liked it a lot actually. So much so, that I'd decided to make it my own house when the time was right. For now, I'd let him think I was in his pocket while taking his cash, fucking the whores he brought here on the weekends and sleeping in his summerhouse whenever I fancied. He'd said I could stay in the manor, but I didn't like the stench of his aftershave which lingered in the place or his wife's boring stories about working as a cabaret girl in Vegas. Maybe I'd bend her over something just before I blew her husband's head off so I could enjoy the horror in his eyes when I fucked his wife, but I reckoned the only pleasure I'd get out of that would be of the sadist variety.

Anyways, I'd taken myself for a stroll on Kaiser's grounds after he'd specifically told me I wasn't to show my face tonight at the manor. That had rung some alarm bells on my account and curious little me couldn't help but take a look. So imagine my surprise when I found Fox Harlequin walking in the front door with my girl on his arm and a while later his ex-brother Maverick Stone had appeared too. Interesting that was, very fucking interesting.

Turned out I wasn't the only pie in town which Kaiser was diddling. I guessed I wasn't surprised he was splitting his bets between us to ensure he came out on top either way when the war was over. Problem was, Kaiser didn't let my men onto his grounds and as hospitable as he was to me most of the time, I knew he wouldn't hesitate to turn his henchmen on me if my finger got twitchy on the trigger of my shotgun and I accidentally took Fox's head from his shoulders during his fancy party tonight. So I decided to lay low and gather a little intelligence instead.

I'd followed Rogue and Maverick out to the graveyard at the edge of the property and now I was hiding in the shadows behind a tall statue of an angel, my gaze fixed on them.

I'd learned three things while I was standing there:

There was something hella important in that crypt which I was now exceedingly interested in.

Maverick was one dirty fuck up of a man and it was delightful to see how broken he was first hand.

Rogue was a little slut as expected and Fox was not gonna be pleased to learn his girl was fucking the enemy.

I chewed over these facts and devoured each one slowly. I never acted rashly or emotionally to situations – emotions were for the weaker species. No, I bided my time and waited for things to fall into place for maximum damage and drama. So I'd think on what I'd learned for now.

Rogue lifted a necklace from her throat, pulling it over her head and my eyebrows arched as she took hold of the key on it. She'd told me it was the key to her grandma's liquor cabinet but unless that cabinet was located inside that big beasty of a crypt, I had to suspect she'd lied, because as I watched, she slid one of those keys into the lock and it fit like a dream. They spoke for a moment then Maverick shoved his tongue in Rogue's mouth while she was crying and I half hoped he'd start fucking her so I could make a video which would break poor Fox's heart. Unfortunately, they broke apart then started walking back to the house and I stared after my little whore with my cock throbbing and a smirk on my lips.

I might drive into town with some of my men later tonight, round up a few sluts and take 'em to the woods to be fucked until dawn. Yeah, I needed the outlet and I had a gifted bottle of whiskey from Kaiser that would appreciate being licked off of some perky tits.

When I was sure they were gone, I headed over to the crypt, taking in the door and running my fingers over the five key holes. Rogue had a key, so where were the other four?

I started laughing as I realised who might have the answer to that. My little pretty eyed boy down in Kaiser's basement. When the party was over, I'd pay him a visit and see if I could crack him once and for all. I wouldn't ask about the keys until he'd started singing about his favourite Fox though. I had to play this right, because Chase would close up tighter than a mollusc's asshole if I gave too much of this away. Of course, he was already going full mollusc on me, so I really need to crack him open with a knife soon.

I was a patient man, but we couldn't play this game forever. I was going to need some information or I'd have to get rid of him. I guessed I was hesitating to do it yet because I really enjoyed being the centre of his miserable world, loved the feeling of power I got when I drove my knife into his flesh and boy did I adore a challenge. Pretty eyes had turned out to have zero regard for himself, which either made him a sad little fool or braver than any man I'd destroyed before. I twisted the leather bracelets on my wrist which I'd stolen from Chase – my Chaselets if you will – as I thought on him.

I'd slowly been increasing the levels of torture I subjected him to, building to the beautiful crescendo I had planned. When I was finished breaking him and leaving my scars on the inside of his flesh as well as the out, I'd have one of my men record me taping a bomb into his mouth then drive him out to the woods.

Once we were there, I'd tie him to a tree and send the Harlequins the video, giving them the coordinates and fifteen minutes to find him. They'd discover their sweet friend was alive only to lose him all over again. Because no matter if they got there in time, that bomb was going off. I'd make sure of that. I just really hoped they were there to see his head go boom.

CHAPTER SIXTEEN

We slipped back inside the house and headed to the game room together, Maverick hounding my steps like a dog, his breath brushing the back of my neck and the weight of his eyes on me making my step falter more than once.

He wound an arm around my waist, grasping the door handle as we reached it, his chest pressing to my back as he caged me there for a moment and his stubble grazing the skin right beneath my ear as he leaned in to speak to me.

"I'm getting tired of waiting around for you, Rogue," he breathed. "And I'm not used to waiting around for what I want. You're starting to seriously test my sanity here. We need to figure this out fast, or I might just go on a Harlequin killing spree to reclaim my queen."

He swung the door open ahead of me so that I didn't have the chance to respond and I blew out a breath to expel the taste of him from my skin as I walked into the room like nothing had happened.

But the buzzing feeling he'd left running all over my body only intensified as I lifted my gaze and found Fox staring at me from across the room.

I swallowed a lump in my throat and raised my chin as I strode straight towards him, refusing to let myself get flustered by these boys. Though as my gaze travelled over the way Fox's muscles bulged against his shirt, I knew I was playing fast and loose with the term *boys* these days. Still. I could remember when Fox was eight and he fell off the monkey bars and skinned his knees. Granted, he just cursed out everyone who had seen it happen then instantly climbed them again and hung from them upside down to prove a point to anyone who thought seeing him bleed equalled seeing him being weak. But I still remembered his nose being dusted with freckles and his eyes bright with questions before every innocent thing about him had been stripped away. He wasn't going to intimidate me.

I made it across the room to Fox as he just stood there, waiting for me, but instead of the jealousy or anger I expected to find in his green eyes when I arrived, I found a heat which scorched me from the inside out.

"Hey," I said, my voice coming out all breathy for some fucking reason and he arched a single brow at me.

"Been having fun?" he asked.

"Just checking that our old secrets still remain hidden," I explained.

"And?"

"Looks like it."

Fox nodded then turned away from me and fell into conversation with the mayor. I blinked at the shift in his attitude but slipped closer to him anyway, taking his arm in mine and squeezing his bicep affectionately.

Fox leaned closer to me and I looked up at his strong profile, not sure what I was expecting him to say though it certainly wasn't what escaped his lips.

"Grab me another drink, yeah?" He gave me a nudge towards the fancy bar area set up towards one side of the room and I blinked up at him in surprise. "I'll come find you in a minute."

The mayor gave me a bland smile and I was left with a choice between obeying and causing a scene. One glance at the armed men in the room reminded me that I shouldn't really be looking to make an enemy for the Harlequins here, so I shot Fox a scowl as I was forced to obey him.

I strode across the room in my stiletto pumps, trying to ignore the way they reminded me of being trapped in that safe for hours on end. But I'd decided I couldn't go my whole life without wearing heels ever again - I mean sure, I *could,* but if I wasn't going to let all the other shit in my life destroy me then I certainly wouldn't be bowing to the flashbacks of that fucking place. That said, I wasn't likely to pick shoes that buckled around my ankles the way the ones I'd been wearing in that hell had and I could easily kick these babies off if I needed to run or even if I just wanted rid of them for comfort purposes.

I ordered myself a shot of tequila then ordered some girly pink thing with an umbrella for Fox as a fuck you for his bossiness.

"Drinking alone, gorgeous?" a smarmy voice questioned and a wash of expensive aftershave half choked me as I turned to find Kaiser Rosewood leaning into my personal space.

Curls of dark chest hair bristled out from beneath an admittedly expensive looking eggplant coloured shirt. But expensive clearly didn't equal nice. I plastered on a smile as I turned to look at him, waving the bartender over for more tequila.

"I'm never alone," I assured him. "I have a hundred friends in my head who are always willing to play with me." Not even a lie, I'd made up a whole ton of imaginary friends in my dreams and fantasies over the last ten years when I found the real people I was interacting with to be seriously lacking. The only problem was that they inadvertently all ended up with the face of one of my boys after spending a few hours in their imaginary company, and I had to banish them to the corners of my mind alongside anything else that had reminded me of this place.

Kaiser laughed like that was freaking hilarious, his clammy hand landing on my thigh just above my knee, but below the hem of my dress. *Err, fuck no.*

I rather unsubtly crossed my legs away from him, forcing his hand to fall free as I flashed him a shark's grin which would be his one and only warning with me.

"Great party," I commented as surprise flickered through his gaze. I was guessing his name and money meant he didn't get the brush off all that often, but he could go suck a dodgy whelk if he thought I'd put up with him pawing at me or worse just because he was dripping money like it was going out of fashion. And speaking of things going out of fashion - were those gold chains dangling on his fancy loafers? *Shudder.*

"I do enjoy a little shindig," he replied, clicking his fingers at the bartender like a total douche canoe and pointing at his empty glass. "And you've certainly been cleaning up nicely on the table."

I flashed him a smile. Because fuck yeah I had. I'd won so much of these rich asshole's money tonight that I'd lost count of it. Okay, that was a lie - I knew exactly how much I was owed down to the dime so that I could be certain they paid the fuck up before I left but yeah, I was killing it as standard. Poker was my game.

"I like cards," I said with a shrug. "At least if they're going to fuck you over, they tell you to your face and give you plenty of warning about it."

Kaiser bellowed a laugh and although I was hella funny, it was definitely overkill. I arched a brow at him as he stepped closer and slid a smarmy arm around my back, his hand clamming its way over the material of my dress at the base of my spine.

"Dude, I'm having fun at your party and all that shit, but I'm not a hooker and I'm not looking to buy what you're selling," I said in a hard voice.

Kaiser blinked at me, but before he could fully process that, Fox's loud laugh broke the tension and the bartender arrived to offer Kaiser a glass of something from a fancy bottle which smelled powerful enough to catch in the back of my throat even without me drinking a drop.

Fox's arm slipped around my ribs and he tugged me closer to him, forcing Kaiser to drop his arm as I kept a blank stare on my face.

"What did you say, sweetheart? It's a little loud in here," Kaiser said, pushing a hand through his slicked back hair and flashing me a set of bleached teeth. The scent of a dead worm clung to his skin beneath the overbearing stench of all that aftershave. I couldn't say I'd ever sniffed a dead worm before, but I just knew that was what he smelled of.

"Just saying what a great party this is," I replied sweet as pie.

Kaiser licked his lips and glanced between me and Fox, his little eyes flaring with a hunger for something far more dangerous than sex.

I slid Fox's pink drink towards him and he didn't even bat an eye as he tossed the umbrella aside and sank it in one hit. *Asshole.*

"I had some business dealings I wished to discuss with Luther tonight," Kaiser said to him. "Perhaps we could talk in private? Assuming you really can speak on behalf of the Harlequins and I'm not just wasting my time by not speaking to the man in charge?"

"Well my father wanted to come, but he doesn't make a habit out of spending time around men who are late in paying their debts to him," Fox said in a flat tone. "It makes him a little stabby."

Kaiser laughed loudly but his eyes darted left and right nervously like he didn't want anyone to overhear that. "Yes, yes, that matter is all well in hand. But I actually needed a chat about some other things…"

"We can talk," Fox agreed, though he didn't look particularly keen to do so. "What are you interested in?"

"Not here," Kaiser said, knocking his drink back and gesturing towards the door. "We can have a private discussion in my office."

Fox nodded, urging me along with him as he started to follow Kaiser's lead, but the smarmy asshole cleared his throat, a frown pinching his brow.

"I'd really rather keep our discussions on this between us," he said. "I'm already allowing a lot of leeway by speaking to you instead of Luther and-"

"That's fine by me," I interrupted as I felt every one of Fox's muscles bunching in anger, knowing he was about to insist on me being present, but I doubted there was any need for me to attend some stuffy chat with this creep and it sounded like a snoozefest to me anyway. "I need to use the restroom."

Fox still looked inclined to protest as we stepped out into the garishly decorated hallway, but I just tiptoed up to place a kiss on his cheek.

Fox wasn't having that and instead of allowing me to pull away again, he pushed me back against the wall, fisted my bun in his hand to force my head back and took my mouth hostage with his.

He kissed me with a brutal, demanding need, his tongue taking control of my own as his powerful body crushed me against the wall and a soft moan of surrender burned through my throat.

His free hand grasped the back of my thigh, fingers pushing between the slit in the material where Kaiser couldn't see what he was doing and a gasp escaped me as his fingers twisted into the wet material of my panties.

"I'm getting sick of this game, Rogue," he growled low, his words just for me as his mouth moved to my ear and I panted desperately against the press of his fingers against my aching pussy through my underwear. "I'm starting to think you *want* me to force your hand in this."

He flexed his fingers against me, making me whimper as my legs threatened to buckle beneath me, but then he was gone, striding away with Kaiser Rosewood who was making crude jokes while I just sagged against the damn wall.

Fuck him.

Shit, that was a bad choice of suggestion to make, because now all I could think about was what it might be like if I *did* fuck him and all the ways he might throw me around the bedroom while trying to control me the way he was so desperate to.

I glanced back towards the room where most of the party goers were still talking bullshit and drinking, my gaze falling on Rick who now had an arm curled around Mia the clam vag as he spoke with some asshole in a suit.

The wildly violent look in his eyes told me he'd just seen Fox pin me to the wall and I was willing to bet he wouldn't have nice things to say on that subject if he got me alone again. But as he was currently all up in the clam, I wasn't gonna have to deal with him playing hypocrite with me, so I just turned away and decided to do some exploring instead.

I wandered along the corridors which had once been so familiar to me when Miss Mabel had been alive, missing the simple, traditional decor she'd enjoyed and knowing she'd have fucking hated every garish choice that had been made in these so-called renovations.

I tried doors as I went, casual as fuck, finding most of them locked or otherwise boring, but in a drawing room which hadn't been touched by the renovation fairy yet, I found some old photographs in a drawer.

I smiled as I flicked through the pictures of Miss Mabel which dated back over the years, some of them faded and brown but showing a time when she'd been happy, laughing with a handsome man. I paused as I found a photograph of her cradling a baby in her arms, the look of serenity and peace on her face making my heart twist. Where had that baby been when I'd known her? She'd been so alone, so where was that child?

A noise from back in the corridor made me jump and I hurriedly shoved the photographs back in the drawer, whirling around with some bullshit line on my lips to excuse my nosy wanderings. But I found Fox standing there watching me instead of some random asshole and my posture relaxed.

"Found anything interesting?" he asked curiously.

"No," I replied with a shrug. "Just some old memories."

I crossed the room to join him and we headed back out into the corridor as I fell into step beside him.

"What did Kaiser want?" I asked when he failed to fill the silence. The space dividing us seemed to crackle with expectant energy, but for once he was making no attempt to cross the divide.

"Just a load of bullshit that comes down to a price. He wants to buy protection and loyalty from the Crew. Of course, it's pretty clear to me that he's looking to make that same deal with The Damned Men, so I don't feel all that inclined to offer him much loyalty. But we'll take his money all the same."

We turned down a narrow corridor which I remembered from my youth and I glanced around at the dim space as we moved towards the door which led to the basement. JJ had chased me down there once and scared the crap out of me when he'd jumped out from behind an old suitcase.

But as we reached the door to the basement, we found it all locked up with several bolts and a large padlock. Three separate padlocks secured it with heavy bolts like Kaiser was keeping a monster in there.

"Ten bucks says he's got his collection of butt plugs locked away down there," I joked, flicking the padlock with my fingers so it smacked against the heavy wood of the door.

"Or maybe that's where he keeps the dead bodies," Fox teased, laying a hand against the wood above my head and peering down at me.

"Nah," I disagreed, turning towards him and pressing my back to the wood as I looked up at him. "That guy isn't the kind to get his manicured hands dirty like that."

Fox twitched a smile at me, his gaze moving down my body for a moment before fixing back on my eyes.

"And you prefer a man who gets his hands dirty then, do you?"

"Let's see." I took his free hand in mine, lifting it up and inspecting it closely. There were scars all over his knuckles which spoke of the violence that touched his life all too often and callouses lining his palm which proved he wasn't afraid of hard work. I trailed my fingertip around the curve of the infinity tattoo on his thumb and glanced up at him questioningly.

"I got that for you. Because I never gave up on finding you and I knew I never would. Now that I've found you again it isn't about the search. It's about the life we're owed. And the forever I know we'll claim."

I licked my lips as I looked up at him, wanting more of his mouth on mine and knowing that wasn't fair while I knew I couldn't ever be what he wanted me to be.

"Say it," he growled, watching me like I held every answer to every question he'd ever wanted to ask on the tip of my tongue.

"No," I replied because I couldn't. I just wished I could make him understand why.

Fox growled in frustration and shifted forward, grasping the backs of my thighs and lifting me so that I was pinned against the basement door with his hips between my legs. He leaned in and my lips parted in anticipation of a kiss he didn't offer.

He paused there, holding me in suspense and looking me in the eyes as he smirked, his mouth just out of reach of my lips and his breath tasting like every sin I wanted to commit with him.

A muffled thump sounded from somewhere close by, but with Fox stealing every inch of my attention, I couldn't spare a moment to wonder about it.

"I warned you, hummingbird. If you don't ask for it soon, I'll end up taking it. But sometimes I think that's what you want, isn't it?" Fox asked darkly.

I shook my head as I gripped his biceps, physically forcing myself not to close the distance between us and let him win despite the ache I felt to do so.

He leaned in even closer and my traitorous lips parted as a soft whimper escaped me, the feeling of his solid cock driving against my panties making my fucking brain melt away and leak out of my ears as every single reason I had to try and fight this slipped out of my grasp.

"Liar," Fox breathed before stepping back suddenly and dropping me to my feet again.

I gaped up at him and he smirked down at me. "Asshole," I hissed, trying to pull off a scowl but I sagged back against the door and my chest heaved as I tried to fight off the effect he had on my body.

"You only have to say the word. Or we can keep playing this game until one of us snaps." Fox smirked at me like the cocky bastard he was and I straightened my spine at the challenge.

My gaze trailed down his muscular physique to the more than tempting bulge in his pants and I groaned again, knocking my head back against the basement door and laughing.

"I never lose, Badger," I said, trying to show more confidence than I felt but he only laughed too.

"We'll see."

CHAPTER SEVENTEEN

"Fox!" I shouted against the gag in my mouth as I kicked the edges of the wooden chest Shawn had locked me inside hours ago. "Rogue!"

I could hear them, they were so close. I'd thought I was just imagining it at first, sure my mind was playing cruel tricks on me, but they were there. Right upstairs in this fucking house.

"Miss Mabel!" I cried, my voice nothing but a muffled sound and no answer came from her. She'd told me Kaiser always slipped her a sedative whenever he had guests over and tonight was clearly one of those fucking nights.

I kicked, shouted and thrashed as Rogue's soft laughter called to me and my heart fragmented at that noise. Seeing her face again would be everything. I pictured her mouth pulling up in a smile and her eyes full of light, the endless depths of them possessing me.

Maybe I really am going mad.

But then they were talking again and I was sure, so fucking sure that they were there. I couldn't quite make out what they were saying, I just knew it was them. I could sense them up there like they were pulling on some cord tethered to the core of my being.

"Fox!" I yelled against the fucking gag, kicking harder, but I couldn't move properly in the tight space. My muscles were cramping and my back was in agony where it was pressed to the side of it and my legs were forced to curl to my chest. My hands were bound behind me and I fought with all my strength to break the rope binding them, but it just wouldn't fucking give.

The sound of their voices started drifting away and I bashed my head back against the box so hard I saw stars.

"Fuck, no, *please*," I begged to any god who might be listening. "Rogue!" I roared so loud it burned my throat, but between the gag, the box and the steel door locking this room, there was no chance of her hearing me.

Their voices faded away and my muscles shuddered as I continued to kick and the rope bit into my wrists. I heaved in air, the taste of it stale from being in this box for so long and my heart split open. I didn't know what they were doing here, but the idea of them being so close was the final straw for me. I'd lost hope the moment I'd been brought here, but having a piece of it handed to me for a few sweet seconds only to be taken away again was too much. I didn't even know if they wanted me back, or if my death was a relief to them after all I'd fucking done. Would Fox care if he knew I was here? Or was Shawn just doing to me what he hadn't been able to in the end?

I fell still, my only company the thundering of my pulse in my ears and the press of the wooden chest on all sides. The last shard of my resolve crumbled like sand before me and I descended into a frighteningly dark place that was full of bad memories.

I'd die a cornered boy who was never worth loving and that was that. My existence had had no value and I was so fucking tired of being here. I just wanted it to be over. I wanted the silence and the eternal embrace of a deep grave. And I wanted Shawn to make it hurt, because pain had been my lifelong companion and I wanted to go into the dirt with at least one friend there to watch me go.

CHAPTER EIGHTEEN

I drove us home in my truck and Rogue bobbed her head to Wildest Dreams by Taylor Swift while my mood started to slip over Maverick. I wasn't sure how to deal with him, but what I did know was that anything I'd done so far hadn't worked. And I was starting to think it wasn't going to. Rogue seemed to draw closer to me, only to retreat all over again until I was left feeling like I didn't know what she needed at all. I'd always been convinced I was the best thing for her, that I could provide for her in all the ways she needed and make sure she never had to worry about anything. But Rogue didn't want to be looked after, at least not by me. And it wasn't like I wanted to stifle her, I just had no idea how to be what she needed. Maybe I'd been an idiot to think I was the right thing for her, but I still couldn't shake the feeling that we were meant to be together. And I wasn't giving up yet, I just needed to figure out how to be the man for her, and how to get rid of the one trying to steal her from me.

"What's going on in that head of yours, Badge?" she asked. "You look like you've got a storm brewing up there. Is it Chase?" she lowered her voice on his name and my chest tugged painfully.

It's always Chase.

"No," I said and silence pooled between us. "What do you want, Rogue?

You want Maverick? Are you hoping I'll let you go to him?" *Because I never will.*

"You don't *let me* do anything, Badger," she said in a warning tone, but she didn't answer my other questions.

My grip tightened on the steering wheel and I fought to keep my temper in check. In all the visions I'd imagined of her coming home after ten years, this was not one of them. I'd always thought that once she was back, I'd figure out a way to make her mine. But the more I tried to claim her, the more she seemed to pull back even further, despite the fact that her body gave away exactly how much she desired mine.

Now she was fucking Maverick right under my nose and I just had to suck it up until I could figure out how to get rid of him. But what if she fell in love with him before then? What if she already was? Did he care about her like that? I couldn't see it. Not after everything I'd witnessed Maverick do in Sunset Cove, the men he'd killed, the trail of blood he'd left in his wake. He'd changed, and I didn't want her falling for some illusion he was painting for her.

JJ had told me Maverick had eyes among my men too, and that was seriously unnerving. How could he have turned a Harlequin? Maybe it was just a bluff and he was trying to fuck with my head, but I'd have to question all of my men and try to figure out if it was true or not regardless.

"Maverick isn't a good man anymore," I said, trying to keep my voice level. "You don't know what he's done."

"I'm well aware of what he's done, but I don't see how it's any worse than what you do in the Crew," she said lightly.

"I don't make deaths bloody unless I need to," I said. "I swear Maverick does it because he enjoys it."

"Well maybe I like that he's not afraid to show his monster," she tossed back and my shoulder muscles bunched. "Who knows? Maybe I'd like you a bit more if you showed yours more often." The comment was off hand, but it made a growl build in my throat. I didn't show her that side of me much because that was the last thing I wanted her to see me as. I'd done things in the past ten years that could put even Maverick's dirty work to shame, and I didn't want her witnessing that. I wanted her to see the good left in me, but maybe what remained just wasn't all that appealing anymore.

Although, whenever I pushed her boundaries and showed her exactly how much power I could seize over her body, she always seemed to like it. I was starting to think she really did want me to take the decision away from her and bend her to my will, and the idea of that got me seriously hot. But I wasn't gonna do shit unless I could be sure that was what she wanted. Or maybe I was just deluding myself and she was planning to shack up with Maverick as soon as she got the chance. *Over my dead body.*

We arrived back at Harlequin House and I drove us down into the garage, switching off the engine so quiet settled between us.

"I'm not going to stop fighting for you, Rogue," I told her, gazing out the window instead of at her. "I can't, it's in my blood. But I'm starting to wonder if the battle's already lost." I shoved the door open, stepping out of my truck and heading upstairs into the house. I unbuttoned my shirt as I marched up to my bedroom and headed inside, tossing it into the laundry hamper and unbuckling my pants.

This house felt suffocating lately. I could feel the press of Chase's room across the hall from mine like it was pushing the walls toward me inch by inch. We'd stopped sleeping in there, leaving it as a sort of shrine to him, but one day I knew we'd have to go in and clear through his things. I just didn't want to. I hadn't even thought to do it after I banished him from the Crew, let alone now that he was dead.

My grief welled up again and I walked into the bathroom, resting my hands on the sink and staring myself in the eye, facing the consequences of all the decisions I'd made in relation to him. I had to own it all, every ounce of regret, every pound of hurt. The choices I'd made were the right ones, I had to believe that. It was the only thing that allowed me to lead within the Crew, because if I ever stopped to question my actions, I'd spiral out of control.

You did the right thing.

It's not your fault he's dead.

My eyes looked darker than they had when I was a kid, the green in them seeming to deepen a shade every year I tainted my soul with more bad deeds. This was my burden to bear for my position and I'd accepted that there was no other life for me anymore. But the one thing which had always kept me resilient was my family. Knowing JJ and Chase were at my side had been a constant reassurance that I was making the right choices. Because since I'd lost Rogue then Maverick too, I'd made it my life's mission to keep the last of my family close and ensure no harm ever came to them. But I'd failed. I hadn't listened to Chase when he'd needed me. His struggles had been right there in front of me since Rogue had come home, but I hadn't listened, too blinded by my love of my girl to even hear a single word spoken against her. He wasn't right in what he'd done, but if I'd just tried to handle things differently…

I hung my head then splashed my face with cold water, knowing another restless night awaited me in my bed. Whenever I closed my eyes, all I saw was Chase on his knees with my gun aimed at his forehead, the way my finger had tightened around the trigger, how close I'd been to really doing it. It made me fucking nauseous.

"Fox?" Rogue's soft voice called from my bedroom.

I turned and pushed out the door, frowning as I found her there with Mutt hugged to her chest.

"Are you alright?" I asked.

"Yeah, but um, can I stay in here tonight?" she asked hopefully. "I still get nightmares about Chase when I sleep on my own."

I frowned, hurting for my girl and knowing that pain as well as she did. "Sure, baby."

She turned around, pulling her hair over her shoulder. "Could you unzip me? I can't reach."

She placed Mutt on the bed and I moved toward her, taking hold of the zip and drawing it down the length of her spine, a shiver dancing across her body at my touch.

My gaze flicked to the mirror on the wall in front of us and she caught my gaze there before shrugging out of the dress and letting it drop down to her ankles, leaving her in her pale blue panties and matching lacy bra. Her nipples were pressing against the material and my cock hardened at the perfect sight of her, my breath hitching in my throat. It was a dare, a fucking challenge that persuaded me a little more that she wanted me to claim her.

Her eyes moved onto her own reflection and a frown creased her brow as she kicked her dress away.

"What are you thinking, baby?" I asked, leaning down to speak in her ear. We weren't touching, but we were so close that I could feel the pull of her like the most powerful magnet in the world.

"I'm thinking about how I've used this body to survive all these years," she said, then held a hand to her chest. "But what was I even protecting, Fox? It's just flesh and bone, the house of a worthless girl who doesn't belong anywhere."

"You belong here," I said fiercely then took hold of her chin to make her look herself in the eyes in the mirror. "Your worth has nothing to do with this shell you're in, you were born worthy and you'll die worthy, Rogue Easton. You could rule the whole world if you'd only see how powerful you are." She tried to look away, but I didn't let her.

"Bullshit. I'm disposable, I've never known anyone who hasn't thrown me away. You might want this body, Fox, but you don't really want *me*."

She tried to pull out of my grip again, but I wrapped an arm around her and pulled her back against me in a tight hold.

"I don't want you because you're beautiful, baby, I want you because our souls are forged of the very same thing and they've been fighting to get back to each other for ten years. You can't tell me you don't feel it." I ran my fingers over her flesh, along her stomach then up between her breasts before dragging my thumb up the length of her neck. Goosebumps rose all over her body and she melted back against me as a shaky breath left her.

"That's how I know you're mine, hummingbird." I bit down on the shell of her ear and her ass ground against my hard cock, making both of us groan. I slid my hand over her right breast, squeezing and circling my thumb over her peaked nipple through the lace of her bra. "I feel you even when you're not here. But when you are, it feels like this all the fucking time." I ran my free hand down her stomach, making her inhale deeply as I trailed my fingers over the outside of her panties and her hips bucked a little with need.

"I'm the crime you're tempted to commit," I growled as she whimpered for more of my touch. "And you know once you give in, you'll commit it again and again because of how good it feels to sin with me."

"*Fox*," she half moaned, half begged and I got so hard for her at the sound of her saying my name like that that it practically hurt.

I slid my fingers down onto her clit through her panties and a heady moan left her as I circled them once, giving her just enough to know how good this could be.

"Fox, wait," she panted as she reached a hand back to cling to my neck, her hips rocking to try and force me to contradict her complaints. "We can't. I can't be all in with you."

I tugged on her nipple and she released a desperate noise in her throat, her nails digging into my neck.

"Stop," she panted.

"Stop enjoying it," I countered.

"I'm not yours," she said breathily. "This doesn't make me yours."

"I'm only touching your bra and panties, baby, seems like it doesn't count to me," I said, leaning down to bite her neck hard enough to mark her.

"You mean that?" she demanded, her back arching and her whole body coming alive for me. It felt so fucking good and my head was so far gone. I needed her so bad. And I needed her to know what this fire between us felt like when we poured a little gasoline on it.

"I mean it," I said firmly, taking my hand from her breast and tugging her hair to make her look at me in the mirror and see the truth in my eyes. She sucked her lower lip and I ran my middle finger up and down over her clit, her hips chasing the movement as she tried to steal a kiss from my lips. I didn't let her, tightening my grip on her hair. This was for her. And she was going to witness every second of it.

I angled her chin so she looked down at my hand on her pussy before dropping my other hand and squeezing her breast in a firm, possessive grasp. She shuddered, leaning back against me and I swear I could feel the heat in her veins, the electricity charging every particle in her flesh.

I needed her to feel good for me, I needed her to see why we were perfect for each other even if I still couldn't truly have her. I scored my thumb over her nipple, making her moan for me once more and she arched back against me, gasping, panting, falling apart for me. I worked my fingers faster on her clit and she moaned my name again, making an animal growl leave me as I held her upright.

She shivered and tipped her head back against my shoulder and I moved my hand from her breast to her mouth, stifling her cry as she came for me and feeling the warmth of her breaths against my palm, making my cock throb in desperation. God, it felt so fucking hot having her like this. I swear I'd die happy if I could make her mine for even a damn hour.

When her shoulders relaxed, I slid my fingers down between her thighs, rubbing my hand over the wet patch on her panties with a smirk, my head buzzing over the fact that I'd done that to her.

Her cheeks were flushed as I let her go and she turned to me, raising her chin. "You swear that didn't count towards your delusions that I'm yours?" she demanded and I gave her a sideways grin, painting a cross over my heart.

"Promise, baby."

"Good." She walked to my closet, grabbed one of my shirts and disappeared into the en suite, kicking the door shut behind her just like that.

The shower started running a second later and I looked to Mutt who was glaring at me and I rolled my eyes at him before stripping out of my shoes, socks and pants then getting into bed.

I leaned over to open the drawer in my nightstand and pulled out the new toy I'd bought for the little bastard. It was a seagull with a squeaker inside and as he both loved chasing seagulls and had recently finished destroying the duck version of this exact same toy, I was pretty certain I was about to buy my way back into his good graces.

"What's this?" I said to him, shaking the toy and squeezing it a few times to make his ears perk up. He looked between me and it and I smirked in triumph as I shook it a couple more times then tossed it to him.

The stuffed seagull smacked him in the side of the face as he made zero attempt to catch it then fell off the bed with a soft thump.

Mutt glared at me and I huffed at him in return.

"Seriously?" I demanded. "That's like an exact copy of your favourite! Plus it's a freaking seagull – what more do you want from me, dog?"

Mutt cocked his head at me then hopped off the bed. I smiled victoriously as he picked up the new toy, watching him as he trotted over to the door with it before he dropped it down and peed on it. Then he turned his back and kicked his feet at it like he was trying to kick it away and promptly moved to curl up on Rogue's discarded dress without offering me another glance.

Little asshole.

I grumbled at him, calling him out on being a dick while he continued to ignore me, and I had to get out of bed to clean the fucking puddle off of my floor and toss the brand new toy in the washer.

By the time I returned to my room the little bastard was snoring softly like he was totally at peace with the world.

"I should just drop you to the pound because you won't house train," I grouched at him and I swear he farted at me in a challenge.

Before I could get anymore riled up at the little dog, the sound of Rogue singing in the shower drew my attention away from him and I groaned as I came up with all kinds of fantasies about heading on in there and fucking her against the wall of my shower while she was dripping wet.

I cursed my fucking life as I fisted my cock through my boxers, half tempted to just jerk off to relieve some tension, but finding I didn't want to. Nothing aside from the hot heat of her body was going to be able to satisfy this need in me tonight and fucking my hand alone did not appeal.

I needed a fucking distraction, so I hooked the Dark Fae book off of my nightstand and continued reading. I was right at the end of the book and shit was going down. To be honest, I was confused. The girl seemed to be lusting after all four guys and refusing to choose between them even though Gabriel was obviously her one and only. I guessed she'd pick him eventually, I'd just figured it would have happened by now.

When Rogue reappeared, I got somehow even harder at the sight of her in my shirt, her hair twisted up into a colourful knot on top of her head.

Mutt started wagging as she approached, like he wasn't a devil in dog form and she tickled his ears before climbing into the bed with me and the scent of my body wash on her skin made me feel so fucking good. My instincts were burning, telling me she was mine and urging me to try and claim all of her, but I'd made her a promise that tonight didn't count. And I wasn't gonna be an asshole about it. I was just glad to have taken my first orgasm from her at last.

She rolled towards me, her head resting on the pillow beside mine and I studied her face as she closed her eyes.

"Stop staring, Badger," she said and a grin hooked up my lips.

"I have a question."

"What is it?" she asked sleepily.

"What do you want?" I shifted closer to her. "I think I forgot to ask before now."

She cracked an eye, frowning at me before shutting it again. "That's a big question with an impossible answer, Badge."

"Answer it anyway," I urged.

She remained quiet for a while like she wasn't sure if she wanted to tell me, but she finally did. "I want what I had when I was fifteen, riding waves with my boys and knowing no matter what happened, we'd be okay. Because we had each other."

I sighed, rolling onto my back as a crushing weight fell on my chest. "So you want the one thing I can't give you."

She shifted closer, wrapping her arm around me and laying her head over my heart. It eased the cloying despair in my chest so I just held her, closing my eyes and pretending we were at Sinners' Playground, sleeping between the Pac Man and Space Invaders machines. But then I thought of Chase there too and I held her even tighter, my jaw clenched as I tried not to lean into that pain and just steal some peace with Rogue for once.

"I know you need it too," she whispered just as I was falling asleep. "I'm sorry I can't give you it either."

"Shit, we need to put everything back where we found it and get the hell out of here," JJ said in a panic.

I stared at the symbol on the medallion in my hand in fear before looking around at my friends' pale faces.

"Um, guys, it gets worse. Far fucking worse," Chase called and I looked over to where he was standing peering in a doorway with a cigarette between his lips. We moved after him and I smelled the death before I saw it. He pushed the door wide and I took in the bodies lying everywhere in there, bloody and mutilated, their faces twisted in death.

"Oh fuck," Rogue gasped and I reached for her hand, stuffing the medallion into my pocket as I tried to remember exactly where we'd found it.

"Holy shit, look at his." I turned at Maverick's voice, finding him with a bottle of vodka in his hand with what looked like a thumb floating in it.

"Put it down," Rogue hissed like she feared his fingerprints being on that thing and she pulled out of my grip, taking it from his hand. A large wave rocked the boat at that moment and it slipped from her fingers, crashing to the deck and vodka spilled across it along with the severed thumb.

JJ bumped into Chase and I moved to brace them, but my foot slipped on the vodka and I crashed to the floor, taking Chase out with me. His cigarette popped form his lips, hitting the deck in a shower of sparks and the vodka caught alight in a blaze.

JJ hauled us upright as another wave made the boat rock wildly and Rogue and Maverick clung onto each other so they didn't fall.

"I told you there was a fucking storm coming in tonight," JJ said in alarm. "We shouldn't have come out here."

"Keep your panties on," Maverick barked, but the fire flared in his eyes and we all scrambled to get out of its way, scrambling towards the stairs that led back up to the top deck.

The fire flared hotter and Chase pushed me along as we all started running up the stairs, the heat of the flames washing over my back.

I kept my gaze on Rogue ahead of us as Maverick clung onto her hand and we all gasped as the boat rocked wildly once more. I leapt up a step, cushioning Rogue as she skidded sideways towards the wall. My head impacted with it but she thumped harmlessly against my chest and I pushed her up the next step, encouraging her to keep going as Maverick tugged her along. I threw a glance back to make sure Chase and JJ were right behind me, my heart thrashing at the sight of the spreading flames at their heels.

"Go!" JJ cried and I damn well did, racing along with all of them as we made it to the top deck and dove over the railing. I plunged into the ocean and the moment I resurfaced, we all started swimming for my dad's speedboat which we'd tied off beside the yacht.

Maverick heaved himself up first, pulling Rogue after her before they both worked to help the rest of us out of the water. Chase ran to start the motor *and we tore away toward the shore, staring back at the yacht as the fire crept into view on the top deck. I wrapped my arm around Rogue's shoulders and JJ took her hand on her other side while Chase and Maverick closed in tight around us.*

"We're fucked," JJ whispered.

"We're not," I growled fiercely. "Only we know we were there. So all we have to do is never tell another soul. Swear it."

"I swear," they all said straight away, and I felt the power of that oath binding us somehow deeper than we already were.

I left Rogue to sleep in my bed while I went for a run in the morning, shaking off the ghosts of the past as I soaked in the morning sun and reminded myself our secret was still locked firmly away in the Rosewood crypt. When I got home, JJ's voice carried to me from the patio.

"-yeah like that. Can you feel me inside you so fucking deep?"

My heart lurched and some crazy, wild thought entered my head that had no fucking place in existing. *There's only one girl in this house right now.*

I ran to the kitchen, stepping out onto the patio and my eyes fell on JJ laying on a sun lounger in some hot pink shorts with a burner phone tucked against his ear.

"Call me by my name, big boy," he purred then smirked as he noticed me and hit the speakerphone.

"Hung," a man's voice said breathily.

"My full name," JJ growled in a domineering tone then casually sipped some coffee from his bright yellow Pikachu mug. He'd lost his shit when Rogue had almost smashed his Charmander one a few weeks back. I'd never seen him move so fast to catch something. I swear he'd take a bullet for one of them.

"Hung Likahorse," the guy groaned.

"Take my fifteen incher, you dirty little stallion," JJ growled and the sound of the guy coming made my nose wrinkle as I turned and grabbed some coffee from the kitchen. When I returned to the patio, he'd killed the call and had a frown forming on his brow.

"You alright, man?" I asked as I took the sun lounger beside him, figuring I'd drain a coffee then start on my laps in the pool.

"Yeah, I just…" His gaze moved to me and I saw darkness there. I wasn't exactly surprised, we all had this aura about us since Chase. Like every smile was harder to summon and whenever there was a pause in conversation or we were left alone to our thoughts, they always turned to *him*. But something in JJ's expression told me there was more going on than that.

"You can tell me anything, you know? I got you," I said, not liking the idea that he was keeping something from me.

"It's the escorting," he said on a heavy breath. "I stopped doing it ages ago."

"What?" I frowned in surprise. "But you rely on that money, why the hell would you stop?"

"I just don't wanna do it anymore." He placed his mug down and scraped a hand through his hair. "It feels wrong."

"Why didn't you tell me?" I asked in confusion.

"I dunno, I just thought you'd be mad that I couldn't make my cut and I didn't want you to bail me out. I…worked for Jolene doing some fetish shit for a while." His expression pinched in regret and my lips parted as I stared at him.

"JJ what the fuck?" I demanded, not because I gave a shit about Jolene, but because I wanted to know why he'd stooped that low instead of just talking to me.

"I'm sorry, I just thought if I could handle it myself then-"

"You don't ever need to handle stuff alone." I swung my legs over the side of the lounger and stared at him intently. "You know we've got your back – I mean I do." I'd meant Chase and I hated that I'd meant Chase. The look in JJ's eyes said he knew that too.

"Chase did help me out for a bit," he admitted in a mutter.

I gaped at him for a moment, hurt cutting through my chest. "But you didn't think you could tell *me*?"

"I didn't wanna burden you," he said but I didn't buy it.

"It's not just that," I said. "I know it's not. What aren't you saying?" I pressed, trying to keep the bite from my tone because I knew JJ wouldn't do anything intentionally to piss me off. That wasn't his style. He was always looking out for everyone in our family. But I didn't like that I'd been on the outside of this knowledge for so long. Chase had been gone for weeks and weeks now, so all this time JJ had just been struggling to get by right under my nose.

JJ swallowed hard. "Don't get mad, alright?" he asked and I took a long sip of coffee before nodding. "Since Rogue's been back you've been seriously on edge. I get that you wanna protect her, keep her in town, all that shit. But the way you've handled it…"

"Spit it out," I pushed, sensing I really wasn't gonna like what he was about to say.

"You're acting like your dad," he said in a low voice, his brows pulled tightly together. "You're trying to control the whole world and everyone in it. But we all need to be able to breathe, to make our own choices, to go after our own wants, and we shouldn't have to fear what you think about all that. And by we I mean *us*. Your family. Me and Rogue. The three of us are all that's left, Fox. I didn't wanna tell you my shit because frankly I knew you wouldn't let me deal with it. You'd make plans and run extra jobs and not let me have a say in any of it. So I did what I did and maybe it was fucking stupid now I think about it, but I guess I was tired of being told what to do. You might be my boss, but you're my friend first. And I think you've forgotten that."

I didn't immediately explode, though that was my auto reaction, so I had to fight hard to keep myself in check. I tried to hear what he was saying, because he was my brother and I knew he wouldn't bring it up at all if he didn't really feel that way. I'd argued with him at the wreckage of The Dollhouse and I'd seen the anger in his eyes at me then. I hated him looking at me like that. And I was starting to fear he was right about me. I just didn't know how to do better. I was so caught up in trying to protect the final members of my family that all I ever seemed to do was lose more of them. And I couldn't lose another one, not for anything.

"I'm sorry," I sighed, rubbing my eyes. "You're always my friend first, J. You're my brother. I don't wanna be the asshole you avoid because I can never switch off boss mode."

"It's okay," he said with a slight smile. "And I'm sorry…so fucking sorry." He shook his head, glancing away then back to me.

"You don't have anything to apologise for. I know I'm an asshole sometimes. From now on, in this house I'm not your boss. We've been taking business to the clubhouse lately anyway, so we'll stick with that. And unless we're working, you don't have to do shit that I say," I promised.

"Ooh does that apply to me too, Badge?" Rogue appeared in my t-shirt and my throat closed up at how fucking edible she looked with her bed hair and sleepy eyes. I eye fucked the hell out of her as she walked over to join us with a steaming coffee in JJ's Squirtle mug. "Oh wait, I don't give two cat shits if you order me to do exactly what I wanna do. I still won't."

"Hilarious," I said, but I couldn't help a dark smile as I thought about her panting for me last night.

"Careful with that mug, pretty girl," JJ warned as she sat down beside me and sipped her coffee.

"I'm always careful," she said.

"You're a mug murderer." He smirked and she right smirked back.

"It does apply to you by the way, even if you don't listen to me anyway," I answered her earlier question, nudging her with my elbow.

"First a key to the house, now I'm free to speak my own mind? Wow, it's like going through the women's liberation movement at record speed," she said, arching a brow at me.

My gut tugged over all that fucking Shawn had put her through, keeping her to himself and goddamn emotionally abusing her. It made violence lick against the inside of my skin. I wanted to strike up a bargain with the Devil to give me his death.

I didn't wanna be like Shawn. I'd never wanted to cage her, I just struggled to trust that she wasn't going to vanish the second I lost sight of her. It was always the same. The moment she was out of view, there was a warring panic in the back of my mind that I needed to hunt her down, bring her home. I'd lived in that state of panic for ten whole years, never able to reclaim her. But now she was here, the habit died hard, because how could I really trust that she was going to stay? I guessed JJ was right though. I couldn't control her, and the tighter I held on, the less she seemed to want to be anywhere near me. I had to work harder to loosen my grip and let her be, but with the new fear that Shawn could snatch her up out on the streets, it was impossible to simply let her go off alone anytime she liked. If he got hold of her, I'd never forgive myself.

JJ headed off to get himself more coffee and I turned to Rogue, cupping her cheek to make her look at me. "You're free, baby. I swear I'll never trap you again. You know that, right?"

A little V formed between her eyes as she searched my gaze for a lie. "I think the Cove is my chains, Fox. I think we're all tethered here to live and die on this soil and that never used to scare me growing up because there was nowhere else in the world I wanted to be, even when we made up adventures in our minds and thought about sailing beyond the horizon. I think I was always bound to come back. None of us can escape it for long."

"Maybe it's not chains, hummingbird. Maybe it's simply our home," I said, trailing my fingers down to where her pulse thumped in her neck like soft wings.

Her breath hitched and I felt a burning path of fire tracking down my spine as she leaned in a little closer like she couldn't resist the call of my flesh any more than I could resist hers. The world around us blurred to nothing until it was only us and I could no easier fight this urge than fight the rising sun tomorrow.

I closed the distance between us, kissing her hard and tasting coconut and desire on her lips as they parted for me. I slid my hand around the back of her neck, gripping tight as I pushed my tongue between her lips and she responded to me like she couldn't resist this fire either. It raged between us like an inferno, fuelled by our hunger for each other as it grew and grew until I was sure it was going to consume everything inside me. She could have all the corrupt pieces of me, and I'd fight to be worthy of her with every breath in my lungs and every beat of my heart. She was the sole reason I lived on this earth. To serve her, worship her until she realised she had always been a goddess made to rule me.

We broke apart an inch and her eyes locked with mine, wide and unblinking telling me she'd felt that as sharply as I had. I couldn't get air in my lungs as I held onto her and fought with the raging urge in me to assert ownership of her. My dick was iron hard and aching for one girl only and she was it. The single creature who I'd ever truly desired.

"I'll give you some space," JJ's voice cut through the air and I released Rogue, turning to him where he stood in the patio doorway staring at us. His jaw was tight and Rogue pulled out of my grip as I adjusted my swelling dick in my shorts and gave JJ an apologetic look.

"Stay, man," I encouraged. "We won't be all over each other while you're here."

"Nah, I've gotta drop by the club anyway. It's payday," he said, a huge smile breaking across his face, but it didn't seem to touch his eyes. Had I pissed him off?

"We'll run a new job soon," I said. "If you want?" I added quickly and he nodded, but he seemed distracted as he turned and walked away.

"Wait, JJ," Rogue called, pushing to her feet.

"You alright, baby?" I asked with a frown, the sound of the garage door reaching us as JJ left.

"Yeah…I just needed a word with him," she muttered distractedly.

The rumble of his car engine swiftly followed and I got up, diving into the pool and starting my swim. Rogue headed inside and Mutt appeared with a yawn, jogging around her ankles as he looked for a tickle, but she didn't seem to notice him there.

She disappeared out of sight and my chest knotted as I wondered if she was angry that I'd kissed her. It hadn't exactly been a choice though, more of a fucking need written into my damn bones. I couldn't have fought against it even if I had the strength of a titan. So maybe I was just over thinking things because for once because me and Rogue seemed to be on the right track at last. And if I was lucky, everything was gonna work out for us like I'd always hoped.

I just had to prove I was the better option than Maverick - plus deal with that motherfucking distraction to her regardless - then once she realised I could be all she needed, there was nothing else that could possibly go wrong. And after ten years of suffering, I was ready to get started on our happily ever after.

CHAPTER NINETEEN

I snatched my phone and jogged up to my room with Mutt scurrying around my heels, a soft whine escaping him as he looked up at me.

"I know, boy. I'm on it," I promised him, slipping into my bedroom and hitting dial on JJ's number.

I leaned back against the door, listening to it ring and ring and ring before the voicemail eventually cut in. I dialled again. And again. On the fourth try, the call cut off halfway through the second ring and when I tried again it went straight to voicemail. *For fuck's sake.*

I tossed my phone down at the foot of my bed then quickly stripped and changed into a shorts and crop top combo before tying my hair in a high ponytail and jamming JJ's pink sunglasses onto my face.

I kicked on a pair of white sneakers then snatched my phone, keys and the flick knife I now carried everywhere before hurrying back downstairs.

Fox was still swimming laps out in the pool and I chewed on my lip as I stood watching him for a few moments. In theory I had more freedom now. I could come and go when I wanted, but he also sent a platoon of Harlequin thugs to follow me wherever I went 'for backup' in case Shawn showed his face. Though I guessed there wasn't anything weird about me heading up to

Afterlife, so I decided not to make any attempt to shake off the escorts for my trip. I had no desire to give Shawn any kind of chance to strike at me if I could avoid it.

I grabbed a notepad and quickly jotted down a message for Fox, telling him where I was going then snatched a can of Coca Cola from the fridge and headed for the garage.

It was as hot as a crab's left butt cheek today, so despite the puppy dog eyes Mutt shot my way, I told him to stay where he was in the aircon rather than bringing him out to bake with me. Then I jogged down into the garage, hopped into my red Jeep and headed onto the drive.

I had to give my entourage a couple of minutes to jump in their own cars. Unfortunately, the death glare I shot the guy who tried to climb in with me wasn't enough to get him to leave me driving alone and Eddie just gave me a flat look as he reclined in the seat beside me.

"You know the rules," he said with a shrug. "No point taking it up with me if you don't like them. Talk to the boss."

"Yeah, yeah," I sighed, making a mental note to tell Fox I didn't appreciate having a passenger in my car with me when I went out. Surely the entourage following me was enough. Though in all fairness, Eddie seemed nice. So I guessed I could have had a worse bodyguard.

As soon as the gates rattled open, I took off down the winding streets which hugged the cliffs before cutting a beeline to Afterlife.

JJ's orange Mustang was parked out front, half blocking the entrance to the place and I blew out a frustrated breath as I swung my own car around back and took a space in the crowded lot.

There was a show on today and it looked like there was a big turn out for it, but this conversation couldn't wait and if JJ wouldn't even pick up his fucking phone, then he was going to have to have it in person.

I hopped out of my car, striding towards the entrance with the gang of Harlequin goons trailing me like shadows. It put me on edge, mostly because I knew they had good reason to be there.

My gaze skipped between the crowd of people who were sitting out on the terrace which overlooked the distant sea and I couldn't help but hunt for Shawn amongst them. He'd have to be damn insane to show up at a Harlequin stronghold like this, but I was well aware that he was more than a few screws loose of a full set, so I wasn't gonna underestimate the levels he'd go to in hopes of winning this war.

An excited squeal announced my friends before I was bundled by them, Di and Lyla smooshing me in a hugathon as they bounced up and down, making me laugh.

"I'm so ready for your life dramas to chill the fuck out," Di groaned. "You missed a killer party on the beach last night - Carter tried to go surfing in the dark while shit faced and almost drowned. Jake had to haul his ass out of the water and give him CPR. It was freaking hilarious."

I smirked at that visual while Lyla started filling me in on some of the gossip from around the trailer park. I still didn't know all that many of the people she was referring to, but I snorted a laugh as she told me about a fight that had broken out between two of the guys over a girl who they'd both thought was their girlfriend. It turned out she'd been playing them both and robbing them blind as well and she'd taken off while the fight was still in full flow and hadn't been seen since.

Bella was working behind the bar and she flashed me a smile, her eyes bright for once, lacking the added dullness she usually brought on by self-medicating.

The music changed and Lyla groaned. "That's our cue," she said, pointing towards the stage out in the sun which was looking suspiciously empty. "We'll be working a long shift until later tonight, but you should stay and get drunk. We can have a party for four back at your trailer afterwards and you can catch us all up on the Harlequin D you've been bagging."

I scoffed lightly, glancing over my shoulder towards my bodyguards but they'd all spread out around the bar and none of them were lurking too close by.

"I've got some damn good stories for you," I agreed. "But right now, I need to find JJ."

"He's in his office," Di said, pointing across the room to a door marked for staff entrance only. "Showed up a while back looking pissed as all hell. Came out back to the dressing room and warned all of us to put on a damn good show today because he was in the mood to fire people then stormed off looking like he had a porcupine wedged up his ass."

"That porcupine would be me," I sighed. "Wish me luck."

The girls did, but they looked more than a little nervous on my behalf as they hurried away to take their places on the stage. I pushed through the crowd, lifting cash from a few pockets as I went, before remembering I'd promised JJ I wouldn't do that here and doubling back to return said cash to said pockets with a pang of regret. It was probably best I didn't piss him off any more than necessary though, so I waved goodbye to my easy money then strolled right on past the goon blocking the door to the staff area of the club. He gave me a healthy dose of side eye, but he clearly recognised me so didn't make any move to stop me.

It was a little quieter back here away from the music, though I could still hear it thumping through the walls.

I kept walking all the way to JJ's office, pushing the door open without bothering to knock when I got there.

Johnny James was sitting behind his desk, a bunch of paperwork spread out before him while he ignored it in favour of drinking tequila straight from the bottle and scowling at nothing.

He paused as he looked up and found me lurking on his threshold, his eyes brightening then darkening as he set the tequila down with a heavy thump and settled back in his chair, folding his arms across his chest.

"What do you want, Rogue? I've got work to do."

"Looks like it," I agreed, striding into the room and kicking the door closed behind me before snatching the tequila and taking a hit from the bottle. It burned like a motherfucker on the way down and I scrunched my face up as I smacked the bottle back down on the table.

Silence fell between us while JJ just continued to scowl at me and I huffed out a breath of frustration.

"Just spit it out, JJ. Whatever it is is clearly eating you up, so just give it to me straight."

"Shouldn't I be asking you to do that?" he asked bitterly. "Or were you planning on stringing me along a little longer before you told me you'd decided on Fox in the end after all?"

"What the fuck are you talking about?" I snapped. "I've made it more than clear to you that I want you. But you know how complicated it is with me and the others too. The five...four of us are so tangled up in each other that I don't think the knots will ever come free. So why is me kissing Fox suddenly the end of the fucking world?"

JJ winced at my slip over Chase, but he clearly wasn't going to let his grief get in the way of his anger.

"Because I know what Fox wants from you. I know what he'll *demand* from you. And I'm more than used to watching him get his own way every fucking time. Don't get me wrong - I love the bones of that man, but as much as he might be my brother, he's also my fucking boss and he's made that clear to me time and again ever since the day we were initiated into this fucking gang."

"Fox might control you, but he doesn't control *me*," I growled.

"Sure. Not now. Maybe. But I know how this goes. I remember how he was with you when we were all kids. He used to scare off every and any guy who even thought about trying to get close to you. And he might have been okay with the three of us hanging out with you alongside him, but he always made it more than clear that the future he saw was one with you and him together. You're his end game, Rogue and you always have been. So where does that leave me?"

"Do you think I don't know that that's what Fox wants from me?" I demanded. "I get it. He's told me. And I've told him that I'm not ready for that. That I'm not looking for monogamy or any of that bullshit yet and-"

"See, there it is," JJ snapped, shoving to his feet. "Yet. You're not ready for that *yet*. Which means eventually you will be. You'll be ready to pick and settle down and have a fuck ton of kids and that one little word tells me you already know that it'll be with him whether you've admitted that to yourself or not."

"No it doesn't," I snapped angrily. "I didn't mean that. I don't want that. Haven't I proven to you enough times how much I care about you?"

"By spreading your legs and showing me just how much you enjoy my cock? Yeah, sweetheart, you're real good at showing me that. And I'm fully aware that I'm a damn good lay. But fucking me and loving me are two different things, aren't they?"

My lips popped open at the slap of those words and I just stared at him for several seconds. "JJ, you know I love you," I said in a low voice but he snorted derisively.

"Yeah, you love me," he agreed scathingly. "You love the boy who used to find seashells for you down on the beach. The asshole who made you that fucking bracelet you keep on your wrist. The kid who stole doughnuts with you and laughed with you and surfed with you every morning at dawn as often as he could. But you're not *in* love with me, are you?"

"JJ," I breathed, my heart thrashing in my chest as I stared at the cold, hard look on his face and tried to hunt for the boy beneath the Harlequin who stood before me with his muscles bunching and a coldness in his eyes which bit right down into my heart. "You know why I can't tell you that. You know that I-"

"I love you, Rogue," he snapped. "I love you and I want you and I fucking need you. But loving you feels like loving sand I'm gripping tight in my fist while the tide rushes in to claim it. And as much as I want to be able to hold onto you, every time a wave hits, a bit more of the sand is stolen. How long until he takes every piece of you from me? I can't fucking stand it. I can't survive it."

"You're seriously saying all of this to me over one kiss?" I asked him incredulously. "When you've literally watched me fuck Maverick? You've shared me with him, touched me at the same time as him and you never once showed even the slightest hint of jealousy. But now-"

"Are you kidding me? Of course I'm fucking jealous when I see you with Rick. Especially after finding out that you fucked him when we were sixteen, but it's not the same as-"

"I never fucked him back then," I growled furiously. "Chase got that shit wrong. And if he or you had wanted to know the truth about that then you should have just fucking *asked* me. And if you're so desperate to know about me losing my virginity then you'll be pleased to hear that it wasn't with anyone you know. It was just some asshole who I dated when I was homeless and alone and desperate for someone to love me. Which he didn't by the way - he just liked fucking girls my age. And when he shoved his cock into me it fucking hurt, and I mostly just waited for it to be over, which thankfully it was fast enough. Does that make you feel better?"

"Of course it fucking doesn't," JJ snarled, placing his palms flat on the desk and glaring at me over it. "Nothing that happened to you while you were gone makes me happy, Rogue. It haunts me at night, and it consumes me during the day. When you tell me stories like that, they cut into me and make me fucking bleed for you. Because I love you, Rogue. I've been in love with you since before I was old enough to even understand what love was. You're it for me. I've always known that. But if we keep doing this and I have to watch Fox take you from me it's going to destroy me, and I can't fucking survive that."

"I'm not going to-"

"I know Fox. He always gets what he wants. And that's you. All of you. Not the bits and pieces you're willing to share. And I saw the way you were looking at him when he kissed you. You want that too, you want him and maybe you want me and Maverick as well, but that's not how these things work out, is it? One day you're gonna want the whole picket fence and two point four kids thing, and the stripper who makes you laugh and fucks you like a pro won't be the choice you make."

"Name one single thing about me that makes you believe I want a freaking picket fence?" I demanded. "None of this is on me. It's just your insecurities. I've made it pretty goddamn clear how much I like you - how much I want you-"

"How much you want my cock you mean," he sneered. "Don't think I don't see it in your eyes. When you fuck me, I'm it - the only thing in your pretty little world, but the moment we finish, that look goes away. I lose you every single time as you retreat back behind your walls and push me firmly back out. But that's not how you look at him. You look at him like he's half way through carving a door for you to step through. So I think it's better we squash this now."

"Are you saying you don't want to be with me anymore?" I asked, something fissuring inside my chest and stopping the air from making its way down into my lungs as pain pressed in on me from all sides.

"Be with you?" JJ scoffed. "You were never mine though, were you? So maybe it's best if I just get back to my job and you can get back to your destiny of becoming the Harlequin princess Fox always knew you'd be."

"Your job?"

"Yeah. I don't fuck for free, Rogue, and you knew that well enough when you dropped your panties for me." JJ snatched a piece of paper from his desk and started writing on it aggressively. "So there's the time on the hood of Fox's truck. The carousel, my bed, my shower, the train car, your bed, the trip out to Dead Man's Isle..." JJ kept jotting down each and every place where we'd had sex while I just stared at him in confusion, my heart thrashing painfully as I tried to understand what the hell he was doing until he tallied off the number at the bottom and scribbled down a figure before striding around his desk and slapping the piece of paper against my chest.

"Here's your bill, sweetheart," he said in a cold, hard tone, his eyes dark with fury as my fingers automatically curled around the piece of paper and I just stared up at him in shock. "And to be honest, I charge by the hour so you're getting a bargain there, because I've given you all the sleepovers and cuddling and all of that bullshit for free."

He shoved away from me, ripping open the door to his office and slamming it behind him as he stormed away.

Pain ripped through my heart as I stared down at the bill he'd given me, each and every moment we'd shared in each other's arms tallied and accounted for like he'd been keeping score the entire time. Like I was nothing but another day's work to him and now he wanted his frigging pay day.

I stared at the figure scrawled at the bottom of the page, my eyes burning with tears which I blinked away aggressively. Because no. Fuck no, he wasn't getting my fucking tears. If that asshole wanted to charge me for his motherfucking time like I meant nothing more to him than any one of his paying clients, then he could have his well earned money.

I didn't even know why I was surprised. Of course he hadn't wanted to keep me. No one ever wanted to keep me. And as the pain of that oh so miserable fact of my life tried to drive its way into my soul, I felt the curtains closing in around my heart. The same ones I used to draw close when Shawn would call me a whore and tell me I was only good for taking his cock. The same ones I'd relied on to keep my feet moving forward day after day while I was all alone and had nothing to live for aside from the sad fact that I didn't want to die.

So I focused on the one clear thing I had to work towards and blocked out the agony trying to consume me as that little lost girl started begging for attention from deep inside me. I wouldn't let her out. I couldn't. I'd bury her just like I'd learned to a long time ago and I'd take JJ's bill as the wakeup call I'd needed. Of course he hadn't just stopped escorting for me. Of course this was all I was to him. And maybe he'd tricked himself into thinking I was something else for a while there but now he'd figured it out. I wasn't worth loving. I wasn't worth any more than any of the women who had paid their way into his bed and now he was rectifying the mistake he'd made by giving me this. So he could have his fucking money. I wouldn't owe any man anything ever again. Least of all JJ Brooks.

I just had to figure out where the hell I was supposed to get twelve thousand, three hundred and sixty-four dollars from. The asshole had even added a surcharge for sucking his cock. *Damn we'd had a lot of sex.*

I ground my teeth, folded the piece of paper up and shoved it into my back pocket before snatching my phone out and calling Luther.

The pain inside me was threatening to drown me but I just forced it back, retreating from it and numbing myself to it until I couldn't feel it anymore. Until I couldn't feel anything and nothing mattered aside from my goal. I'd get his money then I could lose my shit after that if I had to.

"Wildcat," Luther answered, a curious lilt to his voice. "Do you have good news for me?"

"Not yet," I replied. "I just need some cash. Do you still run a chop shop up on Sailor's Street?"

"We do. We can turn around pretty much anything there. But if you want some real money, I have a request for a Maserati Gran Tourismo. Fox tells me boosting cars is your talent. I'll give you a cut of ten grand if you can secure one in prime condition."

"Twelve thousand, three hundred and sixty-four dollars," I demanded, the figure from JJ's bill burned into the inside of my skull.

"Fine," Luther agreed with a snort of amusement. "But only if you can get it today."

"Consider it done." I hung up on the leader of the Harlequin Crew like a bitch with a death wish then dialled my new, ultra-rich bestie.

"Hey, Rogue, what's up?" Tatum asked as she answered my call and a little bit of the pain roaming beneath my skin eased at her friendly tone.

"I was wondering if you're up for hanging out with a criminal tonight? I need to boost a car from your end of town and figured you might wanna come play with me?"

Tatum laughed as a deep, male voice said something on the other end of the line which I failed to catch.

"I've actually just finished up a dinner date at Andre's. Do you know it?" she asked. "I could come meet you-"

"That's just down the road from me. I'll come to you," I said decisively because pulling this job would be a whole lot easier without a Harlequin entourage tailing my ass so ditching my car here was the best move I could make.

"Okay. We'll meet you in the parking lot," Tatum agreed.

"I'll be twenty minutes tops," I promised, cutting the call and opening the office door.

JJ had fucked all the way off and I swallowed down the lump that rose in my throat at him just walking out on me like that. But he'd made his choice and the bill in my back pocket was proof enough of that. So if he wanted to go around making grand statements about our relationship or lack of then I was going to take him at his fucking word.

I slipped back downstairs but instead of heading into the club, I jogged along the corridor towards the dressing room where the dancers all got ready for their shows, easing the door open as I reached it and walking inside.

A couple of the guys were laughing loudly in the back corner of the room and I ducked low, grabbing a blonde wig and a pair of rollerblades from the rack of costumes to one side of the space.

I slipped out the back door and sat my ass on the sidewalk as I switched out my sneakers for the rollerblades then tucked my rainbow hair away into my wig and pushed myself upright with my sneakers gripped in my fist.

I didn't have long before my Harlequin escorts would come looking for me, so I had to hurry. After a few slightly wobbly attempts at taking off on the skates, I got into the swing of it and started picking up speed as I headed away from Afterlife in the direction of the burger bar Tatum had mentioned.

My heart felt a little lighter as I moved faster, letting the curve of the hill take me as I gave myself to the moment and forced a smile onto my lips. It didn't sit there as easily as it would have before JJ had dumped me like a chew toy he was bored of, but I kept it in place until I could almost believe it was real. I was pretty much a pro at that these days anyway.

I shot around the corner in record time, finding the burger joint easily and groaning at the scent of fries on the air. I skated round back to look for Tatum, my eyebrows going up as I spotted her leaning back on the hood of a classic white Cadillac with a dude's head buried beneath her long skirt.

I smirked to myself at the opportunity that gave me, switched the rollerblades for my sneakers then jogged back around into the crowded burger bar.

"Order for Karen!" a guy yelled as I made it to the end of the serving line and I swooped in like a hungry seagull to snatch the paper bag and drink he held at the ready. The guy gave me a look which said he questioned my Karenness, but I was already heading on out the door.

I jogged back around to the parking lot and checked out my haul, tossing the cheeseburger to an alley cat who looked half scandalised and half pleased before I grabbed the large portion of fries, dumped the bag and headed back over to the Cadillac.

I took a long sip of my vanilla milkshake as I walked, awkwardly holding it alongside the fries in my right hand so that I could start eating with my left.

Tatum and the boyfriend I'd nicknamed Tats on account of the ink he had covering his skin were just finishing up with plenty of moaning and praising names as I arrived and I grinned at them as he emerged from beneath her skirt.

"Jesus," Tatum gasped as she spotted me, a laugh escaping her as she fell somewhere between embarrassed and amused at my arrival.

"You all done?" I asked around a mouthful of fries.

"No," Tats grunted but I just smiled wider at his frustration, averting my eyes from his pants to make sure I didn't make eye contact with any unsatisfied bulges. That would be hella awkward and though this one of Tatum's men was rougher around the edges and more suited to my usual tastes, I had girl code to stick to, so he was nothing more than a heavily inked potato as far as I was concerned. And no matter how hot that potato may or may not have objectively been, I wasn't gonna be noticing shit about it.

"Well it's a girls' night, so it's not really about you, dude," I pointed out, slurping my milkshake. "You ready to come cause havoc with me, Tate?"

"Yes," she agreed with a grin. "Are you cool to meet me at home, baby?" she turned the doe eyes on Tats and he sighed.

"You just expect me to let you go off with this criminally inclined girl who we barely know and break a bunch of laws with her?" he asked.

"Yeah. Don't wait up." Tatum tiptoed up to kiss his cheek then grinned at me as she hopped into the Cadillac. I didn't need telling twice so I jumped in the passenger seat and relaxed back into my chair as I continued with my meal.

"Where are we headed?" Tatum asked.

"I need to find a Maserati Gran Tourismo. I figured the most likely suspects in town to have one will be over your way."

"Hang on, I'll call Saint. He'll know who has one."

"Is he a car buff or something?" I asked.

"Err, no, he's more like a walking talking map of everything. He literally remembers every detail about all kinds of random shit. He'll be able to tell you who owns one of those cars, give you the registration for it and give you a bunch of reasons for why he hates whoever happens to own it." Tatum called him as she spoke and the sound of ringing filled the car speakers before a clipped, posh boy voice answered the call.

Tatum filled him in on what I was after and within a few moments we had the full details of some guy who owned the car I was looking for who had offended Saint by wearing his cap sideways. Apparently backwards was just about acceptable, but sideways was an unforgivable crime. I wasn't sure where the logic was in that, but I was willing to go with it.

"So why do you look like someone took a dump on your favourite shoes today?" Tatum asked me as she drove us towards my mark and I sighed audibly before slurping the dregs of my milkshake through the straw.

"Man issues," I muttered.

"I've had more than my share of those," she replied.

"Who hasn't?" I agreed. "My...well I dunno what he was because we weren't putting labels on it exactly, but he used to be a sex worker. Or no, I guess he *is* a sex worker, but he went on a leave of absence while the two of us were hooking up. Only now he's gotten it into his head that I'm gearing up to leave him for someone else, so despite everything I had to say on the matter he basically just dumped my ass and slapped me with a bill for his services."

"What do you mean a bill?"

I took the itemised list from my pocket and began reading it out to her while her eyebrows raised all the way up into her blonde hairline.

"Wow," she said as I finished. "So what are you gonna do in response to that?"

"Pay the fucking bill of course. The asshole thinks he's being all dramatic and trying to make me feel like I've done something wrong when it's his own insecurities that are causing the problem here. So fine. If I'm nothing but another client to him then I'm sure as fuck gonna pay my bill. I'll even give him a tip. Like, P.S. you're an asshole and you should work on that."

"Are you sure that's the best way to-"

"Totally sure. If he wants to play this game with me then he will get precisely what he's asking for."

"So you don't want this other guy? Because if you want to have a relationship with-"

"Believe me, I'm not having any kind of relationship with anyone," I growled. "My damage runs too fucking deep for that shit. No one would want me once they got close enough to see that, and JJ just proved it. So now I'm gonna pay my bill and get shit faced - in that order. The rest of it is tomorrow's problem anyway."

Tatum gave me a sympathetic look but before we could get any deeper into it, we pulled up outside a huge house where the car I needed was parked up beneath a fancy looking carport.

"You wanna come back to mine and talk boys some more when you're done here?" Tatum offered with a grin as I grabbed the door handle, preparing for my next move as I eyed my fancy new ride.

"I think I'd be bad company tonight," I admitted because no matter how hard I was trying to keep the smile on my face, it just kept slipping and I was fairly sure I was going to lose my shit soon.

"I can be your getaway driver," she said with a grin and I laughed.

"How about we rain check it for tomorrow when I've got my shit together?" I offered.

"I'm actually going to a cage fight tomorrow, but I could get you a ticket?" she suggested, her eyes lighting with excitement over that.

"That would be a fuck yeah. I'll see you tomorrow then," I promised, hopping out and glancing around for any signs of additional security systems surrounding the property I was planning to hit, but lucky for me, I couldn't see any cameras or anything like that.

Tatum drove away and I released a low breath as I composed myself. I needed to focus on the job at hand, not let the pain in my chest over JJ distract me from it. Besides, fuck him. Fuck him for not listening to a damn word I'd said and double fuck him for giving me a fucking bill. Who the hell did he think he was? I just hoped he enjoyed his fucking pay day because I was seriously done with his shit. I had Jack the Licker and Vlad the Impaler mark two sitting at home with new batteries just waiting for me to use them, so I had no need of his mega cock. Especially if it came with a fucking price tag.

I threw my head back to the sky and screamed in an attempt to banish some of the anger from my body then forced all of my feelings down into a teeny tiny box deep within me and crossed the road to go get my car.

Luckily the owner of the house and vehicle hadn't heard my little outburst and as I approached the building, I soon realised they weren't home at all.

There wasn't a scrap of movement through any of the windows and there wasn't a sound to be heard anywhere.

I did a quick look around the building, peeking through windows and double checking the doors were locked before stopping and looking up at a slightly open window on the first floor.

I glanced around to double check there wasn't anyone about to see me, then grabbed hold of the drainpipe and started climbing towards it.

I kept my eyes on my goal, ignoring the drop below me as I focused on the open window. Why the fuck were so many people dumb enough to leave windows open when they weren't home? Honestly, I'd never figure it out, but I was glad they were because this was basically the way I'd been earning a living for the last ten years and it kept me fed most of the time. And I was not a girl who enjoyed going without food.

I reached the window and pulled it open, my heart leaping as my foot slipped but then I grabbed the windowsill and heaved myself into a bedroom where I dropped to the floor with the perfect grace of a ballerina. Or maybe it was more like one of those new born foals who fall on their ass a lot, but I was still taking the win. The Green Ranger would have been proud. I mean, not so much of all the stealing and shit, but I liked to think he'd understand my reasons for my criminal behaviour and would wanna be my bestie despite my flaws.

I glanced around the room, spotted a fancy looking necklace on the nightstand and quickly put it on before heading out onto the landing and continuing down the stairs.

One glance around showed me the hook full of car keys and I grinned as I snatched the one I was looking for, opened the front door and hurried over to claim my prize.

The engine purred beneath me as I started it up and I sighed as I leaned back into the leather and hit the gas, roaring out of the driveway and tearing through town to the chop shop in style with my blonde wig blowing in the wind from the open window.

Luther was waiting for me to arrive, sitting out back with a few of his men while they smoked and talked shit together. He got to his feet as I pulled in and I couldn't help but look smug as fuck as he let out a low whistle of appreciation for the car.

I climbed out with a swagger in my step, moving towards him and handing over the keys as he pulled a thick envelope filled with cash out of his pocket and handed it over.

"Nice work, wildcat," Luther commented.

"Don't sound so surprised, grandad, you tossed me out on the streets with nothing for ten years. I had to figure out how to survive somehow."

"Watch your mouth," Luther chastised in a low growl, but he didn't really mean it. Or maybe he did and I was just playing make believe with the idea that he thought my attitude was cute and I'd end up dead for it one of these days. Maybe I didn't really care about that anyway though.

I hopped up onto the hood of the car and folded my legs as a couple of the other Harlequins came to inspect my fresh steal and I began counting my money.

"Don't you trust me?" Luther asked.

"I only trust two things in this life," I replied. "Death and cash. And if

I'm looking one in the eye then I'll make sure I get to know it properly before I make any deals with it."

I kept counting out the money, trying not to overthink the insane amount of it so that the temptation to keep it didn't eat at me. I didn't think I'd ever earned this much in one job, let alone held it in my hand and it was seriously tempting to go all squirrel over it and try to smuggle it away.

"What's up with you?" Luther asked, moving closer to me while I continued to count. "You don't seem as perky as usual."

I blew out a breath, trying to force all of the bad shit back down, down, down into that tiny box. But JJ had cracked it open and I could feel my hold on my emotions tearing apart. I was gonna break tonight and when I did it was always fucking messy. But not here. Not now.

"People aren't always as they seem on the outside, Luther," I said, glancing up at him. "Maybe I smile a lot and crack jokes and try to make the best of things, but that doesn't mean I'm not all fucked up inside. Damage isn't always that easy to see and mine runs thicker than blood in my veins. It's just showing a little more than usual because I've had a shitty day."

Luther glanced between me and the cash I was holding, swiping a hand down his face in a way which was reminiscent of his son while I went back to counting every last dollar.

"I feel you on that," he muttered. "But I've gotta know if this sudden need for all that money has anything to do with you and Fox. Because despite the ties I've placed on you by bringing you into my Crew being reason enough, you know I can't let you run if that's what you're thinking. For his sake. Sending you away broke something between me and him a long time ago. Hell, I think it broke *him*. And Maverick...let's just say they need you. And I think you need them too. It might be hard and you might wanna hate me for it for the rest of your days, but it's true. And I can't let you leave again, wildcat. You get that, don't you?"

There was a warning in his voice though I almost imagined there was a hint of concern there too.

I pursed my lips at the feeling of more ties being placed upon me, but I shrugged the feeling off. I wasn't staying here because Luther Harlequin demanded it. I was staying because for better or worse, this was my home. I had no idea what that meant long term, but I could reassure him on that much.

"I'm not going anywhere," I promised, closing the envelope as I finished confirming that all my cash was accounted for. "You don't need to worry about that."

Luther nodded, accepting my word and I slid off the hood of the car, heading towards the exit.

"It's not safe out there for you with Shawn still lurking in the shadows," Luther called, moving into step with me and pointing to his truck which was parked up outside. "Let me give you a ride home. Fox is losing his shit over you giving his guys the slip earlier anyway."

"You know about that?" I asked.

"Yeah. And don't worry, I told him you were running a job for me, so he isn't tearing the Cove apart. But I should get you home safe."

I nodded, climbing into his truck. For a moment I considered asking him to take me to Rejects Park instead of Harlequin House, but I held my tongue. I had one more thing to achieve today and the rage burning inside me wouldn't stand any chance of lessening until I did it.

Luther dropped me to the front door and I used my key to let myself inside, the darkness in me building and building with every step I took as I withdrew into myself.

Fox and JJ were both sitting at the kitchen island as I walked in and they looked around at me with a mixture of relief from Fox and barely concealed rage from JJ who I guessed had been called home following my disappearing act.

I didn't give a shit if he was angry at me for running off though. In fact, I no longer gave a single shit about him at all. If I was nothing more than a client with an unpaid tab to him then he would be nothing but the memory of a long-lost boy to me.

Fox wrapped me in his arms and a little piece of my heart tugged as the familiar scent of him coiled around me and my heart ached to take comfort from him. But that was the mistake I'd made with JJ. I'd let him in and now he was done with me all over again. I couldn't keep being a playing piece for these boys and their wayward emotions. I couldn't keep letting them in when all they ever did was hurt me.

Just be a good little whore and we won't have any problems, will we, sugarpie? Shawn's voice echoed in my ears and I knew he'd seen something in me when he'd spoken to me like that. He'd seen my worth and it had amounted to what lay between my thighs and how much control he could take of it. Which seemed to be pretty much the same as what these men saw in me these days too.

I withdrew from Fox's embrace, my gaze falling to my feet as I tried not to listen to the memories which were creeping in. All the worst thoughts and feelings I'd ever had about myself and all the ways Shawn had made sure I knew that was what he thought of me too.

It hurt. It fucking hurt because I could see it in them now as well. JJ didn't think I was worth more than the value of the cash I had wedged in my back pocket and I was still struggling to figure out what Fox wanted me for.

"Are you okay, hummingbird?" Fox asked, seeming to catch on to my mood without me even saying anything. "You want me to run you a bath or something?"

"Yeah," I agreed, biting down my anger with JJ because of course I couldn't just tell Fox why I was so pissed at him thanks to all the bullshit secrets we'd been keeping. "That would be nice."

"I'm on it." Fox pressed a kiss to the top of my head and I was so glad that he'd reined in his freak out reaction to me going missing that I caught his hand in mine for a second, squeezing his fingers briefly before forcing myself to let him go.

Fox hesitated, glancing at JJ like on some level he could feel the tension burning between us, but then he just turned and headed upstairs.

Mutt licked my ankle quickly then turned to glare at JJ with his upper lip peeling back in a snarl like he knew it too.

"You shouldn't have run off from the club like that," JJ hissed as soon as he could be certain Fox was out of earshot.

"Well you didn't give me much choice," I replied icily, stalking towards him as I pulled the envelope from my back pocket. "I needed to make sure you got paid for all of your hard work after all." I slapped the envelope against his chest and he caught it automatically, staring down at the cash as several hundred dollar bills tumbled to the floor from the impact. "Now we're square, yeah?"

"Rogue-" he began, snatching my wrist in his grip as I tried to turn away from him, but I cut him off as I whirled back to glare up at him.

"What's wrong? Were you hoping for a tip?" I asked in a mocking tone. "Because I have to say, Johnny James, I think you over charge. So don't worry, I won't be coming back for any repeat custom in the future. But I'm sure you're satisfied now that you got what you wanted from me."

His lips parted and something in his gaze tore through my heart, but I didn't care and I didn't want to hear it. He'd made this choice when he reduced our entire relationship to an itemised bill.

"Fuck you, Johnny James," I hissed. "All you did today was prove to me that I was right when I said I never wanted to come back here. I hope that money helps make up for what you lost when you started turning down clients in favour of me, but don't worry - you can go back to your day job now."

I whirled away from him, yanking my wrist out of his grasp and stormed after Fox, ignoring JJ as he called me back and silently thanking Mutt as he dove between us to stop him from grabbing me again.

Tears were burning the backs of my eyes and I knew I wouldn't be able to keep the nightmares out tonight. Because everything I'd been working for was fucked. Chase was gone, JJ was done with me, and I could never be what Fox wished I could be. And Rick…Jesus, Rick might even have been more fucked up than me and I knew I wasn't ever gonna be enough to fix him.

Fox was about to step out of my room as I burst through the door and as he caught me in his arms, my self control fell apart. My lips found his and a sob escaped me as tears rolled down my cheeks and met with his skin too.

Fox groaned as he gave in to what I was taking from him, his strong arms banding around me and dragging me closer as he kissed me back.

I wrapped my arms around his neck and deepened the kiss between us as I jumped up and wound my legs around his waist. He walked me to the wall and pinned me against it, his hips shifting between my thighs and making me moan.

I needed to stop. This was selfish and stupid and it would only make things worse because I still couldn't be what he needed me to be. But as his tongue raked over mine, I found myself wishing I could be. That was all I'd ever wanted. To be everything to him and to all of them the way they were to me. But that wasn't a reality which I would ever be able to own, and I couldn't make Fox the promise he needed me to make him.

"I can't," I sobbed, forcing myself to break our kiss even as my fingernails dug into the back of his neck and I began to fist his shirt in my hand. "If I don't stop now, I won't stop at all. Please don't let me hurt you like that, Fox," I whispered as he began kissing my neck and the feeling of his mouth on my skin set my entire body alight.

He stilled at my words, sighing as he took them in and slowly pulled back enough to look me in the eyes.

"I'm more concerned about hurting you while you're feeling like this," he murmured. "But I promise not to let this go any further if you let me stay with you tonight. I don't know what's happened, but that pain in your eyes hurts me too, hummingbird. Let me look after you."

I wanted to say yes, but the idea of that terrified me even more than the idea of being alone. Because if I let him hold me while I felt like this and let him see the person I was beneath all of the bullshit and bravado and the mask I let the world see, then he wouldn't look at me the same anymore. He would know exactly why he shouldn't want me, and he'd understand precisely what I meant when I kept trying to warn him about how damaged I was.

"I need to be alone," I breathed, dropping to the floor and balling my hands into fists as I fought to hold myself together for just a few more minutes despite the tears which wouldn't stop rolling down my cheeks.

Fox hesitated but I pushed him towards the door determinedly and he gave in despite the fact that he clearly didn't want to.

I couldn't look him in the eyes as I closed the door between us and my heart hurt even worse knowing I was hurting him by shutting him out. But I couldn't let him in. If I did then I knew I'd be lost to him, and I just couldn't let that happen. I couldn't let any of these men take my heart again or I knew I'd be lost to them forever.

I turned the lock on the door then turned and ran for the en suite, dropping to my knees beside the bath and plunging my head into the hot water Fox had run for me as I let myself scream where no one could hear me.

But I could still hear them. All the memories of all the worst things I'd lived through. The people who had hurt and used me and the whispered words Shawn had driven into my soul like nails driving into rotten wood.

I was the girl no one wanted.

I was the whore they all discarded.

And worse than all that, I was the dead girl who didn't know how to die.

CHAPTER TWENTY

Today I was playing the regret game again. My stupidity was at the forefront of this one. Ten years. Ten fucking years I'd believed Rogue had chosen Maverick, had given herself to him behind all of our backs and made the decision that would end us for good. I'd harboured so much anger over that, let it bleed into everything I was until I was tainted by it. And all for something that had never been true in the first place.

My dad was right, I was a dumbass kid back then and it looked like nothing had changed. If there was a god up there in the sky, I guess he was confused as fuck over how one person could make so many stupid decisions in their life. When I mapped it all out, I wasn't even surprised I'd ended up here. Something had to give eventually. So now I was in purgatory, waiting to be shipped off to hell, but not before every regret of my life stared back at me out of the dark and called me a fool.

The one thing I realised about my youth, was that I'd always been happy before I'd thought Rogue had chosen Maverick. I'd been content with her not choosing, because I'd known I was never going to be the choice she made anyway. So long as she didn't pick, I still had her and my boys. I got to hold onto them all and that was the only thing I'd ever wanted. Us and Sunset Cove.

At least she has that now even if I'm not a part of it.

The sound of the door opening upstairs drew me out of the dark trance I was in and the heavy stomp of boots came this way.

"Morning, Mabel," Shawn called. "Ain't that shirt real pretty on you. Now close those withered ears of yours. I won't be held responsible for traumatising an ancient lady. Unless of course, maybe you're into hearing him scream, you dirty old bird."

"You stay away from me, you codswallop of a boy," Mabel crowed and my skin prickled at the idea of him hurting her.

But Shawn just chuckled as he switched the light on in my prison then unlocked the door and stepped into the room. I didn't bother to open my good eye as I rested my head against the wall and felt the darkness creeping under my skin as keenly as the cold.

"Now, now, pretty eyes, I'm getting tired of this no reaction bullshit. I dressed up real perdy for you today. Have a look."

I looked up just to make him shut up. Not that he ever did for long.

He was wearing jeans and an open checked shirt, his abs on display and a sledgehammer slung over his shoulder. I gave him a dry expression as he did a twirl for me, swinging the hammer through the air. Maybe I should have been afraid of that thing, but all I felt was numb. I was tired of the games, tired of the dark. He'd started leaving me here without the light on and days would slip by where I was caged in my own mind, facing all my poor life choices, unable to do anything but pick them apart piece by piece and accept the torture of my countless failures. That was far worse than anything this asshole could do to me.

"Come on, sugar, gimme a scream. Try to run. Do *something*. You're not makin' this fun for me anymore. And if I get bored, you know what that means." He wrapped a pretend rope around his throat and made a noose out of it, sticking his tongue out and rolling his eyes back into his head.

"You know what to do then," I said flatly. "Make it slow or fast, or whatever the fuck you like, I don't really give a shit, Shawn."

He went quiet for a moment which was saying something for him then he leaned down, holding out a cigarette and pushing it between my lips. "Have a smoke with me, pretty eyes." He lit up the end and holy mother of a fuck,

I wasn't strong enough to resist the taste of the tobacco on my lips. I inhaled deeply, dragging in the sweet toxicity and letting it rush down into my lungs, a buzz quickly chasing it. It woke me up, pulling me out of the black depths I'd descended to within my own mind and reminding me of all the rare delights in the world which I'd never had enough off.

"Death tastes good, doesn't it?" he said, pulling the wooden chair over and sitting down in front of me, his head haloed by the lightbulb hanging from the ceiling and throwing his features into darkness.

He puffed on his own cigarette as he laid the sledgehammer across his knees, his blue eyes turning red under the glow of the cherry. He looked like the demon he was for a moment, all shadow and fire.

My gaze moved to the gun at his hip and his eyes followed as he laughed low in his throat. "Now that's more like it, pretty eyes, I awoke a little fight in ya. Try and take my gun, go on, I dare you."

My fingers itched as no fear awakened in me. I was an animal at the hands of a butcher, already long dead. This skin didn't feel. *So fuck it.*

I lunged for his weapon and his other hand came up fast, a knife in it which slashed across my bare chest in a furious swipe that made me curse and lose my chance as he drew the gun and pressed it to my forehead.

"Sit back and smoke your cigarette, boy," he warned, his finger tight around the trigger as blood ran down to my stomach and soaked into the dirty grey sweatpants I wore. The wound wasn't too deep, but it stung like a motherfucker.

I wasn't afraid to die, but I sure as shit would prefer to take him out before I went. So I didn't see the point in goading him into pulling that trigger today.

"So how are you, pal?" he asked casually as I sat back and took another toke on my cigarette, savouring every toxin that rolled over my tongue and ran deep down into the depths of my unfeeling body.

"I'm not your pal," I growled as I released the smoke between my teeth.

"Don't be like that," he said with a taunting smile that made hatred rise in my blood. "You and me have a bond now, see? All this torturing's gotta count for somethin'."

I took another drag, shutting my eyes and remembering all the times I'd sat on Sunset Beach smoking with my friends, sunlight seeming to spill into existence behind my eyelids for a second. The nicotine in my blood unlocked a thousand good memories, but a thousand bad ones too. I smoked to forget, smoked to celebrate, smoked to smoke. I guess I'd been punishing myself my whole life, knowing every inhale brought me a little closer to death. But damn did it taste sweet. And that was probably the point. I always squeezed a little more sugar out of the good, and a little more poison out of the bad.

"I'm going to be the last face you see if you don't give up the secrets in your head, Chase Cohen. I mean sure, I have a great face, but do you really want it to be your last? How about you and Fox, huh? Don't you wanna be underneath the weight of all that pure golden tanned muscle when you go outa this world?"

"He's not my boyfriend," I said dryly, though frankly at this point I didn't really give a fuck what he thought.

"Well not anymore," he laughed obnoxiously, inhaling another breath of smoke. "He kicked you out, didn't he? Got rid of you for being a bad boy. I'm still waiting to hear what you did to deserve that." He cupped his hand around his ear, but I remained silent. I expected him to start the torture then, but he didn't, just continued to smoke and look at me like I was a puzzle he needed to solve before he cut up all the pieces so they never fit together right again. "I have a feeling it has to do with the little whore he stole from me, hm?" He eyed me closely for a reaction and my jaw tightened involuntarily. "Yeah." He smirked, pointing at me with his cigarette. "That's it, isn't it? I always did have to keep on her a tight leash. Did Fox catch you with your pants around your ankles while Rogue choked on your cock? She's got a damn talent for that after all."

"Fuck off," I snarled, my temper rising and a part of me relished the heat that rage brought to my veins. I was always so damn cold, always so numb, but I'd defend her until my final breaths. And a part of me was glad the fire that burned in me for her hadn't gone out. If I was lucky, I could take it with me when I died.

"That wandering pussy always gave me trouble," he mused. "I had to keep an eye on her so she didn't spread her legs for my men, that's the kinda girl she is."

"She's not a whore," I spat. "Shut your filthy mouth, you don't know her."

He grinned, continuing as if I hadn't spoken, "Oh I know her alright. I know how she feels on the inside, I know how she moans and begs and-"

"Shut your goddamn mouth!" I roared and he twitched the gun towards my face again in a warning.

"You're like her in ways. You've both got this aura about you, it's like…" He thought on it for a moment, wetting his lips. "Like you're missing vital pieces. And something about that just draws me in. I wanna get into those voids and etch my name against their walls."

I glared at him, my eyes moving to the gun in his grip as I wondered if it was worth attempting to get hold of it again. I'd relish shooting him, seeing his blood splatter the room, watching the smile on his face shatter into a thousand pieces of broken teeth.

"Lemme tell you a secret…" He leaned down, stubbing out his cigarette on my thigh and I gritted my teeth through the pain as he flicked the butt away and placed another cigarette between his lips, lighting it up with my Zippo. "I like being the centre of your world, Chase Cohen. Just like I enjoyed being the centre of hers. It gives me a high like no other, knowing you're down here locked away just waiting for me to come back and tear your flesh apart. You don't know if I'll kill you, but you know I can any time I fancy. That's how it was with her. She had bite in her at first just like you did, but I know how to break the strongest of backbones. And I enjoy every crunch of each vertebrae beneath my heel." His eyes flashed with something truly evil and my upper lip curled back with hatred. I knew then why Rogue was shattered inside, why her trust in us could never be restored. We'd taken a few pieces of her heart when she'd left Sunset Cove, but this monster was the one who'd made sure to break the final ones beyond repair. And I found a purpose in that, something to keep living for down here in this cage. Because I simply *had* to live to kill this motherfucker deader than dead. It was the only thing that mattered. The one good deed that might just make all my shitty actions in my short life worth something.

"She made me promise to be loyal to her," he said with a smirk. "Which made it much more fun fucking other women in secret while she waited at home for me, fingering that tight pussy which was reserved solely for my cock. She was obsessed with me. I was her one and only. It was fucking beautiful, and when I get her back, I'm gonna tie her to my bed for days and-"

I lunged at him with a roar of fury ripping from my throat, my fist cracking against his face as I reached for his gun, my hand clamping around the barrel.

The pistol went off and my ears popped with the blast of the shot. For a heartbeat I thought it was game over, but then Shawn yanked the gun from my grip and kicked me away, levelling it on me once more.

"Do not interrupt me while I'm speaking, boy," he snarled in a tone worthy of my damn father, carefully pushing his hair back into place with his free hand.

My chest heaved as I glared at this fucking monster and my limbs trembled from the exertion. I didn't get enough food down here and this was why. He kept me weak so I couldn't win against him, but all he had to do was make one mistake and I'd destroy him. I may not have had my strength, but I had something fiercer than that. A promise to Rogue written into the essence of my flesh. *I'll kill him for you, little one. I'll speak your name just before the light goes out in his eyes.*

"Anyways, you and her are not the only broken toys I've laid a claim on, pretty eyes. I like seeing Luther's little Fox crack and fall apart too. And I absolutely *love* how Fox despises him. They think I don't know that. Acting like they're unified whenever they're on the front line, but I see the way Fox looks at his daddy and I hear rumours on the wind that confirm it. That hatred makes me very happy, Chase Cohen, you know why?"

"'Cause you're an asshole?" I guessed dryly.

"Well obviously," he roared a laugh. "But it's more than that. Daddy Harlequin owes me a debt, see? A blood debt." His eyes deepened a shade as a touch of pain entered his gaze that I'd never thought he was capable of. He ran a thumb along his lower lip as he thought on his next words, a thick silence forming between us. Shawn talked his mouth off to me but I had a feeling this was crossing a line, unveiling a piece of himself that he possibly hadn't unveiled to anyone else before. It probably meant I was a dead man, because he wouldn't spill his secrets to me unless he was planning on making sure I could never tell them. But I was curious all the same.

"Oh yeah?" I murmured to prompt him on and that was apparently all Shawn needed to keep going.

"Luther Harlequin took someone from me who I was very fond of, and there ain't many people in this world I've ever been able to say that about, pretty eyes," he said. "Most people are only useful or not useful. For example, my daddy wasn't a nice man, but he taught me the ways of violence when I was just a kiddie. He wasn't good for much else, the only thing he brought to my home was screams. Mine, my brother's and my momma's. So when I was ten, I took his pistol and pressed it the side of his head while he was sleeping on the porch, blew his brains out and tossed the gun down beside him. When Momma came running and found me covered in blood, she thought he'd killed himself right in front of me and so did everyone else. That was the first murder I got away with." He inhaled deeply through his nose. "I can still smell the blood if I focus on it hard enough, I can feel my momma's hands sliding over my eyes too, the way she tried to shield me from the slaughter. But I liked it, pretty eyes." He licked his lips slowly. "I got a taste for it that day. I felt this rush like my daddy's power was filling me up, that hunger in him for bloodshed offered to me instead. I'm not a spiritual man, Chase, but I do believe one thing. The people I kill give me a piece of them when they go, a slice of their power." He reached out, trailing the barrel of his gun down my cheek in an icy caress. "I wonder what I'll get from you."

I glared at him, hating that I shared something in common with him, having lived in a house with a man like that, dreaming about placing a gun to his head and pulling the trigger. Shawn had done what I'd hesitated to, and this was what he was because of it. Would I be like him if I'd acted on one of those violent urges?

"So this is all some revenge plot against Luther?" I asked, giving him a cool look as I steered the conversation back to the Harlequins.

"Nah, not all of it. I love chaos for the sake of chaos's sake." He shrugged. "But Luther's had it coming for a long time, and I enjoy watching his whole world crumble. Fact is, he took my brother from me, so I took one of his boys, and I plan to take the other one just as soon as I can."

I frowned, my ears pricking up at that. "What do you mean you took one of his boys?"

Shawn smiled broadly, clearly having been baiting me for that very question. He took another slow drag of his cigarette to build suspense, ever the fucking storyteller and I waited impatiently as he blew out a few smoke rings before he went on.

"My little brother was my favourite person. He was everything a little brother is supposed to be. Cruel, cold-hearted, bloodthirsty, funny, and downright loyal to his big brother." He smiled at some memory and rolled up his sleeve to show me a tattoo of a bloody heart that had the name Nolan weaved through the jagged crack down the middle of it. "He could skin a bastard with more skill than I have ever seen. He didn't have my way of talking though, he liked the quiet, only spoke to me mostly, but when he got to killin'…damn, it was like he came right out of his shell and painted the world red just for me. It was a sight to behold I tell ya. You'd have been lucky to die by his hand. Anyways, he got caught up with Luther and some of his boys one time, he was outnumbered and King Harlequin made me watch while he slit his throat." His upper lip peeled back and my mouth hooked up at the corner to drive that pain a little deeper.

"Don't you fucking look at me like that, sunshine." His hand crashed against my cheek, fucking bitch slapping me then he went on with his story like nothing had happened. "After that, I swore I'd fuck with Luther real good. Killing him wasn't good enough, he took my brother, so I decided to take his kids. But death's too easy sometimes, you can only break a man while he's still breathing." His eyes glinted with some dark secret and I found my lungs constricting as he twisted the gun in his grip. "I was in the state penitentiary when Maverick Harlequin was transferred there from juvie."

My mind whirled at that news and I found myself falling very still as I listened to his story.

"I was in for petty theft – well alright it wasn't that petty – but anyway, I paid my way into a decent cell block and befriended me a few dirty guards by lining their pockets. They liked me, I always did have the knack to talk my way outa anything, and they fell for all my smooth talking as easily as everyone does whenever I turn on the charm. Those boys turned out to be real handy, because they did whatever I said. I never saw Maverick on account of us being in different blocks, but I sure did enjoy the tales the guards brought back to me about him. They agreed to take him from his cell night after night and beat the living hell outa him. But that wasn't fun enough, so I had them tell him they were Harlequins sent there by his sweet old daddy who'd put his ass in jail in the first place. The guards told me he was ignoring all correspondence with the outside world anyways, so he was primed for being fucked with. It was too easy, pretty eyes, they even brought me a few photos to lighten up my afternoons, especially after they put him in a cell with a rapist." He barked a loud laugh as the weight of those words crashed against my heart. "Can you imagine, poor little Maverick Harlequin all alone in that place, facing night after night with all the worst kinds of animals, believing his own daddy had sent them after him? It was fucking poetic, I tell ya."

"You fucking monster," I spat as he got to his feet, holstering his gun and weighing the sledgehammer in his hands.

"Yeah, I'm a monster," he said, letting the cigarette fall from his lips so it hit the ground between us in a shower of sparks. "I'm Freddy Kruger, your living nightmare. Whenever you shut your eyes, I'll be there until I'm all you can see. And when you go outa this world, you'll go with my name scarred on the inside of your flesh. You'll know who broke you, pretty eyes. I'll be the most significant person in your life." He leaned down, swinging the sledgehammer up to rest on his shoulders. "Or you can start talking about those friends of yours who tossed you away like the trash you are, hm? Maybe there's a place in my gang for a man who's not afraid to bleed."

"I'd rather carve out my good eye," I hissed at him and a sigh left his lips.

Before I could act, he swung the sledgehammer and it cracked so hard against my shin that a roar of utter agony left me as the bone shattered under the impact. I curled in on myself, clutching the injury as I clenched my teeth through the pain, white spots exploding in front of my eyes and bile rising in my throat.

"Motherfucker," I snarled as he started whistling casually.

Shawn's boot slammed into my face, knocking me onto my back and he placed the hammer down on my chest, leaning his weight on the top of it to keep me pinned there.

"As I was saying," he said calmly as I bit my tongue over the agony coursing through my fucking leg. "I got those guards to get themselves Harlequin tattoos to make sure the lie was swallowed nice and smoothly by Maverick. And you know what?" He glared down at me, grinning as his light blue eyes glittered. "I never got to tell anyone that. I thought the secret would come out after a while, but I couldn't believe my luck when it didn't. I got outa jail long before he did, but I couldn't wait for the day he returned to Sunset Cove, and when I heard Maverick had moved to an island and started up a whole gang of his own to destroy Luther, Fox and his boys, well let me tell you I laughed my ass off." He took his gun from his hips, twirling it on his finger before pointing it at my head. "But now my words have to die with you I'm afraid, pretty eyes. I'm done with your tight lips and all those secrets locked up in your head. I wonder if they'll splatter across this room when I blow your brains out."

I breathed through my teeth against the pain in my leg and shut my good eye, filling my head full of Rogue instead of this asshole, making sure she was the last thing I saw, not him. He was nothing. And he wasn't going to steal her from me in my final moments.

"Do it," I gritted out. "Do it you fucking asshole. But know that my family are gonna kill you. They're gonna kill you so fucking good and I'll be there to greet you in hell."

My heart thrashed as I waited for the bang and for everything to go black, for the world to finally give me some goddamn peace. *Don't think of him. Don't let him take her from you.*

I focused hard, bringing her to the forefront of my mind and finding peace within the chaos.

"Are you sure it's deep enough?" Rogue asked, standing beside me on the railing at the far end of Sinners' Playground.

"I swear it," I promised, offering her my hand and she wound her fingers between mine, making my heart thrash. She was smiling wide and there was a wildness in her eyes that I was captivated by. The drop didn't scare me, but she did. She made my heart thrash and fill with this absolute fear that one day I was going to lose her. I held her hand tighter, wishing I could bottle this moment and keep it forever, so when a day came that she wasn't there, I could

still find her.

"Ready, little one?" I asked and she nodded keenly.

We leapt forward at the same time, hurtling through the air before colliding with the water and sinking deep into the blue. All the noise in the world was stolen away and it was just me and Rogue beneath the waves, floating in the endless sea.

"Shawn?" a man called from somewhere upstairs. "The hookers are here."

"Ooh hookers." The gun pulled away from my face and I cracked open my only working eye and found Shawn standing up with a childish grin on his face. "You can have some time to enjoy that broken leg, pretty eyes. I'll kill you the next time I'm here." He made sure to kick my bad leg before striding to the door and I bit down on a pained yell as I almost blacked out from the agony.

He headed upstairs and I was fairly sure I passed out because the next thing I knew, soft hands were pushing some hair away from my forehead and I found Mabel there.

I looked at her in surprise as she took my hand, unsure why she hadn't seemed to think any worse of me even after I'd told her what I'd done to Rogue and my friends.

"We'll find a way out of this, Chase," she said assuredly, but as she glanced down at my fucked up leg, her brow furrowed with a look that told me exactly how condemned I was. I knew it. She knew it. Fucking Shawn knew it. And it was soon going to be time to face the music.

I realised leaving her down here was one of the worst things about Shawn coming to kill me the next time he was here. She didn't deserve that. She had a good heart and had lost the final years of her life to this prison.

"I'm sorry I can't get you out of here," I whispered to her and she squeezed my fingers.

"Oh sweet boy," she sighed. "Life is too short to be sorry for things that aren't your fault."

CHAPTER TWENTY ONE

I stood in front of the mirror in my room at Harlequin House, fiddling with the tumble of curls that I'd styled my rainbow hair into as I got ready for my night out with Tatum.

Today was a better day.

I was wearing a pair of pale denim dungarees, the strings from the shorts part trailing down my thighs and tickling my tattoos. I'd opted for a no bra situation despite the way my brain kept filling with thoughts of what fucking Shawn would say to the side boob I was currently flashing.

I hated that he still lived in my head like that sometimes. I couldn't even figure out if I was showing more skin to prove a point to myself about not having to bow to his bullshit anymore, or if I was just picking something I wanted to wear for myself.

Mutt whimpered from his position on the bed as I fell into the trap of my reflection, and I swallowed thickly before taking the flick knife Fox had given me and slipping it into my pocket.

Tatum was going to swing by and pick me up in half an hour on her way to the underground cage fighting place and I was caught between excitement over going and the crippling need to crawl back under my bed covers and cry some more.

But I'd done enough of that last night. I'd fallen into the dark in me and I'd let myself feel all of that emptiness inside me. I'd drowned in my grief over Chase, and I'd fallen apart until I was certain I'd never be able to pull myself back together again. But then I had. Somehow, I'd dragged my shattered pieces together when the sun rose and I'd forced myself to function once more.

I'd gone down to the beach for a surf with Di, Lyla and Bella and though they'd noticed how quiet I was, they hadn't pushed me on it. And the sea had been the balm my soul needed to hold myself in place despite the mini platoon of Harlequins who had been sent with me to keep an eye out for Shawn from the beach.

I ran my fingers over the key to the Rosewood crypt which still hung around my neck, my mind trailing to Chase's and Rick's which I'd hidden beneath a floorboard in the corner of the room. I needed to speak to Fox about them. This weight which hung around my neck would never go away while our secrets stayed buried in that crypt and I was pretty certain it was time for us to cleanse ourselves of them once and for all.

It had been a long time since we'd buried those memories in there and had sworn never to speak of them again, but now that place was a burden. We needed to exorcise our demons and destroy the things we'd hidden in there so that there was no chance of them ever seeing the light of day again.

When we'd been fifteen that had seemed impossible, but now I knew we would be able to do it. And once those secrets were gone, maybe there would be some hope of us finding peace again.

I blew out a breath, painting some cotton candy lipstick onto my lips then turned and headed for the door.

Fox and JJ were talking out by the pool and my heart twisted as I hesitated by the foot of the stairs.

I hadn't seen Johnny James since I'd paid my debt to him and I had no desire to see him now either. But that wasn't going to happen. He lived here and I did too - at least part time. And Fox couldn't know about the two of us, so I wasn't going to be able to just freeze him out. Not as thoroughly as I'd like anyway.

Mutt licked the backs of my ankles as he passed me and scurried out to the pool, glancing back as if to say 'come on, bitch, you can't let that asshole win.' And he was right.

I took my phone from my pocket as I went, tapping into the speakers by the pool and starting up Montero by Lil Nas X, letting the music sink into my skin until my plastered on smile felt a little more real.

Fox and JJ looked around from their sun loungers as I strode out with something of an extra swing in my hips, because fuck letting Johnny James see me hurt for him. In fact, I planned on ignoring him as much as possible from here on out. I didn't have to be good enough for him - I just had to be good enough for myself and I happened to think I was pretty damn awesome most of the time. At least on the outside. The broken mess of a girl who I kept locked in a box on the inside didn't count. Appearances were everything and I was happy to fake it 'til I made it real. Or real enough anyway.

"Hey, hummingbird," Fox said gently, pushing himself to sit up as I approached.

He was looking at me like I might break at any moment and I cursed myself for not just going back to the fucking trailer last night. I'd tried to hide as much of my meltdown from him as possible, but I was willing to bet even the sounds of my muffled sobbing into my pillow had travelled.

"Hey, Badge," I said brightly, giving him a wide smile which only made him frown harder.

"Look, I know you're all perky again now," Fox began slowly, cutting a glance to JJ which I automatically followed.

The moment my gaze met JJ's honey brown eyes my heart imploded like I'd just run smack bang into a wall at high speed, so I reached out for Fox's beer and quickly downed the half he'd had left in the bottle.

"But I think we should all talk about last night," Fox pushed on, eyeing me with concern.

"I'm going out tonight," I said, ignoring him and tipping my head back as I began to dance to the music.

"We heard you crying. We sat outside your room so you wouldn't be alone," Fox tried to go on, his hand catching my thigh and his fingers curling tight around the back of it as he tried to force me to face his questions.

"Well I warned you," I replied a little harshly. "I told you I was all fucked up inside, but you didn't wanna hear it. So now you know. Now you've seen it for yourself. And *now* I wanna go out. So what's it to be, Badger? Are you gonna come watch some cage fighting with me and help me drink my pain away or are you gonna keep on with this bullshit and make me run again?"

"Rogue," JJ growled behind me and I whirled on him.

"What?" I snapped as I turned to glare down at him. "What is there that you wanna add to this conversation so desperately, Johnny James? Is there something you wanna say about me too? Are you going to impart some great knowledge upon me over my mental state and give me some advice on how I could be better?"

"Stop it," JJ snarled, lurching to his feet and glaring down at me.

Tension crackled between us, my heart twisting and aching as the space that divided us felt like this endless abyss of pain waiting to swallow me whole, then I just laughed. I tipped my head back and laughed, spreading my arms wide and wishing for rain which wouldn't come.

JJ tried to catch my wrist in his hand but I jerked my arm away, turning and striding into the kitchen again as Mutt shot forward to intercept him, snarling and baring his teeth when he tried to follow.

"What's up with you two?" Fox asked, getting to his feet too.

"I broke his Pikachu mug and he's all butt hurt over it," I called over my shoulder.

"What?" JJ asked in confusion but I'd made it to the kitchen so I just grabbed the mug in question, gave it a silent apology then tossed it down on the tiles. "Rogue!" JJ cried as it shattered but I ignored him, grabbing a bottle of rum and unscrewing the top. I ignored the sad little kicked puppy look he was sporting over his mug and turned my head sharply away.

"Someone tell me what this is about," Fox demanded but I left that little mind fuck to JJ as I took a long swig of my booze.

"She's just pissed because I didn't wanna hang out with her at the club yesterday. Now she's being a brat," JJ said coldly but there was something in his eyes which said he was hurting just as much as I was. But that was on him, not me. I wasn't the one who decided he wasn't worth the effort anymore.

"Rogue, we need to talk about last night," Fox said firmly, striding into the kitchen and looking all big bad boss man. He looked seriously hot when he did that, but it also wasn't gonna fly with me today.

"You said you weren't gonna play the Harlequin prince when we were in this house," I said to him before he could continue with that train of thought. "So here's my counter offer. I'm a big girl. I've been alone and dealing with my shit for a long fucking time. Did I fall apart last night and scream into a bathtub full of water for hours before crying all night long? Who can say for sure? Am I standing here right now, telling you that what I need is to go out and have some fucking fun if I want any hope of not falling into that darkness again tonight? Yeah, I am. So you can either come out and play with me or you can keep pushing me on this and I'll go find someone who's willing to give me what I want."

It was a low blow. I was a grade A asshole and I knew it. But I couldn't do this with him right now. I couldn't even face all of the hurt in me without bringing JJ into it at the moment and I definitely couldn't do that. I might hate the prick right now, but I wasn't going to throw him under the bus. I'd seen what Fox did to his brothers when he thought they betrayed him and as angry as I might have been with Johnny James, I refused to hurt him like that.

Fox hesitated and I could see the struggle in him as he battled against the desire to force what he wanted from my lips, but I could see that resolve cracking and he glanced at JJ before swiping a hand down his face.

I stayed where I was as Fox approached me, his hands landing on the work surface either side of me as I leaned back against it and his forehead pressing to mine as he exhaled slowly.

"Yeah, I'll come play with you, hummingbird," he murmured. "I promised you I always would."

I swallowed as the weight of his presence settled around me and my racing heart slowed a little. He'd seen it now. I knew that. He'd gotten a good look behind my bullshit and he'd seen the gaping hole inside me, but he was still here.

My fingers trembled where I held the bottle of rum and he eased it out of my hand before placing it down beside us.

"I'm here, baby," he promised in a low whisper just for me. "I'm not going anywhere and I'll be what you need me to be. You wanna go out and play? I'm in. But if you wanna scream and cry and rage at the world then I'm here for that too. You don't have to hide any of it from me. I swear. I'm here. No matter what."

I nodded slowly, trying to accept that as my fingers landed on his forearm and I brushed them over the hummingbird tattoo he had inked there.

"I need to fake it, Fox," I breathed. "I need to laugh and smile and dance and just keep faking it until it starts to feel real again."

"Then let's go out," he agreed heavily, lifting his head and placing a kiss against the top of my hair. "Give me five minutes to get changed and I'll take you wherever you wanna go."

I nodded silently, expecting him to leave, but he wound his arms around me and pulled me close instead, crushing me against his chest and showing me how strong he could be for the both of us if I'd just let him. And I wanted to do that. I wanted it so fucking bad. To just fall apart in his arms and let him find a way to put me back together again.

Only I couldn't. Because as much as I might have wanted to, I still couldn't trust these boys with my heart. And I couldn't accept his either because he was asking me to choose him alone. Even with the choice JJ had made, I couldn't give him that. My heart had always belonged to all of them, and I needed Maverick and Johnny James just as much as I needed him.

Fox released me when I managed to stop shaking and he headed upstairs to grab a change of clothes, leaving me standing there alone. Or at least, I thought I was alone until JJ spoke from the side of the room, making me realise he hadn't actually left.

"See, pretty girl? You were always gonna end up in his arms."

His words struck me with bitterness and rejection and all the hurt he was feeling, but I didn't have anything left in me to be able to take it on. The void inside my chest was opening up and threatening to swallow me again and I just felt numb to it. Numb to him and his words and the pain in his eyes. Numb to the memories which haunted me and the damage which scarred me. I was his and he didn't want me. Story of my life.

I just stared at him impassively, letting that numbness travel all the way through me until I didn't care anymore then I dropped his gaze, took my phone from my dungaree pocket and sent Tatum a text telling her I didn't need the ride and that I'd meet her there.

JJ walked away while I was still typing and each of his footfalls echoed through my brain like a death toll, but I still didn't look up.

This was just what happened to me. I was trash with a shine on it. Something about me drew people in but in the end, they realised I was worthless and tossed me aside again.

By the time Fox had reappeared, I'd painted a new smile on for him and he hesitated a moment as he approached me. He was wearing a pair of black sweatpants and a grey tank top with long arm holes which showed off enough of his cut abs and chest to be distracting.

"You don't have to do that," he said to me as he moved to take my hand.

"Do what?"

"Fake smiles for me."

"How can you tell it's fake?" I asked brightly, accepting his hand and winding my fingers between his as I started backing up towards the garage door.

"I can't. That's the problem. If I didn't know how you'd been last night, then I wouldn't have any idea there was anything wrong."

"Good," I replied, tugging him after me. "I spent ten years perfecting this mask, Badge. I'd be pissed if there were cracks in it."

Something shattered in Fox's gaze at my words so I booped him on the nose then turned and ran for the door. I snatched the key to his truck from the hook and sprinted down to it without bothering to switch the lights on, ducking down beside his vehicle and waiting for him to appear.

Fox flicked the lights on as he followed me, his footsteps approaching across the concrete and I crept around the truck as he rounded the hood, staying out of sight.

"Come on out, Rogue," he called and I smirked to myself as I kept going, staying low as I circled his truck.

He started heading for the back of it by the time I made it around the hood again and I leapt at him with a laugh, landing on his back and locking a hand around his throat.

"Oh shit," I gasped. "Did I just take out the great Fox Harlequin?"

He breathed a laugh as he caught my thigh, dragging me around his body and pushing me against the door of his truck the moment we were face to face.

"You always were my weak spot," he admitted, studying my face for a long moment. "Just tell me your smiles aren't always fake."

My amusement stuttered for a moment before I shook off the feeling that I was disappointing him. After all this time of searching for me, he'd just realised I wasn't who he'd been looking for anymore.

"Not all of them," I agreed softly and he nodded before dropping me to my feet and opening the door for me to get in.

I did as he wanted and he climbed in behind me, taking the key from my hand before tugging me close so that my thigh was pressed to his as he started the engine.

"Well I guess I'll just have to keep working on that until you don't have to fake them anymore at all," he said.

I didn't say anything to that, but I dropped my head on his shoulder as he pulled away, enjoying the feeling of his skin against mine and stealing a little bit of his strength while he wasn't paying attention.

We drove into the heart of the Cove. Not the flashy, prissy side of town where rich assholes liked to swan about in their luxury cars with their bleached teeth and even more bleached assholes acting like they shit hundred dollar bills for fun all the time. No, we headed into the real heart of the town. Where the streets were painted with every colour of graffiti you could imagine, alleyways made up homes for folk who were down on their luck and you could buy just about every kind of sin, if you could only figure out where to find the cash.

Fox seemed to know exactly where he was headed even though I couldn't say I'd personally ever been to this club. In fact, I was fairly sure this place hadn't been here when I was last in town at all.

We pulled up on a side street, Fox's shiny truck looking a little out of place amongst the half rusted shit heaps that surrounded us, but I did notice a few other cars with a little bit more value to them parked here and there.

We got out and Fox slung an arm around my shoulders as we started walking towards the low thump of bass which was rattling the windows of the club up ahead.

It wasn't much to look at from the outside. Just a lone black door with a line of people leading up to it as they waited to get in.

"Chase was the one who set this place up," Fox said, grief touching his words for a moment as he guided me right past the queue of people.

The bouncer dipped his head in respect as he spotted us, stepping aside to let us head through.

"Of course this is Chase's baby," I muttered as a girl in a bikini top and booty shorts looked up from behind a desk with a wide smile, holding out a rubber stamp and ink pad as she jerked her chin towards a sign stating it was twenty dollars to get in.

"Oh, sorry, Mr Harlequin," she muttered, taking a step back again as she realised who had just walked in. "Didn't recognise you for a sec. You can just go on in."

"I want the stamp," I said, holding out my hand and digging my heels in a little as Fox made a move to sweep me on through.

He indulged me as the girl quickly obliged, inking the word *Slammers* to my hand with a nervous smile.

I grinned down at the name of the club, wondering why I hadn't instantly realised that this was Ace's place the second Tatum had told me the name of it.

I took Fox's hand in mine, quickly pressing the back of my hand against his so that the ink transferred to him too, just like we all used to do every year when the carnival came. You couldn't go on any of the rides without a stamp to prove you'd paid the entrance fee, so we used to pool our money for one ticket then quickly press the ink to each of our hands before it could dry. Fox and Rick could have just bought their own of course, but they always stuck with us when we were pulling a con, no matter how petty it was.

Fox sighed, lifting my hand and placing a kiss on my knuckles before leading me down a dimly lit corridor into the heart of the club.

The volume of the music rose to a roar the moment we were inside and my eyes widened as I drank in the dark space with my heart thrashing with excitement.

There was a single brightly lit area in the whole room, the large fighting cage at the heart of the space dominating everyone's attention as a blonde dude with a tattoo of a roaring tiger on his bare chest beat the living hell out of his opponent against the wire.

The crowd were screaming and cheering for him and the vibe of the club had my veins buzzing with excitement, making my smile widen even further.

The club had almost entirely standing room only, so I had to push up onto my tiptoes to try and see around a tall fucker when he moved into the space ahead of me.

Fox noticed and tugged me towards him, grasping my waist and turning my back to his chest before ducking down and encouraging me to get onto his shoulders.

I laughed as he lifted me up, his fingers curling around my thighs as he held me in place and I was gifted the best seat in the house as the blonde dude punched his opponent so hard that he fell to the floor of the cage and didn't get back up.

The crowd exploded with cheers as a board flashed up, naming the winner as Simone Dipsicle and I watched as the people who had bet on him celebrated while those who had bet against him cursed and tore up their betting slips.

My gaze caught on a flash of blonde hair and I spotted Tatum on the other side of the cage, jumping up and down and pumping her fist in celebration as the winner of the match was let out of the cage. She raced forward and leapt on him, kissing him passionately despite the blood speckling his skin.

"Onward horsey," I called to Fox, pointing across the crowd to my friend and kicking my legs like he was my faithful steed. "Yah!"

Fox made some comment about him being happy for me to ride him if that was what I wanted and graciously started walking through the crowd while I stayed high above the sweaty bodies on his shoulders.

I kept directing him until we made it to my friend and Tatum yelled a greeting to me over the music as Fox let me down.

"You made it!" she cried enthusiastically, throwing her arms around me and drawing me into a hug.

Fox did some super cool dudebro head nodding and acknowledging of the three guys who were with her while they all clearly sized each other up. Tatum had brought two more of her boyfriends, aside from the one who had just won in the cage and I grinned at Tats as he gave me an indulgent smile.

"Hey, troublemaker," he said to me. "I hope you're not here to try and corrupt my girl again."

"Corrupt? Moi? Never," I assured him.

"Are you in the line up tonight?" Fox asked him, his arm going around my shoulders again as he tugged me close to his side, that whole possessive asshole streak to him coming out to play.

"I'm headlining, sweetheart," Tats taunted. "They like to save the best 'til last."

Tatum scoffed. "No chance of that because I'm up before you. You're more like the filler at the end of the night."

"No fucking way," I gasped in excitement, looking at her with wide eyes. "Are you gonna kick ass up there in that cage for real?"

"Sure am," she agreed.

"Who are you up against?" Fox asked Tats, and I swear to Christ they were both flexing.

"Someone who calls himself Pyro," Tats scoffed.

"You want a real opponent instead?" Fox offered and I froze. No, scrap that, I melted. Because the idea of Fox getting up in that ring and going all wild dog with his shirt off and his body gleaming with sweat was all kinds of intriguing.

"So the rumours are true? The Harlequin prince likes getting his fists wet?" Tats asked, a smirk on his lips as he sized up my man, looking excited about the prospect of that fight.

"Jesus, I'm about to choke on all the testosterone flooding this room," I muttered, pretending to swoon against Fox's chest and he caught me with a snort of laughter.

"Don't you want me to fight?" he asked, sounding disappointed.

"Err, where did you get that idea?" I asked him. "Do you seriously think I would have any objections to seeing you up there shirtless and sweaty, fighting like a motherfucker with your body all oiled up as you roll around with another dude who-"

"There's no oiling up," Fox said, rolling his eyes at me and I huffed.

"Way to ruin my fantasy, Badger. Maybe you can ask around and see if there's a bit of oil going spare anyway?"

"Oooh, then we can film it and make a viral video," Tatum suggested with a giggle.

"Yes! How do you guys feel about doing this naked?"

Fox shoved me playfully while I laughed with Tatum, but I was pretty certain I had him close to convinced on this, so I wasn't giving up.

We all moved away from the cage as another fight started up, finding a spot at the side of the room where we could hear each other a little easier as the drinks began to flow. I mean, mostly they flowed my way because the others were keeping a clear head for their fights, but I did a damn good job of drinking their share alongside Tatum's other boyfriends.

When the time came for Tatum's fight, I was officially half cut, but the buzz I had going was of the best variety and I was front and centre to watch her as she climbed up into the cage in a sports bra and shorts combo which kinda made me crush on her. Damn she had legs for days. I couldn't wait to see her roundhouse a bitch with those things.

The fight was brutal and Tatum fought like a motherfucking badass, throwing her opponent around the ring and taking her own hits like a pro.

I was screaming her name the whole time and when she dropkicked the bitch she was fighting to the ground, I swear I tore my own throat open with my triumphant screams on her behalf.

Tatum headed for the cage door as it was unlocked, swiping blood from her face as her guys hurried around to congratulate her, but before I could follow, Fox caught my waist and spun me to face him.

"Wish me luck," he said in a low voice, making my eyes flick up over his shoulder to the neon board which was announcing the next fight. Big Bad Badger vs Lord Squiddington.

I grinned at the name he'd picked out at my suggestion and Fox caught my chin in his grip as he drove me back against the wire of the cage.

He leaned in and my lips parted automatically at the promise of his kiss. "When I win, I want a prize from this mouth," he growled, his voice somehow reaching me above the roar of the music. "Will you give it to me, baby?"

I licked my lips slowly as I held his green eyes, my skin tingling at the contact with his and a nod making my head bob up and down without my permission. I was pretty certain he was asking for a kiss, but I couldn't help but imagine what else I could do with my mouth for him. And I had to say, I wasn't all that opposed to the ideas that were forming in my mind.

Fox smirked like a cocky asshole before releasing me, leaving me aching for him as a groan escaped me. Why did these boys keep doing that shit to me? I was ad*dick*ted to them and I was starting to think the only answer to that problem lay on top of them. Or under them. Or pinned against something by them. Or in front of them. Behind them. On my knees for-

"Eddie and Tom are gonna stick with you while I'm fighting. Promise you won't give them the slip," Fox said, making me blink away fantasies of my mouth wrapped around his cock and a faint blush lined my cheeks.

"No worries, Badger. I'm not going anywhere. I'll be the one panting over you against the wire while you go full savage in that cage."

His pupils darkened at my joke and I was actually kind of certain it wasn't even a joke at all.

Fox pushed away from me, jerking his chin at the two stooges who had turned up to lurk on me and I sighed as I was instantly flanked.

Tatum caught my gaze from the other side of the cage, pointing to her bleeding nose and holding up a finger to tell me she'd be back once she got that shit sorted out. I raised my bottle of beer to her in a salute as she headed away with her guys to clean up, but I was staying put to watch every moment of this fight.

Tats hopped up into the cage with Fox a moment later and I grinned at my boy as he stood there in nothing but a pair of shorts he'd clearly borrowed, holding his arms wide as the crowd roared at the sight the Harlequin prince taking centre stage.

But one look at Tats told me this definitely wasn't going to be an easily won fight and my heart pounded as the MC started calling out a countdown for the fight over the microphone.

Fox and Tats began circling each other, dark grins on both of their faces like they were eager for the pain and violence of the coming fight and my heart picked up a rampant rhythm as my teeth sunk into my lower lip.

The buzzer sounded to start the fight and instead of pussyfooting around each other, Fox and Tats dove towards one another with a savagery that had my eyes widening and adrenaline surging.

They exchanged blows, each of them blocking and striking just as often as the other before Fox was suddenly uprooted by a leg sweep that seemed to come from nowhere. Tats dove on top of him while he was still down, sending brutal blows into his face and chest and a scream escaped my lips. Not of fear like some dumb bitch, but a roar of encouragement as I demanded Fox beat the shit out of this asshole and show him what people who grew up on these streets were capable of.

I wasn't sure if he heard me or if it was just perfect timing, but Fox found his opening and swung his forehead up to collide with his opponent's nose. Tats reared back a few inches and Fox pressed his advantage, throwing a heavy punch straight at his throat and knocking him clear so that Fox could regain his feet.

The fight only intensified from there and I leapt up and down, screaming my encouragement as their blows picked up pace.

Movement at my side drew my attention from the fight for a beat as Tom suddenly crumpled to the floor beside me.

I gasped as I looked down at him, whirling to look at Eddie on my other side for help and finding him staring at me with wide, panicked eyes and a knife protruding from his neck.

"Hey, sugarpie," Shawn purred in my ear, making my blood chill as his hand slipped around my throat and he tugged me back against his chest. "It's time for you to come home like a good girl."

My lips parted on a scream which was swallowed by the roar of the crowd as Fox and Tats started beating the shit out of each other against the wire of the cage right in front of me. They were so close, yet still nowhere near close enough to hear me over the noise of the music and the people watching their brawl.

Tears pricked at my eyes as Eddie dropped to his knees, clutching at the knife which still stuck out of his neck as blood ran down his chest from the wound and grief warred through me.

My feet scrambled against the hard floor as Shawn started dragging me backwards through the crowd and I quickly lost sight of Fox fighting in the ring as people surged forward to watch. None of them even spared us a glance, all of them riveted on the show with no one seeming to notice what was happening here.

I started to struggle as the shock wore off and Shawn snarled a curse before pressing the tip of another blade to my stomach.

"Don't test me, sweet cheeks," he warned. "I've had a helluva day and I don't have time for any of your shit."

The fight fell out of my limbs and he chuckled in my ear, leaning down to press a rough kiss to the side of my neck which made my skin crawl with memories I wished I could wash off.

"There's a good little whore. Now let's get going. We have some making up to do."

Shawn shoved me through a door against a side wall and my gaze met that of one of the bouncers who had been on the door when I'd arrived here with Fox.

"You're fucking dead," I snarled at the nameless asshole. "The Harlequins will rip the skin from your bones for betraying them."

The bouncer didn't say anything, only slamming the door between us and him as Shawn dragged me out into the night.

"Everyone has a price, Rogue," Shawn cooed in my ear as he hustled me towards a big grey truck which was parked in the shadows down a side alley. "A good little whore like you should know that well enough."

"Fuck you," I hissed. "I've never been for sale a day in my life."

"No? So you haven't been spreading your legs for food and board at Harlequin HQ then? Tell me, which one of them fucks better, Fox or his daddy?"

He paused, drawing the knife away from me as he pulled his key from his pocket and I took my shot at freedom, slamming an elbow back into his gut and trying to break away from him. But his fingernails bit into my throat as he scrambled to maintain his hold on me and I was twisted around before being thrown back against the truck so hard that the back of my head rang from the impact with it.

I screamed for help, kicking and snarling as I threw myself towards him, not even giving a fuck about the knife he held and just needing to get away.

Shawn shoved me back against the truck again before slapping me so hard that my head wheeled to the side and the inside of my cheek was sliced open by my own teeth.

He laughed excitedly, his eyes flaring as he looked me up and down, drinking in the sight of me brought to his mercy as my chest heaved and my mind spun with thoughts of how the hell I was going to escape him. Because I wasn't going back to him. I couldn't. If I became that girl ever again, even for the briefest of moments I knew it would destroy what little was left of me.

"You may be a broken toy, sugarpie, but you're still *my* toy. And I'll have you on your knees begging for my forgiveness before you know it."

"I'd sooner choke on my own vomit than let you near my body again," I snarled at him. "Why the fuck do you even want me anyway? You tried to kill me. You threw me away."

"Aww shucks, sugarpie, did I hurt your feelings? You want me to buy you some pretty flowers before I reclaim that tight body of yours or somethin'? Was me spilling the blood of those men not enough to show you my commitment?" Shawn asked, giving me the puppy eyes like we were just bickering over nothing.

The flick knife in my pocket was purring my name with promises of the freedom I so desperately needed, but as my gaze fell on the blade in his hand, I knew I had to wait. I needed him distracted for a moment before I would be able to make my move.

My gaze darted back in the direction of the club and Shawn laughed. "Waiting for the cavalry? Because they're not coming. And even if someone did show up here to try and save your sorry ass, I'd just kill them too. Because this is war, sunshine."

"You said if I went with you, you'd stop," I reminded him.

"That required your willing cooperation, not me having to kidnap you. Now get your sweet ass in the truck and stop stalling for time." Shawn hit the button on the key and the truck unlocked with a flash of the lights and a dull thunk.

He jerked his chin in a clear command, but I stay rooted to the spot.

"It'll be worse for you if ya keep fighting me," he warned in a low growl, but I just stayed where I was. No fucking way was I climbing in there willingly. "Are you hoping for me to break you in again, tom cat? Because I can be rougher for you this time if that's what you need."

"Fuck you."

"I'm sure you're looking forward to that," he taunted. "Look at you all dressed up for me. I dunno whether to be pissed about you showing so much flesh or pleased to get a look at those perky tits of yours again." Shawn moved his blade, dragging the tip of the knife down the open side of my dungarees and smirking as it caressed the side of my breast. "Are you as wet for me as always, sugarpie? Have you been aching for me as much as I've been aching for you?"

I spat at his feet and he lunged at me, snatching my hair in his fist as he shoved me towards the back of the truck. But as he spun me around, I snatched the flick knife from my pocket and swung it at him with a furious scream.

Shawn lurched back as the blade swiped across his cheek and a hot spill of his blood splattered over my face. But I wasn't a dumb bitch, and I knew that wasn't going to be enough to save my ass so I channelled the badass vibes of the Green Power Ranger and lunged towards him again, sinking the deadly little blade into his side and twisting it sharply before jerking it free again.

Shawn grunted in pain as he took a swing at me with his own knife and I cried out as I jerked away, feeling a keen sting of pain across my right arm as I failed to fully avoid the blow.

But as he lunged towards me again, he stumbled, his free hand going to the wound in his side as his blood pissed down onto the asphalt and a curse escaped him. I'd hit something important there and for the briefest of moments, the tables were turned between us as he found himself dropping to one knee beneath me.

A door banged open somewhere and people started shouting my name just as Shawn reached for the gun he had jammed into the back of his pants.

My heart plummeted into my ass and I leapt away as he raised it in my direction.

A shot rang out as I darted down the alleyway and Shawn's angry shout chased me as I sprinted as far as I could get from him.

"You'll be back, little whore! I'll just keep killing all the people surrounding you until then! And when you're sick of seeing people die for me, you can come on back to me and get on your knees to make it stop."

Another shot was fired and I shrieked in fright before launching myself around a corner and slamming straight into a hard body.

"Rogue," Fox gasped, dragging me against him and crushing me in his embrace.

"It was Shawn," I panted, pointing back over my shoulder with my bloody flick knife still in my grasp. "He killed Tom and Eddie and tried to throw me in a fucking truck. I stabbed him but he had a gun, so I just ran-"

Fox snarled like a beast, pushing me towards Tatum and her boyfriends and warning them to protect me with their lives before taking off running down the alley I'd just appeared from. He was still only wearing the shorts from the cage fight and his flesh was speckled with more than a little blood, but he held a gun in his hand and looked ready to end this fight right now if he could.

I tried to chase after him, but Tats snatched my wrist into his grasp and held on tight. "It's not safe, unicorn," he warned me.

Tatum ripped a strip of material from one of her other boyfriends' shirt and quickly tied it around my bleeding arm. But I couldn't even feel the sting from the cut as my whole body tensed with fear for Fox.

But before I could freak the fuck out and start trying to fight my way out of there to go after my man, he reappeared.

"There was a big fucking puddle of blood but no truck and no fucking Shawn," Fox growled, shoving between the others and taking my face between his hands as he stared down at me. "I would have torn the world apart to get you back," he swore to me as I was taken hostage by the desperation and fear in his green eyes. But there was fury there too, a rage that had no outlet now that Shawn had run back to his hole like a rat in a storm and I knew he needed to vent some of the violence burning through his body.

"He had help," I breathed, sincerely hoping Shawn was currently bleeding out in a ditch somewhere, though I doubted fate would be that kind to me. "One of the bouncers in the club sold me out. He must have let Shawn in through a side door and he let us back out of it too. It was one of the guys who was on the door as we came in."

The roaring inferno in Fox's eyes turned to a simmering pit of fury and he kissed me hard, his mouth bruising and punishing against mine as his hands gripped my face firmly enough to hurt.

He broke away from me so suddenly that I was left reeling, my lips burning from the heat of his kiss as he took my hand and led me back to the club.

He made a call as we walked, telling the person on the other end of the line that they were to secure the two doormen immediately or face the wrath of the Harlequins.

Tatum and her men followed behind us, but as we reached the entrance to the club where people were pouring out of the door in a tidal wave, Fox turned to look at them.

"This is the part where you leave so that you don't witness anything else," he said firmly.

"You sure you've got it handled from here?" Tats asked, his eye swelling from their fight, though there was no animosity hanging between the two of them.

"Yeah. We'll have to finish that fight another time. I was enjoying beating your ass," Fox told him and Tats laughed loudly.

"In your dreams, big boy."

Tatum gave me a quick hug, making me promise to get my arm looked at by someone with medical credentials and I promised her I would before the four of them turned and left us to it.

The club was just finishing emptying out and Fox took my hand as he led me inside.

We strode straight into the huge room where the fights had been held, the lights now bright and the space looking decidedly less cool with beer bottles and empty glasses scattered about the place.

Two men were kneeling on the sticky floor beside the ring, a dozen Harlequins standing around them menacingly.

Fox looked to me in a question and I didn't hesitate for a second before pointing to the motherfucker who had sold me out to Shawn.

The guy whimpered and started begging, making excuses and generally acting like a total pussy.

Fox snapped his fingers and one of the Harlequins gave the other bouncer a shove to get him moving and send him on his way out of here.

"String him up," Fox commanded in a low voice and the guy's pleas turned to screams and begging as the Crew quickly stripped him down to his boxers and tied his hands to a rope one of them slung over one of the roof beams.

They hauled him up until he was hanging by his wrists with his feet only just touching the floor and Fox gently took my chin in his grasp, turning my gaze from the show until I met his eyes.

"I'm going to make you hurt for putting my girl at risk like that," Fox told the guy while he continued to beg and sob. "I'm going to make you bleed and break and beg for death. But there's no point in you begging for it from me. She'll be the one who decides when enough is enough." He pushed the pistol he'd been holding into my hands, the green in his eyes seeming to brighten as I accepted it without hesitation.

"You want me to be the one to finish him?" I asked in confirmation, weighing the weapon in my hand and wondering if I was really capable of that. I'd done it before. I'd killed Axel, but that had been different, he'd been hurting me, trying to assault me and I'd been fighting for my life at the time. This would be in cold blood. And as much as I was certain I wanted Shawn to die by my hand for all he'd done to me, this wasn't the same as that.

"Either do it yourself or hand it back to me when you want me to stop," Fox replied, his fingers pushing into my hair. "Either way, he's dead. No one gets away with hurting you, hummingbird."

"She's just some piece of ass," the bouncer whimpered. "Just some whore he wanted back. He paid me ten grand for her. How was I supposed to know you'd give a fuck about it? There are a thousand more like her. I didn't know she mattered. I didn't know!"

My grip on the gun tightened and a cold detachment filled me as I accepted it. Up until then I'd been letting myself think this asshole might not have been a total sack of shit. Luckily for me he'd just proved me wrong.

Fox gave me a dark look which really shouldn't have turned me on, but I had to admit, that fucked up little heathen in me didn't mind it one bit when he told his men to go wait outside and turned his attention to the job at hand.

I watched as he punched, kicked and beat the motherfucker for far longer than I needed to let it go on for. Time ticked by and my blood pumped with a dark kind of hunger as I watched Fox mercilessly beat the fuck out of him.

This was the beast that had been lurking beneath his skin. The part of himself he'd been trying to protect me from.

But as I watched him set his monster loose and break the man who'd put me in harm's way, there wasn't a single piece of me that thought any less of him for it. In fact, my heart was racing as I watched him. The way his muscles bunched and flexed and the sweat gleamed on his bare skin from the exertion made my own flesh tingle with an ache I'd been fighting since the first moment I'd laid eyes on him again.

Fox Harlequin was brutal, savage and utterly intoxicating. And the more he made my enemy scream for him, the harder I fell into the dark with him. Because this was where I belonged. Down in the pit with the monsters. Deep in the heart of this chaos. The Harlequin Crew had been my worst nightmare for so long that it had taken me too long to realise this, but they'd clearly been my destiny all along too.

And when I finally had enough of hearing the man shriek and cry while his bones cracked and his body was broken, I raised the pistol in a steady hand, locked eyes with Fox, and pulled the trigger without hesitation.

CHAPTER TWENTY TWO

"**A**re you watching, baby?" Mia called from her bed as she rolled in the sheets with some naked chick.

I was on my phone, Googling *can people die of boredom?*

The answer wasn't even a resounding no. Apparently long-term boredom increased your chances of premature death, but that wasn't good enough. I needed boredom to make my brains shoot out of my ears right this second because I'd agreed to watch Mia fuck a girl after she'd been begging me to for a week. I was officially done with this relationship, especially as Mia waved her naked ass in my direction and fingered Miss Who-Knew-Her-Name so hard I was pretty sure she wasn't enjoying it.

"Look, baby!" Mia cried, doing some sort of ass shake thing before going down on the girl who was mewling like a cat in heat.

"Uhuh," I grunted, opening my old Facebook account and scrolling through photos from my youth.

I paused on one of me and Fox with Rogue standing on our shoulders on the beach. Her hands were raised in the air like a cheerleader as we each held one of her ankles and my lips twitched at the memory. She'd watched Bring It

On and had been so convinced she could do one of the moves that we'd worked all day on Sunset Beach to perfect it. She had this big ass grin on her face, her eyes full of pride at pulling it off and I swiped onto the video beside it.

"Go on, Rogue!" JJ called off camera and Chase whistled his encouragement, the sound so loud he must have been the one filming. Rogue ran down the beach towards me and Fox, did a cartwheel toward us and we caught her as she flipped over, throwing her up into the air and supporting her legs as she landed on our shoulders and whooped. I replayed the video a couple of times, trying to drown in that memory but Mia kept moaning so loudly she was pulling me out of it.

"You're not even watching!" she shrieked and I looked up.

She had her ass on the girl's face as she crouched over her like fucking Gollum, pawing at her own tits. I could see the porno title now: *Gollum gets his one ring destroyed by busty Orc.*

I checked the time on my phone, finding we only ten minutes before we needed to leave. Kaiser had invited us over for dinner and I was ready to be done with Mia and her whole goddamn family at last. Tonight, I'd be walking into that house with a grenade hidden in my pocket and I was going to blast my way into the Rosewood crypt, get the stash inside and get the fuck outa there. I'd lock down my island so hard that Kaiser would have to declare war on The Damned Men if he wanted to have it out with me, and frankly I didn't give much of a fuck what happened after that.

"She's doing a shit job. I'll eat your ass good tonight when we get home," I said as I pushed out of my seat and Mia's eyes lit up like a Christmas tree.

"You will?" she gasped, losing her balance and ass-planting the girl so she got buried between her cheeks and started screaming, the sound muffled by the amount of ass she was lost in.

"Yup." *Nope.*

I walked out of the room, grabbing my leather jacket on the way. "We're leaving in ten minutes," I barked and Mia squealed in excitement.

It wasn't long before we were heading to the mainland and I pulled off the boat with Mia on the back of my motorcycle in the bitch seat – its name apt for once. I drove through my side of town and circled around to the Rosewood Manor while Mia whooped like a school girl. I was pretty sure she was on something tonight, she liked popping pills from time to time and it made her clingy as fuck. The girl she'd brought to bed was likely high as well, so maybe she wouldn't remember the assmageddon she'd lived through this evening. Kinda fucking funny if she did though.

We reached the gates and I flipped up my visor so the guard could see me and he nodded, letting us through onto the property. I accelerated up the drive with a roar of the engine, parking outside and waiting for Mia to get off the bike before I did too. We left our helmets on the bike and I wrapped my arm around her waist, keeping her close as we walked up to the door.

My heart warred excitedly as we passed another set of guards and I felt the time ticking down to when I'd be free from this charade at last. No more Mia in my bed, no more fake smiles or fake politeness with her father. No more pretending I gave anything of a shit about them or their damn allegiance. I was making an enemy out of them tonight and I looked forward to the backlash.

We were taken into the dining room for dinner and we sat opposite Kaiser and his wife as they talked money and more renovations to the grounds and manor. They told me about building a giant chessboard out in the garden which made me almost throw up my starter from how tacky that idea was, then went on to say they were planning to demolish the summerhouse which made me sick for a whole different reason.

A thousand memories of my childhood lived in that summerhouse. It was a place I'd only known good things to happen, where we'd sipped fresh lemonade made for us by Miss Mabel, and spent hours lazing there playing cards or just talking shit. It was where I'd seen Rogue's tits for the very first time too.

When I was officially done with their bullshit, I excused myself to the restroom and adrenaline rushed through my blood.

And so the fun begins…

I tried to exit through the side door I'd gone through with Rogue the last time I was here, but found my way blocked by some security asshole so I doubled back before he spotted me and slipped down another corridor.

This house was stupidly large and I was definitely pushing the limits of my restroom break already. They either thought I was doing the biggest shit known to man or were gonna start getting suspicious. So I needed to hurry the fuck up.

"Where's the fucking exit?" I snarled in frustration as I walked down yet another hall.

"Hello?" a distant male voice called and I glanced at a door opposite me which was locked with several bolts and padlocks.

I figured that was none of my fucking business and I was on a time limit, so I started walking again, but the voice called out once more and my blood froze in my veins.

"Is someone there?" he yelled and my brain rattled.

I just stood there like my legs had turned to stone, glancing back at the door as a frown tugged at my brow.

Not possible. I'm hearing things.

But I found myself drifting back towards that door with my pulse drumming in my ears and hope tearing a hole in my chest.

"Hello?" I called back.

"Maverick?!" Chase's voice came, sounding desperate and doubtful at once.

Not. Possible.

I stood there for two endless seconds then gripped one of the padlocks on the door, the cold metal kissing my skin.

"Rick is that you?!" he called, pain in his tone and I knew it was him. I didn't know how, but it was. He was in there. Chase fucking Cohen had either risen from the goddamn dead, his ghost was trapped down in the basement of this house, or he was fucking alive.

"Are you still there!?" he called, panic in his tone like he really believed I'd left him. "It's Chase!"

I tried some of the bolts on the door before yanking on the large padlock, but the door was locked up like an ogre lived down there. My mind worked over everything that was happening and I came to a terrifying conclusion that was the only one which made sense. Chase was here. Alive. And a prisoner to Kaiser Rosewood. I had no fucking idea how those facts had come to be true, but they had. *Holy fuck. He's alive.*

I rested my forehead to the door, cursing under my breath as emotion ripped up through my being and I shook my head at myself as I made the most stupid decision of my life. I took the grenade from my pocket, wedged it under the doorhandle, pulled the pin and ran away.

The boom that rang through the house was followed by the fire alarm going off and sprinklers turning on over my head. Chaos descended in seconds, and I was now fully invested in this choice.

I ran through the massive hole blasted in the remains of the door and the wall surrounding it, knowing I had so little fucking time to act that I was probably a dead man already.

I reached the bottom of the stone stairway, finding an old woman there sitting in a wooden rocking chair, fast asleep and I skidded to a halt as my eyebrows shot up in recognition.

"Miss Mabel?" I rasped in shock, my head spinning, but then the hammering of fists on a steel door to my left brought me back to my senses. *Is everyone from my past rising from the dead tonight??*

There was a bolt on this side of it and I unlocked it, wrenching it open and Chase slumped through it at my feet. The inked map of Sunset Cove on his back was intersected by old wounds and fresh ones, the Harlequin tattoo on his shoulder had been burned clean off and a myriad of cuts and bruises lined the rest of his arms. My gut tightened as I took all of that in within a single torturous second.

I fell to my knees, pulling him up as fear split me open and he stared up at me through his long hair, looking so fucking pale. My gaze settled on his mutilated right eye, a gruesome X carved through it so it was now sealed shut by a savage cut that split through his eyelid. My chest crushed and I found it hard to draw in a single breath, but when I did, I spoke his name.

"Chase?" I gasped, unsure if I could even believe it was him. Not that I cared but fuck it I did.

"Don't leave me here," he said in a tight voice like he thought I was really about to turn tail and run. But I hadn't risked everything just to abandon him, so I hauled him to his feet.

He groaned in agony, unable to put weight on his left leg at all and I could tell it was broken. *Fuck. Fuck. Fuck a duck.*

I slung his arm around my shoulders, supporting him as I moved. We were dead. Absolutely fucking dead. But I was in for the ride now, so we might as well make a run for it and see how far we got.

"Maverick," Miss Mabel croaked, coming to as she blinked groggily and I moved toward her, not knowing how I was going to carry both of them, just sure I had to do it. "No." She held up a hand to stop me trying to help her up. "You have to run. I can't come with you," she said firmly.

I didn't know how the fuck she was even alive, but I needed to get her to her feet.

"Come on, don't be stubborn." I reached for her, but she batted my hand away weakly.

"No. You need to go now. There's no time and Kaiser gave me a damn sedative. If you can get onto the grounds, head to the fountain in the walled garden," she said, her eyes fluttering shut for a moment before reopening. "There's a tunnel beneath it. It's been there since the prohibition days. Press the stone with the Rosewood crest on it to open it and it will lead you to the woods beyond the grounds. Now go." She pointed and I growled under my breath, seeing she was a lost cause and vowing I'd get her out of here somehow, but I couldn't waste any more time and she clearly wasn't coming.

"I'll be back for you," I swore as she seemed to fall asleep again, the drugs she'd been giving seizing control of her body and I turned, practically carrying Chase up the stairs.

His head lolled and I was pretty sure he passed out at some point. He was a heavy motherfucker, but I'd become the strongest man in the room a long time ago and I wasn't going to let him fall for anything.

I made it to the top of the stairs and by some miracle there was no one there yet. So I turned left down the hall and dragged Chase along as he mumbled something incoherent and half helped me for a moment before sagging against me once more.

I made it to a window and forced it open, poking my head out and finding grass below it. I shoved Chase through and he hit the ground with a pained groan which was muffled as he face planted the dirt.

"Asshole," he grunted.

"I'm saving your ass, but I didn't say I'd be gentle about it, Ace," I muttered as I climbed after him, shutting the window and heaving him back to his feet.

His fingers dug into my shoulder as he held on and we managed to move at a fair speed as we headed for a group of trees a few hundred yards away. Shouts went up before we got there and I swore colourfully, moving faster and making Chase hiss in pain.

"Stop!" some asshole called, but fuck if I was going to listen.

Chase slumped against me once more, almost taking me to the ground, but I manged to hold us upright, clamping him tight to my side and moving as fast as I could as we made it into the trees.

Flashlights swung our way, but somehow none landed on us as I moved, my muscles bunching and flexing and sweat trickling down my neck as I worked tirelessly to keep going.

We reached the walled garden and more shouts went up as I led Chase toward an archway. A bang sounded as a gun went off and a chunk was shot out of the stone wall as we made it through, making my heart jackhammer.

"Fuck you for being alive," I hissed at Chase.

I didn't have to get him out, I didn't have to waste my one goddamn chance at opening the crypt. But here I was apparently insane enough to get shot for this prick.

"Sorry for the inconvenience," he tossed back, but the strength was failing in his voice again and I tried to ignore the tug in my gut over that.

We reached the fountain and the sound of pounding footsteps made my adrenaline surge as I half considered drawing my gun and seeing how many I could take out. But that option ended in both of our deaths for sure. So now I was going on the word of an ancient woman who was apparently part of the Not Actually Dead Club she'd formed with Chase and I started looking for the fountain.

We staggered through another archway and gunshots rattled in my head, somehow defying all laws of the universe and missing us by millimetres.

I gritted my teeth as I spotted the round stone fountain ahead of us, needing to get into the secret tunnel before a single asshole saw us do it.

I rounded the fountain, hunting the edge of it in desperation and as I spotted the crest on a brick near my feet, I kicked it hard. The flagstone to my right lowered in the ground, revealing a hidden stairway and I shoved Chase down it as the thump of boots ran this way. He made no sound as he went tumbling into the dark so I was pretty sure he'd passed out again as I dove after him, running down a few steps before shoving the flagstone back into place above me. I waited in the absolute darkness, listening to the men somewhere above us as my pulse crashed against my eardrums.

"Where'd they go?" one guy barked.

"Split up!" another shouted. "They can't be far."

I didn't breathe until the sound of their movements carried away and I rubbed a hand over my face as I accepted what I'd just done. What I'd risked. What I'd lost. For fucking Chase.

I pulled my phone from my pocket, turning on the flashlight and finding Chase laying on the stairs unconscious. Some piece of me fractured at the sight of him like that and I dropped down beside him, wanting to hate him, but finding something far more dangerous than that making me bleed instead. I knew in some part, I was responsible for this. I'd set in motion the path that had led him here. I'd wanted him punished for what he'd done to Rogue, but not this. Never fucking this.

I couldn't examine any of these unwanted feelings too closely as I lifted him to stand and he managed to wake up enough to lean on me for support.

"Rick," he murmured. "Tell them I'm sorry."

"You'll tell them yourself," I growled, carrying him along down the damp tunnel that seemed to go on and on forever.

We eventually reached a hatch that led us out into the woods beyond the Rosewood Manor and by the time we got out, Chase was unconscious again. I panted as I stood over him, resting my hands on my knees as I shut the hatch then grabbed a large rock which was vaguely in the shape of a star and placed it on top of it. Then I leaned down, lifted my ex-friend and threw him over my shoulder, locking my arm around his thighs.

"Come on then, asshole," I gritted out, starting to walk. There was only one place I could go and getting there without being shot was going to be an absolute challenge, but I always had thrived on being pushed to my limits.

It was nearly half an hour before I made it out of the woods and started taking the old route me and the others used to take to get up here when we were kids. The backstreets were mostly quiet and I only passed the odd drunk who didn't seem lucid enough to recognise me, one of them even making jokes about me taking my boyfriend home for a pounding.

I was soon deep into Harlequin territory, and I was probably the most fucked I'd been in my life as I carefully picked my way through the streets, waiting for people to clear out before hurrying down them and hugging the shadows.

I was breathless, gasping for water and my shoulder was ready to drop off by the time I was a street away from Harlequin House. I lay Chase down in someone's doorway as I sat beside him and kept my head down as I took a break. We probably looked like a couple of hobos at a glance, but anyone looking closer would likely shoot first and ask questions later. So how was I supposed to get him to the Harlequin front door?

I waited for an opportunity to present itself and it came in the form a pizza delivery driver on a moped. He stopped up the street, jumping off and buzzing the door to a block of flats. I picked Chase up with a grunt of effort, running across the road and snatching the helmet on the handlebars just as the door opened for the guy and someone stepped out to take the food from him. I shoved Chase onto the back of the bike, slapping him to wake him up before forcing the helmet onto his head and sitting in front of him. He sagged against me and I wrapped one of his arms around my waist before kicking up the stand and turning the key to start up the moped.

"Hey!" the driver cried in panic as he spotted me and I turned the moped around fast, racing down the street and clinging onto Chase's arm as he started tipping violently to the right.

"Hold on, you motherfucker," I demanded, my stomach clenching as I turned down the street towards Harlequin House and loosed the throttle, going as fast as this piece of shit could go. Which was around thirty miles per hour. *Fuck.*

I approached the Harlequin gates and eyed the armed guards in front of them. One of them looked me in the eye and I cursed, knowing I should have taken the damn helmet, but it was that or risk Chase's head cracking open on the pavement when I dropped him off. And seeing as I'd just hauled his ass miles across town with a bunch of gunmen hunting for us, I figured killing him now would be kind of fucking pointless.

I shoved him off the bike and he hit the road in front of the Harlequin gangbangers with a yell of pain. A gun was fired and I ducked my head, turning down the next street and cursing Chase out as I made my getaway on a goddamn moped through Harlequin territory.

You're welcome, asshole.

CHAPTER TWENTY THREE

Gunshots and yells tore through the air outside and I leapt out of my bed as Mutt barked in alarm. I'd been just dozing off with dreams of sinner boys and bad deeds filling my mind and the sudden buzz of a fight breaking out had my pulse scattering.

I scrambled to my nightstand in the grey wifebeater I'd stolen from Chase's old room, snatching out the gun Fox had given me and flicking the safety off before kicking on my sneakers as I ran to the door.

It burst open before I could get there, Fox's eyes wild for a moment before they landed on me. He was only wearing a pair of shorts and he held a pistol in his hand. JJ was right behind him, his gaze meeting mine for a moment before he looked towards the corridor instead.

"What's going on?" I demanded.

"Something is happening at the main gate," Fox growled. "I want you to lock yourself in the-"

"Fuck no," I snapped, shoulder checking him as I made it to the door and pushing my way out into the corridor between him and JJ. "I'm not hiding like some little bitch. Besides, the safest place I can be is with you assholes."

Neither of them seemed to have an argument for that fast enough to talk me out of my decision so I took off down the corridor, forcing them to follow.

Mutt took point as Fox caught my shoulder and pushed me behind him.

"Stay close," he commanded.

"Yes, sir," I snarked back and JJ cursed.

We hurried downstairs where the sound of gunshots had come to an end and someone started hammering on the door frantically before we could reach it.

"Boss!" one of the Harlequins yelled from outside. "Boss, you need to come see this!"

Fox moved to the side of the door, checking through the peep hole to make sure it wasn't some trick before wrenching the door open and looking at the man who stood there.

"What is it?" he barked.

"Maverick Stone just tossed him from the back of a bike right outside the gates," the dude panted and I peered around Fox to get a look outside.

My heart was thrashing to a heady beat as I spotted the group of Harlequins who were all crouched around something in the road right outside the gate, an innate sense of need urging me closer to it.

"What the fuck are you talking about?" Fox demanded but I pushed him aside, the gun falling slack in my hand as I spotted a body between the crowd of Harlequins, a mess of dark curls covering his head.

A strangled cry escaped me as I shoved my way outside, my heart forgetting to beat at all as I broke into a sprint with Mutt at my side.

"He's alive," someone gasped as I raced towards the figure laying on the floor. "Holy fuck, call an ambulance."

I skidded to a halt as I passed through the gates, the gun falling from my hand as I dropped to my knees with a sob escaping my lips. It couldn't be real. How could it be real? And yet I was looking right at him and that broken, lost piece of my heart seemed to have just come alive inside me once more.

"Chase?" I breathed, snatching his hand in mine and squeezing it so tight that it must have hurt. But I couldn't help it. I had to be sure he was real. That this wasn't some cruel twist of my imagination and that the boy who owned a piece of my soul really was right here before me.

Mutt started barking at him, nudging his face with his wet nose and licking his cheek like he was trying to get him to wake up too.

A groan passed Chase's lips as he rolled his head towards me and a cry of grief escaped me as I caught sight of his face. He was bruised and battered, a scruffy beard covering his jaw and hair clinging to his sweaty skin. But the mangled destruction of his right eye made my whole body freeze with horror.

"Holy fuck," JJ gasped as he dropped down beside me and Chase groaned again as he was half lifted from the ground and into JJ's arms, forcing Mutt to scamper aside.

Fox threw his arms around them too, a grieved noise escaping his throat as I just kept hold of Chase's hand and his gripped me back like a vice.

"How is this possible?" Fox breathed.

Chase made a pained sound and both Fox and JJ released him with apologies, the two of them talking a mile a minute as they asked question after question. But I couldn't hear any of it and Chase didn't seem to be able to give them the answers they needed either. He just met my gaze with his one blue eye, the two of us staring at each other as so much hurt and loss and pain and love passed between us that it didn't even need words.

"We should gather the Crew and head straight to Dead Man's Isle and kill that motherfucker Maverick for this," one of the Harlequins snarled.

"No," Chase grunted, the first word he'd managed. "Rick saved me. This was all Shawn."

A sob caught in my throat at that because we should have known. We should have been hunting for him all this time instead of grieving over a death that had never occurred. I'd been down in the bottom of The Dollhouse with him and Shawn right before it collapsed. We'd known Shawn had escaped, so why the fuck hadn't we ever considered this?

"I'm so sorry," I whispered while a whirlwind of motion took place around me and I wasn't even sure if he could hear me anyway.

Red and blue lights flashed as the ambulance showed up and suddenly there were more people moving around us, more questions, more noise.

Chase was being hoisted up and onto a gurney, but I still held onto his hand with an iron grip which he returned even when he seemed to pass out, his fingers tight around mine like he never wanted to let go.

I climbed up into the back of the ambulance with him, hardly hearing the EMT who directed me into a seat at his side, Fox and JJ telling us they'd be following right behind us.

I didn't hear any of it. See any of. Because all that was here in this moment with me was the boy who'd held my hand the first time I'd jumped from the end of Sinners' Playground. The boy I'd boosted my first car with. The boy I'd been aching to rescue every single day I'd known him. And the man who had broken me when I thought he was lost.

I paced outside the operating theatre, not knowing how long I'd been doing it aside from the fact that the sun was now rising beyond the window and my legs were burning from the constant movement.

Fox and JJ sat against the wall opposite the door, their faces painted with worry for the man inside that room.

I hadn't fully taken in the list of injuries that had been reported to us by one of the nurses, but I'd heard her talking about a broken leg and his eye needing major surgery alongside some broken ribs, a lot of wounds which needed stitching and a serious burn.

The police had showed their faces a few hours back, but one harsh threat from Fox had sent them packing. We didn't need their help with this shit anyway, though I was sure they were lurking in wait to ask their questions again as soon as Chase came out of surgery. But it wouldn't be the cops who would get justice for this. We'd be doing that ourselves just as soon as we were certain Chase was alright.

The double doors swung open and the various surgeons and nurses strode out, one of them heading over to us to give us an update on what Chase had had done.

All I took in was the fact that he was still breathing, leaving Fox and JJ to listen to the details of the kind of recovery and aftercare he'd be needing as a bed was rolled out of the room next and my gaze fell on Chase.

His eye was all bandaged up now, his left leg elevated and in a cast.

More bandages and dressings plastered the rest of his bare chest than I could easily count.

I ran to his side, taking his limp hand from the blankets and keeping hold of it as the porters wheeled him down the corridor. We headed into an elevator and I just kept my eyes on his face, drinking in the sight of him and the feeling of his hand so warm in mine. He was here. He was real. He was alive. And no matter what else had happened to him, I was just going to cling onto those three most important things. Because until he'd been brought back to me, I'd been staring at an eternity without him in it and as much as I'd been trying to cope with the reality of that, it wasn't a life I'd wanted to exist in.

We arrived in a private room and I just stayed beside him, holding his hand while he was hooked up to all kinds of machines and a drip was attached to his other hand. Fox and JJ arrived not long after, but the nurses warned us we could only stay for a few more minutes.

I looked up as the two of them came to stand on the other side of the bed and the door finally fell closed behind all of the hospital staff, leaving us in silence alone with the boy we'd all thought we'd lost.

"Shawn had him for weeks," I breathed, my voice cracking and guilt warring through me as I stared down at the broken body of the man I'd loved for as long as I could remember. "Weeks and weeks of torture while we were all grieving him like he was already dead and gone and-"

"Don't do that," Fox snarled, reaching across the bed and taking my free hand in his. "This isn't on you or any of us. Shawn is the one who will pay for this."

"His fucking eye," JJ murmured, his voice cracking as he reached out to grasp Chase's shoulder. I'd heard the doctors saying he'd been blinded in it, but right now I could only be thankful that he was alive. The horror of his injuries felt like a distant whisper of a problem I couldn't face right now.

"When we get our hands on Shawn Mackenzie he'll be begging for death," Fox said fiercely. "And we'll make him feel the pain of it ten times over before his wish is granted."

"That's enough," a nurse barked firmly as she pushed the door wide, looking in at us. "Mr Cohen will be out of it for hours and he needs his rest if he's to start the path to recovery. The police are waiting downstairs to take your statements too."

She gave us a look that was judgemental as fuck but I didn't have it in me to take offence. No doubt she was judging us and what we were, blaming us for what had happened here but right now I could only really agree with her on that.

Fox cursed but nodded in acceptance, leading the way towards the door while swiping a hand down his face like he wanted to wipe the feeling of this day off of his flesh.

A tear ran down my cheek as I made a move to leave too, despite the hurt in my heart which demanded I stay precisely where I was. But before I could take so much as a step away from him, Chase's fingers locked tight around mine and I jerked to a halt, looking down at him in surprise.

His one good eye remained closed, his face expressionless as the drugs kept hold of him, but his fingers were tightening in a clear demand for me to stay.

I glanced up at the nurse, setting my jaw in determination as the heart rate monitor began bleeping faster, like he could sense me pulling away from him and that was causing him some distress. That was all the encouragement I needed from him and I set my feet as I made the decision not to move a single inch from this spot for however long he needed me to stay.

"I'm staying," I said firmly, squeezing Chase's fingers in reassurance just in case he could hear me.

She didn't look happy about it, but either the look in my eyes, the gun jammed into JJ's waistband or just the sense of threat hanging in the air between the three of us and her made her nod.

"Fine. Just you. And don't be a nuisance."

Fox glanced between me and Chase, nodding once and muttering about him and JJ staying downstairs if I needed anything.

The door closed again as they left and another tear slipped down my cheek.

I hesitated for a moment before climbing up onto the bed beside him, being careful not to bump or jostle him too much and I curved my body against his, placing my head down on his chest and listening to the solid thump of his heart beneath my ear.

I curled my arm across his stomach, holding him close and breathing him in as the piece of my soul which belonged to him settled back into place.

This was fucked up on so many levels and I knew that nothing about it was alright. But I had him back. He was here in my arms.

And for now, that was the only thing in the world that mattered.

CHAPTER TWENTY FOUR

I'd had a rough few fucking days. It had started with me getting stabbed by my ex-bitch, followed by me laying on a kitchen table being stitched up by one of my more valuable men, then spending my time getting through the pain of my injury on nothing but pot and hard liquor. I was on the move again at least, my side bound in white bandages and my anger at an all time high. The stab in the side wasn't even what made me the most vengeful, it was the cut to my goddamn face that pissed me off to high heaven.

No one cut my fucking face and got away with it. So Rogue Easton was officially in my bad books, and I was gonna enjoy breaking my sugarpie all the more because of it. Don't get me wrong, I was enjoying seeing the fight in her. The more backbone she displayed, the more hungry I was to shatter it under my boots, but she had gone too far. I was torn between wanting to return the favour in kind and wanting to fuck the life out of her. Maybe I'd settle on both when I got the chance.

Luckily for me, I had someone to take my anger out on waiting for me in the Rosewood basement. My pretty eyed boy was gonna die real good today and I'd twist the blade in Rogue's chest nice and slow by making sure she saw his bloody remains. Yup, it was gonna be a bloodbath alright. I'd changed my mind on taping a grenade in his mouth and leaving him in the woods to be found by the Harlequins. Because today, I wanted to colour myself red and feel every snap of bones and splash of blood as he died for me. I'd tie him to a tree then skin him alive while I fed the live video to my enemies.

I drove through the Rosewood gates in a black Ford. I had to change up my vehicle often so none of those Harlequin boys could track me around town, but I missed the power of my SUV and the purr of her engine beneath me.

I parked up and headed to the trunk, whistling as I took out a bag with some rope, my shotgun and some knives in it. I was gonna cut off a few fingers before I moved Chase to the woods. I needed his screams to sate the angry monster in me this morning, so I'd be sure to pull them from his lips as soon as possible.

I walked inside and headed through the huge entrance hall, upping my pace as excitement twisted through me.

"Oh – er- Shawn!" Kaiser Rosewood called out from behind me and I snapped around in frustration, knowing I had to pander to him for now. He was in a purple dressing gown that was hanging open to reveal some gold silk boxers. I didn't entirely hate everything he wore, I reckoned I could pull it all off a lot better than him though.

"Morning, Kaiser," I said, tipping an imaginary hat to him. "I've got a lot of work to do today. My little secret in the basement ain't gonna be a burden on you no more."

He cleared his throat, toying with a gold chain around his throat. "Yes, er, about that. Unfortunately there was an incident last night and um…"

"An incident?" I echoed coolly, assessing him as I tried to read what he was saying from his eyes. "Are you tellin' me he's dead already?"

He swallowed hard, raising his chin as he tried not to be intimidated by the look I was giving him. "It was all pretty shocking. I was betrayed by my stepdaughter's fucking boyfriend."

"Keep talking," I gritted out, sensing I wasn't gonna like where this was going.

"Well…it seems Maverick Stone isn't a man to be trusted. He released your prisoner and they-"

"Do not let the word 'escaped' pass your lips unless you're ready to face the consequences of that reality," I warned, coldness washing over me.

He cleared his throat. "I'm sorry, Shawn, I'll compensate you of course."

I inclined my head, working over everything he'd said and deciding what I was gonna do about it. Then I slapped on a wide smile and opened my free arm wide.

"Well ain't that a doozy, Kaiser?" I clapped my hand down on his shoulder overly tightly as I continued to smile big.

"You're…not angry?" he confirmed.

"Accidents happen," I said, then inhaled deeply through my nose. "Oh my, is that breakfast I smell? You don't mind if I join you and your family for the most important meal of the day, now do you?"

"Of course not." He returned my smile, seeming to think everything was just dandy as he turned and led me back in the direction of the kitchen.

My smile flattened as I followed and I gazed at the back of Kaiser's head, picturing a bloody hole in it.

"Must be nice being the man of a house like this," I mused, my tone light, my expression dark. "Your balls must feel real big between your thighs, hm?"

Kaiser chuckled. "They do when they're slapping against the round ass of a twenty year old." He laughed louder and I echoed it. "Don't tell the wife though, the hookers are our little secret." He tossed a wink back at me over his shoulder and I mimed zipping my lips and throwing away the key.

We stepped into the huge kitchen with one violent orange wall and a large oval island in the middle of it with a black worktop. Kaiser's wife Jasmine was sitting there eating half a grapefruit in a transparent black robe that showed off a lot of tit. Beside her was a girl who I guessed was Kaiser's stepdaughter Mia, but I hadn't had the pleasure of fucking her yet – I mean meeting her.

She had a dark black bob of hair and full lips that looked like they'd seen plenty of cock. They weren't full of filler like her mother's and that made her all the more appealing to me. I liked my girls natural.

"Oh Shawn, we weren't expecting company," Jasmine piped up, looking me over appreciatively. I dumped my bag down on the table with a smirk, unzipping it as Kaiser moved to pour me some coffee. "Do I need an invitation to enjoy the pleasure of your company, Jasmine?" I purred and she blushed, waving a hand at me with a chuckle as my eyes slid onto Mia. "I don't think we've met in this life, angel, but I think we musta met in another, because I'm just tingling with recognition."

Mia frowned, not swallowing my lines as easily as her mother did and she sat up a little straighter in her seat, giving me a view of her tits in the grey teddy she wore. *Mm, come to daddy.*

"I'm gonna go back to bed," she muttered, pushing out of her seat, a bit of a pout about her lips. My eyes trailed down her as she moved towards me and I casually slid my shotgun out of my bag and swung it sideways to block her path, the barrel knocking against her chest.

"No, no, sweetheart, I want breakfast with the whole family," I purred as Jasmine shrieked and Kaiser took a step towards me in alarm.

"Drop it, Shawn, what the fuck are you playing at?" Kaiser demanded as I pushed Mia back by the tits and she hurried away to sit with her momma again, staring at me in fright.

I turned my attention to Kaiser, swinging my gun up to point at his fat head, watching all the blood drain from his face drop by drop. *That's it, sunshine, you're realising who the real power in this house is now, aren't you? Shouldn't've invited me in. I'm a vampire hungry for blood and there's no way I'm leaving without my fill of it.*

I swiped up a piece of French toast from his plate, taking a vicious bite out of it as I gazed at him. "Now that is delicious. Who made it?"

"M-mia," Kaiser stammered.

I finished the toast, licking the cinnamon off my fingers as I stared at Mia's tits. There was a little rage in her eyes as I glanced up and I smirked, looking forward to crushing that out of her.

"I'll call my men," Kaiser warned. "One shout from me and they'll come running."

I nodded, considering that as I slid my finger onto the trigger. "But if you shout, your head will go boom." I shrugged. "So I think you're gonna stay quiet, don't you?"

He swallowed then nodded quickly. "What do you want?"

"I want my name on the deeds of your house, old boy. How quickly do you think you can pull that together?" I arched a brow, expecting him to start begging and doing all the boring shit where he tried to make me change my mind. But he didn't do that, Kaiser nodded several times, eyeing the gun in my hand which was apparently enough to make him sell his whole empire to me. *Chicken shit.*

"Lead the way then," I said. "One wrong move and I'll shoot your arm off. Two wrong moves and it'll be your head."

He scurried toward the kitchen door and I jerked my chin at his wife and stepdaughter to make them walk ahead of me too, my gaze dropping to Mia's fine ass as I followed. I slid my gun under her teddy as we walked, pulling it up to bare her naked flesh to me and her shoulders stiffened.

"You were Maverick Harlequin's girl?" I asked and she glanced back at me with fear in her eyes, nodding once as I withdrew my gun.

"Stone," she corrected.

"Darlin', he's a Harlequin down to his core. So tell me, did he seem to enjoy it when he fucked that ass? I guess it made a change for him, being the one on top. Or did he make you wear a strap-on and do some prison roleplay with you?"

"Leave her alone," Jasmine hissed, pulling her daughter closer and I ran my tongue over my teeth.

"You don't give me orders around here, Mrs Rosewood. Oh and by the way, how does it feel knowing your husband fucks girls younger than your daughter?" I asked lightly. "He looks like a sweaty, grunting boar when he does it though, so maybe you're happy he sticks his dick in anyone but you. Are you faithful while you're away and he's here fucking barely legal pussy?" I asked, using my gun to brush a lock of hair from her shoulder.

"You're lying," she snarled.

"Am I liar, Kaiser?" I called and his shoulders tensed, not looking back as he muttered something under his breath. "Couldn't quite catch that, old boy, and I think the French toast is making my finger a little slippery on this trigger."

"He's not l-lying. I'm sorry, my love," Kaiser choked out and Jasmine raised a hand to her mouth in shock as she clutched Mia closer.

"Come now, don't be like that. You musta known on some level." I pushed my way between Jasmine and Mia, laying my arms over their shoulders as Kaiser unlocked his office and led us inside.

He started rifling through drawers looking for the deeds to this place and I looked at his wife under my right arm as tears ran down her cheeks. "You knew, come on. Kaiser's a dirty pervert, anyone can see that. Tell me you've at least been getting yourself some decent cock while you've been off on your sailing trips?"

She shook her head, silently sobbing and I gave her a pitying look. "Well honey, you sure made yourself available to me, didn't you? I'd only have had to unbuckle my belt and you would have dropped your panties for me, wouldn't you? Am I too late to take you up on the offer? Revenge fucking is the best kind."

She released a suppressed wail and shook her head. "Please, let Mia go," she begged.

"Aw, ain't you a good momma? My momma's good too, bless her heart. I think she'll like this place, not the décor though, it's fucking hideous," I said, pushing her away from me so she staggered into the desk. She hurried around it, staring back at us as I lowered my hand to Mia's ass and squeezed tight.

"Get off of me," Mia hissed.

"Just gimme a kiss, sweetheart. One kiss and maybe I won't blow your mommy and step daddy's brains out." I looked down at her, drawing her hard against my side as her hand splayed over my chest to try and hold me back. I winced as she pressed against the wound on my side and released a hiss through my teeth.

"Careful with me, sunshine, I've got a few battle wounds from a round with a feisty little rainbow shark. Now where's that kiss?"

She glanced over at her family then back at me with tears in her eyes then leaned up to peck my lips.

I chuckled as she drew away, fisting my hand in her hair and driving my tongue between her lips, taking a filthy fuck of a kiss in front of her parents as my cock twitched with interest. She was too easy right now though. I didn't bend girls over and fuck 'em until I was the centre of their universe.

But as I was waiting for my real challenge to come home, this one did look like a fairly interesting distraction to keep hold of until then. I reckoned a few weeks would have her falling to her knees for me and begging for my cock. That was how I liked them, destroyed from the inside out, then tethered to me in ways they couldn't even imagine. I got deep into women's minds and hooked them on me like a drug. I made them love me, obsess over me and then I fucked them like the good little whores they were whenever I felt like it. That was my favourite way to fuck a girl, when they were broken and confused, their thoughts not even their own anymore, and the one true thing they knew was that I was their rising sun. They wanted to worship me because I was their god, the one who gave them purpose. Who struck them down when they were bad and lifted them up when they were good. There was no rush quite like that, and nothing better than girls who claimed to hate me turned into pliant little whores who spread their legs on command.

Rogue had been the only one I'd never felt I fully owned. She'd never given me that look of love, though she'd been good enough at taking my cock. But I hadn't ever quite achieved the euphoria of knowing she was utterly and undeniably beneath my spell which was why I'd kept her around for so long. Of course, all good things came to those who waited and now that she'd risen from the dead for me, I was more determined than ever to finish what I'd started with her.

When I yanked my mouth off of Mia's, I shoved her to the floor, swinging my gun around to point at Kaiser. "What's taking so fucking long?" I barked and he jumped, his hands shaking as he yanked a document out of an iron safe on the floor.

"H-here," he stammered, picking up a pen and working to sign the property over to me.

I moved around the desk and leaned over his shoulder, making sure he did it right. When he was done signing everything into my name, my gaze hooked on a journal as he tried to quickly stuff it under a pile of papers. I shoved his hands away, plucking it up as my eyebrows arched.

"Now what do we have here?" I flicked open the brown, leatherbound journal which had Kaiser's name scrawled in the front of it, finding page after page of locations crossed out and hand drawn maps from places around Sunset Cove with huge Xs through them.

"What are you looking for, eh Kaiser?" I elbowed him, tapping the shotgun against his temple as I waved one of the pages in front of his face. "Start talking."

He huffed out a breath and I saw a demon in him then, not a scared little boy who was close to pissing his panties. Whatever it was he was hiding, he did not want me to know about it.

"Tick-tock," I encouraged, swinging my gun onto his wife instead. "Or we'll all find out if Jasmine's face makes a nice wall hanging."

She shrieked, ducking behind the desk as if that would save her from my wrath.

Kaiser kept his lips sealed and my eyebrows kept climbing. *Very interesting.*

"What's he looking for, Jasmine?" I stepped around the desk to point the gun at her and she trembled as Mia screamed, begging me not to shoot.

"Please!' Mia cried.

It was like a little preview of what she'd sound like when she was begging for me to fuck her raw. I winked at her as her mother shook her head several times.

"I don't know, I swear I don't know. I've never seen that journal before."

I chuckled, looking to Kaiser again. "You're a bad man, ain't ya Kaiser? Guy after my own heart. But why oh why would you hide this journal from your one and only?"

Kaiser's eyes darted from me to Jasmine and back again like they were playing a game of pinball. "I'll talk to you alone. You and me, Shawn. Man to man."

"You won't talk in front of your own wife? The woman you vowed to love and to hold and all that bullshit?" I tutted and he gave me a pleading look.

"Alright, alright, me and you," I agreed but then he lunged at me, making a grab for the journal and I fired my gun. The blast went off with a boom that made my whole body tingle and Jasmine's head was splattered across the room as Mia's screams tangled with the air. Pure music that was.

"You bastard!" Kaiser roared, lurching toward me in a clear attack but I just turned the gun on him and he backed right up to the wall as Mia's wild screams turned to sobs.

Goddammit, now he'd gone and made it harder for his stepdaughter to obsess over me. Not impossible, but definitely more of a challenge.

"Yeah, I'm a bastard, old boy," I agreed. "My daddy never made an honest woman outa my momma, but it never did me any harm. Now shut your stepdaughter up or she's gonna eat the next round."

"Mi-Mi," Kaiser sobbed. "Stop, honey, you need to stop."

Mia managed to stifle the noise coming outa her pie hole and I could think a little clearer again at last. I wound my finger through the air as I gave Kaiser a hard look.

"I'm gettin' bored, so tell me about the meaning of that journal or we're gonna have a lot more mess for your boys to clean up in here. Speaking of which…" I heard the shouts going up in the house and the boots coming this way in response to the gunshot.

"I'll be needing you to tell your men to hold fire." I directed Kaiser to the door and he stumbled that way, calling out to them as he made it there.

I stole a moment to kick the safe door wider and found myself a bunch of cash from his latest poker night. I gathered up as much as I could in my arms then an animal attacked me from behind. It was a feral girl with sharp teeth that dug into my shoulder. Mia punched me right in the wound in my side and I bellowed in pain as she tore at my flesh. I twisted around and hit her hard enough to drive the breath from her lungs, making her crumple to the floor in a heap.

I drew in a breath through my teeth as I clutched my side and growled through the pain.

"Jesus Christ, are all the women in this town raised by wolves?" I released a heady laugh as I scooped up the cash once more then followed Kaiser to the door where he was telling his men to back down. I pressed the shotgun to the side of his head as I kept my other arm locked around the money and smiled at the men there.

"Hey boys, this house is under new management. How much has Kaiser here been paying ya?"

One of the bolder ones stepped forward with a frown. "He's meant to pay us every Friday, but he owes us two weeks."

"I told you I just needed a little longer," Kaiser said in a panic.

I shook my head. "Oh dear, Kaiser. You've been holding out on your boys, sitting on all this cash while the wind whistles through their pockets. And if there's one thing I learned a long time ago, it's that if you're buying loyalty, you'd better be a generous boss who pays on time, and gives nice, juicy Christmas bonuses or you might just find yourself with a knife in your back while you're sleeping."

I tossed the cash at his men's feet, doing a sweeping count of all eight of them. "You can call that an advance on your pay or a ticket to fuck off outa here and never come back. You're either a Dead Dog or you're dead to me, so what do ya say?"

They glanced between one another and just like babies bribed with candy, they all swooped down to grab the cash.

"Wait, please," Kaiser gasped as I barked a laugh.

"Okay boys, fuck off." I jerked my gun and they headed away, all loyalty to Kaiser gone just like that. I felt Kaiser trembling and leaned in to whisper in his ear. "What are you looking for? Last chance to tell me, old boy." I pressed the journal to his chest and his hand slithered over it. "Then we can go looking for it together. You and me. I like ya, Kaiser. You and me could be real good friends, what do ya say?"

"You killed my wife," he choked out, though I didn't see any tears.

"I know, I know," I said, patting his back. "But listen, I've done you a favour, see? Cut you off from the old ball and chain. Now you're free to get a new wife, a younger one with perkier tits, or one of those twenty-year-olds you like so much. We could be kings in this house, parties every night, snorting cocaine off the asses of premium hookers who'll let you fuck 'em any way you like. That's what you really want, ain't it?"

He looked to me with a hopeful expression, showing just what a dirtbag he was as he saw a glimmer of a new, free life in my eyes where he could really be a king.

He swallowed hard then drew me out into the hall away from the sobbing Mia and licked the sweat gathering on his lips.

"There's a lost family fortune," he said in a rush of words, his eyes darting all about the place.

"What kinda fortune?" I asked, leaning in closer as he piqued my curiosity.

"Diamonds," he hissed, his eyes sparkling as if those diamonds lived right inside his eyes.

"Keep talkin'," I urged, my heart rate picking up a little, because fuck me, I liked the sound of this.

"Five of them, worth millions each," he said, his hungry eyes widening.

"You don't say…" A smile pulled at my lips. "But you don't know where they are?"

He shook his head. "All I know is they're hidden somewhere in Sunset Cove. This journal documents the places I've searched. I hunted hard back in my youth, but Luther Harlequin kicked me outa town after I, well…" He cleared his throat.

"You what?"

"I asked for his help to kill a bunch of men I owed money to," he said tightly, as sweaty as an old lettuce leaf.

"You were in debt? Now why doesn't that surprise me?"

He shrugged. "Anyway, I couldn't pay him either, could I? And he was gonna kill me real good so I told him about my diamonds. Said he could have them if he let me go, but I just needed some time to find them. He agreed, and I planned on skipping town as soon as I dug them up, but I couldn't fucking find them. So Luther ran me outa town."

"So how comes you're back then?" I frowned curiously, slotting all this information away for later.

"I won a bit of money in a poker game and I offered it to Luther if he let me move back here to keep looking for them. I said I wanted to be home to look after my old aunt."

"Who you keep in your basement?" I sniggered.

"She's a pain in my ass," he muttered. "She was meant to up and die but she just keeps on living, doesn't she? I haven't got the heart to kill her, but I needed my inheritance, so I put her down there and faked her death. I figured she had a few years left in her at best, but hell sometimes I think she's gonna live forever."

"Mmhmm." I clapped his face as I thought on that. "Well alrighty then. Looks like I've got a lot of work to do, doesn't it?"

"I can show you the places I've checked, and I've made a list in the back of the journal of where I'm going to look next. The Rosewoods used to own some land on the edge of town where an apartment block is now, I've been trying to work out a way to get access to the basement but-"

I pulled the trigger of my gun and blasted a huge hole in his chest, showering me in blood as he crashed to the ground before I stooped down and plucked the journal from his twitching fingers.

"Thank you kindly, Kaiser. I'll be sure to take it from here. But I'm afraid there's only room for one king on the throne of Sunset Cove."

Mia was screaming again and I kicked the office door shut to drown out her wailing, turning the key in the lock and pocketing it. I'd have one of the men put her somewhere I couldn't hear her crying because Lord have mercy, that noise was giving me a headache.

I caught sight of myself in a mirror across the hall, covered in blood with the cut across my cheek still shining as it healed up from Rogue's knife slash.

I ran my finger along it with a sneer, picturing exactly what I was gonna do to her in penance for that when she came to me. And while I was waiting, I'd move my army into my new castle and start looking for my diamonds.

I guessed things were looking up.

CHAPTER TWENTY FIVE

Darkness encircled me and a weight seemed to press down on my chest, keeping me in place. The soft brush of fingers ran over my temple and I thought of my mother, wondering if she was here somewhere, drawing me to her.

My mind was a groggy haze and the closer I came to surfacing from the thick, unshakeable sleep, the colder I got. I started to shiver and suddenly a voice reached me along with the scent of coconut and a thousand regrets. *She's here.*

"Nurse!" Rogue shouted and the heaviness of my left eyelid eased enough for me to open it, but I couldn't quite remember why the other one didn't work right then. "He's shivering. What's happening?"

"It's alright, dear, it's quite normal."

The light was too bright for a moment as the nurse moved into view and I blinked, trying to hunt for the girl I'd just heard, fearing I'd only imagined her.

"Can you see me alright, Mr Cohen?" the nurse asked and I nodded vaguely, trying to crane my neck to see past her, but she wouldn't budge.

My teeth were chattering and the woman started laying blankets over me before doing some checks. Pain swam through my left leg and a curse escaped my lips. The nurse fiddled with an I.V. beside me and the morphine slid into my veins, starting to take the pain away, but it made my mind fuzzier too.

"Where is she?" I demanded. "I heard her."

I've lost my mind. She's not here. Why would she be here? She despises me.

My mind hooked on Maverick, the fragments of my memories drawing together to paint a picture of him saving me. That didn't sound right, but somehow I knew it was. And it was the only thing I could grasp right then that was definitely real.

The nurse finally stepped back and my gaze fell on Rogue, standing there in one of my grey tank tops, her eyes puffy, her hair pulled into a messy ponytail. My heart thrashed with the need to get closer, but I was still fairly sure my mind was playing tricks on me. This was a pretty illusion, one of the thousands I'd had down in the basement at the Rosewood Manor.

"I'll let you two have some privacy." The woman patted Rogue's arm as she headed away and I took in every detail of my little one's face just in case she disappeared.

"Chase," she broke the silence, her voice half a sob, half a laugh. She climbed onto the hospital bed, wrapping her arms around me and a manic sort of noise left my throat.

Very funny. This isn't real.

My head was a swirling mist, trying to pull me back down into the dark away from her. But I was going to cling to this perfect daydream for as long as I could.

I pushed my hand into her hair and felt her teardrops on my shoulder like hot wax, trickling over my flesh in a burning trail.

"Don't cry, little one," I murmured, drawing her closer as I stole a moment in this fantasy.

I drew her chin up, finding her mouth and stealing a kiss that tasted all too like reality. Her fingers knotted in my hair and I kissed her harder, biting her lip and enjoying the sweet illusion my mind had conjured. The dark was pulling me down again so I was gonna forge a memory I couldn't forget even when I was lost to the nothingness.

"You said you love me, little one," I spoke against her full lips, sea salt and sugar rolling over my tongue. "Can you imagine what a mess we'd have been together if that was true?" I laughed, delirium crawling through my mind.

"Ace," she breathed against my mouth. "I'm so sorry I didn't look for you. We thought you were dead."

"But I am dead," I said, a dark smile twisting up my lips before it flittered away again. "Shawn said I didn't get a grave, is that true? I always thought gravestones were pointless anyway. Countless memories, loves and hates then you're just reduced to a few words on a rock. What would my words be, little one? Here lies a failure?"

She released a cracked sob, her fingers trailing along my cheek. All too real, all too perfect. *I hope she stays forever.*

"You've got a lot of drugs in your system," she choked out. "You're not thinking clearly. The doctors had to operate. But you're okay, Ace. You're right here in Sunset Cove with me. You're home."

Home...

Home was where three boys and one girl sat in the sand with me. This wasn't home, it was a place I couldn't stay.

I stared into her blue eyes which were always so much brighter than mine. The sky didn't compare to these eyes.

"And where are we going next? On a boat to dive at the Mariner's shipwreck?" I mused, memories sliding through my mind of doing just that. I'd spent too much of my adulthood being a dull fuck. I missed going on adventures with my family, I missed swimming as deep into the ocean as I could before I was forced to come up for air.

"Is that where you want to go?" she asked, curling up against me.

"As long as you're there," I muttered, carving my fingers down each rivet of her spine.

My mind started to catch up a little more to everything and a deep chill set into my bones as I remembered Shawn. I tried to shut him out but he drove in deeper, the ghosts of every piece of me he'd killed now living beneath my flesh to haunt me.

"Shawn Mackenzie's a demon," I whispered and Rogue clutched me tighter. "I never believed in monsters until I faced him in the dark. And now's he's here..." I walked my fingers up to my chest, tapping them hard against the bone. "Here to stay."

"Don't say that," she gasped, staring up at me from where she lay against my chest.

I stroked my thumb along her cheek and up to her temple. "But you know anyway, don't you? Because now he's left his mark on me, I can see him in you too."

She swallowed hard, then nodded in admission, turning her head into my palm to lay a kiss there. Where her lips touched, the cold was burned away and for a moment I didn't feel Shawn's hold on me at all. But the second her mouth parted from my flesh, the cold dug in deeper and I could hear his laughter echoing in the back of my mind.

"That's what he does," I said. "He's a master at burrowing beneath skin and bone, finding unhealed wounds and peeling them further apart to make room for him. But you survived him, little one."

"You did too," she said fiercely, her eyes watering again and I cocked my head as I gazed at her, not wanting to talk about Shawn anymore.

"You're my biggest regret," I said in a low voice, darkness curling through the corners of my mind. "You're a goddess forsaken by a fool. And he bled, and bled, and bled for you in penance, but it was still just the blood of a fool."

"Chase, don't. You need to rest, you need to get better. You're not thinking straight," she urged.

"What would I get better for?" I murmured as sleep tried harder to claim me, but I didn't want to go back to the dark. That was where all my fears lay. I wanted to stay here in my daydream and hold onto a forged reality where Rogue rested her head on my chest and things didn't seem so bleak.

"For me," she said. "I'll break if you leave again. Please don't go."

"Wouldn't want that," I said sleepily, my eye sliding closed as sleep fought to kidnap me. "But I'm good at breaking things. Don't always mean to, but they tend to end up broken anyway."

"Just rest," she urged.

"Only if you promise you'll be here when I wake up." I didn't hold much hope of that, but even just a sliver of it was enough to help me let go of the fantasy I was trying so desperately to keep alive.

"I'll be here." She hooked her little finger around mine and kept it there as the drugs washed deeper into my veins, and soon there was only black.

CHAPTER TWENTY SIX

I paced the hall leading to the front door, Mutt looking from me to the door with a low whine in his throat. He was missing Rogue and fuck, I was too, even if she did hate me. And I'd been anxious as hell since Chase had shown up and been admitted to hospital. I didn't sleep, I just festered, waiting and waiting for them to come home. And today, after five days in hospital with Rogue never leaving his side, he finally would.

How could this have happened?

We'd stopped looking for him. We should have been looking all this time. *All this time.*

Fox had agreed he could stay here at Harlequin House for his recovery period but that was it. I couldn't even think about him leaving again though, I just needed him here in this house. I needed to see him and convince myself he was actually still in this world. Because frankly I was having a hard goddamn time believing it.

Fucking Shawn had had him and we hadn't known. Rogue had kept Fox informed on anything Chase said, and Fox always filled me in. And we'd all been stunned silent when we'd found out Miss Mabel was still alive, locked down in a basement by her asshole nephew. It was sickening, and we were definitely going to do something about just as soon as we could figure out how.

My mind turned to my brother again. I felt like I'd failed Chase. I'd never felt the finality of his death even after all these weeks. Maybe I should have realised he was out there. Maybe-

"They're almost here," Fox's deep voice came from behind me and I twisted around, finding him standing in the shadows with his shoulder propped against the wall and his eyes on his phone.

I had no idea how long he'd been there, but I guessed it was long enough for him to see what a wreck I was. Rogue was bringing Chase back in a wheelchair accessible cab that Fox had booked for them and my heart was lurching in every direction as I waited for them to arrive.

"He's not back in the Crew, JJ," Fox said in a low voice as he tucked his phone away.

"I know," I said quickly.

"Just don't get attached to him being here. I know what you're like."

"The guy's been captive to fucking Shawn, Fox," I took a step toward him as I bristled at those words. "I thought he was dead. What do you expect me to be like?" I'd barely slept since we'd left him at the hospital, working extra hours just so I could try and keep myself busy and not think about all the shit that must have been happening to him at Shawn's hands.

Rogue answered my texts about him with one word responses, clearly still pissed as hell at me and I couldn't even blame her. I'd been a fucking asshole, and I'd felt like a dick about it ever since, but I didn't even know what to do to fix it at this point. She'd moved closer to Fox every day since we'd called it quits just like I'd known she would, and the worst part about that was that I'd driven her there. Maybe it was better this way, ripping the Band-Aid off myself rather than letting her do it for me down the road. I just wished it didn't feel like fucking dying.

I felt like utter shit any time I thought of giving her that stupid bill to pay for my services. It had been so immature and every time I remembered her paying me the money, I wanted to destroy something. She'd been so angry with me and who could blame her?

I'd shoved the cash in my nightstand drawer, not touching a single dollar of it since, but every time I slept in my room I could feel it there. And it felt like regret and shame.

Fox swallowed and I could see how hard he was trying to mask his own pain over Chase. The day we'd come home from the hospital after we'd found him, we'd just sat up all night talking about Chase and Shawn and all the things this could mean. We'd drank our weight in Chase's favourite rum and ended up falling asleep out on the sun loungers, sharing in our relief, our pain. But since then, he'd shut down again, sliding his Harlequin armour back in place.

"We have to be careful. We don't know what he's told Shawn," Fox said, a crease forming on his brow.

"He wouldn't sell us out," I scoffed in disbelief.

"I don't know what he'd do anymore," he muttered. "He already betrayed us once."

"Fox…" I started, but the sound of a car pulling up outside the door reached me and I ran forward, wrenching it open as Mutt started barking.

Rogue was already out of the cab, grabbing the wheelchair from the trunk and Chase pushed the door open and hopped out. He dropped into the chair as Rogue rolled it up to him. She propped up his left leg which was in a cast, and I took in the gauze he had taped over his left eye too.

He wore a simple white tank top and black shorts, but wherever I could see exposed flesh there were cuts, old wounds and burn marks. My heart broke all over again and I found myself just standing there, frozen in place as Rogue greeted Mutt then moved to wheel Chase towards the house, ignoring me entirely. The dog immediately jumped up onto Chase's lap, making him curse as he made his bad leg jolt and the dog sat facing me as he used Chase like a moving throne.

"Hey," I said hoarsely as Rogue pushed him right up to me and I knew I was blocking the way inside, but I still couldn't make myself move.

"Hey," Chase said with the ghost of a smile on his lips, but it was quickly swallowed by the darkness in his gaze and a look of utter fucking horror which hung about him. I needed to make that go away, I knew it in my soul. It was my damn duty to heal that pain somehow, but I didn't know where to begin.

"I was just telling Chase how badass he's gonna look with an eyepatch," Rogue said, her gaze glinting but I didn't miss the ripple of pain that ran through her expression. "Don't you agree, J?"

She was playing the I-don't-give-a-fuck act again, talking to me like nothing had happened between us and that was worse than being on the receiving end of her anger. At least when she was shouting at me, I knew she cared. But when she was like this, it was as if the two of us had never even happened.

Right now, I needed to put on a brave face for Chase, so I slapped on a grin that stretched a little too tight across my skin and nodded my agreement. "Yeah, it'll be cool, man. You'll be like Nick Fury from The Avengers."

"You don't have to do that," Chase said, looking away from me. "I'm not a kid. I know what this is gonna be like and it ain't nothing good."

Rogue flicked his ear. "Don't be a Debbie downer. Scars are hot."

"Mm," he grunted and I smirked.

"She's right, dude, you're gonna get so laid," I said, aiming to cheer him up but he just looked empty and that killed me. The sheer fucking happiness and relief I'd felt at having him back was now being wholly swallowed by that void in his gaze. What had Shawn done to him? Was he ever gonna be alright again?

I finally got out of his way and Rogue pushed him up to the front door and I lifted the wheels to help him into the house.

Fox stood staring at Chase for an endless moment where the world was entirely silent and I felt the tension rolling through the air like toxic fumes.

"You can stay here until you can walk again," he said eventually, his voice hard as he turned away and Rogue started pushing Chase along after him. "You'll stay in your old room. The rest of this house is off limits."

"Badger," Rogue started in a growl.

"Those are my terms," Fox barked and I gave Rogue a look that told her not to push him on this. I was all for doing it soon, but at this second I just wanted Chase home and I'd figure out how to keep him here later.

She rolled her eyes at me, but didn't say anything more as we reached the stairs and Fox looked anywhere but at Chase as he pointed up them.

"Thank you," Chase said quietly.

Fox's gaze slid onto him and his jaw ticked for several seconds as he took in his broken brother. "Did you tell Shawn anything that will harm anyone in this house or anyone in my Crew?" he demanded.

"Of course he didn't," I growled.

"I didn't ask you," Fox shot at me, still glaring at Chase.

"Nothing," Chase said and my heart tugged. "I swear I didn't tell him anything."

Fox nodded stiffly then moved forward and offered Chase his hand. "JJ, help me bring him upstairs."

"I can manage," Chase started, but Rogue flicked his ear again.

"What are you gonna do? Crawl up there like a zombie?" she asked and he huffed, their little back and forth so familiar that it made a smile twitch at my lips. What I'd give to go back to it being all four of us in this house, even when Chase had acted like he hated her.

Mutt jumped out of Chase's lap, growling at Fox before running off upstairs.

Chase muttered something incoherent, but let Fox help him out of the chair and slung his arm around his neck as he balanced on his good leg. I drew his other arm over my shoulders and locked my arm around his waist to support him - and fuck it, I took a tight hug too because I'd seriously missed him. He didn't smell right though, he smelled like hospital chemicals and eucalyptus. It wasn't him. And that choked me up inside. This wasn't the man I'd known before Shawn had taken him, he was changed in ways I could probably never understand. And it was destroying me.

Rogue hovered behind us as we made it to the landing and practically carried him to his room. Inside, we laid him down on his bed and he sighed in a way that was full of complete relief, his good eye closing and a moment of peace passing across his expression.

"I'll bring some food and water up," Fox murmured, striding quickly to the door but I didn't miss the agony in his expression before he left.

Mutt reappeared, jumping onto the bed and laying down next to Chase, resting his chin on his stomach and Chase brushed his fingers over his fur in a fluid motion.

"Do you need anything?" I asked as Rogue moved to prop Chase's broken leg up on some pillows.

"No, this is just...perfect," Chase breathed and I was pretty sure he fell right asleep.

"It's the pain meds," Rogue explained, moving onto the bed and brushing a few dark curls off of Chase's forehead. "I think I only got him to take them because he was too weak to fight me off. But they make him sleepy." Her voice broke on the last word and suddenly she was crying and I rushed onto the bed too, wrapping her in my arms as I felt my own heart breaking in time with hers.

I knew she hated me, but I just needed her to be okay, and frankly getting Chase back put so much of my petty bullshit into perspective. She resisted my hold for two seconds before she just clung onto me and tried to hide her face against my chest so I wouldn't see her cry.

"He'll get better," I promised.

"I can't bear it, Johnny James, all this time he was alive, suffering, thinking no one was coming for him. That no one even cared."

I held her tighter, my breaths harder to grasp at the thought of that. "He's here now," I rasped. "We just have to focus on getting him back to himself."

She nodded, sniffing as Mutt moved to lick her arm and whine gently like he was trying to comfort her too. She pulled away from me at last, wiping her tears as she curled up beside Chase and didn't look at me again. She'd slipped into my embrace and now that she was absent once more, I felt her missing from me like a vital organ.

Chase was out for the count, but there was no way I wanted to be anywhere away from him, so I lay down on his other side and Mutt curled up between him and Rogue.

Rogue gently pushed her fingers through Chase's hair, staring at his face like she was afraid he might disappear if she blinked. My mind spun and a veil seemed to lift from it that had hidden the truth from me this whole time. Because I suddenly understood everything so fucking clearly in that moment, understood all she'd been trying to tell me, understood how it made absolute sense when it came to all of us even if it didn't make any sense to the rest of the world.

"You and him…" I started, unsure how to say it, but her watery eyes snapped to mine and the truth was right there in the depths of them. She didn't even try to hide it, she just nodded, but then doubts flickered over her features and she looked back at Chase.

"We kissed," she admitted and I was surprised at how little that bothered me after the anger I'd felt over seeing her kiss Fox. Though that was more to do with how much I feared losing her to him. He'd openly loved her his whole life, decided they were destined to be together, but I didn't factor into that plan and I knew he'd do anything to make sure it happened. And why wouldn't she want Fox? He could provide her everything she'd ever need. He was gonna be the king of this whole town one day and why would she choose to settle down with some sex worker over him?

"When Fox banished him, I went to see him at Raiders Gym. We were both so angry at each other, so hateful," she whispered, her voice thick with emotion. "But that's the problem, JJ, I think part of the reason I hate him so much is because I don't hate him at all."

"He doesn't hate you either," I said in a low voice. "Ever since you got back, he's been acting like a kid who can't handle his emotions. But that's what he is, Rogue. He never did learn to handle shit because he never had anyone to teach him how. And after you left, he shut down. He didn't talk to me and Fox about his pain over you. He just started drinking, numbing it out and refusing to deal with everything he was harbouring. But sometimes he'd get so drunk, he'd tell me how broken he was inside, how he didn't think he'd be whole again unless you came home, and how he was afraid that if you did he'd lose you anyway because he was never good enough to have you."

She sighed, resting her head on Chase's shoulder as she gazed at him. "Why is everything such a mess?"

"I don't know, pretty girl," I said sadly, even though she hadn't really been talking to me.

Her gaze slid to me and I got caught staring at her, an ache of regret in me over what I'd done. Chase showing up again made me realise how fucking juvenile I'd been, how things could be so fucking bad at the turn of the wind.

Words burned in my chest which I was desperate to say, but somehow I couldn't force them out. Because I couldn't take back what I'd done. I'd fucked my one chance with her and shattered her trust all over again. *I'm sorry I've been an asshole, I'm just afraid to lose you.*

I couldn't make my tongue bend around those words though, because they weren't enough. So I just pressed closer to my brother, shutting my eyes and bathing in the feeling of having him home. There was a wedge cut out of my heart in the shape of him and now that it was back, I was going to fight to keep him here for good. I wasn't sure how I was gonna convince Fox of that, but I'd damn well figure it out. The four of us needed each other, he had to see that. And surely Chase had paid plenty for his crimes against us now. The problem was, Fox was one stubborn asshole and I had the feeling convincing him would be about as easy as moving an immovable wall. But I'd try. I just had to try.

I woke to a crash and jerked upright, pushing Chase's arm aside where it was stretched over me. The lamp had been knocked over and had smashed to pieces.

"Turn the light on!" he barked.

"Woah, woah," I tried to calm Chase down as he shoved me and fought me, his nails digging into my skin.

He tried to scramble his way over me to get off the bed and I forced him back, but he didn't stop fighting me, seeming to be in some frantic trance.

"It's me, man," I told him, trying to see him in the darkness and his hands eased up on me, starting to shake instead.

"The light," he begged. "Put the light on, JJ."

I got out of bed, striding across the room and switching it on, just as the door flew open and Fox stood there in his boxers with a gun raised.

"It's alright," I said, knocking the gun aside and he lowered it, looking from me to the bed where Rogue still had an arm draped around Chase's heaving chest, fast a-fucking-sleep.

"What's going on?" Fox growled, stepping into the room and looking to me for an explanation, avoiding Chase's pinched expression.

I didn't exactly have an answer so my lips just sort of hung slack and Chase answered for me.

"He left me in the dark a lot," he muttered. "For a second I thought I was still…" he trailed off, his jaw ticking and a flush of embarrassment sliding into his cheeks. Anger knotted my chest at that and I strode back to him, kneeling on the bed and getting in his line of vision.

"You're home, Ace," I said firmly. "You're not going anywhere."

I felt Fox bristling at those words, but he didn't say anything to contradict them and I was thankful for that. Chase's frantic gaze eased and he leaned back against the headrest with a sigh of relief, placing his hand on Rogue's back. She'd shimmied out of her t-shirt at some point so she was just in her sports bra and panties. She nestled closer to him in her sleep, her fingers tightening on his flesh as she murmured his name.

I looked to Fox, finding him fighting a war in his eyes before he turned and marched away in the direction of his room, leaving the door wide open.

Chase's good eye was scrunched shut as he held Rogue to him in a way that said he'd be hard pressed to let her go.

I moved to the far window, twitching the curtains open and gazing down at the patio area, the sky just beginning to pale. My heart weighed a thousand tons as I stood there, hurting for Chase and knowing that he was never going to be same after what had happened to him.

I soon found myself sliding back into bed, breathing in the scent of him and trying to find peace in the fact that the four of us were together in this house again. But somehow all I could find was turmoil. Because Rogue was angry with me, Chase was broken, Fox would never let him stay here long term, and Maverick was severed off from this family like a limb that could never be reattached. I felt the weight of all that following me back into sleep, where only nightmares waited for me.

The days slipped by and we fell into a routine where Fox avoided Chase as much as humanly possible, bringing food and drink to his room whilst refusing his requests for cigarettes and booze in place of his painkillers. Chase only took the meds if Rogue was there, letting her push them between his lips and swallowing them down with a glass of cold milk. Every time she did that, she kissed his cheek and something told me that was the part he did it for.

Whenever I watched him with her, it was clear to me beyond a shadow of a doubt that he was in love with her. I guessed I'd always known that, yet it had never been as plainly obvious to me as it was now. Something had shifted in him since his time with Shawn, and he didn't fight his urges to watch her anymore. Now his gaze followed her like he was the earth and she was the sun, the centre of his universe, the reason his world kept turning. And the only thing I found myself feeling about that was sad. Because Fox was going to send him away again, and he knew that. It was probably why he was letting himself look at her so much, because his recovery period was all he had left with her. And if I'd been locked up and tortured in a basement for weeks on end, sure I'd never see Rogue again only to find her in front of me once more, I knew I'd want to drink in every moment with her too.

Since I'd been working so much, I hadn't seen Rogue that often. I missed her so damn hard and I hated this tension between us. But I'd probably fucked any chance of us even being friends again. Let alone anything else.

Fuck.

I despised myself over the bullshit move I'd pulled with the bill. What the hell had I been thinking? I'd pushed her away, and for what? She was the best thing I'd ever had and I'd cut her off because I was too afraid to believe she could really want me. The money she'd paid me with was still in the envelope she'd given me, sitting in my top drawer and making me feel sick every time I looked at it. The idea of what we'd had being reduced to a transaction tore into the most broken parts of my soul but I was the one who had done that. Not her. And I didn't know how to take it back.

After I'd helped Chase have a shower and put him into some shorts for the day, I propped him up against the pillows on his bed and changed the dressing on his right eye, taking in the savage X cut through it as I did so. The doctors had repaired it as best they could and it was healing up well, but he was never gonna see through it again, the best he could hope for was flickers of light. It hurt me, all of these wounds, each one like a knife in my chest, but somehow this one was the worst of all.

I should never have stopped looking for him.

"You should talk to her," he said after a while, making me frown. He didn't say all that much since he'd come back and the first thing I thought was how fucking good it was to hear his voice, but then his words settled in and I knew he'd picked up on the rage between me and Rogue. I mean, I guessed it wasn't that hard to detect with the way we kept sniping at each other and subtlety had really never been her thing.

I sat on the edge of the bed as I finished redressing his wound.

"Who?" I muttered, playing dumb and he cocked his head to the side, giving me a dry look that was so Chase it made me crack a grin.

Fox was out for his morning run so it wasn't like I needed to watch my mouth, and Chase knew about us anyway, I just hadn't wanted to talk to him about this shit because I knew how he felt about Rogue. And I wasn't gonna be an asshole and ask his advice on how best to get her back to being with me, not when he was lying in bed here like this.

"We're fine. We just had a disagreement." I shrugged it off, but he caught my arm as I went to get up, making me look back at him.

"Don't let her go, JJ," he growled fiercely, a dark and urgent need in his expression. "She deserves someone like you. You're the best guy I know, the one of us who kept a piece of the kids we all were. You're the right choice for her." He didn't have to say it, but those words spoke of the thing he wasn't saying anyway. That *he* wasn't the right choice. That he never had been. And I could see plainly that he'd given up on ever claiming her for himself.

"Don't say that," I hissed, aware that Rogue was only downstairs making coffee and she could return at any second. I tried to pull my arm free of his grip, but his fingers tightened to the point of pain as he gazed at me in desperation.

"I have to say it. And I need you to hear it," he said, darkness unfolding within his bright blue eye which was pinned on me. "You can give her what she always wanted. She needs a home. This is it."

"And what about Fox?" I whispered. "Where does he factor in? Because the last time I checked, he was willing to kill to keep anyone else's hands off of her. Maybe you were right before, Ace, maybe what I did is gonna destroy us. Or maybe we're gonna forget we were ever together and she'll end up in Fox's arms and he'll never let go."

"Bullshit. She looks at you like you're breaking her heart. So stop breaking it and just work it out. Find a way, JJ," he growled. "And make Fox understand."

"He'll shoot me," I scoffed.

"He didn't shoot me," he tossed back.

"That's different," I murmured, my temple pulsing at the memory of seeing my brother on his knees.

"Well tell me this, J, are you gonna just let her go? Give her up and forget you ever loved her?" he asked with a razor sharp edge to his tone.

I was already shaking my head. "You know I can't forget her."

"So take it from someone who knows what regret is, if you love her then find a way to keep her. And if you love Fox, then find a way to keep him too. Clearly I don't have advice on how to achieve any of that. But I suggest you start by doing the exact opposite of anything I'd do."

"Ace…" I sighed, but then the door pushed open and Rogue appeared with a tray of coffees and Mutt bounding along behind her.

Chase gave me a look that told me to talk to her as she placed the coffees down on the nightstand.

"I got you a gift," she said, biting her lip as she looked at Chase and reached into her denim shorts' pocket. She produced a black eyepatch, dangling it on her finger enticingly.

"No," Chase said dismissively as he stared at it and I snorted a laugh.

"Oh come on, it'll suit you, Ace, and you can only keep that dressing on like another day anyway," she insisted. "Ooh unless you wanna go all Scarface on the world?" Her eyes lit up at that idea, biting her bottom lip as if she liked it. He thought on her words before snatching the eyepatch from her and staring at it in his palm with a dark frown.

My chest tugged at his expression and I hated how he looked so disgusted by it. Then he shoved it under his pillow and looked away from her. She grabbed a glass of milk from her tray along with two pills, moving onto the bed beside him and pushing them between his lips. He didn't look at her as she poured the milk into his mouth and his throat bobbed as he swallowed. But then she leaned in, pressing her mouth to his cheek and his good eye slid onto her, staring, fucking captivated and shattered at once. Then he looked at me with an expression that told me to fix my shit with her and I couldn't deny him anything in that moment.

I took her hand as she leaned back and Mutt jumped up, settling himself in beside Chase and shutting his eyes, not quite touching him as he stacked his little front paws on top of one another.

"We need to talk," I told Rogue, tugging her to her feet and she looked about to protest but I just towed her out of the room and didn't give her the choice.

"Sorry I'm all out of cash, JJ, I can't afford a fuck this morning," she said bitterly as I walked her straight into her room and kicked the door shut behind us.

I let her go and skirted around her to my nightstand, taking out the wad of cash she'd given me to pay the bill I'd handed her. Fuck, I felt like a cunt for that. I had to try and fix it.

"Here." I strode around to face her as she folded her arms and glared at me.

"No thanks," she said lightly as I held it out to her.

"It's yours. I'm not keeping it. I was a fucking piece of shit to you, and I wish I'd never handed you that bill. It was a shitty thing to do."

"Yup, it was," she said and I waved the cash at her again. She turned away from it and I caught her hand, trying to press it into her palm. "No, JJ. I don't want it." She smacked it out of my hands and bills cascaded everywhere, raining down on my bed.

She strode past me, trying to make it to the door but I stepped into her path, barring her way out.

"Please, just wait. I'm sorry," I said on a heavy breath, tasting her on the air and instantly hungering for more. "I was an asshole. The biggest fucking asshole in the history of assholes and I'm so damn sorry."

"Correction, you *are* an asshole," she said, her chin rising.

"Yeah, but you gotta forgive me, because every day you keep looking at me like that is destroying me and I know you're hurting too. I know I deserve this pain and I know I have no right to make you stay here and hear me out, but I need you to, pretty girl. Please."

I walked towards her so my chest pressed to hers and she moved onto her tiptoes, leaning back as she tried not to stumble from the pressure of my body against hers.

"Fuck you," she hissed, a wall in her eyes and frustration raced through me.

"You know what Rogue?" I stepped forward, making her stumble but she pressed right back against me like she could possibly move me. I was a force driving her toward the bed and unless she could stop me, that was where we were headed.

"What, Johnny James?" she asked venomously.

"You and me never made sense back when we were kids," I growled. "I was the nice one of the group, and you always needed someone edgier than that. But I'm not nice anymore, pretty girl. Haven't been for a long time. I might joke and laugh with you, but on the inside my soul is painted black. My wings got cut off the first time I sold my body and ever since then I've been walking the road to hell. But now I'm bad, I'm not bad enough."

"What's that supposed to mean?" she scoffed.

"It means you need more than that," I growled. "Like luring me to Dead Man's Isle to share you with my enemy."

"You seemed pretty happy to play along at the time. I didn't drag you into the water. You've got weird lines, J. Kinda confusing for a girl, wouldn't you agree?"

I pressed harder against her, making her stumble again and she slammed her hands to my shoulders, trying to keep me back but she wasn't really trying all that hard.

"Sharing you with a guy – who fucking hates me by the way – is far more than confusing. It's a headfuck."

"So you don't hate him back?" she asked lightly and I bared my teeth.

"Of course I do," I growled, but there wasn't an edge to my voice like there used to be when I said that. Hate was a big word for someone who'd once been like a brother to me. "But we're getting off topic."

"Seems pretty on topic to me. You know this is a headfuck for me too, right? I'm not exactly Miss Pornstar here shooting Fifty Shades of Cock, I don't know what I'm doing."

"That's the problem," I growled, forcing her back another step and pinning her between me and the bed, the backs of her legs bowing ever so slightly as she fought to stay upright. "We're all lost again, just like we used to be. Fox tries to control the whole world so he can live under the illusion that he's in command, Maverick pretends there aren't any rules except the ones he makes up, Ace fought against every instinct in his body to try and hold onto the only people he was sure would stick around, and I'm here trying to prove to you that I'm a man when inside all I feel like is a stupid boy who didn't know what to do with you as a kid and still doesn't know what to do with you as a man. And *you*," I snarled, fisting her shirt in my hand and yanking her up so she was on the very tips of her toes. "You're just trying to find your way back to a home that doesn't look the way it did when you once lived in it. But it's still the same home, still the same boys. The problem is, we all put on different kinds of armour that are keeping us from recognising each other. But I see you, Rogue. I see your walls and your damage and I feel the weight of the baggage that ten years gave you. So I'm lenient because maybe you do need Maverick as well as me, and maybe you need Fox and Ace too. But we all know there's no future that exists where that works, so what are we gonna do about it?"

Her eyes searched mine, her breaths falling heavily against my mouth as I held her almost off her feet. She looked so fucking hot like that, caught in my trap, panting for me. I'd been hard for her the moment I'd walked into this room, but we were teetering on the edge now, either about to fall all the way into this messed up relationship that didn't look like any other I'd ever known. Or we were going to pull apart and keep moving in opposite directions, ripping out each other's hearts all over again. And really, it was her choice. Because I may have been angry, but I was still hers to do what she wanted with.

"I want to tell Fox," she admitted. "But I can't lose him."

"If we stay together, we lose him, if we don't, we lose each other," I said, anger twisting up my insides. It wasn't fucking fair. Ten years I'd waited for her and now keeping her meant losing my brother. And neither reality was bearable.

"What's the answer?" I demanded of her in a snarl, furious at her, at Fox at the whole fucking universe.

"I don't have one," she said, her eyes blazing with emotion. "All I know is I want you, I want you so fucking bad Johnny James, but sometimes I want him too. And it can't come to me choosing, I won't. Because if I have to, the choice will come down to it being all of you or none of you. Like it always was."

"Goddamn you, pretty girl," I growled, tugging on her shirt and forcing her lips up against mine. "You know how this ends." Our lips grazed, tasting like coconut and temptation and as my cock drove against her, I knew where this was headed because I couldn't resist her. When we were this close, it was like the moon driving the tide. Nothing could stop it crashing against the shore, pulled by forces beyond our control.

"I can't keep away," she croaked, her fingers moving up to knot in my hair and she kissed me, trying to tease my mouth apart, to let her in and I just remained there as I enjoyed her wanting more from me.

I slid my hand down her spine and squeezed a handful of her ass so tight she gasped, her lips parting and I drove my tongue between them, kissing her with all the blinding fury building in my chest.

"Maybe Chase was right, maybe you are our downfall," I sniped at her and she clawed at my arms with a growl.

"Fuck you," she snapped. "It takes two to fucking tango."

"Not when you tango with me, pretty girl." I flipped her around by the hips in a dance move that made her suck in a sharp breath, yanking her back against me. I moved my mouth to her ear, rocking her hips in time with mine as I forced her to dance with me, grinding my cock against her and giving her no choice in the matter. "I'm not blaming you, in fact, this is me officially taking the blame from your shoulders. Because I'm no longer offering you a choice in this relationship."

"JJ," she panted and I spun her back around to face me, swinging her low across the bed and yanking her up to meet my mouth.

She was slack in my arms, letting me move her body how I liked and I fucking loved it. I kept one hand firm on her ass, guiding her hips as I pressed my knee between her thighs and made her grind on me in a rhythm that fit the music in my head. But I needed that music to spill beyond my flesh and fill this room to the brim. So I slid my phone from my pocket, hooking it up to the Bluetooth Beats Pill in her room and playing the song rolling through my mind. I See Red by Everybody Loves an Outlaw.

I fisted my hand in her hair, tugging backwards and running the tip of my nose up her throat. Then when she was bent backwards to her limit, I let go of her so she fell onto the bed beneath me onto all the cash and it pooled around her like a green sea. I ground over her, rolling my hips in time to the sultry music and she carved the heel of her palm down my spine as I fed on heat of the dance, lost to the beat as I enjoyed my two favourite things in the world.

I hooked her legs around my waist, rocking my hips as her back arched and her tits were pressed to my face. I forced her sports bra over them, sucking her left nipple into my mouth before dragging the thing over her head and tossing it away. Her thighs locked around me and I stood up as I held onto her, pressing her to me with a hand on her spine and spinning her around as she clung to me. The bass of the music pounded in my skull so loud it was all I could hear and as she dropped to her feet, I caught her hand and spun her in a pirouette, grabbing hold of her little denim shorts in the same movement and ripping them clean from her body, making her breath hitch. She didn't have any panties underneath them and I growled my approval as I spun her back into my chest and her hand fell against my shoulder as she looked up at me. I ran two fingers down her spine, her naked flesh hot and perfectly silken against mine.

We both stopped moving and she reached for my shorts, unthreading the drawstring while our eyes remained locked and my heart hammered just for her. I couldn't look away, falling so deep into the blues of her irises I didn't think I'd ever get out. And suddenly I was moving, shoving her back onto the bed and climbing on top of her as I claimed her mouth with a dirty, desperate kiss. I was lost, my mind a haze of her and nothing else as I pushed my shorts down and slammed into her in one furious drive of my hips.

A gasp escaped me as I fisted my hand in the pillow above her head along with several fifty dollar bills, realising way too fucking late that I'd forgotten a condom for the first time in my life. She was so wet, so tight, so hot.

"Oh fuck," I groaned.

"Don't stop," she demanded, her mouth finding mine and I automatically obeyed, my hips rocking as I groaned at the sensation of her pussy around me, flesh on flesh.

Screw condoms. Screw every fucking condom in the world. I was never, ever using one again with this girl.

"Fuck, Rogue, oh fuck my fucking life," I cursed as I moved faster, gripping the backs of her thighs and driving so deep into her that she started screaming. She was so slick and silky and clenching me so fucking sweetly. I wasn't gonna last, I was a goner already.

Sweat beaded on my brow as I clung to the backs of her legs and fucked her brutally while she met every thrust with cries of encouragement, the headboard smacking against the wall and making sure Chase knew exactly what we were doing even if her cries hadn't given us away already.

Her nails tore into my back and my forehead fell to hers as we just became this one, perfect creature made of nothing but pleasure. The cash stuck to our flesh, getting everywhere and this was one fantasy I'd never realised I'd had as Rogue lay on a small mountain of money while we fucked like animals.

I needed to stop. I had to fucking stop. But I couldn't, she was too wet, too good and I was gonna go mad if I didn't finish inside her. I had to know what it felt like to do that, I just couldn't stop myself. I'd thought sex was amazing, but I'd been fucking delusional my whole life. Because without that sheath of latex between me and her, sex wasn't amazing it was *everything*. It was one helluva reason to fucking exist.

"Oh fuck, you feel so good," she moaned, her head falling back and rainbow hair spilling everywhere.

"I'm gonna come," I growled, my fingers clawing into the pillows as I tried to slow down, tried to force myself to pull out. But then she dug her heels into my ass, making me sink into her even deeper and my cock nearly burst with how perfect that felt.

"*Rogue*," I warned, but her lips met mine and I upped my pace, losing my mind and giving no fucks if I got committed after this. She was my reason for insanity and I fucking pleaded it.

Her pussy clenched my cock so hard, I knew she was coming before she even started moaning and fisting her own hair. I grabbed the headboard, rearing above her and finishing with a firm thrust that blew my fucking mind and my cum spilled deep into her pussy without anything to stop it.

"Fuck, fuck, fuck," I panted, my eyes scrunching up as the best orgasm of my life ripped through my cock.

I held my weight off of her as I just felt the hot, sticky mess between us and my face split into a wicked grin as I stared down at her. "We should have done that sooner."

She nodded mutely, pushing locks of hair out of her eyes. "Fuck me, Johnny James. I think your cock's been a prisoner to rubber for too many years

and now it's a free man making up for lost time. And do you dip it in honey
every morning because damn it's fucking smooth."

I pulled out of her, rolling onto my back beside her as I started laughing,
plucking a hundred dollar bill off my pec and tossing it away so it fluttered
down to land on her thigh. "No more condoms. I'm gonna burn them all."

She laughed, slapping my chest. "And what if I get pregnant?"

"You like kids, right?" I said and she slapped me again with a snort
laugh.

"No way, not happening."

"I can't go back, pretty girl. I've felt the greener grass," I said with a
smirk. "Your pussy's my new addiction."

"I think I'm getting a little ad*dick*tion of my own – get it a-*dick*-tion?
Like addiction but-"

"I get it, pretty girl," I chuckled.

She turned her head to grin at me but our smiles melted away as we just
stared at each other and my hand found hers on the bed, our fingers winding
together. I felt like that kid again, and for once I didn't mind that so much.
Maybe it was okay to be him sometimes, the boy who loved a girl a thousand
miles out of his league. Because that kid had been happy and maybe it was
time to claim that happiness for myself again, for however long it might last.

I reluctantly headed to Afterlife in the evening, the stack of freshly fucked-on
cash stashed back in my nightstand again. Rogue had refused to take it back
out of pure stubbornness and I wasn't gonna keep it out of pure pride, so for
now it would just sit in my drawer until I could figure out how to do something
with it for Rogue.

When Fox had returned to the house in the morning, I'd told him me and
Rogue were going surfing and technically we had been, only we'd stopped off
at the clinic on the way to get Rogue officially on the pill. Girl was as scatter-
brained as a dodo though, so I'd set up daily reminders on her phone to take

them too. Because I sure as fuck wasn't going back on this no-condom deal now I'd driven my cock into her bare. Johnny D had ascended to a higher plane of existence which was worth more than all the gold in the world, and he sure as shit wasn't gonna be convinced to go back.

I felt so good tonight, the best I'd felt in a long damn time actually. Chase was home, Rogue was no longer angry with me and things seemed to be getting back on track at last. I still had the massive issue of Fox to deal with, but for now I was just gonna appreciate everything else that was going right and figure out how best to handle him later. Because I was out of my mind in love and there really was no more going back for me at this point. There were complications, sure, but what relationship didn't have problems? Not that I really knew anything about a normal one of those, but this was never going to be normal. Nothing about our group was. Which was why I knew we needed a different kind of relationship that might just solve all of our problems. I mean…Fox was gonna be hard pushed to agree to it, and Chase's stance was yet to be seen, but if anyone could figure it out, it was me. I was the escort after all. I was open minded by nature. The main issue was that I was dealing with a couple of the most possessive guys I'd ever met. But we'd managed to share in the past, and Maverick clearly still had it in him to do so, maybe the others did too.

Of course, Rick would also likely shoot me dead if he got bored of our situationship, but I had a feeling he wasn't inclined to do that considering he'd lose Rogue over it too. So yeah, things weren't perfect, but maybe they could be, or maybe I was just a lovestruck idiot whose head was clouded by the delusional optimism that came with that love. Either way, I had a badly thought out plan and a lot of motivation, so how far wrong could it really go?

I used the back door to enter the dressing room at Afterlife and my eyebrows arched as I found Jessie running back and forth between the guys, shaking a bowler hat at them.

"Lucky dip, the one with my name on it gets a BJ!" she said excitedly, popping a bubble of gum and grinning at Texas as he plucked a condom out of the hat. "No peeking!"

He kept it in his fist and Jessie ran over to Adam where he was oiling up for the show by his dressing table, shaking the hat under his nose. His cheeks pinked and he shook his head, but she just rolled her eyes and grabbed his hand, pushing it into the hat.

"Come on, sweetie, I promise you'll like it if you win," she encouraged, pushing a condom into his hand then running away again.

Di laughed, shaking her head at her. "Well this is isn't fair, who's handing out free pussy licking for the girls? I've had a long day."

"You don't need to win a game for that, I'll eat you out all day and all night, honey," Texas said, adjusting the towel around his waist and Di tossed her hair.

"You'd better get a hat and some condoms then, Texas baby," she purred back and he jumped to his feet, heading to his dressing table to do just that.

"Okay, has everyone got one?" Jessie asked, bouncing on the balls of her feet then noticing me and running forward with a squeal. "There's one left, boss, it could be your lucky day!" She batted her lashes at me and I quirked a grin.

"No thanks, sweetheart. Give Adam double chances."

Adam's throat bobbed as Jessie bounded away to place the final one his hand.

Bella was sitting on Ollie's lap, the two of them kissing so filthily I was pretty sure it was gonna descend into a sex fest in here at any second. And that wouldn't be the first time. I'd only ever accepted blowjobs from Jessie in the past, my dancers needed to respect me as their boss and as I was basically everyone's pimp too, we'd needed some boundaries that ensured we could keep working together without things getting messy. Now I was a taken man and that felt so fucking good, I wished I could tell everyone in here. But instead, I just had to keep that secret buried down inside me which was just plain sad sometimes. I wanted the whole fucking world to know Rogue was my girl, even if that meant the world knew she was Maverick's too.

"Someone gimme a drumroll!" Jessie cried and Texas swung his hips side to side so a slapping noise sounded within his towel as his dick slapped between his thighs.

"Dude," I laughed as Ruben cracked up behind him.

"Look at your condoms," Jessie demanded, her eyes dancing with excitement as she bit her lip and looked between the guys who had one in their palm. I noticed Kevin the janitor was standing by the wall with a mop in hand and his face fell as he found his condom lacking Jessie's name.

"Well? Who has it?" Jessie pushed as Texas and Ruben showed her blank condoms with disappointed expressions.

My gaze swung to Adam who was being suspiciously quiet and Jessie ran over to him with a skip in her step, peeling his fingers apart to get hold of the two condoms there.

"Adam has it!" she announced, waving the strawberry condom in the air before grabbing his hand and towing him toward the costume closet.

He glanced back at me in alarm but the massive bulge in his boxers said he wasn't fighting that hard to get away.

"Adam, Adam, Adam," I started chanting and everyone else took up the chant too, making a shy grin split across his lips as Jessie stole him away into the closet.

"Right, my turn." Texas waved a baseball cap around and Lyla and Di plucked a condom out each, giggling together just as Estelle walked into the room. "Grab a condom, Momma Stelle."

"Do not do that," I warned her.

"Oh are we playing a game?" Estelle asked keenly, pressing a crease out of her buttoned up red shirt.

"Stelle, don't do it," Lyla laughed.

"Do it Stelle," Texas urged, a look of mischief in his gaze.

"You're a sick, man," I said with a snort. "I forbid you from offering that hat to Stelle."

"Don't be a bore, Johnny," Estelle said, waving a hand at me and snatching a condom out of the hat.

"Don't look at it yet," Texas commanded before wafting the hat in the direction of Bella on Olly's lap, but Olly swatted him away then slid his hand between Bella's thighs, making her moan and kiss him once more.

Ruben dove at him, snatching a condom from the hat before Texas could stop him and barking a laugh. "You'd better suck my cock good if I win, Texas."

"Shut up, asshole. This is for the girls," Texas said dismissively, but his gaze lingered on Ruben for a second like he wasn't entirely opposed to his offer.

I pulled my shirt off as I headed to my dressing table, grabbing my almond oil and starting to apply it to my skin.

Texas swung his hips again to start up his twisted little drumroll before telling everyone to look at their condoms.

"I win!" Di cried.

"Me too." Lyla frowned.

"Ooh, what do I get?" Estelle asked, waving her winning condom.

"Hang on, I won too," Ruben said, arching a brow at Texas.

"Did you write your name on all of them, dickwad?" Di demanded, throwing her condom at Texas so it bounced off his chiselled chest.

"Yup. Who's first?" He licked his lips and Di and Lyla squealed as he ran at them, running for the door as he chased them down. Ruben tore after them and Estelle frowned in confusion as they sprinted away.

"Did I just win something dirty?" Estelle asked.

"Texas is offering out oral," I told her and her eyes widened.

"Well damn, if he wasn't twenty years younger than me I'd take him up on that offer," she chuckled as she turned, heading back into the bar and I laughed.

As quiet fell, the sound of Adam groaning came from the closet and I connected my phone to the Bluetooth, playing Peaches by Justin Bieber, Daniel Caesar and Giveon as I got ready for the show.

My gaze fell on Sparkle in his tank by the window and I headed over to see how he was doing. There were no more remnants of moustache in the tank now because damn, this little starfish was becoming a hungry carnivore and I was gonna start training him up to devour more than just moustaches soon too. He'd take some fingers next, then a toe, we'd work up to a hand and maybe I'd bring him a few more friends so they could work as a team to destroy human body parts. One day I'd have an army of flesh-eating starfishes and my enemies would fear their tiny gaping mouths.

"Good boy, Sparkle." I sprinkled some fish food into the tank as a reward, but he just sat on his rock and didn't look at me. He had such a sense of humour.

The show went off without a hitch and I had women pressing their numbers into my hands on napkins by the end of it, all of which I tossed into the trash backstage without a second glance. Tom Collins had been in tonight, cheering me on from the bar with that bright eyed look he always gave me. I had Estelle ply him with free drinks because he'd tipped all the wait staff fifty dollars each and had left a hundred for me behind the bar too. Damn sweetheart he was. I hoped he went home, lubed his cock up real good and had a happy time thinking about me tonight. I really did. Bless his heart.

I washed off the oil in the shower, feeling good for the workout as I pulled on a bright pink tank top and black sweatpants, ready to head home. Rogue would likely sleep in with Chase again tonight and I was aching to be with them too. Maybe we could watch a movie and cuddle like idiots, because that was basically all I wanted to do with Ace lately. It might have been weird, but I just needed to be touching him to remind myself he was still here. After thinking he was dead all this time, I needed the reassurance that he was home, alive and safe. So I wasn't gonna worry about it, because he seemed to like me being a clingy weirdo at the moment.

Having my pretty girl in a bed with us was just the best feeling in the world. I wished Fox would join us though. I knew he sometimes crept into the room at night and watched us sleep. Whenever I woke up and sensed him there, a smile pulled at my lips because it gave me hope that he was coming around to the idea of Chase staying.

I'd tried to talk to him about it a couple of times so far but he'd just dismissed me, said there wasn't a discussion to be made, and that Chase had to go. But surely he didn't mean that. I could see the way he looked at him, the way he ached to forgive him and let him stay. So why couldn't he just allow himself to do that and let us all be happy at last? Chase had been through enough as far as I was concerned. And he'd saved Rogue at The Dollhouse. Surely Fox could forgive him now that he knew that?

I waved goodbye to everyone as I pushed my phone into my pocket and headed out the back door into the parking lot, the night air warm against my cheeks as I headed towards my GT. A whistle caught my hear and I turned sharply, regretting not having a gun on me a moment before my eyes fell on Fox leaning against the side of his truck. Since Shawn had gone quiet after Rogue's stabbing, I'd gotten a little complacent lately but I definitely needed to stop that, because I didn't for a second believe that asshole was dead. His men had been sighted on the edge of town, lurking like stray dogs and we knew they'd have moved out by now if their mutt boss had upped and died.

"Wanna go make some money with me, brother?" he asked and my heart lifted.

"Yeah, sure, what's the plan?" I headed over to him instead as he pushed off of the truck and unlocked it. He wore a white tank top with jeans and had a gun stuffed into the back of them.

"You know that Tatum chick Rogue's been hanging out with?" he asked and I nodded. "Well one of her boyfriends has a job for us."

"One of them?" I asked in confusion. Rogue hadn't mentioned that part. This girl had multiple boyfriends? Wasn't that like, my new dream?

"Yeah," Fox snorted. "Can you imagine sharing one girl? I'd end up killing all the other boyfriends."

I released a nervous laugh as I headed around his truck and got in the passenger side as he got in the driver's seat.

"I mean, it's not the worst idea," I said and Fox scoffed.

"Doesn't make sense to me at all. It's like that book you leant me, right? The fucking drama of the girl not choosing is great for a story, but she'll end up with Gabriel in the end and that'll be that. They're destined."

"What if they're all destined for her?" I asked with a frown.

"It doesn't work like that. You can only have one star-bound mate in the world of Solaria, and Gabriel can see the future. He already knows it'll be him."

"Well maybe the stars shouldn't get to choose," I bit out harsher than I'd intended. "Maybe the girl should get to choose."

"She will choose. And she'll choose Gabe," Fox said with a shrug.

"Don't call him Gabe," I growled and Fox's head snapped around to look at me.

"What's your problem? Is he not your favourite? Dante's a good second choice, but he seems too willing to share her with-"

"Maybe that's the point, Fox. Maybe they should share her. Maybe fate shouldn't decide," I said angrily and a crease formed between his eyes.

"That's ridiculous." He waved a hand in dismissal, starting up the truck and heading out onto the road. "That would never work."

"You said yourself that Tatum girl has a few boyfriends. Clearly it can work in real life, or they wouldn't be together."

"Look, don't get me wrong, they look happy and all. But-"

"But what?" I asked coolly.

"Well, how can those guys be genuinely satisfised with that situation? Some of them must get left out, she probably has a favourite and the others are just there to fulfil some group sex fantasies she has."

"Why is it so impossible for you to believe she loves them all the same?" I demanded.

"Dude, I didn't think you even knew the chick."

"I don't," I snapped. "But maybe it works."

"Yeah, I guess." Fox shrugged. "It's just hard to get my head around. I'd rather die than share my girl."

"Rogue's not your girl," I muttered.

"What?" he growled and my heart pounded furiously.

"She doesn't wanna be owned."

"I know that. I'm not trying to buy her," he said dismissively. "I'm trying to love her."

"Well maybe you should ask her what she needs to be loved," I said, softening my tone.

I didn't wanna fight with Fox. And I really didn't wanna fight with him over Rogue. That was the thing I was trying to avoid most, if only I could figure out how to make him see that her loving me didn't mean she didn't love him too. Because I was starting to understand that her wanting Fox didn't take away from how much she wanted me.

"I know what she needs," he said arrogantly and I took a breath, not wanting this to descend any further into a fight.

We drove down to a dark street leading to Sunset Beach and Fox got out of the truck, beckoning me to follow him. We walked down onto the sand and my gaze hooked on a bonfire further up the beach which we started walking towards.

The lap of the waves against the shore tangled with moans carrying on the wind and I squinted out to where some rocks sat in a semi-circle in the water, making a little calm, secluded area in the sea. Some dark shapes moved there and another female moan carried to us as I squinted out at the bodies pressed together in the water.

One of them peeled away and a large, tattooed guy emerged from the water, heading up the sand as the light of the fire spilled over him and he nodded to us in acknowledgement. He had a pair of white swimming shorts on and holy fuck they were clinging to his monster cock which was currently saluting the moon. I had to smother a laugh as Fox folded his arms beside me.

"Hey assholes," he said but in a way that was friendly more than insulting.

"You could have called to give us the job info instead of inviting us to your beach orgy," Fox pointed out.

"Saint's always bugging my calls, and this has to be kept secret from him," the guy said seriously.

"Isn't he here?" Fox looked towards the water as another loud moan carried from out there. Jesus.

"He'll be here later, but he had a business meeting."

"I've got a relationship to uphold with him," Fox said. "Is this job gonna jeopardise that?"

"Naw," he said dismissively. "He won't know you guys were involved. It's just part of a little family joke. Nothing harmful. And I'll give you three grand for it." He smirked enticingly.

I glanced at Fox hopefully, the sound of that green cash making me hungry. "We in?" I asked Fox and he turned to me with a nod.

"Alright, if Saint gets pissed it's on you though," Fox said and the guy nodded.

"I'll take the heat if it comes to it. Cross my heart," he said with a smirk. "Here's what I want." He picked up a duffel bag from beside the fire, taking out a phone and showing us a picture on the screen of a white squid statue in a playground in the centre of a grassy park. "They just installed it in the Blue Springs park in the Upper Quarter."

"What the fuck do you want that for?" I snorted and the guy chuckled.

"I think it'll make a great addition to Saint's music room," he said with a shrug. "I've left the side gate open at home. No one will be there for a couple of hours so once you've got it, just sneak it in around the side of the house and leave it under the tarp I left behind Tatum's Porsche. I've left the cash for you there in an envelope too."

Tatum's moans started building to a crescendo and the guy looked over at the water with heat in his eyes. "We all good? Because I've gotta go make her moan louder than that to prove whose cock she prefers."

"Yeah, we're good." Fox said, shaking his hand and we turned as he walked back off into the water, swimming under the waves as he headed towards his girl and whoever was out there making her make moan.

A little pang of jealousy ran through me at how easily it obviously was for them to all just be together. Couldn't Fox get onboard with that? It looked hella fun. And I was already conjuring up my own little fantasy of bringing Rogue down here into the water with Fox. Couldn't he just be a possessive asshole while I was there too tonguing Rogue's clit? Was that such an awful situation to be in?

The set of Fox's brow said he was currently confused as fuck over what he'd just witnessed though and I reckoned sharing my little fantasy with him would end in a bullet between my eyes.

"What do you think the squid's about?" I murmured to Fox as we headed back to his truck and got in.

"No fucking clue," he said, starting it up.

"I bet it's a sex thing," I said thoughtfully. "All those tentacles, you know?"

"I don't know, J." Fox looked over at me with a laugh.

"Maybe Tatum's into tentacle alien porn."

"Who the hell's into stuff like that?" Fox scoffed and memories prickled at the edges of my mind from working at The Dollhouse.

"Well you'd be surprised what kind of stuff some people are into."

"Do you think Rogue's into weird shit like that?" he wondered aloud.

"Nah, she likes it rough and I reckon she'd fuck anyone wearing Green Power Ranger shit but-"

"What?" he cut over me in a snarl and I realised I'd just blurted that out like a fucking idiot. "How would you know what she likes?"

"Because she tells me shit," I said quickly, shrugging and he huffed.

"She never talks to me about anything."

"That's because you're too busy bossing her around to hear her speak most of the time."

He sighed, his fingers flexing against the steering wheel and my gaze hooked on the need burning in his eyes, making my chest tug. I knew he loved her as deeply as I loved her, and I wished there was something I could do to make him come around to the idea of her being ours. Not just his. But it was gonna take a miracle to convince him of that, and I was fresh out of those. Maybe I'd get lucky and find a genie in a bottle on the beach one of these days, then I'd get to wishing for our family to reunite so tightly that nothing could break us. Not even this.

CHAPTER TWENTY SEVEN

I was a coward. A big fat coward. Or...maybe I was just an asshole. Yeah, that fit pretty accurately too.

I glanced back over my shoulder as the cool morning wind tangled my hair behind me and the boat zipped over the waves at high speed. Mutt stood on one of the padded seats to the right of the speedboat with his nose to the salty air and his ears flapping in the wind.

Any moment now, Fox and JJ would be home from their run. They'd head back into the house, find my note on the kitchen island and-

My cell phone started ringing in my pocket and my gut twisted in anticipation of the coming explosion.

"Hey," I answered brightly, glancing towards the horizon where the rising sun was making the sea glitter like diamonds.

"What the fuck kind of note is this?" Fox demanded.

"I thought it was pretty self-explanatory," I replied.

"'Gone to tea with Rick?' The same Maverick who is out for our blood, who hates all of us and-"

"Saved Chase's life? Yeah, that's the one. I brought him a fruit basket from all of you to say thanks. And might I add that the three of you should actually be delivering this thank you yourselves. I mean, I'll let Chase off due to his incapacitated state and all that, but you and JJ owe Maverick now and you know it."

The line was silent for several seconds though I was almost certain I could hear the sound of Fox grinding his teeth.

"I want you back by nightfall."

"And I want the moon to come live in my pocket. Dreams are pretty things, Badge, but I haven't quite figured out how long I'm gonna be visiting with Rick for so just calm your onions, trust me like you say you do and enjoy a few hours of peace. Or days. Whatever. I'll keep you posted."

"And what exactly am I supposed to do in the meantime while I'm freaking out over what you might be doing over there?"

"Well, Chase needs a sponge bath," I suggested. "You could take care of that and maybe make a slow-motion video of it for me while you're at it. Soap him up good, Badger. I know you're the perfect man for the job."

Fox agreed vehemently - or started cursing me out. Hard to tell with the roar of the speedboat's engine and the crash of the waves. So I just cut the call and bit my lip while I gave that fantasy some solid air time in my mind.

Mutt yipped excitedly and I looked his way, a grin splitting my cheeks as I spotted what he'd seen. A dolphin leapt up out of the water beside the boat, another right behind it and my heart swelled as I caught sight of more and more of them chasing along in my wake.

I started snapping photos and sending them to the group chat I'd made with the boys. It was designed to give Chase a little peek out of his window at the world while he was recovering, and I'd bought him a new phone especially for the job. Okay, okay, I'd stolen it. From a kid. But seriously, that kid needed to spend less time on his phone and more time enjoying the world, so I'd done him a solid in hindsight. Besides, Chase needed it more and I wanted him to remember there was lots to smile about even when the dark crept in on you, because that was the only way he was going to survive the darkness that Shawn had tried to stain his soul with. Only me and JJ actually sent anything to the chat though. Fox was still playing the grumpy asshole and Chase was clearly not interested - except I could see that they both saw the messages. Every single one always lit up with that little notification to show me they'd read them within seconds of me sending them, so I knew deep beneath their cool, bad boy exteriors they were squealing over the dolphins with me too.

I took a few selfies with the dolphins in the background and squished my face beside Mutt's and even took a quick video of me conversing with the dolphins in their native language.

JJ sent me a voice note of him cracking up at my spot on impersonation and I enjoyed the company of the dolphins for more than half of the trip across the water before they peeled away from me as I approached Dead Man's Isle.

The armed thugs raised guns and shouted shit at me while I waved enthusiastically and brought the boat up to the end of the jetty. I tossed the mooring rope into the face of a guy who was pointing a pistol at me, and he snarled angrily as he caught it.

"Hey, Dave!" I said with a grin as I lifted Mutt off the seat and helped him up onto the jetty. I had to clamber over my surfboard and the sick new board I'd bought for Rick to follow him, and the fruit basket was one heavy bitch, so I passed that to a reluctant Dave before climbing up myself.

"My name is Rupert."

"Dude, it's my accent. You can't blame me for a slight twang on the pronunciation," I said, waving him off as I turned back to the boat and leaned down to start dragging the surfboards out.

"Well look what the tide washed up," Rick's voice called to me as I was ass up in my white sun dress and half falling into the boat. I whipped around so fast I fell back on my butt on the wooden boards.

Maverick stood there, arms folded and scowly, wearing a pair of black shorts and a black tank with a pair of dark shades on his face. Honestly, that dude was a walking talking cliche, but he made it look hot as fuck so who was I to complain?

I abandoned the surfboards and leapt to my feet with a little bit of a squeal, breaking into a sprint as I raced for him and a bunch of his asshole Damned Men raised their weapons.

"If any of you aims your gun at her again, I'll-" Rick cut off as I leapt on him, arms and legs going fully around him and my weight hitting him at speed so that he stumbled back a step before managing to balance us. "What are you-"

I shut him up with my lips on his, kissing him hot and hard, my fingers fisting in his hair as he gripped my ass and kissed me back with equal ferocity.

Fuck, I'd missed him. I hated this water that divided us all the goddamn time. I hated knowing he was so close and so far away all at once. Sunset Cove may have begun to feel like home again for me, but it would never truly be that while he remained away from it. From me. From *us*.

Rick broke away from my lips and I dropped my mouth to his neck, my skin heating and burning beneath his touch as I kissed and bit at his flesh, the scrape of his stubble against my lips making me moan.

"Fuck off," he barked loudly to his men. "Every last one of you."

There was a flurry of movement all around us, but I was blind to it as Maverick used his grip on my ass to rock my hips over the thick bulge of his erection between my thighs.

He turned us towards a small lookout hut at the end of the jetty where it met with the sand of the beach and slammed my back against it hard enough to force the breath from my lungs.

"I've missed you, baby girl," he growled against my lips, his hand shifting beneath the hem of my skirt as he found the string securing my bikini bottoms at my hip. "I've missed those ocean blue eyes of yours. These filthy lips." He bit down on my bottom lip to accentuate that point and I moaned for him as he yanked the bikini string undone. "I've missed that round ass." He slapped it hard enough to make me gasp, while his hips kept me pinned against the hut and his other hand yanked the other side of my bikini bottoms undone. "I've missed your perfect fucking tits," he added, tugging my dress down hard enough to make them spill out the top of it before his mouth closed over my nipple and his teeth dragged across the diamond hard point of it. "And I've missed this wet, wet, pussy." A cry escaped me as his cock drove into me without any fanfare or build up and he sunk it all the way to the base with the kind of brutality I fucking adored from him.

"Jesus, Rick," I gasped, my head falling back as the sun beat down on us and the sea lapped beside us.

"Fuck, you feel like heaven," he groaned, drawing almost the entire way back out of me before driving in again hard. "This is for sure the closest I'm ever gonna get to it anyway."

"I don't want heaven, Rick," I moaned. "I like the dark too much for that."

Maverick laughed darkly, his hands repositioning to grip my ass as he drew back again and looked me in the eyes. "Say it."

I bit my lip as I looked at him, moving my hands to toy with my breasts and tugging on my nipples while he watched like a hungry wolf. "You own me, Daddy," I teased. "So prove it."

Maverick's eyes lit with fire and he slammed into me again with such force that I knew my cries were being heard by every single one of his gang no matter how far away they'd scurried at his command. But I didn't care because he did own me and if he wanted the whole world to know that then I was going to let him show them.

Maverick fucked me harder and harder, my fingernails biting into his shoulders while I drove my heels into his ass to encourage more, my pussy gripping his hard length tightly as each thrust pushed me closer and closer to oblivion.

He kissed me like he was trying to devour me, his tongue worshipping mine as he drank in the sound of my moans.

He lifted a hand to my throat and the noise that escaped me as he locked his inked fingers around it was pure sex.

His eyes met mine as he drove into me harder and harder, his grip tightening and hips pistoning until I couldn't breathe, and all of my damage was forced to the surface of my skin. But as he looked upon me in that raw, broken place, the hunger in his eyes only sharpened, his dick driving into me even more eagerly until I was breaking for him, shattering, exploding and coming so hard that my vision blacked out.

Maverick kissed me hard as he released his grip on my throat, his cock plunging in and out of me while my pussy spasmed around him and I rode out wave after wave of pleasure.

But before I'd even come down from my high, he was yanking out of me and pushing me to my knees before him.

"Open wide, beautiful," he commanded, a fist in my hair as I blinked up at him through the haze of my orgasm.

I did as he commanded, moaning around his cock as he drove it between my lips and began fucking my mouth exactly how he wanted it. He wasn't gentle with me but that only made it hotter, knowing he was taking what he needed from my body in exactly the way he liked.

His shaft bulged and swelled in my mouth and with a throaty groan, he came hard, spilling his cum down my throat as I half choked on his cock.

He pulled back with a sigh like he'd been needing that more than words could express and I smiled up at him as I bit down on my swollen lip.

"Tell me who owns you, baby," I teased and he smirked at me.

"You, beautiful. Only you. Always you."

Rick tugged me to my feet and I tugged my dress back up to cover my tits while he righted his shorts. The only piece of clothing that had actually made it off of either of us was my bikini bottoms in our haste to reunite and it only took me a moment to resecure them.

I spotted Mutt sitting at the far end of the jetty, looking out to sea with his ears back. He glanced over his shoulder at me, and I swear if dogs could raise judgemental eyebrows then that was what he was doing. But I'd seen him humping a dead seagull the other day on the beach so who was he to judge?

"So are you gonna tell me what I did to earn that little treat?" Maverick asked curiously, his gaze falling to the fruit basket that had been abandoned on the jetty beside my boat.

"You know what you did," I scoffed. "You saved Ace. You brought him back to us."

"I dunno if I'd put it like that," Rick said dismissively. "I just didn't want some other asshole to take away my kill. If anyone is gonna be carving up the Harlequins, then it'll be me."

I ran a hand through my hair and looked up at him, shaking my head in disbelief. "Whatever you wanna tell yourself, Rick. But we both know you can't bullshit a bullshitter. So just cut the crap and enjoy the fruit basket the boys sent you to say thanks."

"If a Harlequin had something to do with the creation of that fruit, then I want nothing to do with it."

"Oh yeah, Fox sprouted a pineapple tree right outa his ass especially for the occasion," I mocked.

"Pineapples don't grow on trees," Maverick grunted.

"Err, yeah they do. Like coconuts," I disagreed.

"No they don't. They grow on the ground on grassy bush things."

"That seems super unlikely, dude. The crows would get them if they just grew on the ground."

"Crows can fly, so if they wanted to eat pineapples they could get them from a tree as easily as the ground," Rick argued.

"So you admit they grow on trees?" I demanded.

"No. Just Google it."

"I don't trust some alien on the internet, Rick. I believe what I see with my own imagination. And pineapples definitely grow on trees." I grabbed the heavy basket of fruit and swung it into his arms before taking out my phone and snapping a pic of him holding it. "Smile, dude, you don't look cool when you frown like that in photos - you just look grumpy."

"Fuck off. Why are you taking photos of me anyway?"

"I'm just sending your gushing appreciation back to the boys. Ah look, here's a reply - Fox says he hopes you don't choke on any of it. Aww, that's sweet."

Maverick barked a laugh, his gaze whipping from me to the boat where he spotted the two surfboards and he fell still.

"What's that about?" he asked, placing the basket of fruit down again.

"Well, I was thinking about that time you kept me prisoner out here on your isle of boredom and how you'd done absolutely nothing fun the whole time we were here. And then I realised I'd never even caught a sniff of some board wax on you, and I realised that you mustn't have gotten around to getting yourself a board yet. So on account of you saving Ace, and me being all kinds of grateful, I got you one."

"I thought the sex was your way of saying thank you," he grunted, his mask a vacant kind of blank that gave me the sudden feeling that he was about to refuse to go surfing with me.

"No, dude. The sex was because you're hot and you have a really big cock. But the surf is my gift to you. So are you gonna come catch some waves with me or are you too chicken shit?" I tugged my dress over my head and dropped it to the wooden jetty so that I was left standing there in my navy bikini.

Maverick still looked inclined to say no so I sighed dramatically and began heaving my own board up out of the boat.

"I guess I'll have to tell the boys you can't surf for shit these days then."

"I haven't surfed since the last time you and me were in the water together, beautiful," Maverick said in a low tone and I stilled, my heart twisting at his words.

He used to love the surf almost as much as I did. I'd be down at the beach every damn morning with my board before school and the others all joined me with varying frequency, but Rick was there most often. We were free when we were out on the water. I knew I'd been missing that like crazy while I was away from this place and I got the feeling he could do with some freedom even more than I could.

"Fine," he agreed at last, nudging me aside as he grabbed both boards and lifted them out of the boat. "I'll come surf with you so long as you stay the night. I'm sick of sleeping in a bed that you're not in and I want unrestricted access to that body of yours all night long."

"Be still my beating vagina," I gasped, fanning myself like I was a fancy lady. "I do believe we have an accord, Mr Stone."

Rick twitched a grin at me and I fell into step with him as we headed for the beach and the waves.

His arm brushed against mine and I closed my eyes as the sun washed over us and the sea lapped against the shore, certain for a moment that I really was home and knowing for once that the smile on my face was one hundred percent real.

I woke suddenly in the night, disoriented at first as I blinked at Maverick's suite and let the memories of yesterday and last night settle in my brain while I took in where I was. There was a dull ache between my thighs which had plenty to do with all the rough sex we'd had, and my body felt bruised and tender in the best possible way. But that wasn't what had woken me.

Maverick groaned in his sleep beside me, tossing and turning violently as some nightmare pressed in on him. A sheen of sweat clung to his skin and his brow was furrowed as a single word escaped his lips.

"Stop."

"Rick," I breathed, shifting towards him with my heart pounding as I tried to rouse him from whatever horrors had crept up on him while he slept.

He thrashed in the bed more violently and I reached out for him, my hand landing on his shoulder as I made a move to shake him. But the moment my skin met with his, a furious roar escaped him and I shrieked in surprise as he whirled on me.

His eyes snapped open but they were blank and void of any signs of the boy I'd grown up with and as his hand locked around my throat, a scream of fright escaped me.

Maverick threw his weight at me, my back slamming down against the mattress as his grip on my throat tightened painfully. He cut off my oxygen as he reared over me, pinning me down with the sheer bulk of his body.

Panic took me captive as I struggled beneath him, my fingernails biting into his hand where he held me and suddenly the darkness in his gaze lifted a little like he'd just realised where he was.

He lurched back suddenly, releasing me as he scrambled to the far side of the bed, looking like he was about to bolt on me.

"Fuck…Rogue," he groaned, his hand opening and closing into a fist as he stared at it like it had just betrayed him. "I'm sorry. *Fuck!*" he bellowed the last word and my pulse scattered, but I didn't retreat any further from him because as terrifying as that had been, I knew it had nothing on whatever the hell was going on inside his head right now. His eyes were wild and he looked haunted by some ghost which had visited him in his nightmares.

"It's me," I said softly. "I'm here. It's okay." I reached out for him, but he flinched back like the idea of me touching him was repulsive.

"Don't touch me," he snarled, making a move to get out of the bed and I quickly withdrew my hand.

"It's okay. I won't touch you," I promised quickly. "Do you want me to turn the lights on-"

"No," he snapped, scraping his hands through his hair and glancing around the dark room like he expected to see something else lurking in the shadows. Or someone else.

"You can tell me, Rick," I promised him but he just shook his head, his hand fisting in his hair as he looked about three seconds away from running.

"When I was nineteen, I slept rough for a couple of months," I said in a low voice, coaxing him back to me by offering him a taste of my own pain, wanting to show him that I understood. That I knew what it was like to feel as empty and lost as he looked right now. "It sucked in all the ways you would imagine. I was hungry a lot and there was no bathroom. The nights were long and cold...but that wasn't the worst thing about it. The worst was how tired I felt all the time. But how impossible I found sleep too. Closing my eyes every night felt like running a gauntlet. Like turning my back on the monsters I knew were lurking in the shadows and just hoping they wouldn't find me in the dark."

Rick watched me in silence for several long seconds, his eyes roaming over me like he was weighing me, judging me and I wasn't sure I'd ever wanted to be found good enough as I did in that moment.

He shifted towards me and I gasped at the sudden movement as he prowled into my personal space, the warmth of his breath brushing over my lips.

"Don't touch me," he warned again in a low growl that sent a shiver running down my spine and I nodded as he advanced on me, forcing me to back up as the breadth of his body engulfed me in his shadow.

I dropped back against the pillows with my heart pounding as he reared over me, his hand settling beside my head as he dominated my space and I bunched my fingers into fists to stop myself from breaking my promise to him.

"I told you about the men Luther sent to punish me night after night," he breathed, his face shrouded in shadow so that his expression was hidden from me.

I nodded slowly, unsure if he would even really be able to see the movement, but he went on so I had to assume he had.

"That wasn't the worst of it though. The beatings, the punishments, all of that was nothing really. Not compared to the place I went when they were done with me."

He reached out with his free hand and touched a fingertip to my lips, tracing the seam of them while his posture remained rigid above me and I hardly even dared to breathe. This was on him. I'd made him a promise and I wasn't going to break it, but the small point of contact he'd initiated between us felt like a raging fire burning beneath my skin.

"They got me transferred into a cell with a monster far worse than them. The kind who saw every spot of light in the dark and devoured it completely."

Maverick's finger drew a line down the side of my neck before tracing over the fabric of my shirt and between the valley of my breasts, my breath hitching with every slow inch he passed as I waited for him to go on.

"His name was Peter Krasinski."

I swallowed thickly, blinking against the dark as Maverick withdrew his hand again, drawing back from me and leaving me there on the bed beneath him. I could feel him pulling away before he even made a physical move to do so and I reached for him, catching his hand in mine and feeling the way he tensed at my touch.

"Show me," I urged. "If you can't say the words then show me what he did to you."

Maverick stilled for an endless moment, the shadows seeming to coil around him as the memories of whatever he'd survived in that place took life in the darkness surrounding us. I could feel the ache of them, the pain, the fear, the shame. Something bad had happened to him in there. Something he wasn't dealing with and had no one to share with. But he could tell me. He could trust me with his secrets and I'd gladly take on whatever haunted him too if that was what he needed.

Maverick's gaze raked over me like hot coals searing across my skin before he swallowed thickly, that darkness in his gaze deepening with some decision. He grabbed me roughly and flipped me over, his hand landing in the centre of my spine and his weight drove me down into the mattress as he exerted pressure.

My heart pounded with uncertainty as he reared over me, the weight of his body driving me into the mattress uncomfortably as he leaned down to speak to me.

"He used to whisper in my ear before he did it," Maverick breathed, his stubble grazing my flesh as he leaned close to do that same thing to me. "He'd call me a pretty boy. *His* pretty boy. Then he'd tell me how much he'd been looking forward to seeing me all day. He'd have his filthy cock in his hand while he said it, pumping his fist up and down so that I could hear the movement and know he was priming himself for me."

I shuddered beneath him as he shifted behind me, keeping me immobilised beneath him while his fingers dragged back and forth across the mattress beside me, imitating that sound, giving me a taste of the pain and fear he'd suffered.

"Tell me to stop," Maverick growled but I shook my head.

"I can take it," I insisted in a low voice, my limbs trembling with realisation as I finally understood what had happened to the boy I'd loved. The one who had tried to come after me. The one who had taken the fall for me. This was my fault. All of it. He'd only ended up in that place because of me and if reliving his nightmares with my body could help him to deal with them, then that was the least I could offer him in penance. "I need to know. And you need to get it out."

Rick grunted something and his weight lifted from my spine as he withdrew his hand, making me think for a moment that he was backing out of this, but as I made a move to lift up onto my knees, he shoved the shirt I was wearing up and yanked my panties down so that they were bunched around my knees.

"He never took my pants off properly," he said roughly, twisting the material of my panties in his fist so that my knees were locked together by them. "I hated that. To this day that still haunts me almost as much as the memories of him doing the rest of it. It was that easy. Just yank my pants down and take whatever the fuck he wanted."

"Rick," I murmured but the pain in my voice clearly wasn't what he wanted to hear, and he gripped the back of my hair in his fist, shoving my face down into the mattress.

"He didn't like to hear me speak," he snarled, shifting his weight on top of me so that the heavy press of his body drove against my ass and my heart began to race at the thought of what was next, but I didn't try to stop him. I just waited, my fingers fisting the sheets as he hesitated there for a long moment.

"He didn't want me to beg or tell him to stop. He liked to think I wanted it. Convinced himself I loved it. I dunno if that made him feel better about it or if it was more that he hated how disgusted I truly was by him."

I expected him to keep going, to pull his pants down and press forward at any second, for the bite of pain I would feel at his rough entry while I let him play out his demons on my flesh and work to banish some of them, but it never came.

Instead he released his hold on my hair, letting me turn my head to look at him in the dark until my gaze met his and I could feel all of his pain and damage as keenly as my own.

"Every night for months," he said in a low voice. "Every fucking night after those guards had their fun beating the shit out of me, that monster would force his body onto mine. He'd take and take and leave me more broken every time. But I had one thing he couldn't take from me, beautiful… I had you."

Maverick's fingers moved to the back of my left thigh where the Damned Men tattoo marked my skin and he blew out a long breath before flipping me over onto my back so that I was looking up at him properly.

"Tell me you ended him," I growled, tears burning the backs of my eyes which I fought off as fiercely as I could. Not because I didn't want him to see me hurt for him, but because I knew he needed me to be strong in that moment. He needed me to take on this burden and prove to him that it didn't change anything about the way I felt for him.

"I realised I had to become the strongest man in the room," he said slowly, peeling my panties the rest of the way off as he shucked his boxers off too.

I took the hem of the shirt I was wearing and tossed it aside to save him the job, my thighs parting for him as he moved between them.

"I cornered him one morning when we were working in the laundry room together," he said in a measured tone, his eyes lighting at the memory as he locked his gaze with mine. "The guards always left us alone in there and it only took a few small bribes to clear the rest of the inmates out."

"Tell me," I demanded. "All of it."

"Does this change things?" he asked, shame colouring his expression and making me hurt for him.

"Nothing," I swore, grasping his cheek so he couldn't turn away from the truth in my eyes and a weight seemed to leave him as he nodded, leaning into my touch. "Tell me what you did to him."

Rick smiled this twisted, broken smile that set my heart racing as he leaned down over me to whisper in my ear like we were two lovebirds sharing secrets instead of a pair of fucked up creatures sharing stories of death and survival.

"I beat the ever-loving fuck out of him. I beat him bloody until he was crying and begging at my feet, I listened to him plead for mercy as he crawled across the ground and sobbed for help." I shivered beneath him, that dark depraved part of my soul relishing this story and drinking in the details of him taking his vengeance on the monster who'd hurt him. "I kicked him until I felt bones shatter." Maverick's eyes lit with the memory and I bit my bottom lip as I listened to every detail with rapt attention. "I smashed his face against one of the dryers until there were no fucking teeth left in his mouth." Rick hooked his elbow beneath my knee and leaned down over me, his lips almost touching mine as he went on. "I drove my thumbs into his eyes until he was blinded." I sucked in a breath as he lined his body up with mine and I pushed my fingers into his dark hair, drawing him closer. "And when he was choking on his own blood and praying for death, I locked his head between my hands and broke his fucking neck."

I moaned as he thrust forward with that announcement, the thick length of his cock driving deep inside me as he leaned down to kiss me so slowly I felt like I was drowning in him.

He didn't up his pace like I expected him to either, his mouth devouring mine as his body took me hostage in a slow and tortuous rhythm that had me gasping for air.

"How did you get away with it?" I asked between moans.

"Luck and a lack of people to give a fuck. The inmates weren't gonna rat me out and that piece of shit didn't have anyone on the outside who cared about a thorough investigation, so they did a shit job of looking into it and it was unsolved."

"Thank fuck for that."

"I would have paid any price for that revenge. His death was so beautifully cathartic. You gave me that strength, beautiful," he groaned in my ear. "Every single day I spent in that hell, you were right there with me, holding my hand in the dark, keeping the last good pieces of me locked away in your keeping. I was lost to the world and everything in it, but I never lost you. You were mine then as much as you are now. And now that I've been given a taste of you, I won't ever give you up. Not until the death I'm waiting on comes and rips me from your arms."

He kissed me again before I could answer that, the two of us moving together like we were one body, one soul, this single entity reunited after far too long of hungering for each other. And I knew then that he was right. That no matter the fissures which tore me apart inside, no matter the scars I bore or the hurt I'd suffered, I'd always been holding onto him too. Deep in my heart when the nights were darkest, my mind always retreated to the one place I'd ever been able to call home and the four boys who I'd loved with my entire being.

"I love you, Maverick," I gasped as his mouth moved down my neck and our bodies tangled as one.

He fell still at my words, lifting his head and meeting my eyes with such weighted emotion that I could barely look at it.

"I'm yours, beautiful," he replied darkly. "Take me, own me, use me, destroy me. Anything you like, everything you want. Just don't ever leave me again."

The speedboat bumped against the jetty hard enough to put a scratch right down the side of it or maybe even knock a hole in it for all I cared.

Out on Dead Man's Isle I'd only been interested in Rick and making sure he saw the truth of what I felt for him. I needed him to see that none of the fucked-up things we'd survived took anything from what we both were to each other. He had to know what he meant to me.

But now? Now I was pissed. I was angrier than I had any memory of ever being in my entire life. I felt more rage an injustice over the things Maverick had survived than I had over anything that I'd ever endured myself. And I felt more guilt over it than I had over anything I'd ever been responsible for in my life either. And I was responsible for more than my fair share of messed up shit.

The Harlequins positioned around the house didn't make any move to stop me as I strode past them towards it, the wind picking up today so that my rainbow hair billowed all around me and my dress whipped around my thighs.

Mutt marched at my side like he was a dog on his way to war too and I loved that he had my back on this. Because even he knew in his little doggy head that something had to be done.

I hammered my fist against the back door as I reached it, fury blinding me to anything aside from my goal. I was going to grab a car, get in it and drive straight over to The Oasis and show Luther fucking Harlequin exactly what I thought of his methods of parenting. Better yet, I was going to take a gun too.

JJ opened the door, frowning at me in confusion as he tasted the venomous hatred on the air, but I just shoved my way past him. I had something to fucking do.

Mutt barked in warning as I strode through the house and the sound of voices gave me a five second warning to the guest they were entertaining before I rounded the corner into the kitchen.

Luther looked up at me from his stool at the breakfast bar as I strode in, half a smile tilting the corner of his lips up just before a scream of fury escaped me and I launched myself at him.

My fist connected with his face before he'd even realised what was happening and my weight collided with him half a second after that.

Luther went flying off his chair and I went with him, the two of us crashing to the ground as I lost my shit entirely and started throwing wild punches at him from my position on top of him.

Luther cursed, snatching my arm into his grasp as he tried to hold me off while Fox and JJ yelled in alarm behind us. But Mutt leapt into the fray before anyone else could manage it, his sharp teeth sinking into Luther's other hand and giving me the opportunity to punch him again.

Blood smeared my knuckles, and my heart was racing with a blind rage that had overtaken me and all I could think of was destroying the man beneath me. Of reaching into his chest and ripping the sorry excuse for a heart he kept there right out of it so that he wouldn't live a single day longer to inflict fear and torture upon anyone.

"Get her the fuck offa me before I have to force her off," Luther demanded, clearly holding back on hitting me because I was a girl or some bullshit. But fuck that. He never cared about that when he ran me out of town and threw me to the wolves.

Fox's arms wound around my waist as he tried to heave me off of his father, but I fought him with everything I had, kicking and thrashing, biting down on his forearm and stamping on Luther's leg as he shoved himself backwards beneath me.

JJ was yelling my name and Mutt went from savaging Luther's hand to attacking Fox as he lifted me full bodily into the air.

Fox swore as sharp teeth sank into his ankle and I managed to lurch out of his grip, throwing myself at Luther again with a furious yell, but JJ caught me before I could reach him a second time.

Fox grabbed hold of me too and the two of them heaved me back again while I continued to fight against them with all I had.

Luther pushed to his feet, drawing a gun and stepping forward to press it to my forehead with a sneer as he used his other arm to swipe blood from his bleeding nose.

"Give me one good reason why I shouldn't put a bullet in your skull right now!" he bellowed, his eyes a dark, furious abyss which hungered for my end.

I spat at him, still struggling against Fox and JJ's grip on me and not giving a single fuck about the gun which was jammed against my skull.

"You should!" I roared. "You should pull that trigger and end me now because if you don't then I'll come for you again and again until you're nothing but dirt in the ground, you ruthless motherfucker. I'll kill you for what you did to him! I'll fucking kill you!"

Luther pulled the hammer back, his eyes flashing with my death but Fox was there first, drawing his own gun and aiming it right back at his father.

"I don't know what the fuck this is about," Fox snarled. "But you know the deal. You touch her, you die. Don't go thinking for a single second that that won't happen."

"What the hell *is* this about?" JJ demanded, his arms tightening around me as he tried to heave me back a step and I continued to fight for my freedom.

"Ask him," I spat. "Ask the great Luther Harlequin what he had his men do to Maverick while he was in prison. Ask him about the four guards he ordered to haul him out of his cell every fucking night to beat him bloody. Ask him about the psychotic rapist cellmate he arranged for him to be locked in with after dark!"

Luther's eyes widened at my accusations, his gun pulling back an inch as he glanced between me and Fox.

"I don't know what the fuck you're talking about," he said, a frown etched into his brow and a flash of fear in his eyes like this was goddamn news to him.

"Liar!" I screamed. "You did that to him. You hated him for loving me. You punished him for trying to come after me. You put him in that hell and when it wasn't enough to force him to come crawling back to you, you upped the stakes. I heard the truth from his own lips, I saw it in his eyes, and I felt it in my soul. He was meant to be your son. How could you do that to him?" My voice was raw and jagged as the hurt of that truth ripped free of my chest and my cheeks felt wet with tears, but they did nothing to lessen this desire in me to rip Luther Harlequin's fucking head off.

"Is that true?" JJ demanded in horror, his grip on me slackening just a little.

"What the hell did you do?" Fox asked his dad, his face written in pain as he raised his gun a little higher, a decision forming in his deep green eyes as his finger kissed the trigger.

Luther shook his head, stumbling for words as he realised his son was really gonna do it. And I was ready to see him die for his crimes.

"Stop!" Chase's voice boomed from the stairs.

I couldn't help but glance towards them as the sound of him half falling down them reached us and he appeared on his back at the bottom of them, cursing his broken leg.

"It's not true," he gasped. "It wasn't Luther - it was Shawn. Fucking Shawn and his mind games. He told me about it while he had me locked up in that fucking basement. He said Maverick arrived at the prison while he was serving time there and he took the opportunity to fuck with the Harlequins. He paid off the guards, made them get Harlequin tattoos so it would be more convincing."

I shook my head as I tried to compute that. It didn't make sense. Why would Shawn have gone to all that effort to strike at Maverick back then? Rick was just a kid, barely a member of the Harlequin Crew at all and no real threat to him.

"Why would he do that?" JJ barked, clearly thinking along the same lines as I was.

"Because Luther killed his brother," Chase explained, gripping the doorframe and heaving himself up onto his good leg as he gave us all pained looks. "Didn't you?"

He turned to Luther who nodded mutely, seeming in shock over the news descending on him, lowering his gun as he looked between all of us. Fox's gun was still pointed at his head and he didn't seem inclined to lower it until he had more proof.

Chase went on, "It's been playing on repeat in my head over and over again since Shawn told me, but I didn't know what to believe. He put so many twisted ideas into my head that they all started banding together. I'm sorry, I should have told you."

"So why didn't you?" Fox snarled.

"Because that motherfucker was trying to get in my mind the whole time I was in there. He told me all kinds of crazy shit. Stuff to fuck with me. Stuff designed to worm its way into my brain and lay eggs there. I don't know what to think of any of it anymore, but it seems to me like this has to be true."

"I only wanted Maverick to come to his senses and realise that family was the most important thing," Luther said in a hollow tone. "I had men inside who were tasked to keep an eye on him, to keep the other inmates away if he seemed to be getting into any trouble and though he refused to have anything to do with my men in there, they reported back to me saying he had no issues with any of the other prisoners..."

"That's because his nightmares were the guards. The only inmate to hurt him did it behind locked doors where no one else could see," I hissed, the rage in me still running rampant through my flesh. Maybe Luther wasn't wholly to blame for what had happened to Maverick in there, but he was still the reason he'd been sent to prison in the first place. And I was the reason he'd felt the need to do that.

The fight went out of my limbs and JJ tentatively released me.

I made a move to walk away and Luther grabbed my arm, making me look up at him as blood slowly trickled down his chin from the wounds I'd given him.

"I didn't know," he said, his voice cracking just enough to show me how much this truth was costing him, but it was all a little too late for that.

"That doesn't fix it though, does it?" I muttered, shrugging his arm off and crossing the room towards Chase.

I wrapped an arm around his waist, noticing the way he flinched at my touch. No doubt his tumble on the stairs made his ribs flare with pain again. He leaned on me as I half heaved him back up to his room, the silence stretching between us as we went and the conversation between the others downstairs breaking out again as they came to terms with what I'd just told them and what it meant.

Mutt scampered along at my heels and I helped Chase back into bed as we returned to his room.

"Rick's right to hate us, isn't he?" he murmured as I headed to his nightstand to get his pain pills from the drawer, knowing he wouldn't have taken them without me here.

"Maybe," I said in a low tone, a frown pinching my brow as I held the pills out for Chase and his lips parted obligingly. "Or maybe I'm the one you should all hate after all. It all comes back to me in the end, doesn't it? Rick went down for killing Axel, you were all forced into the Crew for helping me cover it up. Whatever way you look at it, without me in the picture, things could have been a lot better for all of you."

Chase frowned as I held the glass of water to his lips, swallowing the pills for me before I placed the glass back on his nightstand.

"Without you in the picture, I don't think any of us ever would have gotten a taste of happiness, little one," Chase said, taking hold of my wrist to keep me there beside him.

I sighed, leaning in to place a kiss on his cheek and lingering with my lips against his skin for a moment as my eyes fell closed and I breathed him in.

"Even poison can taste sweet at first," I said in a low voice. "But it will still kill you in the end."

I pushed upright again and backed away from him, trying not to feel the slice of pain in my heart as he looked at me like he wanted me to stay. Because he was better off without me. They all were.

The problem was, I was too selfish to let them go.

CHAPTER TWENTY EIGHT

I rode in the truck beside my dad, feeling like a sixteen-year-old who'd just been grounded. Luther was quiet, I was quiet. And I could feel our shared pain rolling between us in the silence. I didn't want to acknowledge it and clearly he didn't either, but something had to be said. It *had* to be. Because now I knew what had happened to my brother in prison, I felt like I was gonna throw up or destroy something.

"He thought I did that to him." Luther punctured the quiet at last and my chest twisted sharply. For all the things I'd thought Maverick hated our dad for, it wasn't this. I'd never even considered that he'd been harbouring something like that. Sure, I figured prison had been bad for him, had changed him. But this? Never…

I ran a palm over my face and tried to contain the raging beast rising to the edges of my flesh.

"No wonder he hates you," I muttered.

Luther's hands tightened on the steering wheel, the trident he had inked along his thumb turning nearly white with how hard he was gripping it. "I should never have sent him down for Axel. It was only meant to be a couple of years in juvie to straighten him out, show him the consequences of him going against my word when he tried to find Rogue, but then he wouldn't respond when I tried to get him to file an appeal, let himself be packed off to state prison out of sheer stubbornness."

"Maybe if you didn't treat us like members of your Crew and send your goddamn son to prison, this wouldn't have happened," I snapped, the rage in me boiling over.

"But you were my Crew after that night. You initiated, wet your hands in blood for the Harlequins," he barked back. "If I'd showed lenience to him, my men would have lost faith in me, you must know that more than anyone now that you're in a position of power yourself, kid."

"Don't call me kid," I snarled. "And maybe I have done things your way for a long time when it comes to my family, but maybe I'm starting to see that your way just pushes them further and further away from me. You know what JJ said to me the other day? That I'm like you. And that's the last thing I ever wanted to be."

"All I ever tried to do was protect you," he snapped.

"If you think sending Maverick to prison was protecting him then you've got a twisted idea of what being a father looks like."

"And what would you know about that, huh?" he growled. "It ain't easy ruling the Harlequins and raising two boys with equally rebellious souls. I knew you'd leave. Both of you. The second you got a chance to take off with Rogue, I knew you'd be outa Sunset Cove off into some dirt poor life where you had nothing and no one to protect you."

"I would have had *her*," I threw back. "And I would have had my brothers, including Maverick. He despises me because of you."

Luther's shoulders tensed at those words and I knew I'd hurt him and I fucking relished it. "Alright, I fucked up. I know I fucked up. But I'm trying to fix it now. I let your girl in the Crew, I showed her leniency, I-"

"It's ten years too late!" I bellowed. "Do you know what Shawn did to her? Do you have any idea what she's been through because she had nowhere to go and had to rely on that motherfucker just so she had a roof over her head?"

"I'm sorry, alright?" he barked, his eyes pinned on the road.

"It's not good enough," I said bitterly. "I'll never forgive you for it. For all of this. It's *your* fault we're in this mess."

"Come on, son," he tried, his tone softening a little. "There's gotta be something I can do to make this right."

"There isn't," I said coldly. "Unless you can turn back time and take us all back to the day you drove Rogue out of town and pardon her of her so-called crimes against the Crew, there is *nothing* you can do."

He reached over to lay a hand on my shoulder and I jerked it off, looking away from him out the window. He was an asshole, and I made a vow to myself and my family that I would dig out the pieces of him that I'd embodied and destroy them.

"Sometimes hard decisions have to be made. You banished Chase, so you must know-" he started and I cut over him sharply.

"That was different. He betrayed us. He betrayed Rogue. And if you're not getting the message yet, that's where my lines are drawn. When it comes to crossing her, I will show no mercy. And that includes you."

"So this is my punishment, huh?" he muttered. "You're gonna freeze me out for the rest of my life?"

"It's what you deserve," I growled and he nodded, pressing his tongue into his cheek and taking a turning onto the cliff roads.

Silence descended again as we travelled up the winding trail, eventually pulling up at the peak where Shawn had declared war on the Cove. Maverick was already there, laying on the hood of an old green Chevy with a baseball cap pulled low over his face. His chest was bare as he sunned himself, but as casual as he looked, a revolver was gripped in his hand and I was sure he knew we were here. I'd had Rogue call him to meet us, knowing he'd never agree if I asked. But for her, apparently he'd do anything.

"What's the occasion?" he called as we strode towards him. "It's not Thanksgiving already, is it? Or someone's birthday? Shame I didn't bring any cake, I guess you'll just have to have a feast on my bullets." The gun twitched in his grip and I slapped a hand to my dad's chest to stop him from approaching my psychotic brother. Luther shook his head at me, knocking my hand away and kept walking, making my jaw grit as I followed.

If my dad thought Maverick was beyond shooting him then he should have taken a closer look at the scar on my neck that my adopted brother had put there. He wanted us dead, and after what I'd just found out about his time in prison, I was surprised he hadn't fired a couple of those bullets at Luther already.

"I'm only here because Rogue's gonna suck my cock in payment later," Maverick taunted, sitting up at last and twisting his baseball cap around so it sat backwards on his head.

I swallowed the growl in my throat at those words, focusing on why we were here as he sprung off the hood of the car, cocking his head and glancing between us with a sneer on his lips. "Why are you looking at me like that, assholes?"

A ball tightened in my throat as I stared at him and my dad gave me a look that prompted me to answer. I guessed he thought it might be better coming from me, but I hardly fucking thought so.

"Rogue told us what happened to you in prison," I let the bomb drop, figuring it was best to cut to the chase.

Maverick's stony expression didn't flicker, but his eyes did. "Did she now?" he muttered, working over that knowledge. "So you've come here to what? Enjoy the look on my face when you told me you knew my darkest fucking secret? Like you didn't know all this time anyway?" he spat.

"No," Luther growled passionately. He took a step towards him, but Maverick raised his gun to warn him back and he didn't go any further.

"She also told us that you thought those guards were Harlequins," I went on, my skin prickling from what I knew had happened to him and despite the years of hatred between us, I fucking cared about that. Because it changed things, I just didn't know how.

"*Thought* they were?" he echoed with a scoff. "I know they were." His eyes swung onto Luther with seething disgust in his eyes. "You planned to bring me to heel the brutal way, didn't you, *Pa*?"

"Those men had nothing to do with me," Luther said fiercely, his shoulders pressing back. "They weren't Harlequins."

"Bullshit," Maverick snapped predictably.

"Chase found out the truth from Shawn," I said quickly. "Shawn boasted that he orchestrated it. He was in prison the same time you were. He paid off those men to wear the Harlequin symbol on their flesh and fuck with your head."

Maverick fell entirely still, his eyes moving from me to Luther then back to me. "What is this?" he demanded. "What are you after?"

"We want you to know the truth, son," Luther said, his voice full of pain. "And we want you to come home."

I gave him a look that said I was not in agreement with that second part, but my dad just set his jaw and fixed his gaze on Maverick.

"Nah, you're up to something," Maverick growled, glaring at Luther. "You're always fucking up to something. You're the Harlequin King. Lord of the fucking rats and now you've just come up with a new little idea to try and manipulate me into doing what I'm told."

"Why would Chase lie?" I pressed. "He has no reason to."

Maverick wet his lips, looking back at me. "Strange. I thought Chase was dead. You been playing with a Ouija board, Foxy?"

"Oh don't give me that," I laughed dryly. "He told us what you did for him and I'm…grateful." I forced the word out, needing for it to be said even though it was sharp in my throat.

Maverick shrugged. "I didn't do nothin'."

"Are you really so stubborn that you won't even listen to the truth?" Luther interjected, steering the conversation back onto the point of it. "I didn't send those men. I'd never fucking do that. It was only meant to be a couple of years in juvie. I was gonna get you out, but you wouldn't even fucking talk to me."

Maverick's upper lip curled back. "Fuck you, Luther. I see what you're doing and it ain't gonna work."

"Rick," I snapped, his old nickname spilling from my lips before I could stop it and he arched a brow at me in surprise. I took a step forward, desperate for…something. I just needed him to know the truth, because as much shit as there was between us and as much as I knew we were never going to be anything but enemies now, I still couldn't bear the thought of him thinking the Harlequins were responsible for what had happened to him in prison. That he maybe blamed me in some part for it too. Even Luther didn't deserve that. "Shawn Mackenzie is responsible. It was a revenge plot, and this war is another part of it."

"I killed his brother," Luther sighed, like he'd wished he'd stayed his hand so none of this had ever happened.

Maverick looked between us again, his features twisting, revealing something of the hurt inside him that I knew was there. And the old part of me that had once loved him ached. Because he may have been a monster standing before me now, but the person those terrible things had happened to had been a boy. A boy I'd grown up with, who I'd once have done anything for.

"Nope. I'm not buying it." Maverick's expression became steely as he spun his revolver on his finger. "Sorry, old man, I'm not a stupid kid anymore. You can't manipulate me. And even if it was true, it doesn't change shit."

"That's ridiculous," Luther snarled.

"Nah, what's ridiculous is that you came all the way up here expecting a heart to heart that ended in a hug circle." Maverick smirked callously then jerked his chin at me. "You raised your boy in the image of yourself, Luther, but you raised me in the image of the Devil." He opened his arms wide, the sun gleaming off his inked chest. "I'm your creation. And you just don't like that I'm off my leash now, because I'm angry, Daddy, real fucking angry."

"You're not even listening to us," Luther growled.

"I heard every word," Maverick said icily. "But I've got a bullshitometer built into my head these days and it's working on overdrive right now."

"You're just gonna ignore the truth because you don't wanna hear it?" I said in frustration. "Don't you understand? This changes things."

"What things, Foxy boy?" he asked, his gaze full of hate. "You think even if what you said is true it'd change anything?" He pointed at Luther. "That man sent Rogue outa town into ten years of misery, he stole my chance to go after her and put me in a place where I faced hell on earth. I don't really much care if he wasn't responsible for the last part. It's still his actions that put it all in motion."

"You're hardly innocent in this war. You've killed Harlequins. You killed my great uncle Tom," I growled and Maverick shrugged, saying nothing.

"He kills the bad seeds," Luther said darkly. "Don't you, son? I know about all of them. I've even sent men to your door so that you can deal with them for me and you've done it, because you know what they are."

"I ain't done nothin' for you, Luther," Maverick snarled and I frowned between the two of them.

"What are you talking about?" I demanded, hating being left in the dark.

"The Harlequins need cleansing from time to time. It's a part of this world, you always get men who overstep, men who thwart the code. We all walk the line of bad and evil, Maverick deals with the evil. It's what I raised him to do. It was one of his callings in his life. He's made for dirty work, he thrives on it."

"It has nothing to do with you!" Maverick snapped.

"You might not want it to, Rick, but you've been killing the monsters in my gang and keeping it clean for years. I let that information reach you, I allowed you to do what you're best at."

"What about great uncle Tom?" I pushed and my dad frowned.

"He was sick in the head," Luther muttered. "One of my hackers turned up a load of child pornography on his laptop."

"What?" I hissed.

"He did more than just look at it," Maverick sneered, his eyes darkening to pitch. "He acted on those urges."

"And how'd you find out about that, huh?" Luther pushed.

"One of your men sang like a canary when I dangled him off a cliff," Maverick said with a shrug.

"And who do you think sent that man to you?" Luther said, raising his chin and Maverick bristled.

"So you've been using me?" Maverick spat.

"I've been feeding you what you went hunting for anyway," my dad said firmly as I tried to get my head around this. "It wasn't all me. You sniffed out the evil among my people like it was a damn sixth sense. You were born for it, kid."

"Don't you dare, old man," he warned. "We're not about to hug it out and have a heart-warming Hollywood moment."

"Look, I made mistakes, but they were all with the right intentions," Luther insisted, his muscles rippling with tension. "I know I fucked up, kid, but I never wanted this."

"You reap what you sow," Maverick said with a light shrug. "Isn't that the whole Harlequin mantra? Seems like you knew exactly what you were doing, even if you weren't sure how it would play out. You wanted to make puppets out of me and Foxy, and look at him now." Maverick frowned at me like he cared, his brows drawing together as he gave me a pitying look. "I can see your strings, brother. Are you blind to them, or don't you care you're on his hook?"

I glanced at Luther who gave me an imploring look, but doubt washed through my gut. Was I just his little heir, forged in the fire to look just like him?

Maverick boomed a laugh then walked around to open the driver's door to his Chevy. "Looks like you shouldn't be so worried about reclaiming my allegiance, Luther, you should be more worried about those questions I see shining in your boy's eyes. Karma's a bitch, ain't she? Gotta fucking love the way she works though." He dropped into the car, starting it up and revving the engine, making the wheels spin and sending a cloud of dust spewing over us before he released the parking brake and shot away down the road.

"Asshole," I coughed, pulling my shirt over my mouth and nose.

Luther stalked back to the truck and I trailed after him, sensing a murderous air about him that reminded me he was a coldblooded killer. Not that it was particularly hard to forget, only he'd been acting way too fucking nice to me lately and maybe what Maverick said held a ring of truth to it.

"Get in," he growled as we reached his truck and I slid into the passenger seat, pulling my shirt down again as he took off in the opposite direction Maverick had taken. "That was a shit show."

I said nothing, grinding my teeth as I played with my switch knife and we bumped along the cliff roads.

"You're not my puppet, kid," Luther said. "You know that, right?"

"I'm not a kid," I said in a warning tone and he sighed.

"Alright, but answer my question," he demanded, his hands tightening on the wheel.

"I know that I've done things I wouldn't have done if it wasn't for you teaching me to do them," I said darkly. "And I also know I've done things that I chose to do because I can be as callous as you, maybe more so. So no, I don't think I'm your puppet. But if I find out I'm wrong, I'll cut the strings, Luther. Because I'm no one's plaything."

He nodded slowly and as we drove back down to the lower quarter, he took a turning towards the beach.

"Where are you going?" I demanded, wanting to get home to check on the others.

My heart beat furiously as he drove his truck down a little unmade road that was darkened by the shadow of palm trees and old stone buildings.

"Luther," I hissed, sitting upright in my seat as fear snuck under my skin.

He pulled up at the end of the alley and shoved the door open, jerking his chin at me to get out too.

I kept the knife in my hand as I followed, my gaze never shifting from him as he moved to stand in front of the truck where the track turned to sand.

"Put the knife down," he commanded.

"No," I said instantly and his eyebrows arched.

"Don't be an idiot, put it down," he said as he tugged his shirt off to reveal the myriad of ink and scars lining his body.

My fingers twitched around the knife as he kicked off his shoes too and moved barefoot across the sand as he waited for me to obey his order.

He tossed his gun down onto his shirt and figuring he was unarmed, I threw the knife down too, watching him closely as my pulse danced under my flesh.

"Come on, shirt and shoes off. Remember when I taught you boys to fight?" he asked and I frowned.

"You want me to fight you?"

"Yeah," he said with a smirk. "'Cause I'm tired of that look in your eyes. You're angry with me, so come deal with it like a man."

"You're serious?" I balked.

"What? You think you can't take on your old man?" He came at me, shoving my chest and raising his fists as he expected me to fight back.

"You're crazy," I muttered.

He swung a punch at my shoulder, making me stumble back a step with the power behind the blow.

"I'm not fighting you." I folded my arms as I gave him a flat look.

"Because I'm gonna put you on your ass time and again like I did when you were a boy?" he asked, throwing another punch and I jerked aside to avoid it.

"I'd beat your ass these days," I said offhandedly.

"So prove it." He wrapped his leg around mine, trying to knock me to the floor, but I twisted out of the hold and slammed my knuckles into his kidney.

He barked a laugh like he enjoyed that and I figured fuck it and tore my shirt off, kicking my shoes off too. If he was giving me an opportunity to put him on the ground then fine. I'd enjoy every second of it.

"Come on, kid, show me why you're gonna take over the Harlequins one day," he encouraged, taunting me with that damn word again.

I lunged at him, swinging a hard punch and it crashed into his gut as I released my fury. I tried to get in another, but he blocked it, his fist smashing into my chest.

I stumbled back and he came at me fast, but I was ready, locking my leg around his and throwing my weight forward to unbalance him. He fell down, but hooked his arm around my neck as we went, dragging me with him and immediately rolling us, his hands winding around my throat. I broke the hold before he could get a good grip, punching him hard enough to wind him in the next moment and he lurched backwards, giving me room to throw him off of me.

He hit the sand and we both sprang to our feet, falling into a furious rhythm of punches and kicks that sent each of us sprawling to the ground more than once. We were soon sweaty, filthy and more determined than ever to win. He was right, it did feel fucking good taking out my anger on him and as I finally dropped him onto his back and pinned his body beneath mine, my forearm crushing his throat to keep him down, he tapped out and I fell down beside him, panting.

A laugh fell from my throat which he echoed and some of the anger that lived in me ebbed away like the receding tide.

"Fuck you," he said breathlessly through a grin.

"Fuck you back," I said, a smile turning up one corner of my lips.

He reached over to rub sand into my hair like he used to whenever we wrestled like this on Sunset Beach. I didn't hate that. And maybe I didn't really hate him in this moment. At least not nearly as much as I wanted to.

CHAPTER TWENTY NINE

JJ had gotten me crutches so I could move about my room and I paced around often to keep the strength up in my body, hating just lying down for hours on end, especially when I was used to daily workouts at the gym. Though with every day I moved a little further along in my recovery, I knew I was drawing closer to the inevitable. The moment this cast came off, I was out of here. And I didn't know what kind of life awaited me beyond this house.

It wasn't one I wanted, but when I heard the waves crashing against the shore and the gulls crying out in the sky, I knew there were things in this world I still wanted to experience again. Even if they didn't include my family anymore. And there was a resounding purpose in me now to hunt down Shawn and bring him to Rogue. She'd have his death, I'd make certain of it. But I'd sure as fuck be getting in some torture of my own in before he went outa this world too easy.

I did a couple of laps of the room, sweat rolling down my spine despite the aircon and the fact that I was only wearing a pair of shorts. Why was walking so fucking hard even with the damn crutches? I guess I knew the answer to that. It wasn't my leg that was the real trouble, it was the prolonged lack of nourishment and wasting away down in that fucking basement. I had to rebuild my strength all over and I was pushing myself too hard every day so I didn't feel so damn weak.

There was a sheet over the mirror on the wall to my right that I'd asked JJ to hang there. I didn't wanna see my face. I knew I was being a vain asshole, but part of the reason I'd kept the beard and shaggy hair look was because I was hoping it meant everyone would see less of my mutilated eye. I didn't need the dressings on anymore but I kept one on anyway, because unless I wanted to look like a fucking pirate and wear the eyepatch Rogue had bought me, this was my solution.

"I said no," Rogue barked from downstairs and I leaned my shoulder against the wall as I took a break by the door, wondering what was going on.

I propped one of my crutches against the wall and held onto the other so I could try the door handle, checking it was unlocked like I did ten times a day. Being a prisoner for so many weeks had left dents of anxiety in my brain about things like that. Lights on, doors unlocked.

"You can't keep him from me!" Rosie's voice carried up the stairs. "I can't believe no one even told me he was alive until now – he's my boyfriend for god's sake!"

"Sorry, pretty girl. Luther said she could stop by," JJ said to Rogue and I cursed under my breath.

My breathing shallowed and I tried to move, wanting to pretend I was asleep, but I dropped my crutch and as I leaned down to try and get it, the door flew open and knocked me off balance. I hit the floor on my ass, hissing between my teeth as I jarred my leg and Rosie stepped into the room in a bright pink sundress, her eyes puffy from crying.

"Chasey!" she cried in anguish, diving on me and I growled, pushing her back as I fumbled for my crutch. "Oh no, let me see what that horrible man did to you." She practically sat on me and my chest got too tight as I felt pinned down. I couldn't get up and I hated that, it was making my heart riot.

"Rosie, get off," I demanded, pushing her aside and dragging myself backwards to grab my crutch.

Her lower lip quivered and she suddenly reached for the dressing over my eye and pulled it clean off. I stilled, gazing at her in shock at what she'd done, watching as her expression morphed from stunned to horrified.

"He ruined you!" she shrieked, wailing like a baby and I just stared at her, frozen as those words rang in my head, tearing at my insecurities. "Why does everything bad happen to *me*?"

Rogue appeared in the doorway with JJ hot on her heels, taking one look at what Rosie had done then a sneer pulled back her lips. She snatched a fistful of Rosie's hair as Mutt dove on her, biting her arm with a savage growl. Rosie screamed like she was being mauled by a tiger and Rogue dragged her backwards into the hall kicking and screaming.

"Get out of this house!" Rogue roared. "He's not your fucking boyfriend."

"You bitch!" Rosie cried, full on sobbing now. "You kept him from me, you let me think he was dead and all this time he was here after being cut up by Shawn Mackenzie. You had no right not to tell me. And you didn't even warn me downstairs about how he looks so…" She cupped a hand around her mouth, lowering her voice to a stage whisper. "*Awful.*"

Despite how much I didn't give a shit about this girl, her words still sliced into me.

JJ stalked into the room, offering me a hand to help me up. I ignored it, wanting to do it myself, but finding myself just watching as Rogue punched Rosie hard enough to shut her up.

Rosie fell to the floorboards, sobbing into them as her shoulders shuddered. Rogue grabbed her leg, starting to haul her away like a sack of shit and Rosie looked up at me through puffy eyes. "It's okay, baby, you can get skin grafts. Plastic surgery, we'll figure it out. We'll make you *you* again." Mutt ran forward and peed on her face with such accuracy that it got her right in the mouth as she started screaming. But I couldn't even find it in me to laugh as I started sinking into a dark pit inside me, unable to get out.

Shawn was coming. I could hear his footfalls shaking the floor above me, unsettling the dust from the ceiling. I could hear him whistling, the twist of the lock and Miss Mabel begging him to leave me alone. When I'd been down there, all I'd wanted to do was die, but somehow out here, free, it all just suffocated me. I felt the claws of regret digging into my brain over everything I'd done again. I deserved his punishments, every strike, every stab, every burn.

"Ace," JJ called anxiously, gripping the back of my head as he made me look at him.

I was shaking and I wanted to crawl into myself and vanish so he didn't see me like this.

I lifted a hand to cover the destroyed side of my face and suddenly softer hands were on me and she was there, tugging my hand down and laying a kiss directly on the scarred flesh of my right eye. I felt the sting and warmth of that kiss at once and wondered if her stomach churned over touching me there like that.

"Shh," she hushed, crawling into my lap and holding me. "Fuck her," she growled. "She's gone."

I wrapped my arms around her, soaking in the warmth of her flesh and letting her presence banish the dark. JJ's hand pressed to my shoulder and I reached for him too, winding my fingers into his shirt and yanking him closer until his forehead pressed to mine.

"We're here," JJ rasped. "We're not going anywhere, Ace."

"I love all of your scars," Rogue whispered against my neck as she tucked herself closer to me. I felt the absence of my other brothers opening up an age old wound in me, but I had to take what I could get these days and the two of them this close to me was everything I could hope for.

"Keep lying to me," I growled at Rogue. "I like your lies."

"They're not lies," she lied again and I kissed her hair just as JJ did too. I felt a heated energy between us which burned me like hellfire and soothed me like heaven.

"I need to see," I exhaled, knowing it was time to face myself at last. "Pull the sheet off of the mirror, J," I asked and he moved back, frowning at me before nodding in agreement.

Rogue's fingers wound between mine as I took hold of my crutch and heaved myself to my feet. She didn't help me, she knew I didn't want that, but she held onto me the whole time like she was ready for if I tripped. She was a tiny little thing and I'd probably crush her if I fell on her, but I didn't bother to tell her that because I knew she'd never listen anyway.

I gripped the crutch with one hand and Rogue with the other as I made my way to the mirror as JJ took hold of the sheet.

"Do it," I growled and he ripped it off.

Rogue's fingers tightened on mine as I stepped forward and a sharp lump rose in my throat. My chest and arms were a mess of scars and the burn on my shoulder was now reduced to mottled reddened skin. But none of that compared to the vicious X through my right eye and I pulled my hand free of Rogue's as I raised my fingers up to brush them along the mark. It didn't hurt so much anymore, but the skin was still tender and slightly red, my eyelid not opening fully with the lingering swelling.

I turned around, glancing over my shoulder to take in the damage to my back. Slashes were torn through my tattoo of Sunset Cove, scars intersecting it, ruining the artwork. Rogue reached out to run her fingertips along the scars and I shrank from her touch, not looking at her. Somehow seeing it for myself made me feel even more self-conscious about it all. I was hideous. My body wasn't mine anymore, it was tainted by Shawn and there was nothing that would ever fix it.

I gripped my crutch and moved away from them, heading into the en suite and pushing the door shut behind me as my breaths came unevenly. I slumped against the door, lowering myself down to sit on the cool tiles as something in my chest cracked.

"Ace," Rogue called through the door. "Don't shut us out. You know we don't care about the scars."

"Bullshit," I hissed. "I wanna be alone."

"Ace," JJ said gently. "Just let us in."

"Get out of here!" I roared, bashing my fist back against the door, despising the pity in their voices.

Quiet fell and a while later the sound of their footsteps retreated from the room. I was alone. And I sure as shit had better get used to that because one day soon I'd be leaving them for good, and the only life that awaited me beyond this town was a lonely one.

I tried not to let myself think about that too much, but right now that fate was staring at me and I couldn't ignore it.

My father's voice worked its way through my head, but now it had a new lilt to it, like Shawn was there too. And there was nothing I could do to escape them.

I refused to hear the lies Rogue and JJ tried to feed me about how I 'didn't look that bad' and how my scars made me look like a 'hot badass Bond villain.' I didn't live in a fantasy world these days; I knew the reality I was facing. Beyond these walls, I was gonna frighten kids in the street, and people would find me disgusting, terrifying. They'd skirt the sidewalk so they didn't have to come near me. I wasn't vain exactly, but I'd always looked after my appearance, and now that part of me was officially gone, it felt like I'd lost something I'd never really appreciated having until now.

I mean it didn't exactly matter when I analysed it. When I was with Shawn, I'd have paid any price to have some time with my family again and I supposed I'd gotten my wish. So whatever life awaited me beyond these short weeks was gonna have to be good enough, because every moment I got with them was worth the shit storm that was coming after.

It was evening, the sky outside coloured in pastel streaks of pinks and oranges. Sometimes it was hard to believe so much pain lived in this beautiful town; if it leaked from the people living here, the sky would be deepest black and it would always be raining.

The scent of dinner carried from downstairs and I tried to hear what they were all saying between their laughter, but I could only catch the odd word. Sometimes I thought I heard my name, but I wasn't sure if I imagined it or not.

I hobbled back and forth across the room with one crutch, the pain in my broken leg not anything like it had once been. And as great as that fucking felt, it was tainted by the impending doom that came along with it. Soon, my leg would be healed, the doctor would cut the cast off and that would be it. Fox would send me away and I'd never step a foot inside this house again.

I brushed my fingers along the wall as I tried to use the crutch less, partly in case I fell and partly just to feel the cool rivets of the wall beneath my fingertips. Technically, I wasn't supposed to be putting any weight on my bad leg, but also technically I didn't entirely give a shit if I prolonged my recovery period a little.

Being aware of having to leave this place soon sure as fuck didn't make it any easier. Knowing I'd have to say goodbye to them all again made me start to drown in so much anxiety, I was sure I'd spiral if I leaned into it. So mostly I tried not to think about it. I just lived moment to moment, sucking out the good in each one and wishing it could last.

As my hair was so long now, I'd started styling it to one side, trying to cover up my bad eye. Rogue always put the eyepatch out on my nightstand every morning and I picked it up and shoved it back in the drawer every time. I wasn't gonna wear an eyepatch like a fucking pirate. I'd look like a goddamn idiot.

Footsteps sounded upstairs and a beat later, the door pushed open and I was surprised to find Fox walking into the room with a bowl of pasta in his hand and some green juice in the other. He'd been feeding me like a damn deity, everything organic and fresh and fucking delicious. Once when Rogue and JJ had been out, I'd woken up from a nap and opened the door to find Fox fast asleep there with a look of absolute exhaustion about him. I didn't like to think I was keeping him up at night; it probably drove him insane knowing a traitor was back under his roof.

He placed the food down on my nightstand and looked me up and down as I leaned against the arm of a chair by the window as I fought a wince against a shoot of pain in my shin.

"How's the leg?" he asked in a low mutter.

"Getting there," I said with an awkward twitch of my lips.

"Your dad called," he revealed.

I blew out a breath through my nose. "Wow, it only took him two weeks to pretend he gives a shit that I'm alive. Or did he not even bother to put on a farce?"

Fox didn't smile, taking a step toward me before seeming to think better of it and folding his arms instead. "He was asking for a pay out from you actually, said he'd bought a plot for a headstone next to your momma's and he couldn't get the money refunded, so you owed him the cost of it."

Bitterness coated my insides at his words. Shouldn't've hurt. Still did. "I'm surprised he even bought me one."

"He didn't," Fox said darkly. "I checked out his claims, but it was all bullshit. He even forged a receipt and sent it over to me, but knowing your daddy I dug a little deeper just to see if he really did have any decency in him. But he doesn't."

"Well that ain't news," I muttered. "I'm surprised he even tried his luck. He must be up to his neck in debt if he's working that hard to scam me outa a few hundred dollars. So did you tell him to get fucked?"

"No," he said with mischief in his eyes. "I told him you'll be leaving the money in his mailbox at midnight."

I frowned, opening my mouth to ask if he actually expected me to pay up when he went on.

"I paid off a couple of kids to give him a visit at that exact time after I filled their pockets with firecrackers and made them promise they'd get creative."

A laugh fell from my lungs, one of the first in a damn long time and Fox cracked a grin. My laughter soon died away and I dropped my gaze, looking down at my leg with a frown working itself into my brow. "Looks like I'm turning into him, aren't I? Dodgy leg, long hair, and everyone thinks I'm an asshole. I just need the wooden cane, the empty shithole of a house and the yellow teeth to finish off the look."

"Ace," Fox sighed, shaking his head at me, his eyes burning with unspoken words and if I wasn't totally fucking deluded…regret. His throat worked then he dropped his gaze and strode to the door, but before he could leave, I forced out a thanks for the food and he glanced back at me with a tightness to his expression. Something passed between us in the silence, it felt like an apology but I wasn't sure if it was mine or his. Then he was gone and the door swung closed. I automatically moved after him, hobbling along with my crutch as I went and cursing as my leg started to ache. It was not happy with my how much time I'd spent on my feet today. I made it to the door, my pulse wild as I checked it was unlocked and a heavy breath of relief left me.

I ate my food and sat on the bed in the quiet, straining my ears to hear the others downstairs but their voices weren't carrying to me now. I hated when I couldn't hear them. Icy fingers started to creep beneath my skin, finding my heart and squeezing it tight. I focused on the room around me, reminding myself I was home, in a space I knew as well as the back of my hand. But somehow that wasn't helping today. Trapped in Shawn's prison, I'd felt an eerie kind of calm, a disregard for my life. But outside of it, I realised he'd damaged me deep down, in a way I couldn't heal from. The kind of damage my father had left on me, where no one could see it.

The noise in my head grew to a roar and I fisted my hair, clenched my jaw and tried to fight away the dark with nothing but sheer will. It was a part of me now though, it ran in my blood. And whenever it claimed me from here on out, I was going to be torn apart by it. By my father, Shawn, myself. We were all the masters of my ruin and I was the product of that destruction.

A soft voice called to me that cast a ray of sunlight through the dark. Her hands fell on my face, her thumbs scoring along my cheeks.

"Chase, look at me," she demanded as my heart beat a furious tune and I managed to do as she asked.

I found myself staring at the most mesmerising creature I'd ever seen and the darkness within me started to recede, the voices quietening until I could only hear my frantic breaths and feel a burning, desperate hunger in me for this girl. A girl I'd once blamed for every bad thing in my life. But I'd been the culprit all along.

"Sorry," I said, but it came out on a heavy breath that had been locked in my lungs and her expression said she didn't catch it.

"You okay, man?" JJ asked from somewhere close by and I nodded as Rogue's hands slipped from my face.

"I'm fine," I muttered, shame washing over me at them finding me in the middle of a fucking meltdown.

I tugged at my hair, pulling it over the ravaged side of my face and Rogue frowned, reaching out to try and move it away again, but I caught her wrist in a vice like grip, a snarl on my lips.

"Don't," I warned.

Her lips parted and tension coursed through the air dividing us, speaking of the anger that had lived between us before Shawn had taken me. I was well beyond blaming her for my problems now, but I doubted she'd forgiven me for leaving her on that ferry. Which made two of us. But having a frank discussion about that now seemed pretty pointless when I was going to be leaving this place forever soon. What could be said anyway? She'd seen my true colours and she didn't like the pallet. I didn't like it either, but if we started getting into all of my regrets and the things I'd rather change about myself, we'd be stuck here writing the list for a century.

JJ moved to kneel on the bed, peeling my fingers off of Rogue's wrist and they shared a glance like they were communicating something telepathically between each other. She nodded ever so slightly and I frowned.

"Rogue wants to cut your hair and give you a shave, brother," JJ told me, but there was a glint of some wicked thought in his eyes which I didn't understand.

"I'm good," I murmured. "It helps hide the scars."

"That's the point," Rogue chimed in. "I like your scars much more than I like the hobo look. You're giving Carnival Bill a run for his money at this point." I recalled the homeless guy who lived on Carnival Hill with his wayward long hair and mad look in his eyes. Gah.

I clucked my tongue in dismissal. I was like the Hunchback of Notre Dame now, and I'd head off to live in my belltower just as soon as I was forced to leave Harlequin House. It looked like I'd be living on a steady diet of hookers if I ever wanted to fuck again too. But even as I thought of being with some random girl, I shuddered, my skin prickling all over. I didn't want any girl's hands on me but the one right in front of me, so I guessed me and my right hand were gonna be dating for the foreseeable future. *Great*.

I hadn't gotten off at all for months now, but it wasn't like there'd been much to turn me on during the torture sessions at the Rosewood Manor, and now that I was back home, I was under watch twenty-four seven so I had to own my morning glory like a man whenever Rogue slept next to me and ignore the raised eyebrow I got from JJ whenever he noticed.

"Don't lie to me," I bit at Rogue. "I can handle the truth, you know? I don't need to be molly coddled over this. I'm not a child."

"Then stop pouting like one," Rogue sniped back, flicking me between the eyes. *God*, this woman.

"She's right, man." JJ pushed a hand into my hair and I stiffened as he smoothed it away from my face. "You think this is gonna turn girls off? Scars are a kink to a lot of hot chicks."

I glanced at Rogue, unable to help wondering if she was the kind of girl who liked that. But this wasn't just a few battle scars on my chest, this was something she had to look at all the time. Though it wasn't like I could lay any claim on Rogue anyway, so why did I even give a shit?

"Let me cut it," she purred, pushing her fingers into my beard as JJ's grip tightened in my hair. Fuck, why did it feel so good? I'd been touch starved for too fucking long in that basement. Especially of the gentle kind.

"Fine," I gritted out, mostly because I just wanted her to keep her hands on me, and I didn't exactly hate JJ's being there either. I needed them close right now and I wasn't gonna think about it beyond that, because this was all just a sweet, temporary distraction before the time I'd have to let them go again.

They both pulled away and I stared after them as JJ led Rogue out of the room, his hand sliding down onto her ass as they left. Blood was rushing hard and fast to my cock and I squeezed the base of it through my shorts to try and relieve some of the building pressure, swallowing a groan. *This is pathetic.*

They returned a couple of minutes later and I noticed Rogue had stripped out of her shorts so she only wore my white wifebeater with a black skull on it. She had a box of cigarettes in her grip and a smirk on her lips, and my throat tightened as my gaze trailed down to her long, tanned legs beneath my shirt. Fuck, she looked good. Her nipples showed through the white material too, puckering as JJ shifted a lock of pastel blue hair off her shoulder and lay a kiss on her neck. He had clippers and a pair of scissors in his hands which he tossed onto the bed before pulling off his own shirt and throwing it on the floor in a fucking stripper move.

"Where's Fox?" I muttered as Rogue moved forward, taking my hand to guide me off the bed, becoming my crutch for me as I leaned on her for support.

"Out," she said simply before directing me to a wooden chair as JJ moved it to the centre of the room.

I let go of Rogue and tried to walk straight over to it, but my leg said hell no and I cursed as I stumbled but JJ caught me, helping me onto the seat. I muttered a thanks, irritated with myself, but all my embarrassment was forgotten as Rogue swung her leg over my mine and sat in my lap.

JJ passed her the scissors and she smiled innocently at me as she started cutting my beard, letting the hair just fall between us and scatter to the floor.

JJ used his phone to connect to my Bluetooth speaker and played the slow version of Goodbye by Feder and Lyse as Rogue worked to shorten the mess of hair on my face. I couldn't stop staring at her as she sat just an inch away from the bulge in my pants and I glanced at JJ as he drew closer again, wondering if he was gonna stop her sitting on me like this. He pulled Rogue's hair over her shoulders then leaned down and shimmied up the shirt she was wearing to reveal her pink silk panties beneath where they kissed her tanned flesh.

I gave JJ a confused look, my heart beating powerfully as Rogue acted like she hadn't noticed, her legs spreading a little wider as she pressed her tiptoes to the floor.

"Don't let her fall, Ace," JJ warned in a voice full of sin as he took my hand and placed it on Rogue's lower back, before gripping her hips and shoving her forward. I swore as she landed right on my cock and my fingers automatically fisted in her shirt. Her pupils dilated and a breathy noise escaped her, making me grow even harder between her thighs.

I cleared my throat, looking over at JJ and trying to silently communicate that I was having a cocktastrophe right now, but from the smirk on his face, it looked like he knew exactly what I was dealing with.

Confused as fuck, I returned to watching Rogue as she continued cutting my beard until it was short enough to start using the clippers. JJ plugged them in then handed them to her, leaning down to kiss her neck and slide a hand up her top to play with her tits. She gasped, her hips rocking over my rock hard dick and I cursed under my breath, grabbing hold of JJ's arm.

"What are you doing, dude?" I demanded.

He leaned back from Rogue, toying with her nipple beneath her shirt and using his other hand to hold her chin and make sure she was looking at me. She bit her lip, staring right at me as a moan rolled up from her throat and I swear I felt that noise right to the base of my cock.

"Showing you how hot you make my girl," he said with a shrug like this was just another day in JJ land.

"What?" I hissed, figuring he'd lost his fucking mind. I wasn't making

Rogue hot, he was. And I was just a – a fucking seat.

"Touch me," she panted, looking right at me and my throat jammed up.

"No," I growled in refusal.

JJ withdrew and I dropped my hand from Rogue's back, feeling how wrong this was no matter how much I fucking wanted her. She circled her hips in a slow, torturous movement as she turned the clippers on and started working on transforming my beard into rough stubble.

"Little one," I warned in a growl, my fingers biting into her thigh as she rocked herself over every solid inch of me and I had to suppress a groan. "Why are you fucking with me?"

"Why's everything an attack to you, Ace?" she asked in a husky voice that made the head of my cock twitch. "I'm just showing you how your scars make me feel."

"Right. So you thought you'd pity hump me?" I clipped furiously, dropping my free hand onto her other thigh and digging my fingers in as I pushed her off of my cock. She took hold of that very same hand, pressing up onto her toes to lift off of me a little. My breathing hitched as she drew it between her thighs, rubbing my fingers over the soaking patch on her panties. I stared at her as an urgent, almost violent need built in me to push those panties aside and drive my fingers into her wet pussy. But then I remembered this was a cruel game of piggy in the middle and I was the stupid little piggy who wasn't going to get his hands on the ball.

"What the fuck is this?" I snarled, snatching my hand back as the rage that lived in me reared up and tried to take over. But then Rogue settled herself back on my lap and continued working on my beard, trimming it down and rocking her hips to the beat of the music like she was totally fucking innocent.

"Rogue," I rasped, looking over at JJ, but he'd just leaned himself against the wall and was watching the show with heat in his eyes and his cock fully hard inside his shorts.

When she was finished with my beard, she finally stood up and stepped back to admire her work, brushing the hair from the shirt she was wearing before frowning at the remaining ones stuck there and pulling the whole thing off. A jagged lump rose in my throat as she stood in front of me with her perfect tits on full display and her rainbow hair tumbling all around her. My cock throbbed with need and the urge to grab hold of her built in me like a billion gallons of water against a dam. I needed her with a primal intensity that made me furious and thirsty at once. She was dangling herself in front of me like the juiciest fruit on earth and my upper lip peeled back in rage as I tried to shove out of my seat. JJ's hand landed on my shoulder, keeping me down and he slid a cigarette between my lips, lighting it up in the next second.

"Don't tell Fox," JJ said in my ear with a low laugh before looking to Rogue. "Dance for us, pretty girl." The music changed to Lost Cause by Billie Eilish and Rogue smirked as she did as he asked, her hips swaying and her eyes closing as she lost herself to the seductive beat.

JJ suddenly sprayed water on my hair and ran a comb through it casual as fuck as he started cutting it. I dragged in a lungful of smoke and the hit of nicotine made my head spin as I stared at Rogue and refused to blink. This was something straight out of my filthiest fantasies. Her in my room, topless, moving like that. It was enough to drive me fucking insane.

"It looks good a little longer, don't take too much off," Rogue told JJ and I drew in another deep drag of my cigarette, unable to even absorb those words as my gaze travelled over her tight, gold kissed body which I thirsted to wreak havoc on.

She awoke a beast in me that had never been tamed, but I was sure she had the charm to do it, she might just end up with a few claw marks along the way. Because if I ever got to own her body, I'd fuck her breathless and make her work for every second of pleasure I offered her. There was ten years of tension living between us and I could feel it making the air thicker now. It made me angry, hateful, maybe even a little vengeful. And I had no doubt she felt it too. We were perfectly designed to destroy each other and I longed to know what it would be like to burn in her fire.

JJ worked to fix my hair as I smoked and Rogue palmed her breasts and tugged on her nipples, making me harder than I'd ever been in my life. There wasn't anything sexual about hair cutting and yet JJ's hands being on me while I felt like this made it seem like we were crossing some line. I wasn't entirely fucking against it either. Man, it was good to just be touched at all. Like I still meant something to the people in this room. Something important.

Rogue's eyes opened, but they were hooded as she walked towards me, her hips swaying as she leaned over, her hand on my thigh as she plucked the cigarette from my lips and toked on it, leaving me in a cloud of smoke. Her fingers crept up my leg and I reached for her, my hand curling around the back of her thigh and squeezing hard enough to bruise.

"You don't know what you're doing to me," I growled.

I didn't have entire control of the dark in me and it was taking on a new form now which was cruel and depraved, the kind that wanted to bend her to my will and make her hurt in all the right ways.

"I know exactly what I'm doing, Chase Cohen," she said, her eyes locked on mine as she finished the cigarette. She lowered it in her hand and I flinched on instinct as I recalled Shawn stubbing his butts out on me. JJ's fingers locked in my hair and Rogue's eyes widened as she realised why I'd reacted like that.

She went to move away, but I clenched my hand tighter around her leg and snatched the cigarette from her fingers, crushing it in my palm so the fire singed the flesh, proving that I'd happily hurt for her.

"There's no pain I wouldn't weather to have you this close," I told her, tossing the butt away so ash and soot tumbled from my palm.

JJ leaned over my shoulder, sliding his hand around the back of Rogue's neck and sinking his tongue between her lips. I was crushed between his boner and her tits as they came together in a clash of desperation for each other and I growled in frustration, trying to get up, only for them each to press a hand to my shoulders to keep me in place.

"Go to your own room," I snarled, shoving them apart as heat pounded up through my chest. "Fuck your games."

"It's not a game, Ace," JJ growled.

I managed to get to my feet through brute force and elbowed him back, refusing to believe him. Because no one wanted me like this, and if the two of them had come to some twisted little arrangement to try and feign Rogue's interest in me then fuck them.

The words *I love you* flashed through my mind as I remembered Rogue saying them to me, but I blinked that vision away, knowing she hadn't meant it that way. That she couldn't possibly have. Before I looked like this, I was a monster on the inside. And she knew that. She'd seen the worst of it.

I hobbled across the room and gritted my teeth against the agony in my leg as I made it to the chest of drawers and leaned against it, pointing to the door. "Get out. Go fuck each other like you want to."

"She wants you too, man, don't you-" JJ started but I cut him off.

"Bullshit," I snarled. I was just some broken little toy they were trying to pretend was whole, and I wasn't buying any of it. "Go!" I snapped and Rogue caught JJ's hand, towing him from the room, throwing me a look over her shoulder that said I was an idiot.

Sweat was beading on my chest and my cock was still aching, leaving me confused and angry and so fucking turned on I wanted to break something. I wanted to rip this room to pieces if only I had the fucking strength to do it.

After a few minutes, a loud moan sounded beyond my window and I bit the inside of my cheek, staying rooted to the spot before it sounded again. I resisted a little longer before I grabbed my crutch and moved to the window, propping my shoulder against the side of it as I tucked myself in against the curtain.

Rogue was spread out on a sun lounger below me on the patio, fully naked with her fingers knotted in JJ's hair as he went down on her. My breaths came heavier and heavier as I watched, unable to look away and I squeezed my near painful cock in my pants.

Fuck, she was the perfect temptation, the way her back arched and she bit her lower lip, it was the hottest thing I'd ever seen in my miserable life.

Did they even realise this was right outside my window or were they just so caught up in each other that they forgot I could see the whole patio from here?

Rogue tugged and teased her own nipples as her head tipped back in utter pleasure and I memorised every inch of that expression. I'd always fantasised about how good she'd look when she was coming, and two seconds later I got my wish as she reared up, holding JJ's head between her thighs as she cried out and her eyes flashed open at the last second, boring right into mine. I wasn't quick enough to move, so I just owned it and stood there watching as she licked her lips and stared at me like I was the source of her pleasure.

JJ stood up, scooping her into his arms like she weighed nothing and taking her place on the sun lounger, laying back and settling her over his lap as she faced away from him toward me. She took hold of his thick cock and guided it to her pussy, her eyes still locked with mine as he gripped her hips and pulled her down onto him, sinking in right up to the base. She slid her fingers onto her clit as they started to fuck hard, making her tits bounce as JJ supported her hips and made her ride him to the pace he wanted.

She looked so fucking edible that my mouth watered and the way her gaze kept clinging to me made it impossible for me not to relieve myself any longer. I pushed my pants down, freeing my hard cock and gripping it tight as I started stroking it firmly in time with JJ's thrusts, picturing my cock in place of his as I drove it deep into her pussy. I thought of how wet she'd been for me in here and imagined what it would feel like to have her soaked pussy wrapped around every inch of my shaft. I pumped my cock harder, growling deep in my throat as she worked her clit, biting down on her lip as she watched the movements of my arm so she knew exactly what I was doing.

As I watched her enjoy the deep thrusts of JJ's cock, I pictured what I'd do if I got that privilege. I had so much pent up energy when it came to her, I knew I wouldn't be able to be anything but rough. She turned me into a savage and I'd unleash the full force of ten years of rage on her flesh. I'd fuck her like the animal I felt like every time she was close to me, and I'd show her why monsters were best kept in cages.

I tightened my grip on my cock, rubbing my thumb over the head and slicking the precum across the tip as pleasure rolled through my shaft. I stared at her mouth, her tits, then those sea blue eyes which owned me as I ached to own her in return.

She shuddered as she came and I fell apart with her, pleasure rocketing along the length of my cock as my cum splashed against the wall and I kept pumping it until she claimed every drop of it from me.

My breath fogged against the glass and Rogue bit her lip as she watched me, falling back against JJ as he finished with a final hard thrust, forcing her head around to claim a kiss from her lips.

I grabbed a towel hanging on the chair from my morning shower, mopping up the mess I'd made before tucking my cock away and tossing the towel in the laundry. Then I yanked the curtains shut and used my crutch to get back to my bed. My leg was seriously starting to hurt from how much I'd pushed it today, but I didn't give a fuck. I was still riding a high. My head spun from the release and a wave of peace crashed over my chest as I fell down on the mattress. I didn't know what the fuck we'd all just done, but it felt both wrong as hell and seriously fucking right.

I slid the eyepatch out from under my pillow and twirled it on my finger before mentally shrugging and putting it on. I leaned up in bed to check it out in the mirror, arranging my freshly cut hair around it which was curling as it dried. I took in the new me in that glass and found I didn't entirely hate what I saw and when the door opened and Rogue stepped into my room in another one of my shirts, her face lit up at the sight of it.

JJ followed her in with a bundle of snacks in his arms and they both piled onto my bed, acting like we hadn't just all taken part in some weird fuck fest. Mutt came bounding in too, yipping as he leapt onto the bed and snatched a gravy bone from Rogue's fingers.

Rogue tossed a bag of Cheetos at me, curling up next to me and gazing up at my eyepatch with a smirk. "Looking good, Captain Ace."

"Yeah, yeah," I murmured, tearing into the bag of chips while JJ got himself comfy on her other side, his fingers threading between hers.

I stole a look at them both, unsure how they could be so comfortable with this situation but strangely finding it didn't bother me all that much either. Maybe it was because I knew I was on a time limit, and I'd take whatever I could get from Rogue while I was still here. One thing I was sure of though, was that we'd just added to the list of things that Fox could never fucking find out about.

CHAPTER THIRTY

I raced into Chase's room with an excited shriek, throwing the door open so hard that it crashed against the wall and maybe put a hole in it. *Whoops*.

Chase cursed from his bathroom where the sound of the shower running filled the air and I clapped my hands loudly.

"Hurry up, sunshine - we're going to be late."

"Late for what?" he snapped. "And why the fuck are you in my room? I'm naked."

"I'm not interested in seeing your todger, Chase, god. Not everything is about you." I hurried over to his closet and grabbed him a pair of shorts and a white shirt before tossing the shirt back and picking a green one out instead. *Perfect*. "I would have organised this better, but I only just saw the advert online and we have to move our asses if we wanna make it on time."

"What the hell are you talking about?" Chase growled, the sound of the water shutting off following his words.

"He's in town," I said excitedly. "Well not *in* town. He's in town like six towns over. But that's close enough and I'm not fucking missing it," I explained.

"You're not talking sense."

I huffed irritably, adjusting my baseball cap and folding my arms as I waited for him to hobble his way out here. He still couldn't put any weight on his busted leg, so he took his sweet time hopping on out, one hand clutching the towel which he'd wrapped around his waist and his cast covered in a bag thingy which kept it dry.

My gaze slid over his bare chest as a few stray beads of water ran down his skin. The cuts were almost completely healed now, only red lines on his flesh remaining and leaving me free to appreciate his muscular body. JJ had taken pity on him and brought a bench and a bunch of weights up here so that he could at least do chest and arm workouts while he was locked away and his muscles were pumped from the workout he'd done pre shower.

I dragged my gaze up from his bare chest to his face, taking in the black eye patch he now wore to cover what Shawn had done to him.

Chase noticed where my attention had fallen and dropped his head, letting his wet curls fall forward to obscure his eyes and I huffed.

"Did I ever tell you about my pirate sex fantasies?" I asked him, making him look up at me again with a frown.

"What the fuck are you talking about?"

"I'm just saying, I might have to buy you a parrot. You've got the eye patch and the peg leg going for you. If you teach a parrot to say 'pretty Polly' to me then I'll probably drop right to my knees and suck your cock like a good little land wench. It's fantasy law."

Chase scoffed, taking hold of the back of a chair as he hopped towards me. "Yeah, I'm sure that'll be the case. What girl doesn't want a guy with a fucked up face who can't even walk straight? I'm a real fucking catch these days."

I rolled my eyes at him dramatically and he scowled at me.

"Are you gonna fuck off so I can get dressed then?" he asked. *Man* he was a grump this morning. But when he was a grump it usually meant he was in pain so I couldn't be too angry with him.

"No," I replied simply. "I already told you we're running late. I have somewhere to be and you need a round the clock nurse. JJ has shit to do at the club today and Fox is off being all Harlequinish which makes you my problem."

"I can't leave the house, remember?" Chase muttered, making it to the bed and half falling down onto it while clutching his towel tightly in his fist like he was afraid a strong breeze might blow in and steal it. Which was massively unlikely seeing as all the windows were shut and the curtains were permanently closed in here. Supposedly that was to make sure no one saw him here, but I was pretty sure that it was at least half because Chase didn't want anyone to see him period. And I was done with that shit. Especially today.

"Yeah well, I never was one for the rules. And I have a date today which you're going to chaperone whether you like it or not."

"What the fuck are you going on about? You and JJ don't need me to-"

"Err who said anything about JJ? This is a much bigger deal than anything in the damn Cove. This is a live GPR signing event and I'm not fucking missing it because you need someone here to change your diapers all day." I folded my arms to let him know I meant business, but he just seemed more confused than ever.

"A what?"

"Green Power Ranger, duh." I flicked him in the forehead and he jerked away from me.

Understanding dawned and he shook his head with a grunt of irritation. "I'm not going out with you to some dumb signing with a dude from a kids show."

"That would be where you're wrong." I lunged at him with the green shirt in hand and managed to force it over his head before he could fight me off. He was left with no choice but to jam his arms through the holes and he growled at me as he wrestled me back, catching my wrists and pinning me to the bed beneath him with my hands above my head.

"I'm not going out," Chase snarled in my face and I sighed, the fight going out of my limbs as I pouted.

"Fine," I agreed with a sad sniff. "I just thought it might be nice to do something fun for once. I'm so sick of being miserable and afraid all the time. I only wanted to try and have some fun."

Chase frowned down at me as I gave up like he'd been expecting more of a fight and he drew back, releasing me.

I pushed off of the bed and headed for the door, sniffing loudly and swiping at my cheek as I went.

"Wait," Chase called just before I could disappear and I paused with my back to him, a smirk on my lips as I waited. "Is this really that big of a deal to you?"

"I'd give my right eye to go," I agreed, still not looking at him.

Chase coughed a surprised laugh "Wow, you really are an asshole, aren't you?"

"Yeah. But I don't think you'd want me any other way." I looked back over my shoulder, finding his gaze on me.

"Fox won't like it," he warned.

"He'll hate it," I agreed. "But you get off on going against him anyway."

"So do you," he pointed out.

"Well why don't we get off together then?" I teased. "Or do you prefer watching?"

"Fuck you," he replied, his gaze skimming down my body and making heat rush beneath my skin as I thought about what the three of us had done the other night. Or what we'd almost done. I still hadn't quite figured out if Chase had sent us packing because he wasn't into it or if it was his insecurities showing. So for now I was playing it by ear but I seriously couldn't have said I would have minded if he'd chosen to get a whole lot more involved with us than just jerking off while watching us together. Not that I was going to be telling him that.

"Unlikely," I tossed back. "Not unless you get that parrot."

Chase launched a pillow at me from his bed and I laughed as I made a run for it, escaping before it could hit me and charging downstairs.

I grabbed the wheelchair Chase had come home with from hospital and half pushed, half tossed it down the stairs into the garage before somehow heaving the heavy as shit thing up into the back of my jeep. Then I reclined the passenger seat as far as it would go and stuffed a few pillows in the footwell.

I quickly started up the engine then pulled the car out of the garage and parked it outside the front door, ignoring the Harlequins Fox had left manning the gates of the property as they shot me curious looks.

By the time I made it back up the stairs, I found Chase dressed in the shorts I'd laid out for him and smirked as I let my imagination run over how he'd managed to pull them over his leg with his big ass cast stopping him from bending his knee.

"Why are you smiling at me like that?" he asked.

"Don't you like it when I smile?"

"Not like that. You're clearly up to something."

"Duh. We're heading out despite the badger's strictest warnings. Now come and ass bump down the stairs or we're gonna be late."

"I'm not ass bumping anywhere."

I smirked at the challenge that presented me with then darted into his room, snatched his crutches and ran to the window with them.

"Rogue, what the hell are you-"

Chase didn't need to finish that question because I'd already thrown his window open and launched the crutches out of it. They fell into the pool with a loud splash and I slapped a hand over my mouth with an exaggerated gasp.

"Oh my god, Chase, your crutches just committed suicide rather than listen to another grumpy word coming out of your mouth!"

Chase gaped at me for several long seconds then finally broke a laugh. "Sometimes I dunno whether I hate you or love you," he growled at me.

"Loving me is way more fun," I promised, skipping back across the room towards him as the weight of his gaze on me increased and I was pretty certain we were both thinking about those three little words I'd spoken to him when The Dollhouse was caving in. But today was about something far more important than our emotional baggage so I just gave him a nudge towards the door without mentioning it. "I'll ass bump with you. It'll be fun. Besides, I can't support your weight on the stairs and you know it. If you fall over there's no way I can hold your big muscly ass up, so bumping is the safest bet."

Chase grumbled as I guided him down to sit on the top step, but I just knocked my shoulder against his and leaned in to whisper to him.

"Last one to the bottom is a frigid duck." I shoved off the step, my ass hitting the next one down and Chase cursed as he fell for the game, grabbing my arm to stop my advance as he butt scooted past me.

"Hey!" I complained, smacking his hand off of me while he snorted in amusement and took the lead.

Chase kept bumping down the stairs and I smirked at him as I got to my feet and ran after him, leaping over his broken leg and landing at the foot of the stairs while he still had three to go.

"I win," I announced, flashing him a grin as I held a hand out to him.

"You fucking cheated," Chase said, taking my hand in his and letting me haul him back up onto his good leg.

He stumbled as he tried to get his balance and I ended up crushed beneath his bulk against the wall at the foot of the stairs. His hard body was all muscly and tempting and I got way too carried away with my pirate fantasy as he pinned me there like a damsel who'd been found floating out at sea on a piece of driftwood, then hauled onto Captain Ace's ship where he drove his plank into my sunken chest and-

"Fuck. Sorry," he said, shoving against the wall to right himself and quickly running a hand through his hair so that it fell down over his eye patch in some dumb attempt to cover it up again.

"Come on, hoppy, we don't have all day." I slipped my arm around his waist and let him lean on me as we headed through the kitchen and I guided him towards the front door.

"How exactly do you plan to get us out of here past the Harlequins?" Chase demanded.

"Those assholes out there? Easy. Just follow my lead and they'll be putty in my hands."

Chase muttered something about that being highly unlikely and I shook my head at him as I whistled for Mutt and opened the front door.

I guided Chase towards my Jeep, opening the door for him and he grabbed the roof bars, heaving himself up and into the car with a grunt which could have been from pain or irritation as I jogged around to get in behind the wheel.

I helped prop his broken leg up on the pillows I'd piled in his footwell then leaned across him to fasten his seatbelt.

"What are you doing?" he asked.

"Keeping you safe. I'm not losing you again, Ace. Especially not to some dumb accident."

He gave me an odd look and I tilted my head to one side as I looked back at him before reaching out to push the dark curls back from his face.

"Don't," he snapped, quickly ruffling his hair and making it fall back down over his forehead again and I huffed in irritation.

"Why are you so determined to hide?" I snapped right back.

"Because I don't need the whole world gawping at me for being some one-eyed, scarred up freak."

I sighed heavily, biting down on my bottom lip before climbing across the centre console and settling myself in his lap, my thighs straddling his as I took his jaw in my grasp and forced his gaze onto mine.

"Fuck Shawn," I said firmly. "He doesn't get to do this. Tell me you're not going to let him. Because if he does, then he wins. And he isn't going to fucking win, is he?"

"Him winning or losing makes no difference to how fucked up I look," Chase muttered, his blue eye searching mine as his hands tentatively rested on my waist.

"So you're bothered about the one eye thing?"

"I still have two eyes," he grunted.

"Mmmhmm. Why don't you take the eyepatch off then?"

"My eyelid still isn't fully healed," he said firmly though I was pretty sure that was bullshit because JJ had told me he didn't even really need the dressings anymore.

"Do you trust me?" I asked suddenly, knowing that was a pretty big question between the two of us after the stunt he'd pulled abandoning me on that ferry.

"Yes," Chase breathed eventually and I flashed him a big smile.

"Okay. Close your eyes then - or eye. You know what I mean."

He gave me a grumpy fucking look but did what I'd asked as I just stared at him, waiting him out. His grip on my waist tightened as he waited to see what I would do and I quickly turned and yanked open the glovebox, rummaging a bit before finding a silver sharpie in there.

Chase still waited to see what I was going to do, so I leaned in and gently brushed my fingers down the side of his face which had taken on the new scars.

"This is just flesh and bone, Ace," I murmured, trailing my fingers over the edges of the scars that peeked out from beneath the black eyepatch he wore. "And the scars on your body don't make you any less. They make you more.

They show your strength.”

His grip on me grew firmer until he was reeling me in like I was a fish caught on a line and I let him because I wanted him to catch me, no matter how much fucked up juju had passed between us. He was still my boy. He leaned into my touch and I continued to caress his skin while gently drawing what I needed with the sharpie.

“But if you’re really that bothered about having two eyes, then fine. Now no one will know the difference and you can stop worrying about it,” I added triumphantly.

“What?” he muttered, his good eye opening and pinning me with a stare for half a moment before his gaze landed on the sharpie I still held.

“You have real pretty eyelashes,” I breathed and he cursed me, tossing my ass back into the driver’s seat and yanking the rear view mirror towards him so that he could appreciate my artwork while I laughed.

He now had a pretty eye drawn on the material of his eyepatch to match the one that still worked. It was totally subtle. I doubted anyone would even notice he didn’t just have his two normal, boring eyes.

“Rogue, you asshole,” he snarled at me as Mutt yipped at him from the backseat in warning and I started up the engine. “I’m not going out looking like this.”

“Wow, ungrateful much?” I teased, driving away from the house towards the gates so that he couldn’t get any dumb ideas about trying to get out. I locked the doors for good measure.

“I look fucking ridiculous,” Chase said angrily.

“So take the patch off if you’re gonna be all pissy about it,” I suggested, laughing as he lunged at me and snatched the Green Power Ranger cap from my head.

“Fuck you,” he muttered, putting it on and tugging the peak low to shadow his face.

“Aww don’t be a baby about it, Ace. You can draw a cock on my face if it’ll make you feel better?” I offered him the sharpie, but he just snatched it and tossed it back into the glovebox.

“How about I just get revenge some other time instead,” he said and I grinned.

"Bring it on, bad boy. I'll start sleeping with one eye open - unless you've got that covered already?"

"Seriously? You're gonna make this a joke?" He pointed at his face angrily but I didn't care.

I shrugged because yeah, I would be making it a joke and he would stop being a bitch about it. Just like the time I fell off of Rick's bike when I tried to ride it and Chase told me not to be a bitch about my road rash. And that had hurt like a motherfucker.

I was forced to stop at the gates as the Harlequins frowned at us in confusion but luckily Chase didn't seem inclined to make a one legged break for it.

"Hey," Basset said, moving to stand by my window and looking between me and Chase curiously. "I didn't know you were heading out today."

"Emergency enema," I explained, jerking a thumb at Chase who looked a little less than pleased about my cover story.

"Oh tell the whole fucking world then," he snarled, playing along despite the fact that he clearly wasn't happy about it. But we'd set the parameters for running cons back when we were eleven and the rules were clear: once someone started a story you had to stick with it no matter what. No contradictions, no changing it up.

"Yeah well, I'm not the one who has a bunged up back door," I replied with a shrug, leaning towards Basset and lowering my voice. "I told him he was eating too much fibre. Or not enough fibre… I dunno. But there was a definite fibre miscalculation there because he's been squatting on the toilet all of yesterday and all fucking morning too, so the doctors told him I had to rush him in before there was a back up. Wouldn't want it to go bang, you know?"

Basset nodded seriously, motioning for the others to open the gates for us and I flashed him a smile before heading on through.

"Go bang?" Chase asked, half laughing while trying to maintain his broody, moody thing.

"Yup. Poosplosion. Can you imagine?"

"I'd rather not."

"Good point. Shall we grab some food?"

"What part of that visual made you hungry?" Chase demanded and I just shrugged as I headed towards the nearest drive thru to load us up on car snacks for the journey.

"Dude, I was born hungry."

"Everyone was born hungry. That's literally the only thing babies care about," Chase pointed out.

"I'm pretty sure babies care about all kinds of things. Like world domination and cute cat videos and generally trying to fuck with people whenever possible. Anyway, have you got your wallet to pay for all this food?" I asked.

"No, I don't have my fucking wallet. This is your day out, not mine."

"Oh, don't worry. I grabbed it on our way out of your room." I tugged his wallet from my pocket and gave it a little shake to show him as we pulled into the drive thru and I started eyeing the menu excitedly.

"You're a fucking menace," Chase grumbled as I started picking out snacks for us, but I could see the corner of his mouth lifting just a little, so I knew he liked it.

"And you're a buzz kill. But somehow it works, doesn't it?"

I pulled up to the window and ordered us a shit ton of food on Chase and he just watched me like a weirdo the whole time until I was dumping the paper bag filled with goodness into his lap and paying for it on his card.

"You're gonna have to feed me while I drive," I commanded as I pulled away again, heading for the highway and my GPR day of dreams.

I opened my mouth for some fries and Chase cursed me out before shoving a whole handful into my mouth.

I choked around my laughter as I started chewing them and for a moment I could have sworn that Chase actually fucking smiled at me out the corner of my eye.

"Okay, would you rather be a bee who's allergic to honey or an owl who hates rock music?" I asked.

"You really wanna play that game?" Chase asked unenthusiastically.

"Why? Are you chickening out of answering on round one?" I challenged in response and he groaned dramatically before answering.

"The bee."

"Seriously? That's fucked up, dude. What kind of loner bee life would you lead in that scenario?"

Chase threw some more fries at me and I laughed as we sped onto the highway, leaving our troubles behind us while racing to meet my lifelong hero.

It was after dark by the time we got home, and I was fucking exhausted. My Jeep was full of Green Power Ranger merch which had been surprisingly affordable with my five finger discount, and when Fox came storming out of the house to start laying into us for running off, I made good use of him by dumping a heap of sweaters, shirts and a limited edition sword into his arms.

I grinned at him as I started telling him about our day and he didn't even bother to tell me off as he dutifully carried all of my new shit inside.

JJ came out to help Chase into his wheelchair and I flopped down on the couch dramatically, surrounded by all of my new things.

"So how was it?" JJ asked as he wheeled Chase inside and parked him up beside me.

"Fucking epic," I said, smiling so wide my cheeks hurt.

"You weren't saying that when we got there," Chase pointed out and my smile fell from my face.

"That's because it was a fucking joke," I snapped, remembering my fury when we'd finally arrived at the plaza where the signing was taking place.

"What was?" Fox asked, moving to sit beside me and my hoard, handing over a cup of coffee. I groaned as I drank some of it, letting Chase explain the drama.

"The dude was wearing his White Ranger shit doing some talk on a stage," Chase explained.

"White Ranger sucks ass," I growled, folding my arms.

"Yeah, I know. Because you yelled that out multiple times in front of all those kids who were trying to listen to what he was saying," Chase added.

JJ barked a laugh and I rolled my eyes.

"The advert said *Green* Ranger, not White. I wouldn't have gone if it had been the fucking White Ranger.”

“They’re the same dude though, aren’t they?” Fox asked with a frown. “Didn’t he just come back into the show wearing a different colour and-”

“It wasn’t the fucking same!” I barked. “Don’t talk to me about GPR vs WPR, Fox, I swear I’ll lose my shit.”

They all laughed at me and I just shrugged, digging my limited edition GPR helmet out of my pile of swag and putting it on. In fact, it was so limited edition that it hadn’t actually been up for sale, and I’d definitely just stolen it while the dude was taking some photos with some kids.

“Well, luckily he didn’t stay wearing the costume for the signing part,” Chase added.

“No, he just wore stupid jeans and a normal person shirt for that bit,” I agreed. Not that I was bitter. I mean, apparently he isn’t in character every day of his life and that was fine. Lame, but fine.

“So he signed some shit for you?” JJ asked, seeming genuinely interested in my day.

“Yep. And we got to cut the queue because Chase was in his wheelchair,” I added with a grin.

“I felt very used,” Chase agreed. “She literally pushed me through the crowd like I was a human battering ram yelling ‘we need the disabled line!’ until we were ushered to the front. I felt kinda like a terrible person for it, but also the line was like a nine hour wait, so I was down with it. But then Rogue told the guy I was near brain dead after getting hit by a truck and I had to play along.”

“Oh don’t bitch, he signed your cast!” I pointed out the signature on it and Chase gave me a dry look.

“Why does it say, ‘to Shelly Tithole’?” JJ asked as he leaned in to read it.

“That was his cover name, duh,” I said.

“Thanks to you,” Chase tossed back.

Fox and JJ laughed and I tossed the helmet aside before plucking a GPR mug out of the pile and offering it to JJ.

“I got you this to say sorry for Pikachu,” I explained as he took it.

“It’s not the same,” he replied with a sad little frown.

“No. It’s an upgrade,” I agreed though he looked like he didn’t agree.

"So what did he sign for you?" Fox asked me before we had to hear another load of grief over JJ's dumb mug.

"Just a photo and my hat and some merch things," I said, looking through my heap for the photo while Chase piped up with his two cents.

"He refused to sign her tits," Chase said, giving me a flat look and I scowled at him as Fox bristled.

"Good." Fox looked from me to Chase, seeming to suddenly realise that he was hanging out down here like the rest of us and his posture tightened. "You need to go back to your room now anyway. Fun's over. And if you put her in danger by sneaking off out of the house with her again, then maybe I'll have to reconsider how lenient I've been with you."

The fun energy in the room popped like a balloon and I frowned at Fox as he strode away from us.

JJ sighed, reaching out to help haul Chase upright and I got up too but instead of leaving with the two of them, I folded my arms and waited for them to go.

"Seriously?" I demanded angrily as Fox dropped into an armchair and swiped a hand down his face.

"Don't start with me, Rogue, you're just lucky I'm not punishing you for going against my orders today too."

"Oh, so that's it? I thought this house was a democracy. Or does that only apply when it suits you?"

"You know full fucking well who and what I am," Fox growled, dropping his hand and glaring at me. "I might be the boy you grew up with, but I'm a leader of the Harlequins now too. And Chase's fate is a Crew issue. Not an *us* issue."

"Well isn't that convenient. I guess you get a free pass then for this asshole behaviour. Poor Fox just has to follow the rules. He couldn't possibly pardon the man he grew up with after finding out he'd endured weeks of torture without ever once selling you out."

"That's enough," Fox snapped, shoving to his feet and glaring down at me, using all of his big bastard points to try and force me into submission, but that wasn't going to fucking happen.

"Don't try to intimidate me, Badger," I snarled, climbing up onto the couch so that I was just as tall as him as I glared into his eyes. "The only reason you banished Chase in the first place was because of me. I'm the one he left on that ferry and guess what? I'm over it. Was it a dick move? Yeah. Was I pissed as all hell at him for it? Yeah. But do I think that after losing his fucking eye, being beaten to hell and having his leg shattered while refusing to sell a single one of us out was punishment enough? Yeah, I do. So if I can forgive him for leaving me behind on that ferry then why the hell can't you?"

"Because he almost lost you again!" Fox roared at me, lunging forward so suddenly that I stumbled back a step, losing my balance and falling onto my ass on the couch beneath him. "For ten long, miserable years I had to endure a life without you. Not knowing where you were or what had happened to you, worrying about you constantly and knowing I'd let you down in the worst possible way. Do you know how much the last words I spoke to you have haunted me all this time? I made you think that you were nothing to us. Nothing to me. When that couldn't have been further from the truth. I wallowed in the dark and grew into a monster without you here to keep me from the worst parts of myself and he was just going to throw you away!"

Fox's chest rose and fell heavily and he turned away from me, stalking towards the patio doors as he carved a hand through his blonde hair.

I swiped a stray tear from my cheek as my heart raced at his words but as I pushed myself to my feet I refused to back down from my point.

"And now you're willing to throw him away just the same," I said, my voice cracking. "So when will it ever just stop?"

Fox stilled, his entire body going rigid with tension and for a moment I thought he was going to turn back to me, break for me, agree with what I'd said and change his mind about this whole fucking mess and try to fix the family that had been broken so long ago.

But instead he just snatched a bottle of rum which was sitting on the table by the patio doors then stormed out into the dark by the pool without another word.

I drew in a shaky breath, wiping the tears from my cheeks as I decided to go after Chase instead of hounding after Fox.

He needed his meds anyway and I was sick of trying to convince Fox to stop being such an asshole towards Chase all the damn time. I was the one he'd left on that fucking ferry and it wasn't like I was pouting all over the house about it. He needed to drop it so that we could all move the fuck on or he was going to ruin us much more thoroughly than Chase had ever managed.

"I'll talk to him," JJ said as the three of us made it into Chase's room and I pushed the door closed behind us.

"It's fine, man. Fox has made his feelings perfectly clear and I don't even disagree with him. I fucked up. And I keep fucking up. I couldn't even get myself out of that goddamn basement where Shawn was keeping me. I'd have died if it wasn't for Maverick showing up when he did. And Miss Mabel..."

We'd spoken more than once about the fact that the old woman who had once been the only adult I'd ever been able to rely upon was locked up in the Rosewood Manor basement, held by her asshole nephew so he could steal his inheritance before she'd even died.

"You know what?" I said suddenly. "We should go get her out of there today."

"Seriously?" JJ asked, his brow furrowing.

"Yeah. Why the fuck not?" I raised my chin as I made this decision, knowing I wasn't gonna back out of it. "She was always there for us when we needed her. All we'd have to do is sneak in through that tunnel you and Rick used to escape and we can rescue her. Kaiser Rosewood is just some fluffed up wannabe gangster. I'm not afraid of him."

"One problem," Chase said, pointing at his fucked up leg. "I can't exactly show you where that tunnel is. In fact, I was so out of it when I escaped that I don't even think I *know* where it is."

"Sorry, champ. You'll be sitting this one out," I told him, taking my phone from my pocket and shooting Rick a text, telling him what I needed him to do. "But I have someone else who knows all about the secret entrance on speed dial."

"You really think we can trust Maverick to help with this, pretty girl?" JJ asked, the look in his eyes telling me he was in without me even needing to ask.

"Yeah. He's already agreed to meet us there." I held my phone out to show them the message he'd sent just as it pinged again.

"He also wants to remind you who owns your wet cunt when he sees you," Chase said in a pissy tone and I laughed as I glanced at the message Rick had sent detailing exactly that.

"Well, we'll have to see if he does a good job tonight before I start considering a reward system," I said with an innocent shrug while JJ gave me a hungry look that said he was more than happy to take part in that game.

The door swung open behind us and we all froze like a bunch of naughty school kids as Fox glared in at us with his arms folded.

"Were you gonna tell me about this half assed plan or just leave me in the dark?" he demanded.

"Probably the dark thing," I admitted as I turned to look at him, still feeling all kinds of raw and angry about our fight. "On account of you going all Badger on us and trying to say no."

"You think I'd shut you down on this?" Fox asked, emotion flashing in his eyes for a moment before he stamped it down. "You know I care about Miss Mabel too."

I bit my lip, approaching him slowly and taking his hand in mine as I held his gaze. "I'm not asking permission to go, because this is happening," I warned him. "But I am asking you to come help us," I added in a softer tone. "And I'd really like it if you'd say yes."

Fox glanced between me and the others, scraping a hand down his face before he nodded. "Yeah. Alright, I'm in."

I squealed a little bit, leaping up and wrapping my arms around his neck as I whispered in his ear. "We're meeting Rick at midnight."

CHAPTER THIRTY ONE

I waited on the track that led into the woodland surrounding the Rosewood Manor, leaning against a tree in the dark. I could have navigated these woods with my eyes shut, seeing as we'd played here so often when we were kids. It had all seemed bigger back then, an endless enchanted forest full of monsters and adventure. Now it was just trees, and the shadows were just shadows. Growing up was a bitch. It seemed like the world would be far better off if we kept the minds of children.

Anxiety stirred under my skin tonight as I waited to see Rogue again. After I'd told her what Krasinski had done to me, all I could think about when she left the Isle was that maybe once she was away from me, the reality of what had happened would fully descend on her. She'd realise I was dirty, and when she thought of me, she'd cringe. I'd almost played Russian roulette tonight for the first time in a while. I'd held the gun to my head and thought of his hands on me, I'd thought about the way Rogue might look at me the next time we locked eyes. But then I remembered her telling me she loved me and wondered if that could possibly be true. So instead of letting my mind create stories, I'd lowered the gun and decided I was going to see it for myself tonight, look right into her eyes and find out if my demons were too dark for her or if she could really handle them.

It didn't make me feel any less uneasy about seeing her, all I could think about was her face twisting at the sight of me, a look of repugnance taking the place of the desire she'd felt for me before. I guessed fantasies did still exist as an adult, but they were the kind which convinced you that your worst fears could easily be brought to life. Imagination games weren't fun when they were full of your worst nightmares.

The sound of voices reached me through the trees and I remained still in the dark as I listened to Rogue speaking to JJ, curious what they were like together when no one else was around.

"-you'd actually rather have a cabbage for a head than a potato?" Rogue scoffed.

"Potatoes have no personality," JJ argued. "At least a cabbage has a bit of flare about it."

Rogue laughed. "That's stupid. Cabbages have those flappy leaf thingys, at least with a potato for a head you could blend in a little. Put a hat and some sunglasses on and no one would bat an eye."

"Depends if the potato is head sized or potato sized," Fox's voice joined the conversation and anger tore up my spine. What the fuck was he doing here?

"It's obviously head sized," Rogue said in exasperation like he was being slow and a smirk tugged at my lips.

"How's that obvious? You said, 'Would you rather have a potato for a head or a cauliflower?'" Fox tossed back.

"It was implied, duh," she replied.

"Rogue's right." I stepped out of the trees into their path and Fox's hand went straight to the gun on his hip, but he didn't draw it. "Obviously the vegetable would be head sized. And I'd pick a potato clearly, a cauliflower wouldn't withstand a single good punch."

JJ smirked as they all stopped in front of me and my gaze slid quickly to Rogue's eyes, hunting for any source of doubt there about me. But she just strode right towards me, tiptoed up and kissed me like the only source of oxygen in the world right now was in my mouth.

I pressed her to me by her lower back, wanting to make a show for Fox but finding I didn't give a damn about him as I just took a kiss from my girl and tasted her desire for me on her tongue. It soothed the thrashing creature in my chest which was afraid of her judgement and as our lips parted and I stared into her eyes, I found nothing there but the same hunger for me she'd had the last time I'd seen her. *Thank fuck for that.*

"Dammit, beautiful," I sighed. "I think you just swallowed my heart."

She chuckled, stepping back and rubbing her stomach. "Is that what that was? Tasted like a peach."

I glanced over at Foxy, surprised he hadn't tried to kill me for that move, but I found JJ had a tight hold of his arm and Fox's teeth were bared like he was in pain.

"You should try doing some yoga, Foxy boy," I said with a taunting smile. "It might help with the constipation you're clearly struggling with."

He jerked his arm out of JJ's grip, his eyes darkening several shades as he strode towards me. Rogue automatically put herself between us and I noticed she had her own gun stashed in the back of her denim shorts. It was shit hot and I decided I wanted to get her a gun myself, one she could tuck back there between her ass cheeks any time she liked and remember who put it there.

"This is a one night only thing," Fox said. "So I don't want any bullshit from you. We're going in there for Miss Mabel and when we're out, we can go our separate ways again."

I thought on that, rocking my head from side to side. "Nah, actually this is *our* operation. I don't recall you getting an invite. So I say me, Rogue and Johnny James go and fetch her and you can sit here on a rock like an old, angry toad waiting for a rainstorm."

Fox took a step toward me with a growl. "You son of a-"

"Bitch?" I finished for him as Rogue planted a hand against his chest to stop him coming at me. "Maybe. Or maybe she was a sweet little mermaid. No one knows. I could see myself with a seashell bra and a tail though, couldn't you?"

"This isn't helping Mabel," JJ stepped in. "Let's just get moving."

"I'll move when he stops looking at me like he's gonna put a bullet in my head the second I turn my back on him," I said with a sneer, jerking my chin at Fox.

"Unlike you, Maverick, I never wake up planning to kill my own brother," Fox said with an echo of the long lost love between us.

"Not until I fucked Rogue anyway," I mocked and Rogue cursed, slapping my chest hard.

"Would you both just stop it?" she demanded as Fox bristled, his shoulders heaving like a bull about to charge, and I rather enjoyed being the red flag that riled him up. "Miss Mabel is alone in that house with her monster of a nephew and we're the only ones that even know she's alive. So can we just go rescue the only decent adult I ever knew as a kid?" Her expression flickered with emotion and my shoulders sagged as I gave in to those destructively blue eyes.

"Fine, but I still don't see why you brought him along for the ride." I turned around, taking my chances with Fox's anger as I led the way up the track.

"Technically he caught us planning to sneak out and invited himself," Rogue murmured.

"And technically, I wouldn't have had to if you trusted me with things like you apparently do the rest of our family," Fox said in frustration.

"Family," I tsked, shaking my head. "I see you inherited Daddy's delusions."

Fox moved to walked beside me and I upped my pace, sensing he was trying to take the lead even though I was the only one who knew where to find the damn entrance to the tunnel. JJ and Rogue half jogged behind us to keep up as we walked on the verge of running.

"At least I still know the meaning of the word," Fox bit at me.

"And what's that, Foxy? Being bossed around by you all day?" I tossed back.

"No. Loyalty," he growled.

"Yeah, loyalty to you. If your little family are loyal to each other and not you though then it's game over, right?"

"It goes both ways," he hissed.

"Uhuh," I said lightly. "It's cute that you think your remaining so-called brother wouldn't stab you in the back just like the other one did."

"Shut up, Rick," JJ snapped from behind us, but I was on a roll now, enjoying seeing how hard I could get that vein in Fox's temple pulsing.

"Nothing could destroy mine and JJ's bond," Fox said assuredly and I couldn't help a dark chuckle, earning me a jab in the back from Rogue which I ignored.

"You're a king sitting in a falling castle, brother, only you're blind to the roof falling down around you."

"My castle is just fine," he gritted out. "But yours is sure looking pretty empty. You ever think about making nice and coming home?"

My eyebrows arched and I stole a glance at his face, finding an unreadable wall in his eyes. Why the fuck would he go and say that?

"I don't 'make nice'," I muttered. "And there's no home for me in Sunset Cove anymore."

"I think you're afraid," he said in a low voice.

"I'm not afraid of anything," I growled.

"Yeah you are," he pushed. "You can't let go of your anger at Luther or me because that's all you've got left, isn't it? Just you and your Isle and your rage. But it doesn't have to be like that."

"I'm rather fond of my rage, we go way back. But are you actually angling for a makeup hug, Foxy, or do you just want me to get closer so it's easier to slide a knife into my back?"

He shook his head in irritation, saying nothing and I frowned, unsure what the fuck he was thinking until he finally spoke again.

"I guess we both know it's too late for that," he said, lifting a hand to run his fingers over the place on his neck where I'd shot him. My throat constricted like a python was coiled around it and I focused back on the track ahead of us as we all fell silent and marched into the dark.

"You seem a little bitter about me hating you, Foxy," I said after a while and he shrugged.

"You seem a little half-hearted in your attempts to hate me, Rick," he replied.

"How so?" I scoffed.

"Apparently you have eyes among my men watching me. I haven't rooted them out yet, but I have to wonder how you haven't caught me off guard before now if you're watching my movements."

"Nah, it ain't men," I said dismissively, ignoring his accusation. "Might be a bug or two though."

"Hmm." He eyed my expression, clearly trying to work out if I was lying or not. I guess he'd never know.

Eventually I turned us off the main path up into the woods, hunting for the star shaped rock I'd placed on the hatch that would lead us into the secret tunnel.

When I found it, I pulled it open, shining the flashlight on my phone down at the dark steps. JJ adjusted the pack on his shoulders and moved forward to take the lead. Fox caught his arm, pulling him back as he glared at me.

"It's Maverick's tunnel, let him go first," he said firmly, like he thought I might have laid a trap down there.

"It'd be a pretty convoluted plan to lure you all out here and kill you underground," I pointed out. "I could have shot you ten times by now with how often you lowered your guard."

"Then how come when you had the chance to shoot me at Harlequin House you missed?" Fox taunted and words spilled through my head that had no business showing their little lettery faces. *Because I didn't really want you to die.*

"I was untrained," I said coolly. "But that ain't a problem for me anymore." I grinned psychotically just to remind him that I was always the danger in the room, but he just rolled his eyes at me. *Asshole.*

Rogue swept past us, heading straight down the steps into the dark. "I'm bored of you dickwads," she called back. "I'm gonna go save Miss Mabel myself. Come on, J."

Johnny James jogged after her and I cursed as I stepped forward to follow, my shoulder bashing against Fox's as he did the same. We shoved and pushed our way down into the dark, fighting to get ahead, but every time I got a step forward, the motherfucker gained it back until we were both marching along the tunnel side by side as pissed off as two hungry lions.

"Hold up, Rogue," I hissed as we made it to the end of the passage and reached the stairs that led up to the fountain.

I bumped into JJ in the dark and muscled my way past him to catch

Rogue's hand, pulling her tight to my side.

"We gotta be smart about this," I muttered.

"Well I wasn't planning on being dumb about it," Rogue shot back and a breath of amusement left me.

"We need to take the darkest route to the house," Fox said.

"Nah, I opt for the quickest," I argued.

"If we're seen, we'll lose our chance to get to her," Fox said through his teeth.

"And if we're slow, there'll be more time for us to be seen," I pushed.

"I say we take a vote," Rogue said.

"This isn't a democracy," Fox growled.

"Well maybe it should be," JJ piped up and we all turned to him as he glared at us through the light of my phone. "This is a family mission, not a Harlequin one." He gave Fox a pointed look and Fox sighed, looking to the ceiling like some god above could offer him help. But if anyone was up there, I doubted they'd be paying attention to a few ruffians in a hole.

"I'm not a part of this family, so I'm gonna do whatever the fuck I like," I said stubbornly.

"This isn't about you," Rogue snipped, poking me hard in the nipple. *Ow, bitch.* "It's about Miss Mabel. And I say we're voting or I'm going to go out there and get her myself."

"I'll follow her if she does that," JJ said simply. Fucking whipped, he was.

"Fine, we'll vote," Fox decided and I clenched my jaw as the urge to go against anything he said rose in me.

But then Rogue squeezed my hand and I sighed as I looked at her. "Fine," I gave in. "I vote we take the quickest route."

"Darkest," Fox said smoothly.

"Dark is safest," JJ agreed like of course he fucking would and we all looked to Rogue to make her choice. If this was a hung vote, I was gonna take her my way and they could go theirs, I wasn't wasting anymore time down here.

"Dark," she chose and I swore under my breath, not missing the smirk on Fox's face as he got his way.

"Then lead the way, oh mighty king." I bowed with a flourish and gestured for Fox to go ahead.

JJ snorted under his breath as Fox walked by and headed up the stone steps.

We followed, all drawing our weapons as he made it to the hatch at the top and pushed against the stone. It swung inward and he peeked out to check the way was clear before hurrying through it. We all kept close as we followed and I pushed the hatch closed half a heartbeat before a brand new, shiny motion-censor floodlight turned on and we were all lit up in a furiously bight glow.

"Fuck," I gasped, turning back and opening the hatch, but a shot went off and a torrent of men appeared, all aiming guns at us.

"Drop your weapons!" one of them barked and my gut knotted right the fuck up.

Me, JJ and Fox crowded around Rogue instinctively, jamming her between us as we all dropped our guns and raised our hands.

Ah shit. Now what?

CHAPTER THIRTY TWO

Some asshole wearing cheap cologne and a string vest jabbed a gun into my back and forced me to start walking.

Maverick snarled insults at all of them as he closed in on my left side, his arm brushing mine while Fox moved in on my other side, the two of them effectively boxing me between them with JJ next to Fox as we were herded around the house.

My heart pounded as I looked between the men who were corralling us towards the front of the manor, searching for a weak spot amongst them as I tried to think of a way out of this.

"I'm gonna kill you first," Maverick said conversationally, looking at the guy who was still jabbing me with his gun. "I'm gonna take that gun you're so fond of poking my girl with and ram it up your ass before I pull the trigger and watch your insides go boom."

"More like the three of you will watch while we all take turns with your girl here before you each eat a bullet," the man pointing a gun at Fox chuckled.

I swear I could feel the tension that ran through my boys at that suggestion. JJ's spine straightened while Fox and Maverick exchanged a look which promised violence with so much certainty that I could taste it on my tongue.

"New plan," JJ growled. "I'm gonna cut slices off of you and make you watch as I feed them to my pet starfish - he's got a real taste for human flesh now, but it will still take a good few weeks for him to get through your gristly ass."

The men all laughed and I could practically hear their death tolls ringing on the breeze. We just needed a moment to figure out our next move and I was sure their blood would spill before Kaiser even made it out of bed.

We made it around to the front of the house where a set of wide wooden steps led up onto a porch which ran along the entire front of the huge property.

The men holding us captive shoved us apart, forcing us to our knees with guns jammed against the backs of our heads as the door to the house swung open.

My heart leapt up into my throat as Shawn stepped out wearing a pair of black boxers with an embroidered silk purple smoking jacket hanging open across his bare chest which was so tacky it had to belong to Kaiser. He had a cigarette lit in one hand and held his shotgun propped against his shoulder in the other.

"Well looky here what the cat dragged in," he crowed, throwing his head back and laughing like a triumphant asshole as he drank in the sight of us all forced to kneel before him. "I caught me a Harlequin prince, the king of The Damned Men and a juicy little Harlequin side piece to boot," he said, looking between the three men who kneeled at my sides, his gaze raking over them like all of his Christmases had all come at once. But as his gaze zeroed in on me, that smile on his lips grew impossibly wider and he started to advance slowly down the stairs. "Not to mention my very own, pretty little whore, back down in her favourite position on her knees for me."

Fox snarled ferociously as Shawn reached out to touch my cheek, lurching forward with a yell of warning which Shawn answered by swinging his shotgun around to point directly into his face.

"Down boy," Shawn commanded, hesitating with his fingers mere inches from my skin as I held my breath and tried to fight off the terror I felt at being forced beneath him like this after knowing everything he'd done to Chase. "If any of them makes a move towards me while I'm talking to my sugarpie, you will shoot them," he added to his men and I swallowed thickly as they closed in even tighter around my boys.

Shawn reached for me again, the cigarette still smoking between his fingers as he grazed them along my cheekbone in the exact same spot as the red cut I'd put on his face.

"I think I owe you a little payback, don't you, sweet cheeks?" he asked, smirking at me like the cat who'd got the cream.

"What's the matter, Shawn? Don't you like looking in the mirror and remembering the way I beat you?" I glanced at his bare chest where the gown he wore hung open, smiling at the still bandaged stab wound I'd given him. "Though I have to admit, I was hoping you'd bled out in a gutter somewhere after our little altercation."

Shawn grinned at me, but it didn't reach his eyes and he leaned in closer to speak just to me. I noticed one of the men to his right shifting his weight, recognising his second or third or who knew what in command, Travis, as he frowned at me slightly before flattening his features again.

"I'm gonna enjoy breaking you again, sugarpie. I'll take great pleasure in watching you crack for me, beg for me, and come crawling on your knees in hopes of satisfying me. I'll have you so turned around and twisted up that by the time I give you what you want and make you into my little whore again, you'll be singing my praises and thanking me for the attention."

"In your fucking dreams," I snarled.

"Every god given night," he agreed, winking at me and straightening up again. He removed his hand from my face as he took a drag from his cigarette, the cherry glowing in the soulless depths of his eyes as he drank in the sight of me. "Question is, what way shall I start up this game between us again?"

"Where's Kaiser?" Maverick barked as Shawn's gaze stayed glued to me, making my skin prickle with a feeling of being unclean. "We want to speak to the master of the house, not his fucking watch dog."

"Oh, haven't you heard?" Shawn asked, clutching his chest and feigning shock. "Dear old Kaiser fucked up bad. See, he was looking after a little treasure for me. A pretty, pretty treasure with one beautiful blue eye - but he went and let it go. Now, I'm a fair man. All I ask is that people don't let me down when they make me promises. But Kaiser broke his promise, so in reparation for his mistake, he signed this big old house on over to me."

"You're kidding," Fox spat. "Why the fuck would he do that?"

"You'd be surprised what a man might do when he's being given an ultimatum at the end of my shotgun," Shawn said, swinging that gun onto Fox. "For example, if I was to ask you to pick between your life or the life of one of the people kneeling here next to you, I get the feeling you'd be fast enough to let one of them go to the grave. If not all."

"I'd die first," Fox said without a glimmer of doubt in his words and Shawn's eyebrows went up.

"Well shit, I think you might actually mean that, don't ya? Even the traitor?" He swung the gun towards Maverick and my heart lurched with every movement of the fucking thing.

"I gave you my answer," Fox replied firmly. "I'd never save my own skin over any of theirs."

"Even though he's been sticking his filthy Damned Men cock into your girl? Oh – I hope I haven't just shattered your little heart with that truth, but I did see them with my own fair eyes. Practically humping each other right out in the open, they were," Shawn pushed, smirking greedily as he waited for Fox's reaction.

"I told you," Fox replied firmly, not letting a flicker of emotion show on his face to that taunt. "I'd die before choosing a single one of them to take my place."

Shawn seemed a little taken aback by the fact that Fox clearly already knew about me and Rick, but he covered it fast enough as he went on with his endless talking.

"Huh. And there was me thinking men like you and me were all the same. But I know full well I'd sell out every fucker and their dog to save my own ass if it came down to it, so I guess we aren't so similar after all. Aside from our taste in women."

Shawn's gaze fell to me again and he inhaled deeply from his smoke before flicking it at JJ's chest.

"You didn't actually say where Kaiser was," Maverick said loudly, drawing his attention again and I knew he was doing it for my sake, trying to buy us some time and keep Shawn's focus away from me as much as possible.

"Oh, where are my manners?" Shawn said dramatically. "If you just look up, you will see the former residents of the Rosewood estate - at least the ones who took exception to my new position as lord of the manor. Plus a couple who just pissed me off."

I tilted my head back automatically at his direction, knowing I didn't want to see whatever was up there but unable to stop myself from looking all the same.

I blinked at the four lumps of meat which had been impaled on the balcony railings above us, some small piece of me recognising what they were even though they'd clearly been left out to rot in the baking sun for days since they'd been put there.

"Christ," JJ cursed as my stomach roiled and the urge to vomit overwhelmed me.

"It's a little hard to tell, but that central one up there is Kaiser's smarmy head," Shawn explained casually. "The scrap of hair to his left was his dear wife - there wasn't much head left to display sadly."

My lips parted as I just stared between the heads he'd impaled there, their features entirely unrecognisable, the skin sloughing from their skulls and rot and animals clearly having gotten involved in their decomposition already. But as my gaze shifted to the head at the end of the line, I sucked in a horrified breath, tears prickling the backs of my eyes as I spotted the white hair, my stomach lurching with grief as I realised who else must have been up there with Kaiser.

Shawn had killed every last member of the Rosewood family. And we were already too late to rescue Miss Mabel.

"So back to the matter at hand," Shawn said, drawing my gaze down to him as I tried to focus on the present instead of falling into the pain of that discovery. Because if this all carried on the way it was going, there might be four more heads up there before long. "We have already established how far the Harlequin prince will go for his merry men. But I'm not all that interested in muscular blondes, I have to admit. And I can't say I'm much in the mood for dear old daddy to come charging in here with all his men, fucking up my house in some vicious attempt to rescue his boy from my basement. So I guess the only option left to me is death. I'm just trying to figure out where to start."

My heart leapt as he swung his shotgun back and forth along the line of us, his eyes sparkling with the game as he bobbed the barrel between each of the boys one at a time.

"Stop," I demanded, a sob catching in my throat. "Don't hurt them. Just tell me what you want. We can figure this out."

Shawn released a low whistle, his gaze narrowing in on me as a wicked joy lit within his blue eyes.

"What I want?" he asked curiously, rubbing at his jaw as he considered that. "Well, now that you mention it, this has all been a little easy. I was only getting into the swing of this game when you bunch of dumb fucks just came and landed yourselves in my lap. And yeah, it's tempting as fuck to blast all of your heads off and win myself a war in one fell swoop - but it's just so fucking easy that I can't say it's all that alluring."

"Spit it out," I growled, my hands fisting at my sides as I dared a glance to my right where Fox and JJ knelt, their gazes both locked on me. Shawn seemed to notice that I held their attention too and he smiled slowly as he raked his gaze over all of us.

"How about we stick to my former offer, sugarpie? You bring that fine ass of yours over here and throw your lot in with me and I'll let them go. Just like that. Poof. Ready to fight another day."

"You'd seriously let them leave?" I demanded while all three of my boys protested angrily, the men surrounding them swarming closer and waving guns around to stop them from moving out of their positions on the ground. "All you want is me? Why do you even give a fuck about me anyway? You can't seriously need to get laid that desperately."

"It's not about fucking you, sunshine," Shawn purred, stepping up in front of me again and taking hold of my jaw. "I could point a gun at any one of these assholes and command you to suck my cock in payment for their freedom and I know you'd do it. You'd part those pretty lips of yours and swallow me down like a good little whore. But I don't want to force anything from you like that. I want you on your knees for me because that's where you want to be. Where you *need* to be. If you agree to come back to me, I'm not gonna tie you up and fuck you whenever I want. That would be too easy. What I want is so much better than that, sugarpie." He tugged on my jaw and drew me up to my feet, keeping his gaze fixed on mine as he drank in my fear and swallowed it whole. He leaned closer, whispering in my ear so that only I could hear him. "I want to smother that fire in your eyes. I want to tame that spirit. I want to be your entire world, sugarpie, and only when I am, when you're begging on your knees for a taste of me again and I know that you'll die if I don't give it to you - only then will I take your body and own that too. And believe me, sweetheart, when I do you'll love every single moment of it."

He drew back and smiled at me, his mouth so close to mine that I could taste his breath washing over my lips as I suppressed the shiver of fear that ran through me at his words. It wasn't even the threat of them that terrified me. It was the brutal truth of them. I knew him. I knew what it was to be his and I knew how close he'd come to owning me that way once before. He hadn't managed it then because I didn't have enough good left in me for him to corrupt. But now? With my boys back in my life and my heart beating for the taste of freedom all four of them had been offering me. I knew it wouldn't be the same. And I knew he wouldn't be the same. If I agreed to this, he really would own me. And I had no way of knowing how long it would take for him to destroy me just the way he was promising to.

"So what's it to be, sugarpie? Your soul or your sinner boys? Because I'm going to be taking at least one from you tonight."

My pulse thundered as I bit my tongue on the answer I knew I was going to give. The only one I could give. Because when it came down to me or them, I knew who held more value. And it wasn't the girl no one ever wanted to keep. It wasn't the one who had already escaped death once before and had stolen a taste of happiness she'd never been owed. In the question of me or them, it was always going to be them. After all, they were the only things in this world that had ever held any value to me anyway. And I would never trade them for anything.

CHAPTER THIRTY THREE

Panic burned along the inside of my bones as I stared at Rogue, seeing the fight go out of her, seeing her accept the offer Shawn was making. But fuck that. I'd die before I let her walk into that house with him. And if that was really what it was going to take then so fucking be it.

The men pressing in around me, Fox and Maverick were stifling, hot bodies and guns everywhere. But I'd clocked the grenade clipped to the belt of the sweaty dude whose face looked like a granola bar the moment he'd appeared and now he had his machine gun pressed to my side, I was ready to go all in on my death wish.

"Rogue!" Fox called to her. "Don't agree to anything."

"I'll stay here so long as you let them go," Rogue said and panic cut into me.

"No!" I barked.

"You've got yourself a deal, sugarpie. Take her inside, boys," Shawn called, jerking his chin at one of his men and they caught hold of Rogue's arm, dragging her toward the door.

"Let them go - that was the deal!" she shouted at Shawn.

"Yeah, yeah, lemme just say goodbye first, sugarpie," he said, strutting towards us with a smirk. "Hey boys, so this is what a winner looks like." He did a twirl and his men chuckled like he was hilarious.

The sweaty guy's eyes slid to him and I acted in that single second of opportunity, yanking the grenade from his hip and pulling the pin in the same moment.

I threw it at Shawn as hard as I could and the motherfucker snapped out a hand, catching it from the air before launching it away from himself with a curse.

"Move Killian!" the sweaty guy cried as the grenade flew towards a man standing beside Shawn's white SUV and Killian tripped over his own feet as he tried to escape. The grenade hit the car window and exploded with a boom, destroying the car and engulfing Killian in a huge blaze of fire that spiralled up towards the sky, the blast knocking us all flat to the ground and making my ears ring.

"My baby!" Shawn wailed over his car.

I'd been ready for the explosion, recovering faster than most and snatching the sweaty guy's gun, turning it on all of the men surrounding us as I unleashed a spray of bullets with a roar of fury.

One asshole aimed his handgun down at Maverick's head and Fox kicked his wrist as he lay on his back, sending the weapon flying just before I gunned the asshole down and he hit the dirt in a pool of blood. Fox dragged Maverick up by the scruff of his neck and all three of us twisted around with stolen weapons in hand, hunting for Shawn and our girl. I couldn't see our enemy, but Rogue was being dragged behind a truck while the rest of Shawn's men ran from the blaze and tried to pull the injured out of the way of the growing fire.

I sprinted in the direction Rogue had been taken, rounding the truck just as the guy tripped backwards over a body on the ground and Rogue twisted out of his hold in a flash of movement. She grabbed the gun from his grip, turning it back on the asshole and firing three rounds into his skull with a shout of utter fury.

Now was definitely not the time to get a boner, but fuck, Johnny D had a mind of his own.

I grabbed Rogue's hand, whipping open the door to the truck and pushing her inside, finding the keys stuffed up in the sun visor.

"Fox – Rick!" I called, spotting them taking cover behind a stone statue of some ancient Rosewood guy with medals on his chest.

Chunks of stone were blasted off of it as several Dead Dogs closed in on them. My boys returned fire, but it looked like Fox was out of bullets and I cursed as I shoved the truck into drive and slammed my foot to the accelerator.

"Stay down," I commanded Rogue and she ducked her head as a stream of bullets shattered the front window. My heart rioted as I kept as low as possible, somehow avoiding the bullets blasted this way as the truck bumped over dead bodies.

I made it to our boys and shoved the door open beside me in urgency.

"Hurry!" I barked and Fox clambered inside but as I whistled for Rick, he just waved us away.

"Fuck," I hissed as Maverick leapt over the hood of the truck and took the guy in the string vest to the ground, rolling him over and jamming his own gun against his ass before pulling the trigger.

"Rick! Get in the truck!" Rogue screamed, grabbing the machine gun from my lap and aiming it out the window.

She started firing at anyone close to Maverick, the rat-tat-tat of bullets bursting from the gun as she shot anyone who dared poke their head out from where they were taking cover.

"JJ we gotta go," Fox said frantically, pointing back at the house where more men were pouring out of it with guns in their hands.

I caught sight of Shawn poking his head out of the doorway, pumping his shotgun and firing a round into the side of our stolen truck with a grin on his lips like he was having the time of his life.

"You sure keep me on my toes, boys!" he called, clearly enjoying the mayhem.

I hit the gas as a line of men started firing at Maverick, slamming into two of them and knocking them down beneath the wheels of the huge vehicle.

Maverick took the opportunity to run to the gate, jamming his thumb down on a button beside it so they started opening then he took off again. But he didn't run towards us, he ran over to a gleaming black Harley Davidson parked to one side of the drive. He swung his leg over it and I turned the truck towards the gate as we all kept low in our seats and Rogue fired at any motherfucker stupid enough to still be out in the open or who dared point a gun in Maverick's direction.

"You'll come crawling back soon, sugarpie!" Shawn hollered as we made it to the open gates. "I'll make damn certain of it!"

Maverick accelerated off the property on his bike and I tore after him, turning sharply down the road as gunfire ripped through the back of the truck. Somehow, by some miracle, it didn't look like any of us had gotten shot and I had to think we were seriously fucking lucky.

We raced through town, following Maverick as the three of us sat up straighter, the only sound between us our furious breaths falling from our lungs.

Fox pulled Rogue close, his arm locking around her shoulders and she clutched his shirt as she held onto him, grief lining her features.

"Miss Mabel," she whispered, tears gleaming in her eyes. "She's been locked up in that fucking place for years and now she's dead and who knows what Shawn did to her before she died."

My own heart squeezed painfully and Fox stroked her hair, looking full of rage and hate over the loss of the old woman who'd once been so good to us.

"I'm sorry, baby," he murmured.

"I'm gonna kill him," she growled, her lip turned back in a wolf's snarl. "And I'm gonna cut him to pieces before I do."

"We'll all be there to do it, pretty girl," I vowed and Fox nodded, sharing a dark look with me as the roar of Maverick's motorcycle filled the air. "Blood for blood. When he dies, the only thing he'll remember of this life is the meaning of the word pain."

CHAPTER THIRTY FOUR

The adrenaline was still scattering through my veins as we arrived back at Harlequin House and through the rush of the escape we'd made, I'd barely even taken a moment to fully grasp what that meant.

We were home. Safe. But Shawn now held a stronghold in the Cove. Worse, he was in a prime position to head into that graveyard and find all of our most valuable secrets buried in that crypt.

But beyond the danger and threat which had taken root in that place thanks to Shawn killing Kaiser and stealing his estate from him was the soul crushing grief of what had happened to the one and only woman who had ever given a fuck about me when I was a kid. I'd called Chase to fill him in while we were racing through the streets of the Cove so that he would stop worrying, but I was desperate to see him in the flesh, confirm that all of my boys were alive and well.

Fox and JJ were in a whirlwind of rage and phone calls, arranging a meeting at The Oasis with Luther to discuss what this meant now that they knew exactly where Shawn was hiding out. They were talking about launching an offensive against him or even calling in reinforcements from the cartel, but I didn't care about any of that.

All that kept replaying in my mind were the words that Shawn had spoken to me. The threat still hanging over me and the men I kept close to me. I knew he wasn't going to stop with this now. Shawn Mackenzie was like a wolfhound on the scent of an injured deer when he fixed his mind on something.

He lived for games and power and now that he'd decided to come for me, I knew he wouldn't just let the idea drop. Worse than that, I knew he would only keep coming at the Harlequins harder and harder for every day I spent refusing to play his twisted games. And if he was attacking the Harlequins then he was always just one step away from ripping my heart from my chest anyway.

I refused the offer to go to The Oasis with Fox when he asked, not wanting to be a part of whatever plans the Harlequins cooked up against Shawn.

I needed time to think about all of this. I needed time to process what we'd just learned and I needed time to decide on my next move. Because if I could end this war by giving myself up to the man who kept striking at us, then didn't I have to consider that? Didn't I have to put aside my own fear and think about what was best for Fox and JJ? Maverick too. If I could stop this fight then they would be free of it. This threat against them would disband and at least I'd know they were safe.

JJ and Fox left and I headed upstairs to fill Chase in on what had happened, Mutt scampering along by my heels.

I knocked on his door but I didn't get an answer so I let myself in, finding him asleep in the centre of the bed with the lights on overhead, his brow furrowed and his eyepatch missing.

My gaze trailed over the scars that marked his right eyelid, the savage X that cut through his eyebrow and ran onto his cheek. The lines of it were still red but a lot of the anger had gone out of the wound now and I could see how the scar would look once it was finished healing.

He'd always bear that mark now and he'd never regain the sight in that eye, but somehow there was beauty in that. In the way his scar showed on the outside instead of being hidden away on the inside where no one could see like mine were.

I considered leaving him in peace, but Mutt scampered over to his bed, hopping up and curling himself in a little ball by Chase's feet, so I followed his lead and moved further into the room instead.

I slipped into his bathroom, snagging one of his band tees as I went and taking a quick shower to wash the feel of Shawn's touch from my skin before I went to him.

I left my clothes in his hamper, tugging on the tee and padding back across his room on bare feet before crawling into his bed with him.

I laid my head down on the pillow beside his, drinking in the sight of his face and the brief moments of peace it held in sleep. But that didn't last long as tension lined his features once more and a grunt of anguish escaped him, causing me to shuffle closer and take his hand in mine.

He gripped me tightly, drawing me even closer, his forehead pressing to mine as he drew in a long breath.

"Stay," he murmured and I nodded, my mouth brushing against the stubble on his jaw and my lips aching for a taste of something I knew I shouldn't have hungered for.

"I'll stay," I swore in a low whisper but he stilled, that soft noise enough to rouse him fully and his eyes opening as he found me there in his arms.

I met his gaze, my heart racing as I took in the damage to his right eye which had turned a much paler blue thanks to the slice of the knife that had cut into it, the pupil opaque and unmoving.

Chase seemed to realise what I was looking at, cursing as he closed his eyes again and tried to roll away from me, muttering about his eye patch cutting into his face if he slept with it on.

I caught his shoulder and tugged on it firmly, stopping him as he tried to roll further from me.

"Don't hide from me, Ace," I breathed, shifting towards him and gripping his arm tightly. "You know me. You were there when I got my first period. You were there when I stole my first car. You were there when I cried because I missed parents I'd never even known, and I cried because you hated the ones who you had. You *know* me. So look at me. And tell me I'm lying about this." I pushed my fingers into his hair, fully exposing his damaged eye to the light of the room and making sure I didn't hide a single piece of what I was feeling for him as I let the love I held in my heart for him and the relief I had over finding him alive mix with the pride I felt for how strong he was while working to recover from all that Shawn had done to him. I wanted him to see all of that in me and to know with complete certainty that I didn't care about scars or any of that shit, because all I cared about was him.

I leaned forward and pressed a kiss to that damaged skin and his arm moved to my waist as he drew me closer with a soft sigh.

"This isn't something you should be ashamed of," I told him. "You should be proud of it. Not for some bullshit battle scars reason or any of that. But because you're Chase fucking Cohen. And you've never given a single fuck what anyone thinks of you, so why the hell would you start now? You're the scariest motherfucker in the room. Not because of your scars, but because you can beat any man bloody without breaking a sweat and everyone knows better than to fuck with you."

Chase groaned needily, his grip on me tightening until he was propelling me up and onto him so that I straddled his waist and his hands locked around my hips.

"You always could destroy me with that smart mouth of yours, little one," he growled, his hands travelling up my sides until he pushed his fingers into my hair while my forehead remained pressed to his and we hid inside the rainbow locks that surrounded us.

"That's our problem, isn't it?" I murmured. "We find it all too easy to destroy each other."

His cock was hard between my thighs and suddenly this tension between us didn't feel like a game anymore. With JJ here and a few drinks in my system it had all seemed so simple. He'd wanted this, I'd wanted it, we'd just been following the call of what our bodies needed, but this, me and Chase on our own was something different. Something that burned hotter, angrier, was gilded in lies and betrayal and so much heartache that it seared me when I looked at it straight on like this.

He was the boy I'd always wanted to rescue but now the darkness he was running from had found its way within him and I didn't know how to fight it off. I didn't even know if I should be trying or if I should just let myself fall into it and be consumed by it. Or maybe I should match it with some demons of my own and let the whole world burn for us.

"Do you love him?" Chase asked me, his throat bobbing as his hand slid from my hair to my cheek, his thumb teasing my bottom lip like he was committing the shape of it to memory. "JJ."

"Chase..."

"It's okay," he said, his fingers drifting onto my neck as he inhaled deeply. "You make him smile in a way I haven't seen since the day you were taken from us. I thought being a Harlequin broke that in him. I thought what we did to Clive that night out in the woods was the end of those smiles. But it was never about any of that. It was you. It's always been you for all of us. And I want him to get his happily ever after when I'm gone. I want him to have you."

I jerked back as his words hit me and he let his hands fall to my waist as I sat upright, replaying them in my mind and wondering how I was supposed to explain what I felt for JJ to him. What I felt for Rick and Fox and him too. They were my boys, and I was their girl, but I was also the cause of so much bad for all of them. I was the divide in their group, I was the reason for at least as much pain in them as I'd suffered myself while we'd been separated. And now I was a target on their backs, dragging the devil I'd collected along my journey to their front door and hoping they could stand against it while holding the key to drawing it off in my fist.

"Shawn said he'll stop the war on the Harlequins," I said, not answering his questions because none of that mattered. Or it was all that mattered. I wasn't even sure, but what I was sure of was that I could do something to end this violence. "He had us all on our knees tonight, Chase. He could have killed all four of us as easy as breathing and the only reason he held off was because it didn't suit his twisted idea of fun. But I know it won't be that easy next time. And I also know how to stop him."

"How?" Chase demanded, his eyes flashing with violence as his fingers gripped my waist tightly.

"I just have to give him what he wants." I shrugged, trying not to taste the bile that coated my tongue with those words or feel the shiver which danced its way down my spine as Chase shook his head beneath me, knowing what I was going to say before I had even uttered the word. "Me."

"Never," Chase snarled, his fingers biting into my skin like he thought holding onto me tight enough would be all it took to keep me there. "I would die a thousand times over, suffer every day of my life in his torture, do whatever the fuck it took to make sure that never happens, little one.”

My heart leapt at the furious dedication in his gaze but I shoved his hands off of me, moving to climb off of the bed as I refused to let him sway me from what I was thinking.

Chase caught my wrist before I could make it to my feet, yanking me down onto the mattress beside him and throwing his weight over me as he pinned me beneath him with a grunt of pain as he clearly jarred his leg.

“Swear to me that you will stop thinking what you’re thinking,” he snarled. “Promise me you’re not actually considering letting that monster have you for the sake of our stained souls?”

“I could end this!” I shouted, losing my cool and shoving my palms against his chest as I tried to force him back, but Chase might as well have been a slab of rock for all the good it did.

“You think leaving us again would end it? You would destroy us, Rogue. Fox would fall apart completely and Johnny James would be devastated. Who the fuck even knows what Maverick would do, but he’d probably rip the entire world apart in vengeance. I won’t let you even consider it. It’s madness and you know it. Look at me - look at what that animal is capable of!”

Tears burned my eyes as I reached up and cupped the right side of his face in my hand, my thumb tracing over the scars surrounding his eye as his panic washed over me and I found myself nodding, agreeing, promising him I wouldn’t do it. The insanity of that idea fell from my flesh and Chase sagged in relief as he sensed it, dropping down over me and burying his face in my neck as he dragged me against him and I wound my arms around him too.

He was shaking, his heart racing so fast that I could feel it where we were pressed together and I hushed him, whispering more promises to him as I stroked my fingers through his hair.

Relief cascaded through my body as he dropped to the bed beside me, still holding me tightly like he was afraid I might change my mind, but I’d heard him. I’d felt his fear and I couldn’t risk hurting him any more than that, so I swore to stay here and I made him swear it too even though I could tell he didn’t believe in his own words. Because I wasn’t letting Fox get rid of him. There was simply no fucking way. And I was sick of him holding onto that decision like he was the one who got to choose what was right for our family when none of the rest of us had agreed to it.

I fell asleep in Chase's arms with that decision etched into my soul. Fox Harlequin and I were overdue a discussion, and I was going to make sure he saw sense before we were through.

CHAPTER THIRTY FIVE

I worked on a feast for breakfast after my run, making pancakes and laying out bowls of fruit, fresh pastries, yoghurt and cereal on the patio table along with fresh strawberry and kiwi smoothies for everyone. My heart hurt the whole time I did it though and I didn't wanna think about why as I worked to make this the best breakfast I'd ever served.

Mutt was sitting by the pool on a little pillow I'd put under an umbrella for him, his head turned away from the fresh chicken I'd laid out beside him in a bowl. He never had gotten over me shouting at him when I'd had Chase kneel down on the beach ready to die. I hadn't forgiven myself yet for that day either though so I kinda understood his moody attitude towards me. I was starting to get the feeling I'd never win his affection back though.

I closed my eyes and forced away the memories of that awful fucking day, my skin crawling all over as I built my armour back into place and kept moving.

When I was done, I walked upstairs and knocked on JJ's door, waiting until he opened it, cracking his eyes at me, his hair standing up in every direction.

"Breakfast is ready. Be down in two minutes, okay?" I asked and he groaned but nodded as he drifted back into the darkness of his room like a ghost.

I headed to Chase's room next, pushing the door silently open and stepping inside. I often came in here at night, not that Chase or Rogue knew it. I'd sit and watch them until my eyes were sore and the quiet was enough to drive me insane. Sometimes JJ slept here too and I just stared at my family, wishing I could crawl into that bed and join them. But someone had to be the asshole around here, and that someone was always me.

Rogue was curled up beside Chase as usual, her arm wrapped around him as I just stood there and looked at the two of them. I couldn't even find it in me to be jealous of this anymore, knowing how temporary it was and how much they needed each other. It wasn't gonna last, so I'd suck it up. And it wasn't like she was fucking him like she was Maverick. That was the kind of infuriating that burned deep into my flesh. And I was done waiting for her to realise that he wasn't the one for her and I was. I'd warned her the time would come when I would have to force her hand on the issue of us and that time was coming up on us fast. Rogue Easton was mine and I was ready to make her admit it.

The room was bright from the sunlight streaming in through the open curtains, but the lamp beside the bed was on anyway so Chase could sleep without fearing the dark. I hated that he'd been altered by Shawn, I hated that I couldn't talk to him about it, I hated that we were never going to be okay again after all the shit between us. But today I'd try and smooth over some of the hurt, because I couldn't bear the pain lasting any longer.

I moved beside the bed, shaking Chase's arm and he jerked awake, panic filling his expression for a moment before his gaze fell on me and he released a breath of relief.

"Hey," he said in a voice rough from sleep, searching my expression like he expected me to start shouting. When did I become the asshole dad of this family?

"I want you to join us for breakfast this morning," I said, dropping down to sit on the edge of the bed. His fingers tightened on Rogue, holding her against his chest as he gazed at me, trying to work out my angle.

"Okay," he agreed slowly and I laid a hand on his shoulder, staring at him with a thousand unspoken words on my lips before I got up and left him to wake Rogue.

I returned downstairs, sitting out on the patio and drinking my smoothie as I waited for the others to arrive, a storm of emotion swirling through my chest. JJ came down first in his boxers and he dropped into the seat beside mine, groaning hungrily as he took in all the food.

"What's the occasion?" he asked, swiping up a croissant and tearing into it with his teeth.

"It's the carnival today," I said, grinning at him as I pushed away the dark cloud hanging over me.

This had been my favourite time of year as a kid. The end of the summer was dawning and with it came the carnival. We used to go on all the rides until one of us puked, eat so much candy that it hurt and camp out in the bed of my truck afterwards, all of us piled in there with nothing but a bunch of blankets and the stars for company.

"Fuck yes, I can't wait to get there." He checked his phone for the time. "It opens in an hour, right?"

I laughed at his juvenile expression as I nodded. "Are you getting there for opening?" I asked, knowing he would.

"Aren't you?" he replied with a frown.

"I can't, I've gotta go meet Luther, but you could take Rogue and I'll meet you there?" I suggested and he nodded quickly.

"Yeah, I'm down. What about Chase?" he asked hopefully and my brow lowered.

"You know he can't come. He's ex Harlequin, JJ."

"Yeah, yeah," he sighed disappointedly, starting to pile up his plate with pancakes.

Rogue appeared with Chase and he walked with one crutch and his free arm wrapped around her shoulders. I got the feeling he didn't really need her support as well, but I wasn't gonna point it out.

JJ looked to me as he chewed on a mouthful of pancake then back to Chase as he sat down to join us at the table beside Rogue. I noticed his latest eyepatch had a bright eye drawn on it in metallic pen with blue scales all around it like it belonged to a dragon. Every time he got a new one, it ended up drawn on by Rogue while he was sleeping.

"He's eating with us?" JJ asked me like he was a kid and I was his parent.

I chuckled, shrugging. "Yeah, he is."

JJ pounded his fist on the table and Rogue smiled widely as she fought Chase over the only pain au chocolat before he surrendered it to her. She ripped it in half, tossing one piece onto his plate and he looked at her with a blazing expression that made my heart yank.

I ate some fruit, basking in the feel of all three of them here with me and just listening to their idle chat. Chase kept glancing over like he wished he could strike up a conversation with me, but he never seemed to find the words and I didn't have the right ones either.

Their discussion soon turned to the carnival and Mutt scampered over to grab some pancake scraps from Rogue, my fresh chicken apparently not good enough to fill his belly this morning.

"I'm gonna go on the whirl-a-round first, then the waltzers, then the space drop," Rogue decided. "No wait, the waltzers first, then the space drop, *then* the whirl-a-round."

"What about the rollercoaster?" JJ asked with a smirk, spearing a grape on his fork.

"Oh I forgot about the rollercoaster!" Rogue cried. "Okay, that first. But wait, there's only three seats on that one, one of us will have to sit in the seat behind. Or we could go two and two, but who gets the front? The front's the best."

"Chase isn't going," I cut in and Rogue turned her gaze on me with a pout.

"What? That's not fair," she complained.

"It's alright, little one," he murmured. "I know I can't go."

"But I want you to go," she said defiantly, glaring at me. "He's not in your Crew, so he doesn't have to do what you say."

"That's precisely why he can't go," I said, my gaze on my food as I tried not to get into an argument here. "The carnival will be full of Harlequins, and I'm already getting enough shit from the elders about letting Chase stay here after I banished him, he can't be seen out in our territory."

"But-" Rogue started but Chase dropped his hand over hers and squeezed tightly.

"It's fine, little one. I'm good here," he said intently. "Just send me lots of videos in the group chat."

She sighed, clearly pissed at me, but JJ helped draw her back out of her moody shell as he started naming all the things they could do at the carnival.

After a while, they headed off to get dressed, leaving me with Chase and silence fell over us like a lead weight.

I cleared my throat as Chase picked at his half-eaten plate of food and looked to me with a frown.

"Nice scales." I gestured to his eyepatch and confusion gripped his features.

"What?"

"The dragon eye," I said and he pulled his eyepatch off with a curse, looking at it and I took in the scars over that side of his face with my gut tugging.

"She keeps doing that," he muttered, then seemed torn between putting it back on and leaving it off. He clearly felt uncomfortable either way as he tried to position his hair over that side of his face.

"You don't have to hide it from me," I said seriously and he sighed as he left the eyepatch off, but there was a stiffness about his shoulders that made my chest tighten.

I heard the others coming back downstairs and gave Chase an intent look. "Hug them tight when they say goodbye," I murmured.

His throat worked and realisation melted through his expression as he stared at me. He nodded as he quickly worked to hide his pain. I felt that pain right down to the pit of my soul and I knew I wouldn't be able to eat another single bite of food.

"Do you want me to bring back blue or pink cotton candy, Ace?" Rogue asked as she bounded onto the patio in a white maxi shirt covered in yellow flowers and a white crop top with her hair tied in two braided pigtails. JJ wore black shorts and a lemon tank top that seemed to make his tan shine and he had a playful look about him as he geared up for the carnival. He held a baseball cap in his hands and he smirked at Rogue as he showed her the Green Power

Ranger on it before placing it on his head backwards and making her clap her hands in excitement.

"Surprise me," Chase said, pushing to his feet as she got close, dragging her into his arms. He crushed her against him and a splinter drove into my chest as he tried to hold onto her as long as he could before she pulled out of his arms with a grin.

"Painkillers." She lifted them to his mouth and he let her slide them between his lips, waiting for her to hold his smoothie up for him to drink from and wash them down. When he'd swallowed, she leaned in to kiss his cheek, but he turned his head so their lips crushed together instead. I flew to my feet with a growl, but they were already breaking apart and I scowled as Rogue's cheeks turned pink.

"Oops," Chase said darkly, staring at her like he wanted the ground to open up and swallow them both away together.

Rogue cleared her throat, backing up as she touched her lips and I didn't think she even realised she was doing it.

"I'll meet you at the carnival in a few hours," I gritted out and Rogue nodded.

Chase reached for JJ, gripping his arm for a moment before drawing him into a hug.

"Have fun," he said, forcing a smile and I guessed they bought it because they waved as they headed back inside towards the garage with Chase's gaze glued to them until they were out of sight.

"What the fuck was that kiss about?" I growled and Chase looked to me with a shrug.

"Wouldn't you kiss her if you knew you'd never see her again?" he muttered and my chest crushed with the weight of those words.

"Come on," I said in a low voice, moving to lead the way inside and deciding to forget that little stunt. "Get dressed, you've got a hospital appointment in half an hour."

I waited for him as he headed back upstairs and once he reappeared in shorts and a black tank top with a new eyepatch in place, he followed me wordlessly down to the garage on his crutches, tension gripping the air.

We got into my truck and I drove us out of the house to the gates and beyond, taking the roads in the direction of the hospital in the upper quarter.

"I thought we could get some ice cream after you get your cast off," I said and I felt his eyes on me.

"Oh yeah?" he questioned, clearly fucking suspicious and I shrugged.

"If you want?" I asked.

"Yeah…okay," he agreed.

It was a long, quiet drive to the hospital, but we eventually arrived and I parked us up as close to the entrance as I could get before helping Chase out of the truck.

"I'm fine, I've got my crutches," he said and I nodded, knowing that, but my hand still lingered on his back for a second before I pulled away.

I kept to his pace as we moved inside and we were soon led to a room where a nurse worked to cut off his cast. I stood by the door, listening when the doctor came to sign him off and say he'd have a limp which might go away in time, but it was possible it wouldn't. Chase nodded his way through the examination, seeming to withdraw into himself as the reality descended on him that his recovery period had come to an end. And whereas most people would have been overjoyed, he seemed to be sinking away into the darkness and the more I looked at him, the more broken I felt over that.

When I led him back to my truck, we got in and sat there in silence for a long time. Then I started the engine and drove us to the best ice cream parlour in town, got us the biggest cones they sold – Chase's rum and raisin and mine chocolate – then drove us to the cliff view that overlooked the lower quarter.

I took a bite out of my ice cream as I parked up, the sharp coldness making my head hurt as I tried to taste anything but the grief glazing my insides.

"This is the first rum I've had since you asked me to stop," Chase said, taking his time over his ice cream.

"You gonna keep that up?" I asked.

"I think if I drank now, I'd never stop. So I guess you did me a favour," he said and I felt his eyes on me again but I just couldn't look. Because if I looked, I'd shatter like glass struck by a hammer.

"Why do I feel like an old dog that's being treated to the best day ever only to be led out into the woods to be shot?" Chase asked.

"You know why," I said quietly.

We finished our ice creams and the wind rocked the truck a little as it whipped across the clifftop, my eyes following a gull as it fought against the flow of the wind. My life felt like that a lot of the time. Like the wind was always trying to push me one way but duty meant I had to battle against it, and no matter how far I got in one direction, I always ended up aching to just turn my back to the breeze and let it carry me as far as it could go.

"I'm sorry I've been a shit friend," I said after a while.

Chase released a dismissive breath. "You're not the one who betrayed us. You haven't done anything wrong."

"No, I have," I said thickly. "I've done so many fucking things wrong, Ace."

"You're Luther's son, not just my brother," he said. "And you let me come home even when I didn't deserve it."

I shook my head, my gaze on the wide expanse of the ocean ahead of us. "I used to wish sometimes that I was you or JJ, anyone but the one of us who had to carry the burden of ruling within the Harlequins."

"I used to think I'd give anything to take your place," Chase admitted. "I wanted to rule, but that wasn't what I really wanted. I just wanted to be someone. You're Fox Harlequin." He spread his hands in front of him. "Prince of the underworld, destined for greatness."

"It ain't like that," I muttered.

"I know that now," he said seriously. "You always had the short end of the stick, I just thought I did."

"I think we all drew short," I said darkly. "I don't see any one of us winning in this life, do you?"

"No," he agreed. "Do you think that's it? You draw a stick and the fate that's painted on it is the one you're destined for? Or do you think you ever get a chance to draw again?"

I considered that, not really having an answer, not one that was comforting anyway. "I think the older you get, the harder it is to redraw. Maybe we could've once, but now…" I shrugged.

"Yeah." He nodded. "It's all too fucked now, huh?"

"Mm," I sounded my agreement then reached out and pressed a hand to his shoulder.

He clapped his hand to it and we sat like that for several long seconds before we pulled apart and I started the truck.

I turned around and took the road back to the upper quarter before heading onto the highway out of town. We were soon miles and miles away from Sunset Cove and I pulled into a motel at random, driving into the parking lot and pulling up in front of a long stretch of room doors.

I got out of the car, my chest compressing further and further by the second as I grabbed a bag from the bed of my truck filled with some clothes for Chase, a gun and some cash to keep him going for a while. By the time I got around to his side of the car, he was already out and I held the bag up for him. He took it wordlessly, his jaw flexing as he gazed at me like he was trying to memorise my face and I felt a piece of my soul being carved off, falling away from my body with the pain of a sliced open artery.

"I need your phone," I rasped and he pushed a hand into his pocket, taking it out and handing it to me, but there was an envelope tucked against it too.

"Will you give that to Rogue for me?" he asked, his brows knitting like he was worried I'd refuse but I nodded. "And will you…promise not to read it?"

I sighed, shifting my weight from one foot to the other before I nodded in agreement to that too.

"And one more thing." He stepped toward me, anxiety warring in his bright blue gaze and all I wanted to do was drag him into my arms and take him home. But I couldn't, because this was who I was, and this was what happened to traitors. I'd told everyone from day one, the second that cast came off this was how it would be, but fuck did it hurt. Every second I stood there was killing more pieces of me.

"Don't remember me like this," he begged. "Remember us as kids. Remember the days we went swimming at the cove and exploring the smugglers' caves. Okay?"

"Okay," I gritted out and he turned to leave, but I couldn't let him. Not yet.

I strode forward, wrapping him in my arms, my hand crushed to the back of his neck and his forehead pressed to mine.

"I'm sorry," I whispered.

"No, I'm sorry, Fox," he said, his voice breaking. "I'm so fucking sorry."

I nodded, knowing he was but also knowing it was too late to change anything.

"Love her right," he said in a firm growl, ordering me to obey. "You love her and you give her the best of this world no matter what it costs you, you hear me?"

"I will," I croaked.

"You can have it all now, all of you. Just…make sure you stay together, no matter what happens. You, JJ and her. And fuck it, Maverick too if you can."

"We'll stay together," I promised, though I wasn't really including Maverick in that. My brother was never going to come home.

"Swear it. No matter what, Fox," he pushed.

"No matter what," I agreed and he stepped back, letting me go, letting all of us go. I could see he thought this was the right thing as deeply as I did, but why did it hurt so fucking much?

My heart begged me to take him with me, but my brain cried out for me to follow through on my decisions like I always did. This was above even me. This was Harlequin law, and I'd already bent the rules, spared his life, then let him come home when I shouldn't have. And now it was time to follow through on my promises, but I wasn't sure there had ever been one more painful than this.

I pressed my lips to his forehead and let him go, turning away and getting in the truck, not looking back as I started it up and drove away. My black soul got a little blacker and the Devil got his claws in me a little deeper. I was the night in this town, the assured darkness that always claimed the day. And no matter how hard you might wish for the sun to keep shining, the night always had to fall. But this was the darkest one I'd ever known.

CHAPTER THIRTY SIX

The carnival was a riot of bright colours, laughing children and all the best memories from my time here growing up.

I grinned up at JJ around my stick of bright pink cotton candy, watching him as he took pot shots at little red targets, trying to win me a big ass rainbow coloured dolphin teddy which was hanging behind the stall.

The vendor didn't look best pleased to have someone with JJ's skill playing his little game and even with the no doubt dodgy aim on the thing, Johnny James was killing it.

There were ten Harlequin goons lurking around us not so subtly on Fox's command and I was reduced to eye fucking JJ in his loose tank and shorts combo. He still wore my Green Power Ranger cap backwards on his head, knowing full well what he was doing to me by looking that fucking good and combining my GPR love with it.

I slipped closer to him as the targets started whirring faster, tiptoeing up to murmur in his ear while the hiss and bang of the air rifle hid my words from our entourage.

"If you win me that dolphin, I'll suck your dick so good you'll be seeing rainbows of your own."

JJ's grin widened, the gun shifting between targets faster and faster as he knocked them all down one after another and the vendor grumbled curses at him beneath his breath.

When the final target was slammed back on its hinges and every one of them was down, JJ whooped excitedly, tossing the rifle onto the stall and snatching me off of my feet as he whirled me around in triumph.

I laughed as I almost lost hold of my cotton candy and he set me back down on my feet, leaning in for a moment like he was planning on kissing me before catching himself and turning away to claim the prize.

I bit my lip in frustration, wondering when we were going to be able to just be open about what we were to each other. But with so much going on all the time between Shawn, Luther and Chase's recovery, Fox was so freaking stressed out that there was just never a good moment to catch him and lay things out.

I did have a vague plan where I was hoping to ease him into the idea by exposing him to me and Maverick more often. Rick gave exactly zero shits about incurring the wrath of Fox and was more than happy to stake his claim on me at all times. The problem was that Fox had made it clear that he fucking hated that as well as believing it was a purely sexual thing, so it wasn't like he was coming around to anything. But I guessed Rick was still breathing, so it was a start.

Of course, JJ had a whole lot more to lose if Fox turned on him than Maverick did, not to mention the fact that he didn't want to hurt him anymore than I did.

Basically, it was all still fucked, but I was also past the point of trying to un-fuck it. I was taking my shit with each of my boys as its own problem and when it came down to it, me and Johnny James were good. More than good. He made me laugh and smile and come so hard I couldn't breathe. What more could a girl ask for than that?

JJ presented me with the stuffed dolphin, smirking widely as he leaned in to speak with me. "I'll be taking you up on that offer before the end of the day, pretty girl," he promised in a low voice and I licked my lips enticingly as I smiled prettily for him.

"What did I miss?" Fox called loudly, making my heart lurch as JJ stepped back suddenly and we found him striding towards us.

"JJ just won this for me," I brandished my dolphin at him with a grin. "Which officially makes him my favourite again."

"Well we can't have that." Fox slung his arm around my shoulders and turned me towards the Ferris wheel in the centre of the fair, shifting me away from JJ as we started walking.

"Did you do everything you needed to get done then?" I asked him, glancing up as a pained look flashed across his face but he quickly hid it by dropping his aviators down to shade his green eyes.

"Yeah...everything is dealt with now," Fox said easily.

"Did Luther make you do something you're unhappy about?" I asked him, picking up on the dark undertone to his words despite him trying to hide it.

"It wasn't Luther." Fox sighed, glancing away from me before looking back again and knocking his forehead against mine. "Let's just have fun today, yeah? All of our issues can catch up to us tonight, but I just really wanna enjoy this moment."

"I need to talk to you about Chase," I said in a firm tone and he nodded, glancing off again.

"Yeah. We will. Later."

I rolled my eyes at him but agreed, taking the last bite of my cotton candy and tossing the stick in a trashcan as we passed it. The sun was shining and we'd been dealing with a lot of shit recently so I could give him that. Today would be dedicated to fun. No heavy stuff.

We made it to the line for the Ferris wheel, but Fox just walked on past it, shoving a couple of twenties into the hands of the guy running it so he'd let us cut in.

"Hold this while we're gone, yeah J?" Fox asked, taking the dolphin from me and tossing it to JJ. "And maybe do a quick sweep of the area to make sure there's no sign of any Dead Dogs around here too. This is exactly the kind of place fucking Shawn would try to come at us."

"You're gonna make JJ walk the perimeter while we go on a ride without him?" I asked in surprise, shooting a look at my seriously hot stripper as he pushed his tongue into his cheek and waited for Fox's reply on that too.

"Well you wouldn't wanna be a third wheel, would you JJ?" Fox tossed at him, guiding me towards the ride as he grasped my shoulders tighter and I had no choice but to clamber in as JJ gave him a sarcastic salute and stormed off to do as he'd been told.

"That was rude," I grumbled as Fox dropped into the seat beside me, making the carriage bounce as the attendant locked the door and the ride began to turn.

"JJ doesn't give a shit," Fox said roughly, throwing his arm around the back of my seat and angling himself to look at me instead of the view out over the Cove as the ride lifted us high up into the air. "Besides, I've been thinking a lot recently about the future and what it looks like to me. I've been thinking a lot about the discussions we've had about it too."

"I told you I'm not ready to settle down, Fox," I warned, reading the implications between his words as he eyed me from beneath those mirrored shades.

"Yeah, well I've been thinking on that too. And I warned you my patience would wear thin one of these days. I told you there would come a point when I'd get done with waiting for you and I'd force your hand in the matter."

"What's that supposed to-"

Fox grabbed my waist and propelled me up onto his lap, making the carriage bounce wildly as I gripped his shoulders tightly and stole a look at the terrifying drop below us. I was wearing a wrap around maxi skirt but the position he'd put me in meant the split in the fabric was baring my thighs to him alongside my white panties.

The ride stopped with us at the very top of it while people got on and off down below and my heart thundered as Fox eyed me, his tongue wetting his lips and his jaw set with this decision.

"Fox," I warned, but he hadn't been joking about being done waiting and he caught the back of my neck, yanking me down into a hard kiss which I was helpless to resist.

His hand moved between us as his tongue pushed into my mouth and I groaned as he found my clit through my panties, massaging it roughly and making my hips buck.

I tried to push back against his shoulders, but he increased the pressure of his hold on the back of my neck, kissing me harder, demanding I bow for him and as my pussy throbbed with need, I felt myself giving in.

I wanted this. I wanted him. I just couldn't have him unless he understood what I had with the others too. I knew what this was for him. His move. The moment he stopped waiting and took what he wanted, and it was so fucking tempting to just let him. Except Fox wasn't like the others. He didn't know how to share his toys and I knew full well that hadn't changed despite him witnessing what I had with Maverick more than once.

"Wait," I panted, trying to pull back, but he just growled at me, his fingers shoving my panties aside before he sank two of them deep into my wet heat.

"You're mine," Fox said fiercely, his thumb still working my clit as my pussy gripped his fingers like a vice and I could only gasp his name as my body gave him what he wanted without question. "And when we get home tonight, it'll be my dick inside you proving that."

I moaned loudly, unable to help it as I rocked my hips against him, fucking his hand and finally getting a taste of what I'd been hungering for from him. His fingers thrust in and out of me and I forgot all of my arguments as he kissed me again, my pussy pulsing around him as I climbed up to the edge of the cliff, ready to dive right off of it for him-

The ride started moving again and Fox yanked his hand back out from beneath my skirt, his teeth taking my bottom lip hostage before he broke our kiss too and dumped me back in the seat beside him.

"You're not going to come for me until you beg for it, hummingbird," he murmured, leaning down to speak in my ear as I blinked at him in shock, my sex scrambled brain trying to figure out what the fuck he was playing at. "I'll take you to the edge like that over and over and over until you break for me. Until you beg for me. And until you tell me that you're mine. Only mine."

Heat rushed to my face as I realised what game he was playing with me and I slapped him hard enough to leave a print on his cheek, cursing him out as I moved to place a hand between my own thighs and finish what he'd started. I'd been right fucking there, so it wasn't like it would take much anyway.

Fox growled a refusal, snatching my hand into his and smirking at me darkly. "No cheating either, baby. It's time for you to accept that I'm your end game."

"You're a fucking psychopath," I hissed at him, half furious and half tempted to drag him behind the nearest tree when we got off this fucking ride so that he could finish what he'd just started. God he looked good today, his inked arms bulging and his broad chest pressing against the confines of his shirt. It wasn't fucking fair.

"I'm done playing nice," he replied with a shrug. "We've been living in limbo since you came home and it's time for that to end. You know as well as I do that we're destined, hummingbird. And now it's time for you to stop fighting it."

The ride came to a halt and Fox got out, tugging me beneath his arm as we joined JJ again and my over sexed brain drank in the sight of him too. Jesus I really had fallen deep into the dicksand with the Harlequin boys, but it was far too late for me to consider escaping it now. Nope. I was going to die here in cockland where they served orgasms for breakfast and my smiles always came with a side of toe curling moans.

"Anything?" Fox asked and JJ shook his head, eyeing the handprint on Fox's face curiously, but he didn't ask about it.

"No sign of Shawn or any of his men," JJ confirmed, my dolphin hanging loosely in his grip.

I wanted to say something to him, but my flesh was still tingling and I was having a little trouble stopping my knees from buckling right now, so I just bit my lip and eye fucked him instead.

"Good. Let's go check out the hall of mirrors." Fox tugged me along with him and despite my anger at him over that little game, I went.

JJ trailed behind us amongst the Harlequin stooges and I frowned, asking Fox why he wasn't hanging out with us too. Fox didn't give me an answer, but the look he shot JJ made me think he'd been the one to arrange us this way. Like I was here with him alone and J was just a part of the backup in case of trouble. What the fuck was that about?

"You know, you're being an ass and it's killing my carnival vibe," I warned as we passed a doughnut stand and I inhaled the scent of doughy goodness with a groan.

"That's because you're still trying to fight us," Fox said, pausing to buy me a rose from a vendor as we passed him, and I just kind of gaped at him as he tucked it behind my ear.

"So are you a gentleman taking me on a sweet date to the fair or an asshole who edges me in public and leaves me all hot and dick blinded while I'm trying to enjoy a day out?" I asked him icily, earning myself a smirk.

"Both, baby. And don't forget, if you want to finish, I can take care of that for my girl. You've only gotta agree that you're mine." Fox trailed a hand down the side of my cheek and my traitorous skin lit up for him.

I huffed out a breath which wasn't any kind of answer and Fox just shrugged, tugging me into the hall of mirrors with him and leaving JJ out again.

"This place is creepy," I commented as we started moving down the narrow aisles, reaching out to brush my fingers along the cool glass as my reflection echoed on eternally all around me.

"That's a matter of perspective," Fox commented, moving to stand against my back as I accidentally walked down a dead end and found myself caught between three mirrors. "For example, if I were to fuck you right here against this glass, I think it would be pretty hot to watch your body bending to mine a thousand times over all around us."

I bit my lip as I felt the press of his dick against my ass and turned to face him, sliding my hand over the front of his shorts, intending to turn his little edging game right back on him, but he caught my wrist before I could make contact with his cock.

"That's not how this is going to work, hummingbird," he growled, pressing my hand against the mirror at my back as he boxed me in. "I'm not letting you call the shots anymore. Today everything needs to change. It's past time. And that means you're gonna learn how good it feels to bend for me, because I promise that once you do, everything will come together the way it was always meant to."

He ran his free hand over my rock hard nipple, drawing a hiss from my lips as my eyes fell closed and every muscle in my body clenched. I was a strong, independent woman who knew her own mind. But damn, I couldn't deny how good it felt to be dominated by him.

My thoughts scattered as he tugged my crop top down and a throaty moan escaped me as he sucked on my nipple, but just as I was starting to think he was going to finish what he'd started on the Ferris wheel, he released me and backed away.

"Fox," I snarled. "Stop fucking with me."

"Then tell me you're mine."

"It's not that simple," I snapped.

"Yeah it is."

He turned and walked away into the hall of mirrors, leaving me to yank my top back up to hide my nipple before some unsuspecting kid arrived and got an eyeful.

By the time I hurried after him, he was gone and I cursed as I moved back and forth through the maze of mirrors, coming up on dead ends over and over again while the creepy feeling of the place sank into my skin.

For a moment I could have sworn I heard someone calling my name, but when I turned there was no one there aside from the countless reflections of myself.

Fuck, I was so freaking turned on that I couldn't even find my way out of a stupid carnival attraction designed for kids.

I took several more turns, a chill creeping up my spine and when I finally spilled out into the sunshine, a muscular figure was waiting to grab me.

I shrieked in alarm as Fox pushed me up against the side of the attraction and kissed me like he owned me. And despite all of my arguments to the contrary, I gave in, my lips parting for his tongue, hands fisting in his shirt and thighs parting for his leg as he drove it between them.

My hips rocked against him as I groaned into his mouth and I chased some fucking friction to deal with this need in my flesh.

Fox's phone started ringing in his pocket and he dropped me like a sack of shit, backing away as I sagged against the fucking wall and glared at him.

"Yeah?" he answered, his heated gaze locked on me. "Okay. I'll come now."

"You're such an asshole," I panted. Fucking panted. Goddammit.

"Say it," he pushed but I shook my head. Because no. Nope. Not a chance. But Jesus, I was tempted to just nod along and let him carry on convincing me.

I had no idea what had gotten into him today. There was a darkness hanging about him, a ruthless kind of determination that was likely to set my panties alight before I figured out what the fuck had caused it.

He was right of course. We had been dancing around this for too long and I couldn't keep stringing him along the way I was. But that meant he needed to know the truth. All of it. And I needed to figure out what the fuck that meant and what I wanted to come from it.

My gaze flicked behind him at a sign of movement and my heart started pounding as I found JJ there, his arms folded as he watched us, though he definitely didn't look as pissed as the last time he'd caught Fox kissing me.

"I need to go meet my dad," Fox said, waving JJ over as he spotted him too. "He insisted. I just have to go meet him by the haunted house so I can hear what he has to say. JJ can take you on something else while I'm gone."

"Oh so I'm not just another lackey after all?" JJ asked, shooting Fox a scowl which earned him an eye roll.

"You know you're not, man. I just needed a bit of time alone with my girl. Isn't that right, Rogue?"

"I just thought you were being an asshole as standard," I said but Fox only gave me a wolfish grin.

"Well it seems like that turns you on. So I'll make a note to do it more often."

I flipped him off, but he strode away from us, not seeming to give a single shit about how aggravating he was.

"You wanna explain what that's all about?" JJ asked me as I fell into step with him and he led the way out into the mess of rides and attractions.

I glanced over my shoulder to check the other Harlequins weren't close enough to listen in then huffed out a breath. But before I could tell him what had been happening since Fox had arrived, a high-pitched voice caught my ear.

"Rogue?" Rosie called, making me wince as I spotted her pushing through the crowd. "Is Chasey with you?"

"Quick, let's run for it," I hissed, grabbing JJ's arm and yanking him away.

"She's looking right at us," he laughed, running with me anyway while she yelled for us again.

"I don't fucking care. I can't deal with her bullshit. And every time I see her I have to think about Chase fucking her and it makes me wanna stab a bitch."

JJ laughed louder as I broke into a sprint and yanked him around the side of the teacups, ducking down a walkway between food vendors then turning towards a bunch of the smaller attractions once I was fairly certain we'd lost her.

"Come on then, tell me what Fox did to make you slap him," JJ said, looking around to make sure Rosie really was gone. I followed his gaze and wasn't too bummed to realise we'd shaken our Harlequin tails too.

"Apparently Fox is done waiting for me to be his girl," I explained, glancing up at JJ to try and gauge his reaction on that.

"Oh?" he asked, giving nothing away so I went on.

"He err... told me he's ready to force my hand and then went on to prove it by finger banging me on the Ferris wheel until I was about three seconds away from coming - and then he stopped." I scowled and JJ barked a laugh, confusing the fuck out of me.

"So he's trying to push you into making the decision by refusing you orgasms?"

"You're not mad about that?" I asked, arching a brow at him and JJ licked his lips, glancing over my head before jerking his chin towards a tent with a sign for fortune telling outside it. He lifted the flaps and led the way inside just as I spotted a flash of Rosie's bottle blonde hair again.

A woman dressed in draping shawls looked up at us with a smile as we stepped inside, waving her hands above a crystal ball which sat in the middle of a deep purple tablecloth which covered the table before her. "Welcome to Madame Mystery's cavern of-"

"Two hundred bucks for you to let me and my girl have some alone time in here for a bit," JJ interrupted her, pulling the cash from his pocket in offering.

"Two fifty," she replied, dropping the spooky lilt to her tone and smirking at us.

"Done." JJ tossed her the cash and she snatched it up from the table before grabbing a pack of smokes and heading towards a back exit. "Just don't leave cum stains on my tablecloth," she warned and then we were alone.

I fell apart laughing and JJ smirked wickedly as he caught my hips and began backing me up towards the table in question.

"So you were telling me about how Fox couldn't get you off," he prompted, his eyes glinting with amusement as my laughter fell away.

"Well, he certainly enjoyed getting me close," I grumbled, my gaze raking over JJ's features as my mood turned more serious. "I think we need to tell Fox about us."

JJ stilled, frowning down at me as my ass bumped against the table and the crystal ball fell from its stand, rolling away from us before falling to the ground.

"I've been thinking about this a lot actually. Especially since you, me and Chase almost hooked up," he said.

"Chase?" I asked, my mind spinning even more at the addition of his name to the conversation, especially as JJ lifted my ass and placed me on the table beneath him.

"Yeah. And Rick. I mean, it makes sense really, doesn't it? You never wanted to choose between us and I'm pretty sure you liked it when me and Rick both fucked you together." JJ's hand slid between my thighs and he groaned as he felt how wet I was. My panties were fucking drenched between Fox's torture sessions and now him being so fucking close to me and I sighed at the relief of JJ's touch on my flesh.

"That was seriously hot," I agreed, biting my lip as JJ dragged the material of my panties aside and began lazily stroking his fingers around my entrance, making me shudder for him.

"It was," he agreed. "But that wasn't all it was about, was it? I mean yeah, the sex is fucking mind-blowing and watching you take Maverick's cock with mine was like living out every fantasy I'd never even known I had. But it's not about us just fucking, is it? It's about all of it. All of *us*."

"Yes," I panted as he continued to torture me, his fingers drifting up to my clit and teasing it cruelly before he went back to circling my opening again.

"And the more I think about it. You and me and them too, the more right it seems. The more I want it too. I was watching you kiss Fox out there and it turned me on so fucking much, pretty girl. I could see the way he made you feel, and I wanted to keep watching as he made you feel it. I like seeing you with them. When Chase refused to join in with us the other night, I can't tell you how fucking disappointed I was. I don't even really understand it myself, but you and me and them, it just makes sense."

"So you're not gonna freak out on me if me and Fox…"

JJ shook his head, pushing his shorts down so slowly that it could only have been designed to torture me.

"So long as I know you want me just as much," he growled, fisting the rigid length of his cock as he set it free and I moaned at the sight of it.

"You know I do," I panted, gripping the edge of the table and waiting for him to finish this torture.

"Then tonight we'll tell him and we'll make him understand it," JJ said in a deep voice, filled with lust. "But he isn't going to like it."

"I know," I agreed. "But we can't keep lying and-"

"And you can't keep fighting what you have with him," JJ finished for me, pressing his cock to my aching core and making me curse.

"Be rough with me, Johnny," I growled, fisting my hand in his shirt and dragging him closer so that I could reach his mouth.

"Whatever you want, pretty girl," he agreed with a wicked grin, slamming the full length of his dick into me with a savage thrust which had me swearing as the tension in my body was finally rewarded.

He gripped my hips roughly and I moaned as my aching pussy got what I'd been dying for as he drove himself inside me with brutal, punishing thrusts and I met every one of them with a demand for more.

"We need to hurry," I gasped, my fingernails biting into the back of JJ's neck as I held on for dear life while he did exactly what I'd asked and slammed his cock into me in the best fucking way.

"I got you, pretty girl," JJ promised and as his mouth captured mine again, I forgot about hurrying or being quiet or any of the things I should have given a shit about. Because the feeling of Johnny James's body taking possession of mine was just about the best feeling in the entire fucking world and I was loving every filthy second of it.

CHAPTER THIRTY SEVEN

I went to meet my dad around the back of the haunted house and found him leaning against the black wall with a grim expression on his face. He always came here with some of his friends and they drank the afternoon away over in one of the beer tents. He didn't look particularly drunk, but I often couldn't tell with him.

"Sorry to ruin your day, son, but I just got word Shawn has an arms shipment coming in from the sea," Luther said as a ghoulish cackling carried from within the haunted house, followed by a scream. "One of my men got a tracker on the boat before it left a dock further up the coast." He handed me a piece of paper and gave me an intent look. "I want the men on that boat dealt with and the shipment brought home."

I nodded, scrubbing a hand over the stubble on my jaw in frustration. "Right now?"

"Right now," he confirmed and I sighed. This was meant to be my day with Rogue, the start of us officially getting on track. I'd wanted to push her into facing what we were to each other before she had to face the reality of Chase's exile.

For fuck's sake, couldn't we have one day of peace in this town? I'd wanted to make a few good memories today before the inevitable bomb went off in my face tonight. Because as soon as Rogue and JJ found out I'd sent Chase away again, they were gonna lose their fucking shit at me. I was already trying to figure out how I was gonna do damage control on what was coming. It wasn't like I hadn't been straight with them. From the moment he'd come home, I'd told them all exactly how it was gonna be, but was that gonna make the slightest bit of difference? Hell fucking no.

I turned to leave but Luther gripped my shoulder and turned me back, his features lined with tension. "Take a strong unit, Fox. There's several men on that boat and I'd rather you went overprepared than got caught off guard. Especially with the amount of weapons I hear is in that shipment."

"Alright," I promised, feeling marginally better that at least this would be a decent strike against Shawn. I was going to pack up his guns and take them home to my own army, ready to be wielded against him instead.

Luther took a moment to load a GPS app on my phone and linked it to the tracker that showed the boat's location still a fair way out to sea.

"I'll swing by the clubhouse when it's done," I said.

He nodded, letting me go and I headed back off into the crowded carnival to look for JJ and Rogue. I knew she'd wanna stay when me and JJ left and would probably be pissed as fuck if I tried to make her go home. The place was swarming with Harlequins so I wasn't too worried about leaving her here, I'd just make sure there were eyes on her at all times.

I headed back to the place where I'd last seen them, taking out my phone and trying to call JJ, but there was no answer. They were probably on a ride, so I started hunting the exit lanes around me, expecting to see her and JJ appearing from one at any moment. Instead, my eyes locked on Rosie as she jogged out of an exit from the waltzers with Jake and a couple of their dull friends in tow.

"Hey," I barked at her and her head snapped around, her large eyebrows jumping up. I did not get the eyebrow trend with girls lately, it was like they were competing to see who could balance the biggest hairy caterpillars on their face. She smiled, hurrying over to me like an obedient puppy and I folded my arms, disliking having her this close, especially after how I'd heard she'd reacted to Chase's scars.

"I'm looking for JJ and Rogue, have you seen them?" I asked.

"Maybe," she said, fluttering her lashes and reaching out to touch my arm. I looked down at where her hand lay on my skin with a sneer.

"Well have you, or haven't you?" I bit out.

I realised she was drunk as she swayed a little closer and I scented the cider on her breath.

"You look tense," she said huskily, running her fingers higher up my arm. "Do you want to go and talk somewhere more private?"

"I'd rather eat rusty nails, sweetheart," I said dryly, peeling her hand off of me and dropping it so her arm flopped to her side.

She pouted, her lip-glossed lips sticking together. "Well I'm not going to tell you then."

She tried to turn her back on me and the audacity of this girl made me snarl. I caught a fistful of the god awful frilly dress she was wearing and shoved her against the nearest trashcan which was shaped like a frog. The mouth was wide and gaping, big enough to swallow her whole as her hair cascaded into it and maybe it would if she didn't spill their location in the next five seconds.

She shrieked like I'd punched her and the noise grated against my eardrums.

"Don't ever turn your back on me," I warned and she nodded frantically.

"S-sorry," she stammered, fear filling her eyes as she finally sobered up enough to realise she'd made a grave mistake in fucking with me.

"And?" I demanded.

"U-um, and I'm s-sorry Mr Harlequin, sir," she sputtered.

I'd meant I wanted the information, but alright. It was actually kind of fun getting a little revenge on this bitch, so I decided to go a bit further with what she'd started. "It's Prince Harlequin to you. And I think you forgot to bow to me."

I released her, stepping back and jerking my head in an order to do it.

We'd gathered a pretty sizeable audience and a couple of assholes were recording which just meant her humiliation would spread through Sunset Cove within the hour. Perfect.

She stood upright from the trash can and I noticed a half sucked lollipop stuck in her hair alongside several pieces of popcorn and a grotty looking tissue.

"I'm waiting," I growled and she bent her knees a little, bowing her head as she trembled. "Lower."

Her knees continued to bend.

"Lower," I insisted and she went all the way down, kneeling in the dirt with her head bowed. "Keep going."

She lay her hands down on the ground, flattening herself to it and a snort of amusement escaped me. But I couldn't stand around here all day.

"Where's JJ and Rogue?" I growled.

"They went into the fortune teller's tent, Prince Harlequin," she said with a sob.

"Good. Oh and P.S. you have shit in your hair, I'd get that out before someone sees." I walked away from her, the crowd parting quickly for me as I headed in the direction of the tent and laughter rang out behind me. I hadn't really had time for that, but Rosie had been asking for it and I was tired of her bullshit.

"Free shot, Mr Harlequin?" a vendor offered me on the strong man game and I grabbed the mallet from his hands, unable to resist as I whacked it down on the target and the puck shot up like a bullet, slamming into the top of the tower so the bell went off.

"Ah perfect!" the guy cried. "Which animal do you want?" He pointed to the row of teddies hanging behind him on a rack and I smirked as I saw a badger. "That one."

He passed it over and I kept walking, knowing Rogue was gonna fucking love this thing. I passed by a guy with long matted hair and some fishing nets wrapped around him as he waved a jar of seashells at a couple of women. "A dollar for a magic seashell!" he called to them and I frowned as I looked closer at him. *Is that Carnival Bill?* "It'll grant your wishes," he said enticingly and they stepped closer. "Mmm, I can tell you're wishing for a big juicy corndog, aren't you lovey?"

"I am kind of hungry," the girl agreed as she plucked a seashell from his jar.

He suddenly opened his arms so the fishing nets parted, revealing his naked cock poking out beneath his ragged brown t-shirt. It had a stick taped to it and it was smothered in ketchup.

"Here's your corndog!" he cried and the girls screamed, running for their lives as he chased after them, dropping seashells everywhere from his jar.

"Jesus," I muttered, wishing I could scour that image from my mind forever, but it looked like it was here to stay.

I headed up to the fortune teller's tent with the badger toy in my grip, wishing I didn't have to call this day short already. But I'd make it up to Rogue as soon as I could.

A soft moan reached my ears and I frowned, a prickle running up my neck as a horrible feeling of foreboding washed over me.

I pulled the curtain aside and stepped into the low-lit space, my brain taking two long, torturous seconds to catch up to what I was seeing before me.

I came to a halt, staring at JJ as he fucked my girl where she perched on a table, his shorts around his ankles and his face buried in her neck. She was moaning for him, gasping his name and urging him to go harder and he came with a hard thrust as her nails tore into his back and she followed him into ecstasy with a loud cry.

The badger toy slipped from my fingers to the floor as Rogue's eyes opened and her gaze crashed into mine.

My heart combusted, utterly obliterated just like that. One second I'd been fine, the next I was in the deepest realm of hell that existed.

"Fox," she gasped.

No.

"Are you kidding me, pretty girl? It's JJ," my brother growled as he pulled his dick out of the woman I loved and tugged his shorts up. She stared unblinkingly at me as she shoved her skirt down to cover her legs. "Or Johnny James, the best fuck you've ever had, the guy who always rails you into next week, king of the D, you can pick any of those re-" Rogue punched him in the chest to shut him up and shoved his face around to look at me.

My heart was jerking in the most excruciating way as I felt it rip right down the middle and my head filled with a murderous, deafening drone of noise that swallowed everything up.

Suddenly I was moving, my lips curled in a snarl as I grabbed hold of JJ's throat and slammed him down on the table he'd just fucked my girl on. My fists buried in his gut over and over as I hit him before throwing him to the floor and kicking him with every ounce of strength in my body. He didn't even fight back, because he knew, he fucking *knew* what he'd done.

Rogue screamed, pulling at my arms, trying to stop me, but I just ignored her as I beat the fuck out of my apparent best friend who'd taken the one thing from me I'd ever wanted for myself.

"Get away from me!" I roared at Rogue, knocking her back, but she came at me again, clinging to my arm, her nails tearing into my flesh just like they'd been doing to JJ's back two fucking minutes ago but for an entirely different reason.

I leaned down, snatching JJ's shirt in my fist as I slammed my knuckles into his face.

"Why!?" I bellowed at him, agony slicing my insides to ribbons. "Why her?!"

"She was never yours to claim," he coughed out and I punched him again, making his head hit the floor hard.

"Fox!" Rogue screamed as my knuckles bashed against his chest and suddenly she was fighting her way in front of me, lying across him with her hands raised and trembling and I managed to stop my fist from hitting her at the last second.

"I love him!" she shouted as tears splashed down her cheeks, fear twisting up her expression and burning out of her eyes. "I'm in love with him and I have been for a long time. You can kill me too if you're gonna kill him, because there's no life for me without him in it."

My throat closed up and no air could get into my lungs at all. I stood upright, my shoulders trembling as I stared down at the girl I'd been in love with my whole life, her words like an axe carving into my head. She loved JJ?

"Move, pretty girl." JJ tried to push her off, but she wouldn't budge, shielding him from my wrath.

"It's over," I said in disbelief as I told myself more than them. Every hope and dream I'd had for claiming Rogue turned to ash before my eyes. There was no us. It looked like there'd never been any us.

"How long?" I rasped. "How long have you been together? And I swear to God, if you lie to me Rogue, I'll kill him. I won't stop. I won't fucking be able to."

"Since not long after I came back to town," she said, her voice quavering as more tears washed down her cheeks.

I nodded, rage coiling in me like a viper thirsting to strike its prey. All this time? All this fucking time? In my house. With my boy, a person I trusted beyond anyone else. The only one of my brothers who hadn't betrayed me. And now he had. And had been for a long fucking time.

"Let's just go home and talk about it. We were going to tell you tonight anyway, I swear." Rogue reached for me, gripping my hand. "We can find a way to make this work. You, me, JJ, Chase-"

"Chase is gone," I spat coldly. "I drove him out of town this morning, sweetheart. Have you been fucking him too?"

"You did what?" she gasped, her eyes widening in horror and for a moment I relished that pain in her expression. That she was hurting over something, because she clearly hadn't given a fuck about hurting me all this time. She'd played me like a goddamn fool. She'd kissed me with the same lying mouth she'd been kissing JJ with this whole time.

"You heard me," I snapped, my gaze moving to JJ's bloody face as he looked up at me from beneath her.

"Fox, let's just talk about this," he tried.

"There's nothing to talk about," I snarled, looking between the two of them in my shadow. "Because your faces say everything I need to know. I'm the villain in your love story, right? This whole time you've been sneaking around my house and fucking each other beneath my nose, fearing what I'd do if I ever found out. Or were you planning on killing me off one of these days so that I wasn't a problem anymore?"

"Don't be ridiculous!" Rogue cried. "How could we have told you? You think I'm yours, but I never was, Fox. And you had no fucking right to tell JJ he couldn't have me."

I tried to swallow the unyielding lump in my throat, but it wouldn't budge. "Well you never said never to me, Rogue. And I guess you forgot to mention you don't want me while your tongue was in my mouth or when you were moaning my name, huh?" I snapped. "But don't worry, I've got the memo loud and fucking clear now, sweetheart. I was the idiot who fooled myself into thinking it would always end up being us. So I guess I'll get the fuck out of your way so you can enjoy your happily ever after."

I turned, stalking out of the tent as Rogue called out to me again, but I didn't stop walking. I shoved my way through the crowd as I made my way to the parking lot, a deathly kind of rage spilling through my blood as I moved.

When I made it to my truck, I bombed it down the road off of Carnival Hill, tearing into the town and towards Harlequin House.

When I arrived, I picked up a bag of weapons and continued on my way to the jetty out back. I jumped down onto the speedboat, starting it up and checking the tracker location on my phone for where the boat was that Shawn had coming in and raced out onto the water.

Anger clawed and bit and chewed on every organ inside me, devouring anything good that existed in me and tarring it black.

I travelled out a few miles until the coast was a distant mass of land and the ocean stretched out everywhere around me.

All I could see in my mind was Rogue fucking my best friend, the way she'd looked when he'd finished inside her, the way they'd clung to each other like they were the centre of each other's world. This pain was akin to losing Rogue ten years ago, the soul destroying agony of heartbreak tearing me open so all my old wounds bled and fucking bled.

I spotted the catamaran coming this way and aimed my speedboat right for her, flipping on the cruise control as I prepared to become the worst kind of savage I could be.

I unzipped the bag of weapons, strapping a Kevlar vest over my chest along with every gun and knife I could fit onto my body followed by a belt full of grenades.

The bloodlust was rising in me like it never had before and I knew I might just die on this mission without any backup, but I didn't give a fuck what happened anymore. All I knew was that I needed death to appease this monster in me. I needed blood and screams and the pain of my enemies to sate some of its fury. And if it wasn't these assholes right now, it'd be Johnny James.

A shout went up from the catamaran as I sped toward it and I fired my rifle, taking down the man who'd alerted the others. I only had a moment to pull my speedboat up alongside the catamaran and I quickly tied it to a ladder on the side with some rope before climbing up and jumping onto the deck. A gunshot slammed into the Kevlar on my chest and I jerked backwards with a growl of pain as I fired my own gun, taking down the asshole in a rain of blood.

I stalked forward, stepping over him as I shoved the door open to the cockpit and gunned down the captain before he could even try and defend himself. I shoved through the door on the other side, striding back along the deck and a deafening bang rang out as another bullet slammed into my back and hit the bulletproof vest. I stumbled from the impact, but relished the pain of the bruise as I twisted around and fired once more, taking the motherfucker out so hard that he fell over the railing into the water.

I hurried to the nearest cabin, kicking it open and finding three men scrambling to load their weapons. I drew a knife, slashing the closest guy's throat before firing several shots that left the room bloody and silenced their screams for good. Then I turned and marched down to the next cabin with a sneer on my lips, my heart beating to a dark and forbidding rhythm. I tasted blood on my tongue and the weight of heartbreak pressing down on my soul as I shoved the door open to the main cabin, finding a stairway full of men running up towards me. Two bullets slammed into my chest and I cursed, doing the only thing I could and snatching a grenade from my hip, pulling the pin out with my teeth and throwing it down into the stairwell. The explosion ripped through the catamaran, followed by another, then another and suddenly I was thrown into the water by an enormous blast, a blaze of fire twisting up towards the sky all I could see before I hit the ocean.

The weight of all my weapons and the vest dragged me deep under the waves and I had to let go of the rifle as I powered back towards the surface with my ears ringing. The moment I made it to the fresh air again, the scent of smoke and the blinding heat of fire washed over me.

My heart hammered fiercely as I stared at what I'd done, my grenade clearly having set off whatever other explosives had been stashed on that boat. What remained of the catamaran was already sinking, some of the fire going out with a hiss as the hull filled with water.

I started swimming as fast as I could around the wreckage, hunting for my dad's speedboat, but knowing deep down that it was already lost. I spotted the remains of it just before it went under, sinking away into the abyss of the deep blue sea.

My breaths came heavier as I fought to keep afloat with all of my weapons weighing me down and growled as I starting pulling them off of me and letting them drop away into the ocean.

I fought to get the Kevlar vest off too and as soon as it was over my head, I managed to tread water a little easier.

I turned my gaze back towards the distant shore, knowing it was one helluva a fucking swim. And as warmth spread over my shoulder, I raised a hand and felt a lump of shrapnel sticking out of my goddamn flesh as the pain started to find me in the wake of all the adrenaline. Which meant I was now not only in danger of bleeding out, but I might just make a shark's day if he found me before I made it to shore. And as I stared at the faraway mass of Sunset Cove, I knew with a certainty that should have frightened me that it was too far to make it.

The last of the fire on the boat sizzled out behind me as it went under and I was left alone in the dark sea with a thousand hungry predators living beneath me. And I realised I didn't much care what happened to me now, because there was no life waiting for me back on the shore anyway. Maverick was gone, Chase was gone, and Rogue and JJ had all they wanted in each other. So maybe this was how Fox Harlequin died. And maybe I didn't really give a fuck.

CHAPTER THIRTY EIGHT

JJ was tearing through everything he could find in Fox's office back at Harlequin House while I paced the floors with Mutt at my heels whimpering sympathetically.

"There's nothing here," JJ cursed, scoring a hand through his inky hair as he looked up at me in desperation.

"There has to be something," I pleaded, the tears on my cheeks dry now and a cold, hard fury knotting my gut.

I was angrier at Fox than I'd ever been in my entire life. And yet I was filled with guilt and pain over how much I'd hurt him today too. And every time I looked at the myriad of bruises covering JJ's face from the beating Fox had inflicted upon him, that guilt in me only festered.

This was all my fault. All of it.

Chase never would have left me on that ferry if I hadn't come back here and started messing with their lives in the first place. JJ never would have touched a girl who Fox had set his eyes on if that girl hadn't been me. Maverick wouldn't have even gone to prison if there hadn't been a crime to go down for. And Fox wouldn't have had his heart ripped up by a fantasy version of me who I was never going to be good enough to live up to.

"I should have let Axel kill me all those years ago," I muttered, not even really meaning to voice my thoughts, but JJ froze at those words, dropping the pile of paperwork he'd been rifling through.

"What did you just say?" he demanded but I just bit my lip and looked away from him out of the window towards the sea. The Cove. The only home I'd ever wanted and the one place I never should have come back to.

JJ's hand landed on my shoulder and he forced me around, grasping my chin in his hand and making me look up at him.

"Never say anything like that ever again," he growled at me. "You scrub those toxic thoughts from your mind right fucking now."

JJ's eyes bounced between mine as my bottom lip quivered and tears blurred my view of him.

"It's true though, isn't it? There's a reason I'm the girl who everyone always casts aside. I *am* toxic. I'm a curse. All I ever bring is bad luck and Chase was the only one of you who ever saw that truth in me. And look what he got for it. Shawn tortured him because of me, he'll never see out of that eye again, he'll probably walk with a limp for the rest of his life and now the only family he ever had have thrown him away! He's all alone because of me. He's out there somewhere thinking none of us want him, his whole world narrowing down to this helpless, hopeless, lonely place where his mere existence will be the only reason he even wakes up in the mornings. I know - I lived it. And I wish I hadn't. I wish I hadn't survived that night because I just went on to be a curse on all of you and I-"

JJ kissed me so hard he stole the breath from my lungs. My tears coated our lips and his fingers dug into my face in a savage demand which had me bowing to him. There were so many unspoken words in that kiss. So many years of loneliness and longing and hurt but so much heat too. There were days in the sun and laughter on our lips, the taste of salt water from the sea and too many missed moments like this. My racing heart slowed and my fingers knotted in his shirt as I dragged him to me, not wanting a single inch to divide us as I devoured the taste of him.

"Did you mean what you said to him?" JJ growled against my lips and I didn't need to ask what he was referring to, my chest inflating with that feeling as I nodded, looking up into his honey brown eyes which held so much pain.

So much longing.

"I love you, Johnny James," I breathed. "I love you so much it terrifies me. It makes my skin burn and my heart race. But it makes my gut knot and my palms clammy too because loving you means risking my heart on you all over again. But this time I know it's not the same. This time I'm all in, which means that if you throw me away again there won't be anything left of me to keep on going."

"I'm never letting you go, pretty girl," JJ swore fiercely, his grip on my face so tight I felt like a life raft keeping him afloat in a stormy sea. "Never. This - you and me. This is it. Some people say that love is easy, you just open your heart and let someone in. But our love has never been easy. It's been won through battles we fought without armour and earned through wounds that leave scars which forever change us. It's messy and brutal and it hurts so fucking good. I don't want some easy version of love, Rogue. I want to burn in the fire of our family. I want you and me for fucking ever. And I need the others in this with us too."

"It's so fucked, JJ," I said, my voice hitching as the weight of his words wrapped their way around my heart and settled in tight like a whole new wall which I was building for myself. But this one wasn't designed to keep him out, it was there to lock him in. "Chase could be anywhere. How are we supposed to find him now?"

"We'll find him," JJ snarled ferociously but I couldn't help the clawing doubt inside me.

"You never found me," I breathed.

Something cracked in JJ's gaze as he recognised the truth in my words, but he just shook his head vehemently. "This won't be like that. There's a clue here somewhere. There has to be. Besides, when Fox gets home we can force the answer from him if we have to. I don't care if I have to fucking waterboard him - I've done it before and I know how. He'll cool off, he'll realise he did the wrong thing, he'll help us get him back."

I nodded because I knew JJ needed me to agree with that assessment. But I'd seen the monster in Fox's eyes and the determination too. He wasn't going to go back on this decision. Especially not after discovering me and JJ together. There was something broken in him now and I could just chalk that all up to yet another thing which I was to blame for.

"Let's go. We can check out all of our old haunts. If Chase hung around maybe he'd try to use one of them for a bit. Then we can start scouring the towns beyond the edge of the Harlequins' control. We'll find him. I promise you we'll find him."

"Okay," I agreed because there wasn't anything else we could do anyway.

JJ took my hand and led me down to the garage, the two of us climbing into his orange GT with Mutt hopping onto my lap before we booked it out of there.

I'd already dialled the hospital searching for him and they'd confirmed he'd been in to have his cast off this morning as well as telling me they had no follow up appointments confirmed with him as they'd been told he was moving away. Fucking Fox. I wanted to kill him and throw myself at his feet begging for his forgiveness all at once.

This was so fucked up. *We* were so fucked up.

I gripped my phone in my hand and blew out a breath as my finger scrolled though my small list of contacts and I stared down at Maverick's name for a long moment.

He still claimed to hate the rest of my boys, but I knew there was a whole lot more to their relationship than that. He'd searched through the rubble at The Dollhouse for days in the hunt for him. He'd shared me with Johnny James and had even saved Fox's life. He may well have hated all of them, but deep down I was pretty sure he still loved them too. Because I always had no matter how much hatred I'd felt towards all of them over the years.

That was the thing about hate. It kept close company with love. You had to really feel something for someone to hold onto anger and hurt like that otherwise the emotions would fade. Because if you don't give a shit about someone then the energy it takes to hate them becomes too much and you end up indifferent to them at best. I should know. I had enough exes to look back on with hatred if I could be bothered, but I'd let all of that go when I'd left them in my dust. They weren't worth the space they'd taken up in my baggage anyway so why waste a single moment of my energy on hating them? But the Harlequin boys and me, that was something so much more powerful. I hadn't even been able to speak their names. I hadn't been able to think of them at all without it burning me from the inside out. I'd hated them so hard and for so long that I knew the only real reason for it was my love for them.

So I hit dial on my phone and pressed it to my ear as it started to ring.

"How did you know I needed to hear your voice tonight, beautiful?" Rick asked, his voice a little rough around the edges and my heart shattered as I realised his demons had been close and I hadn't been there for him.

"I hate you being away from me all the time," I said, trying not to let him hear me cry as JJ shot me a curious look. I showed him the caller ID and he sighed, focusing on the road again as Rick replied.

"Then come stay with me all the time."

"But then I'd be away from the others," I breathed and a long spell of silence followed.

"What's happened?" Maverick asked darkly and for a moment I didn't even know where to begin.

"Chase is gone. Fox kicked him out and we don't know where he went. I have to find him, Rick. I need him..."

Maverick didn't say anything for so long that I had to double check the call was still connected before a sigh escaped him and he spoke again.

"I'll head to the towns north of the Cove. It's not like he can run all that fast, is it?" he muttered.

A choked, hopeless laugh escaped me as relief pooled in my chest. I knew it wasn't like having one more person on the hunt guaranteed anything, but knowing Rick would be searching too, that he even cared enough to help, set something back into place in my heart.

"I love you," I said before he could hang up and Rick hesitated a moment.

"I'll find him for you, baby girl," Maverick swore.

The line went dead and I dropped my phone in my lap. There was no point calling Fox. He wasn't answering and I seriously doubted he'd be of any help to us right now anyway, though I'd left more than a few pleading voicemails for whenever he decided to check back in.

All we could do now was search every spot we could think of and hope for the best. I wasn't giving up on Chase though. I'd never give up on him again.

CHAPTER THIRTY NINE

I'd been out all night looking for Chase and had only just gotten back to the Isle. I'd wanted to go to Rogue when I'd called her to say I'd found no sign of him and she'd started crying, but she'd been at Harlequin House and it wasn't like I could just walk through the gates and head into my old home, so I'd left her to be looked after by JJ, feeling useless to her, to myself, to Chase. Not that I gave a shit about Chase, but my girl wanted him back so I'd do what I could to make that happen. Fucking Fox and his fucking arrogance. I tried not to think about the fact I'd been the one to tell Fox about Chase betraying Rogue. Of course, I'd thought the guy deserved anything he got back then. Now…well, fuck, I wouldn't have placed his ass with Shawn that was for sure. I should have just gotten hold of him myself when I'd heard what he'd done. I could have dealt with it, given him the punishment he deserved. The eye loss was overkill.

Dammit, I hated fucking Shawn.

I sat down by the Mariner's Grave, the old ship wreck half sunk in the shallow waters of Dead Man's Isle. It was quiet down here, but I guessed this place was always fucking quiet. Especially since Rogue had come tearing back into my life. Now everything seemed emptier when she wasn't around and I half wondered how I'd lived on this island for so many years without losing my fucking mind.

Although, when I thought on that a little more it was clear my mind had been lost years ago. And the search parties had gone missing too.

I pushed up to my feet, growing bored of sitting here with my gaze set on the distant view of the carnival in Sunset Cove. At night, I'd be able to see the lights from here, the way they coloured the hill like a rainbow and made me miss all the fun I'd had whenever it came to town when I was a kid.

As I walked the beach, my gaze landed on a shape further along the shore and my eyebrows arched with interest as I upped my pace to inspect it. As I drew closer, I realised it was a goddamn body and my intrigue piqued further. The fucker was face down, covered in sand and some seaweed too plus he had a chunk of metal sticking out of his shoulder. I kicked him over with my foot and he slumped onto his back, making my heart bunch up into a tight ball as my gaze landed on the guy's face.

Fuck.

It was Fox motherfucking Harlequin.

I fell to my knees, my fingers going to his neck as I hunted for a pulse, my gut lurching violently.

A weak flicker beneath my fingers made me release a hard breath and I took hold of his arm, hauling him up with a grunt of effort and throwing him over my shoulder.

I walked as fast as I could up to the hotel and tried to work out how he'd ended up here and why the fuck I was hurrying inside with him like I gave a shit what happened to him. But maybe I did, Because Fox Harlequin didn't die washed up on a beach, that was too damn easy for him, especially after he'd upset my little unicorn.

I barked orders at my men to bring me everything the asshole would need to survive whatever the fuck had happened to him, then I carried him to the spa where I'd kept Rogue prisoner. My muscles burned with effort as I finally made it there and walked straight into the sauna, laying him down on one of the benches and starting to strip off his shoes, jeans and shirt so he was just in his boxers. I slipped his phone from his pocket, dropping it into mine instead for…safe keeping.

"You don't get to die washing up on my beach like a fucking half eaten dolphin, asshole," I gritted out through my teeth. "You need to wake up so I can kill you myself."

A couple of my men appeared including Nick who'd been a medic in the army and had been useful to me on more than one occasion. I stood strategically in front of Fox's face to hide him from view but as Nick hurried forward with a medical bag in his hand, I stepped back to let him examine the huge piece of metal in Fox's shoulder and quickly sent the rest of my men away.

"Holy shit, that's Fox Harlequin," Nick gasped.

"No shit, Sherlock. Now save his ass or I'll kill you." I drew my revolver, pointing it at Nick's head and his eyes widened in surprise before he set to work removing the lump of metal from my brother's flesh.

"Jesus, a couple of inches to the right and it could have severed his carotid," Nick muttered.

"That bad?"

"Yeah, certain death bad," he said. "Lucky he didn't pull this out himself either."

"He ain't stupid," I murmured and Nick gave me the fucking side eye like he was wondering why I was so desperate to get Foxy boy fixed up. "Just hurry the fuck up."

Nick cleaned the wound then stitched it up before binding it in a bandage that looped under Fox's arm.

"He'll need the bandage changing daily and I'll have to keep an eye on it for infection, but he'll live," Nick said.

I nodded stiffly, my shoulders drooping as I holstered my gun. "Why's he not waking up?"

"I'm not sure…what happened to him?" he asked.

"Fuck knows. He washed up on the beach," I said.

"Right, well then I'd guess he's exhausted, he must have been in the water a while." Nick checked his pulse and I leaned closer to look at Fox's face. He had more colour in his cheeks now and it did something to ease the knot in my chest. Not that I gave a fuck.

"This isn't the best place for him. He needs dry clothes, a warm bed and ideally some fluids. I don't have anything here for a drip, but if he warms up he might wake then he can drink something.”

I nodded, scooping Fox up again with a grunt of effort and Nick trailed after me as I carried him to my bedroom and placed him on the bed. I felt Nick’s eyes on me as I pulled clothes onto my arch nemesis, layering him up with two sweaters, some sweatpants, a beanie hat and three pairs of socks before tucking him under my comforter as well.

Then I stood at the end of the bed, folded my arms and waited.

“It might take him a little bit of time to-” Nick started.

“I get it. I’ll be here when he wakes up. Fetch some water if you wanna be useful.”

He nodded, scurrying away and I remained standing there as I stared at Fox, his expression completely peaceful like he had no fucking idea what was going on. He wouldn’t like it when we woke up and that gave me a little more reason to want to see his eyes open. The only reason, some might say. Because torturing Fox was what I enjoyed best. *So why won’t he wake the fuck up dammit?*

Nick returned with a couple of glasses of water, placing them down on the nightstand and moving to grab a chair like he was going to stay here too.

“Out,” I barked, pointing to the door.

“Oh, right, sure.” He backed away, slipping out of my suite and leaving us in silence.

My jaw ticked as I stood there, my gaze riveted to Fox’s face.

It was another twenty minutes before he finally stirred, his eyes flickering open as a groan passed his lips and confusion crossed his features as he slowly regained consciousness.

“Hello, Foxy,” I purred, moving toward him and handing him a glass of water.

“Maverick?” he frowned then cursed as he sat up and jarred his shoulder, wincing from the pain. “Fuck, what’s going on?”

“Drink,” I commanded, placing the water in his hands and he chugged it down, clearly desperate for the liquid, so I passed him my one too. Because I didn’t want a drink anyway, the tap water on the Isle tasted like an old racoon’s asshole.

Fox gulped that down too then placed the glass on the nightstand and rubbed a hand over his head like it was hurting.

"I always told you you couldn't make the swim from shore to Dead Man's Isle," I said with a taunting smirk. "Were you coming out here for some covert attack bullshit? Because I have to say, Foxy, you get a D minus for effort."

"Fuck off," he snarled, pushing the comforter away and getting to his feet, though he swayed a little as he did so. "I need a boat."

I roared a laugh, stepping forward to get right in his way as I came nose to nose with him. "You're not the king of this island, Foxy boy. In fact, you just wandered right into my domain. So I think you're gonna tell me what brings you here or I'll start cutting off fingers. Was it the shame of sending Chase away and breaking Rogue's heart that made you try to drown yourself?"

He gazed at me with an emptiness in his eyes that made me frown, like he didn't care if I carved him up and baked him into a pie, and that was no fun. "I went out on a job solo, blew up a boat and accidently took my own boat out with it." He shrugged his good shoulder, trying to get past me again but I slammed a hand to his chest as I got close to his face, looking right into his eyes.

"You look sad, Foxy boy, what's going on?" I growled curiously, my mind skipping to my girl.

He wet his lips. "I caught JJ fucking Rogue," he deadpanned. "Happy?"

My brows arched as I absorbed this news that Rogue had forgotten to tell me, then another laugh fell from my lungs as I clapped him on the shoulder. "Oh how very unfortunate, brother." I smiled from ear to ear. "How fucking heart breaking for you. I did tell them it would all end in tears, but would they listen?"

"You knew?" he gritted out and I smirked like an asshole.

"Of course I knew. I know all the dirty little Harlequin secrets. I'm a fountain of knowledge, me."

"You piece of shit." He shoved his palms against my chest and I laughed harder as he went feral on me, nearly knocking me to the floor, but he was clearly tired as fuck.

I whistled for my men and a bunch of them appeared as I pushed Fox back and directed them to tie his arms behind him. He put up a damn good fight considering he was battling exhaustion and a fucked up shoulder, but he was in no position to win so they soon had him trussed up nicely for me.

"Take him to one of the empty hotel rooms," I said with a triumphant smile. "You're officially my prisoner, Foxy boy, and as there's no Harlequins knocking down my door to save their king, I have to believe no one knows you're here. So I wonder what Daddy's gonna think when you don't come home."

CHAPTER FORTY

I felt numb.

I knew it was just me going back to my same old coping mechanisms, but it was what it was. Nothing touched me. The pain of what I'd lost couldn't hurt me. I was just here.

We hadn't found Chase. We'd searched every place we could think of, we'd headed out of town, we'd called around hospitals, hotels, freaking gas stations asking if anyone had seen a dude with an eyepatch but no. Nothing. Chase was a ghost lost to the wind and I was just...empty.

Fox hadn't come back either. It had been ten days and he'd been just as absent as Chase, only texting a few times to say he was fine and that he needed some time alone.

Alone.

Fuck him.

Being alone was the one thing in this world that I knew I didn't want because I knew the taste of it all too well. Chase had feared that too. He'd grown up in a house where he was a one man army trying to fight against the full force of the monster who had fathered him. He'd been alone his whole life growing up in that hell.

Me and him were the only ones who had ever really understood that. What was out there away from the safety and love of our little family. How lucky we'd been to have each other.

And now Fox had taken that from him in my name, like using me as an excuse made it somehow okay despite my feelings on the subject. What had he even thought would happen? That me and JJ would just accept his decision in this? That he could pick and choose who got to be in our family and what they were allowed to do within it.

Then he'd just run off at the first evidence of his control slipping. I'd made it clear to him that I wasn't going to be his girl exclusively. My whole life I'd been telling all of them I'd never pick between them. But the way he'd looked at me when he'd found me in JJ's arms had been filled with this devastated kind of betrayal like I'd broken a thousand promises to him when all I'd done was love one of my boys in a way he didn't want me to.

But he didn't get to choose that for me. And he didn't get to choose Chase's fate either.

Only he had. And we couldn't find him to tell him we wanted him back. I was angry at Chase for that too. Looking back on that morning it was clear to me now that he'd known what was coming. He'd hugged me a little too tight, watched us a little too closely and the brush of his lips against mine now left a taste of goodbye on my skin which would never wash off. So I was pissed at him because he should have said something. We would have stopped this from happening. Or if we couldn't, then we would have gone with him.

But no. He'd chosen for us just like Fox had chosen for us and now I had no choice but to just give up.

"Where is he?!" Luther bellowed and I flinched as I looked around from my spot at the breakfast bar with my uneaten dinner laid out before me.

Luther strode straight into the room, clearly having let himself into the house and JJ got to his feet beside me, positioning himself between me and the leader of this gang of assholes.

"I told you, we don't know," JJ said, raising his hands placatingly, but I could tell that Luther had finally lost his patience and he was done waiting for Fox to come home.

"You must know something!" Luther bellowed. "My son wouldn't just walk out on his responsibilities here even if he did fuck up that job. He won't answer my fucking calls and he just sent me this."

Luther brandished his phone at us and my eyebrows arched as I read the message from Fox.

Fox:

Maybe you should go find a nice girl to bury your dick in and relieve some of that tension you're holding onto, old man. I told you I need a few days off and it seems to me that if you got laid a bit more often you wouldn't be such an unbearable cunt all the time.

"Jesus," JJ muttered while I fought the urge to laugh. Or cry. Who even fucking knew anymore?

"This is on you," Luther snapped, sidestepping JJ to get a clearer look at me as he pointed in my face and my heart catapulted up into my throat. But as he went on it became clear that he still didn't know the reason for Fox going AWOL and I relaxed a little. "I gave you a job to do, yet now one of my sons has gone on a fucking vacation and I still don't see any sign of the other."

"Rick's coming around," I said placatingly, though I wasn't sure how much truth there was to that declaration. "And I'm sure Fox will be back soon."

"I see no evidence of any of that being true," Luther snarled and JJ tried to tug me behind him again.

"It is," I said forcefully. "We're actually heading over to see Maverick tonight. He wants to spend time with me and JJ and the last time we were there he didn't seem against the idea of reconnecting with Fox too. I think now that he understands that the things that happened in prison weren't on any of you, he's starting to look at things differently."

Luther released a harsh breath, some of the tension relaxing from his shoulders as he dropped his hand and backed up a little.

"Good. That's good. You deal with that tonight then and I'll work on finding my other fucking son. If he doesn't get back here soon I'm going to have to make an example of him though. There's only so long that I can lie to cover his absence." Luther strode over to the fridge, muttering something about ungrateful boys being the end of him and I realised he fully intended to stay here for a while.

I exchanged a look with JJ and he nodded to my silent suggestion.

"We're gonna get going then. It'll be getting dark soon and Rick will be wondering where we are," I said and Luther grunted his agreement.

I poked JJ to get him moving and we hurried upstairs where I quickly packed a bag with some clothes and my toothbrush while JJ followed suit.

"So that's the job Luther gave you?" he asked in a low whisper. "To reunite Fox and Rick?"

"Simple, huh?" I said, giving him a knowing look and he groaned.

"More like impossible. Why the fuck would you agree to that?"

"Well there was a gun pointed at me which was pretty motivating," I said. "Besides, I figured if they'd rather let Luther kill me than reunite, I could just run the fuck away."

JJ muttered curses about me being the most insane woman he'd ever met as we headed back downstairs and we said a quick goodbye to Luther.

"Tell Rick I love him," he called out after us. "And I want him home soon."

"Will do," I agreed, holding the door for Mutt as he raced out onto the beach and promptly started chasing his tail excitedly.

JJ gave me a look that said Luther was batshit and I wholeheartedly agreed, but I wasn't gonna be calling the psychopath out on it, so here we were.

JJ led the way down the private jetty outside the house, picking out one of the slightly bigger boats seeing as Fox had taken the fastest speedboat with him when he ditched out on us ten days ago.

I took JJ's hand when he offered it and climbed in behind him, glancing back at Mutt as he took a running jump from the jetty and landed in the boat with a triumphant yap.

I shot Maverick a text to tell him we were coming to see him then I sat back in one of the padded seats as JJ started up the engine and tipped my head back to look up at the darkening sky as we raced away across the waves towards Dead Man's Isle.

Night had fallen by the time we pulled up at the dock and for once, Rick's men didn't start yelling and waving weapons around, instead helping us to dock the boat and even offering me a hand to help me climb out.

"He's waiting for you in the bar," Dave grunted, giving me the stink eye. Fucking Dave. I was going to make a special effort to find his packed lunch and eat it while I was here just for that look.

The sound of thumping music reached me as we started towards the huge hotel complex and JJ threw an arm around my waist, his hand sliding into my back pocket as he pressed a kiss to my temple.

"Fuck it feels good to let the world know you're mine," he muttered as I leaned into his touch, stealing some strength from him and holding onto him tightly as I wrapped my arm around him in return.

I was still all kinds of messed up over Chase and Fox, but JJ had a point. Being able to show my feelings for him to anyone who cared to look felt seriously good after so many months of sneaking about like we were doing something wrong. I mean, the sneaking had been hot in its own right, but I was more than ready to let the entire world know that Johnny James was mine.

I led the way into the hotel, guiding JJ down the gleaming hallway towards the bar. After spending time with Maverick here after Chase had abandoned me on that ferry, I knew the whole complex well.

The music got louder as we approached and Shout Out to My Ex by Little Mix rocked the speakers.

We pushed through the doors and Mutt scampered ahead, rushing over to Rick and licking his ankles where he stood leaning against the bar. He was wearing a pair of black jeans with a short sleeved white dress shirt unbuttoned over his tattooed chest and the look he gave me as his gaze fixed on mine was all animal.

"What's this?" I asked, glancing around at the club lighting and the bottle of tequila waiting on the bar. "A party for three?"

"Well I only wanted to invite people I like and the list is surprisingly limited," Maverick replied, sipping his tequila like that shit wasn't liquid fire. *What a psycho.*

"Oh, sweetheart, I didn't know you *liked* me," JJ mocked, clasping his heart dramatically.

"Well, I like watching you fuck my girl," Maverick corrected. "And I don't find your personality totally abrasive, so there's that."

"Come on, Rick, you can admit you love him. I know you want to," I pushed, closing the distance between me and him as JJ released me to grab himself a drink.

Maverick smirked at me, licking the pad of his thumb before swiping his saliva along the groove of his collar bone and shaking some salt onto the skin. He tilted his head to the side, jerking his chin in a command and I obediently tiptoed up, slowly licking the salt from his flesh and pressing my hands to his abs as they contracted at my touch.

He raised a shot of tequila to my lips and I knocked it back before he held a wedge of lime to my mouth for me to suck on last.

"Hey, beautiful," he said in his deep voice, his gaze devouring me as I licked the last taste of lime from my lips and looked at his mouth.

But instead of giving me the kiss I wanted, he beckoned JJ closer and placed another line of salt on his neck.

"I didn't realise you liked me like this," JJ teased, while Maverick just shrugged.

"I'm testing the waters. But I'm thinking I'll prefer the feeling of her mouth on my body over yours."

I bit my lip as JJ leaned in, making a show of licking the salt from Maverick's skin before accepting his shot and lime. I sucked in a sharp breath as I looked between the two of them and JJ gave me a dark look as he leaned in to kiss me slowly.

"Dance for us, pretty girl," he breathed against my lips.

"I'm too sad for dancing," I murmured.

"Because Foxy boy fucked up your life and sent Chase away?" Maverick asked and I frowned at his candid question before nodding. "I bet you really hate him for doing that, don't you?"

"You know how pissed I am at Fox for doing that. But seeing as he's run off and won't even answer my calls, I'm stuck waiting for him to decide he gives a shit about any of us again and comes back," I snapped, wondering why he felt the need to bring the mood down by rehashing this.

"Yeah, Fox is such a dick. He's turned on all of us now, hasn't he? Goes to show what he really thinks of his so-called family," Maverick said, sinking another shot without bothering with the lime or salt.

"Yeah, well fuck him," JJ muttered, the hurt in his voice clear beneath the anger. "All he really gives a shit about is what *he* wants. He clearly never gave a single thought to what the rest of us need to be happy."

"All I want is for him to see sense and bring Chase home," I said, slamming back another shot too. "That's it. But in this moment that isn't going to happen, so I say we all get fucked up and try to forget about the mess he's left us in for one night. I'm so fucking tired of hurting all the time."

Maverick and JJ exchanged a wicked look before Rick raised his glass in a toast. "To forgetting all about Fox fucking Harlequin then. And being a whole lot happier without him trying to control our fucking lives."

JJ grunted, knocking back his own drink alongside Rick but I just glared into mine. "Fuck that," I muttered. "But I'll drink to forgetting all the things I have to hurt over and trying to chase happiness tonight."

"To emotionless oblivion then," Rick agreed and I snorted half a laugh before downing my shot.

My head spun a little at the onslaught of the alcohol and as the music shifted to So What by P!nk I took JJ's hand and pulled him away from the bar to dance with me.

Maverick watched us with a smirk lining his lips as I pressed my back to JJ's chest and let the music have me. I was so fucking angry and I needed an outlet for it, so I was going to dance with my boys and tell the world to get fucked tonight. It would still be waiting to destroy me in the morning anyway and I didn't have to let it ruin this too.

The music moved on to more angry fuck you break up kinds of songs and I swear they were just playing my pissed off feelings over this whole Fox situation out loud.

Maverick didn't keep his distance for long, pushing off the bar and tugging me against him as the three of us started dancing in a heated, sweaty, press of bodies which made my flesh tingle and burn for them. Their hands roamed over my body and I fisted one hand in JJ's hair behind me while winding my other arm around Rick's neck and pulling him closer in front of me as we just danced and danced.

One song ran into another and their roaming hands tugged at the edges of my clothes while their mouths brushed my neck and jaw, never quite crossing that line while still riling me up until my entire being was reduced to a needy, desperate kind of desire.

When I felt like the tension between the three of us was going to explode and I was about ready to come from the friction of us dancing like that, Rick suddenly drew back, tugging me towards the bar.

JJ started kissing my neck as he followed and a breathy moan escaped me before Maverick tugged me away from him and pressed my back against the bar.

He leaned in like he was going to kiss me and my lips parted hungrily, but he dropped his mouth instead, running his tongue along the line of my collar bone before repeating the move on the other side.

He shifted back and JJ already had the salt waiting, sprinkling some over my skin as I leaned my elbows back against the bar and waited.

"Beg for us, beautiful. I wanna hear how much you love taking us together," Maverick growled, his gaze flicking over my head as a dark smirk filled his lips.

I glanced over my shoulder to see what he'd been looking at and spotted his phone there wedged between two whiskey bottles on a shelf and pointed right at us.

"Are you recording us?" I asked, making a move to straighten, but his hand locked around my throat as he pushed me back to keep me where I was.

"What's the matter, beautiful? Don't you wanna watch the video when we're done? I just wanted some material to jerk off to when you leave me all alone out here again and you know this is going to be more than worth recording."

"You're an asshole," I gritted out, but I was also definitely going to be watching that video myself multiple times because fuck yeah, that sounded hot as shit.

"You are," JJ agreed, shoving Maverick half-heartedly. "And you'd better not show anyone else that thing."

"Who the fuck do you think I am?" Rick asked, giving my throat a squeeze which I felt right down to my core. *Jesus.* "I swear no one outside of our little family will ever see it."

"Okay," I agreed, wetting my lips as I looked between the two of them.

I was so turned on and so full of all this vicious energy that I needed the outlet more than I cared about some sex tape. In fact, the idea of us being on camera made it even hotter and I released a breathy moan as I clamped my thighs together in hunt of a little friction.

The noise cut off any more discussion from the two of them and my heart leapt as their eyes filled with hunger, Rick's dark and endlessly deep and JJ's the most delicious shade of brown known to man.

Their mouths fell to my neck simultaneously, both of them devouring the salt on my skin and making me moan even louder as the scrape of Rick's stubble and bite of JJ's teeth set my whole body buzzing.

Maverick yanked on my shirt, half ripping it off me and groaning at the sight of my bare tits before handing JJ a shot of tequila.

I almost protested before they spilled the glasses down my chest but I ended up gasping and moaning as they moved to lap it from my skin, the two of them sucking and teasing my nipples as I just clung to the bar beneath them.

JJ unbuttoned my shorts and Rick helped tug them down over the curve of my ass, bringing my drenched panties with them as they both dropped to their knees.

They yanked my sneakers off as they tossed the last of my clothes aside and clearly no one gave a fuck about the lime as they pushed my thighs apart and moved in on my throbbing core instead.

I cried out as their mouths both fell on me at once, the two of them forcing my thighs wide to make room for them and my moans getting more and more desperate as one of them sucked my clit into their mouth. I couldn't even tell which one of them it was, and my head spun with the thrill of that as Rick slung my leg over his shoulder and I was left to hold myself up on the bar.

"Fuck," I gasped, my hips rocking into the movements of their mouths before fingers were pushing inside me too, pumping and thrusting and demanding I fall for them. And within a matter of seconds I did, my screams of pleasure rising above the music as I gave in to what I needed, finally finding some relief from all the hurt and heartache I'd been feeling recently.

They got to their feet before me as I sagged against the bar and JJ yanked his shirt over his head while Rick just stared at me hungrily.

"Make her scream, Johnny James. Make sure everyone can tell exactly how much she loves your cock."

"Aye aye, Captain Control Freak," JJ mocked before stepping forward and lifting me up onto the edge of the bar.

He leaned in to claim a needy kiss from my lips then shoved me back so suddenly that I squealed in surprise as my back hit the bar.

He wrapped my thighs around his waist and sank his cock into my soaking heat in the next breath, taking his time and making sure I felt every single inch of him.

Maverick rounded the bar as JJ started to thrust in and out of me slowly, driving himself in with deep, languid strokes as he groaned about how tight and perfect my pussy felt wrapped around his cock.

I blinked up at Rick as he stopped by my head, licking my lips as I reached for his belt, wanting to taste his cock, but he caught my hands and pushed them away.

"No, baby girl. I don't want to come in your pretty mouth today. I'm gonna choke you out while you come all over Johnny James's dick, then I'll be taking that sweet pussy for myself while he fucks your tight ass and you scream for us so prettily. Would you like that?"

Fuck that man had a filthy mouth and I was so here for it.

"Yes," I gasped as JJ slammed into me harder and the breath was stolen from my lungs.

"Beg for it then," Rick insisted and I gave in again because I needed this and I was aching for him to give it to me so who gave a fuck if I had to beg, especially when he loved me doing it.

"I want your hands on my neck while he fucks me," I panted obediently between moans as JJ fucked me harder. "Then I want you both fucking me together and making me feel so fucking much that I can hardly take it."

"Good girl. We'd better get started on that then." Maverick smirked like an asshole as he wrapped his hands around my throat and JJ upped his pace, striking me deep and hard like I needed.

I moaned loudly as I pawed at my tits before finding my clit and rubbing it in time with his thrusts, wanting more and more and more.

"Filthy, perfect girl," Maverick growled, his eyes burning as he watched the show, his grip on me tightening in the way I fucking loved as he took control of my breathing.

"Fuck yeah she is," JJ agreed and I moaned even louder as he drove into me harder and I prepared myself for their destruction on my flesh because this right here was my happy place, and I was going to be spending as long in it as I possibly could.

CHAPTER FORTY ONE

I tugged at the ropes bound around my body and tethering me to an armchair in one of the hotel rooms as I was forced to watch this fucking horror show on a fifty inch TV on the wall in front of me.

At first I'd tried to look away, but the sound of Maverick and JJ fucking Rogue filled the whole room through the speakers and I'd ended up giving in to the inevitable as I watched them all carve my heart clean from my chest.

Rogue was splayed out on a bar and I spat air between my teeth as JJ fucked her hard and brutally, her pants turning to begging as he built her up into a frenzy.

Maverick occasionally threw a smirk over at the camera as he palmed her breasts and rubbed the huge bulge in his jeans, making my skin prickle and burn all over.

"I'll kill you!" I bellowed to no one, because wherever they were it was too far from this room for them to hear and clearly no one was coming to save me from this torture. But I had to let the words rip free of my lungs regardless because I'd felt sorry for Maverick before, even had thoughts of trying to bring him home after everything I'd found out about him, but this? This was the monster he'd become, and he was purposefully stabbing a blade into my chest over and over with this move. I wasn't anything to him anymore, that was clearer than ever. Even being shot at by him hadn't felt as deep of a betrayal as this.

JJ stole a hungry kiss from Rogue's mouth and she held onto him like the world began and ended right there against his lips. I cringed, turning my head but my gaze was only drawn back again, like this fuck fest was a magnet for my unwilling eyes.

My shoulders heaved as my lungs worked harder, dragging more and more oxygen into my body like I was hyping up for a fight. And that was what I wanted, a murderous, bloody battle between me and Maverick, and if Johnny James was there too then all the fucking better.

Rogue moaned in a way that made me hurt and burn at once as Maverick dragged her over the bar, forcing JJ's cock to part with her as they both cried out in anger.

"Jesus, Rick," JJ snarled, grabbing the bottle of tequila and following Maverick to an armchair where he forced Rogue to straddle his lap.

"Asshole," she said breathlessly.

Maverick only laughed as he gripped her hips, unbuckling his belt and freeing his dick from his jeans before lining himself up with her pussy and she sank down onto his cock, her head tipping back in a moan. JJ took the opportunity to pour some tequila between her lips and she swallowed it down in one gulp, the rise and fall of her throat sexy as hell. My anger merged with something darker in me as my gaze hooked on her and her movements alone. She was a goddess working to steal her pleasure from mere mortals and my fingers itched with the longing I'd always had in me to please her. But as my treacherous cock grew hard and throbbing for her, I bit down on the inside of my cheek and looked away, a wave of absolute rage engulfing me. *Fuck this.*

My muscles bulged and the rope bit deep into my flesh as I fought against its hold, knowing the moment I got free that death would descend on this place and Dead Man's Isle would live up to its name. Because its self-proclaimed king would die by my hands for this. There was nothing I had ever been more certain about than that.

My gaze moved back to the screen as it always did and I watched as Maverick's palm scored up and over Rogue's tits to lock around her throat.

A sneer twisted my lips at him touching her like that, the way Shawn had touched her when he'd tried to put her in the ground. But her hips rocked fast and breathless, frantic moans left her lips like she wanted more of what he was offering, more of his demons, more of *him*.

It was clearer than ever that I'd never been the one she wanted. She was lust embodied between them both, her eyes wide and flicking between the two of them like they were the centre of her universe.

She reached for JJ, her fingers grasping his cock beside her as she pumped him in her hand and he knotted his fingers into her hair hard enough to turn his knuckles white. She rode her way into another fucking orgasm and I spat air through my teeth in frustration as I begged any god who was listening to give me the strength to break these binds.

"Fuck you, Maverick!" I bellowed, hatred seeping down into the depths of my being. I was violence brought to life and all I needed was freedom and my bare hands to rain down death on him like a plague.

Rogue gasped just before Maverick cut off her moans, his fingers locking tighter around her throat. Desire flashed in her eyes as she free fell through the final waves of pleasure then Maverick slid his hand around the back of her head and pushed down to bring her lips to JJ's cock. She took it between them without hesitation, still pumping the base as she worked to bring him to ruin. His eyes were hooded with primal desire as he watched her mouth running all over his solid cock and my upper lip peeled back as my own cock started to ache.

Maverick took total control of Rogue's movements, driving her head down over and over as he continued to fuck her with lazy thrusts of his hips. His gaze moved to the camera again and he fucking winked at me with that smug bastard of an expression on his face again. JJ was far too distracted to notice the show he was putting on and he came with a growl of pleasure, her lips closing tightly around the head of his dick as she swallowed down his cum without a flicker of hesitation.

When she lifted her head, her lips were puffy and reddened, her eyelashes low and her gaze full of some eternal craving. She looked drunk, but not on alcohol, on them, and she somehow still looked thirsty for more.

My lungs ceased to work as I just stared at that look on her face, feeling like I didn't know anything about her wants and needs at all. Like everything I'd ever thought I could provide for her was just some foolish dream that she'd never even considered living out with me.

All this time I'd deluded myself into thinking she could really love me. That I was the best thing for her. But I wasn't even on her radar. She'd been fucking JJ and Maverick for God only knew how long – and apparently they were just fine with that messed up arrangement too.

A creature had awoken in me far darker than any of the monsters I'd greeted within my body before. This was the Devil himself, and he was made of purest sin.

My flesh was burning with a carnal ache for the girl in the arms of two of my brothers and my hands were twitching with the need to maim, hurt, and kill them. I was lust and wrath at once and my head pounded with conflicting thoughts, some of me joining them in that room and fulfilling the unmet needs I could still see burning in Rogue's eyes, and the other part of me walking in there with a knife in hand which would soon redden with the blood of those two men.

Maverick stole all of her attention again as he gripped her chin to make her look at him and started driving into her furiously so she had to brace herself on his shoulders. He stared at Rogue, seeming to forget all about me watching as he fixated on her like she was the only thing that mattered to him in the entire world before he grunted and stilled inside her, finishing deep in her pussy without any protection between them.

A growl of fury ripped from my throat as I watched her sag against him, their lips coming together in a sweet kiss that he looked absolutely captivated by. JJ pulled his shorts back on and dropped his shirt over Rogue's head as he tugged her to her feet. She moved into his arms, tiptoeing up and running her fingers into his hair as they kissed too, some shared sadness seeming to pass between them in that moment.

"I'm not done with this. I want us both destroying you together, baby girl," Maverick said as he stared at them hungrily.

"Well I'm not the one who needs a recovery period," she teased, kissing JJ again and making my chest knot up into a ball as she pulled her shorts and panties back.

Maverick stood up, yanking his jeans back into place and yawning obnoxiously in my direction.

Rogue had the bottle of tequila in her grip again, leaning on JJ as she swigged on it and he just held her as the light in his eyes started to extinguish once more.

"Do you think we should start calling around motels again tonight? Maybe one of them will have seen Chase," Rogue said and Maverick chuckled darkly.

"You thinking of another guy already, beautiful? Insatiable you are. Would you take his cock as well as ours?"

"Shut up, Rick," she said with an eyeroll but my gaze snapped to her face as I hunted for the answer to that question. Did she want Chase too? All of them apart from me? The thought was somehow more hurtful than even the two of them having her. Because if it was all of them aside from me, then that made me the exception. The one she didn't want.

"Just curious, baby girl," Maverick said as he approached her, running her hand up her spine. "Or is it Fox's cock you're missing at this party?"

"Jesus, stop it," she snapped. "Why are you being a prick?"

"It's his default setting," JJ said, but when he locked eyes with Maverick they only smirked like they were the best of fucking pals. Great, how long had he been secret friends with Maverick for? Long enough to make a damn fool of me at least.

"Foxy boy couldn't handle this anyway. He's too rigid. And too vanilla," Maverick said with a shrug. "I'm pretty sure Luther shoved a stick up his ass at birth then he spoiled him rotten so he thinks he can have anything he wants at the snap of his fingers, and if people object he just crushes them beneath him."

I ground my teeth, looking to Rogue and JJ for their response to that and they seemed all too quiet on the matter, so I supposed that was agreement in itself.

"Anyway, it's better that he's gone," Maverick went on when they said nothing. "Maybe he'll stay out of town and never come back, that'd probably be best anyway, am I right?"

"Just stop talking, Rick." Rogue pushed past him, moving to the couch and dropping onto it, taking another long drink of tequila as she stared out the window.

JJ moved to join her, slinging his arm around her shoulders and running his fingers back and forth along her arm until she melted against him.

"Oh come on," Maverick said in frustration. "He deserves this. He tried to own you the second you came back to Sunset Cove, baby girl, he bosses you all around to no end. Then he exiled Chase while you were off at the carnival and took the decision out of everyone's hands but his own. Again."

My throat closed up as I stared those truths in the eye, trying not to let his tone cut beneath my skin, but it did. I knew I was strong willed in my decisions sometimes, but I was always trying to do what was best for us all. Clearly my best was everyone else's worst.

I was so done with this game, with having to watch Rogue look like she was breaking apart. I'd burst their little bubble and now I was the bad guy, being punished for loving her too hard and not seeing the blindingly obvious truth right in front of me. That I wasn't her end game.

She'd told me herself, she didn't want to be mine. And all along I'd just thought she meant 'not yet' when what she'd really been saying was 'because I'm someone else's' - two someone else's as it turned out.

Maverick walked over, stealing the tequila from Rogue and taking a large mouthful before passing it back with his brow furrowed. It looked like his game wasn't all that fun to him anymore and I stopped fighting against my restraints as I just felt the pain of my broken heart and hungered for a release in blood that wasn't gonna fix anything.

"Alright, alright, game over then," Maverick said. "If you're both gonna be all moody about it then come with me. I've got something that will cheer you up." He jerked his head and they kicked their shoes back on as he led them from the room and they walked off camera out of sight.

I hung my head as darkness trickled through my skull and blotted out all the light. It was an unending fog of pain and hurt and betrayal, sweeping through my body and leaving me lost.

My pulse thumped unevenly as I suddenly heard footsteps coming this way and a minute later the door unlocked and Maverick stepped into the room.

"Hey Foxy, did you enjoy the show?" he chuckled as a snarl peeled back my lips.

"What?" Rogue gasped, pushing past him and coming to a dead halt as she spotted me tied to the chair.

Her gaze flipped to the screen I was aimed towards and she saw the bar they'd just been in staring back at her, horrified realisation dawning on her expression. I felt her pain in that moment, and despite her lies, I still hurt over that. She'd obviously thought that there was some good to still be found in Maverick, but now she could see exactly the sort of person he was. The kind to use her up, devour everything she had to offer and spit it back out like it was worthless.

"What the fuck, Maverick?!" JJ barked, shoving past him and striding over to me in alarm.

Maverick started laughing loudly. "He needed this. It's exposure therapy. That was what I was giving him."

JJ tried to unbind me as I continued to stare at Rogue, my blood cold in my veins and murder singing Maverick's fucking name in my ears.

Rogue shook her head in disbelief at this situation, her eyes blazing with unshed tears that she refused to let fall. She rounded on Maverick, slapping him hard and he just laughed louder.

"Oh come on, beautiful," he tried but his laughter fell away at her volcanic expression.

"How long have you been here?" JJ asked me frantically, but I didn't answer, I didn't even look at him, my gaze was hooked on Maverick as I waited to be set free. Because I was gonna kill this motherfucker once and for all. There was nothing but a bloodthirsty temper left of me and it needed an outlet.

"Foxy washed up on my island needing rescuing. I may or may not have used his phone to keep you all from worrying," Maverik admitted. "And to deliver a few home truths to dear old Daddy."

"You're insane," JJ snapped at Maverick who just shrugged.

Rogue shoved his chest with a snarl on her lips. "You used me! You fucking asshole. How could you?"

Maverick's gaze moved back onto her and a flicker of concern slid into his gaze as he took in her hurt expression. "It wasn't like that."

"What was it like then?" JJ threw at him, giving up on trying to free me and striding back over to Maverick with his shoulders squared. "Because it's pretty fucking clear what you were doing, motherfucker." He swung a punch at

Maverick and he took the blow to his face, stumbling back a step and dabbing his lip as it split open.

His eyes became two dark graves and he lunged at JJ with a roar, throwing his full weight against him so they crashed to the floor.

"Fuck you, you piece of shit," Maverick snarled as they rolled, punching and fighting with the savagery of wild dogs.

Rogue's took out the flick knife I'd given her, striding over as the name Maverick glinted on it and somehow I hated what that blade probably meant to her now. It had meant something to me too once, but fuck if I cared about it anymore.

"How long have you been here?" She worked to cut the rope holding me down as pain blossomed in her eyes over me. And for a second, the crushing rage in my chest gave way to an ache in me that mirrored hers.

She was cracking on the inside, this situation crushing her just like it was me. But as her gaze met mine, I looked away, turning my head as my jaw ticked. Whatever good had lived between us was broken, and there wasn't a future where we could coincide anymore.

"What's it matter?" I muttered and a choked noise escaped her, but she didn't answer.

That was the worst part of this, losing her all over again, and this time knowing it was for good. There was no coming back from what they'd all done, the choices they'd all made. She'd chosen the boys she wanted and they weren't me. So I had to try and pick up what was left of my pride and bow out, but I had a score to settle first. Maverick had wronged me, toyed with me in this room and there was a price to be paid for that.

The rope finally snapped and I shoved to my feet. Rogue's hand grabbed my wrist and the flick knife dropped to the floor as I looked back at her with a hard wall in my eyes.

"I never meant for this to happen. We can fix it," she begged and a seed of longing within me grew shoots, begging me to listen, to somehow find a way to forgive her. But there was a darker seed inside me that was growing into a vengeful beast, and it doused the other seed in poison, destroying it roots and all.

"There's no *we* anymore." I yanked my wrist out of her grip and turned my back on her, striding over to where Maverick was choking out JJ on the floor and locking my forearm around his throat.

I dragged him backwards off of JJ, hauling him tight back against my body as I used my other arm to lock him in the choke hold and squeezed as tightly as I possibly could. Maverick fought furiously against my grip and Rogue started screaming, throwing her weight at me and suddenly JJ was on me too, knocking me down to the floor so I lost my hold on Maverick.

"Stop it!" JJ barked. "Let's just talk about this."

He threw his weight onto me, letting Maverick get up and pace before me like a wolf hungry for the kill.

"Get off of me," I snarled at JJ, shoving him back but he fought harder to keep me down. I lost sight of Rogue as Maverick glared at me and venom slid into my blood.

"What are you gonna do, Foxy? Kill me?" Maverick taunted. "That won't make her want you, brother. It'll just make her hate you even more."

"I've lost her anyway!" I barked. "So what difference does it make?"

"You'll break her heart," JJ hissed, staring down at me as he flattened his palm to my chest. "Again. And don't you think we've all done enough to that girl? Don't you think she deserves more than this?"

I breathed heavily through my teeth as his words worked their way into my head and I quit fighting so hard to get up. He was right, I didn't wanna hurt her, but I did wanna kill Maverick and maim Johnny James. I stared into the dark brown eyes of my brother as betrayal and hurt splintered under my skin.

"Why did you do this?" I asked in a low voice, needing an answer, though I didn't think that there was a single one in this world which could make things any better.

"Because he loves her," Maverick dropped down beside me, his hand squeezing my cheek and forcing me to face him as his other hand pressed down beside JJ's to keep me on the floor. "And you just don't factor into the equation, Foxy boy."

"Rick," JJ snapped, shoving his shoulder against his. "What the fuck is wrong with you?"

"I'm just saying what everyone's thinking and making sure Foxy gets his just desserts," Maverick said coldly then looked back at me. "You sent

Chase away you piece of shit, who gave you that right?"

I glowered at him, but was surprised by the pain twisting his features for a moment before he hid it away.

"He left her on that fucking ferry. He almost took her from me all over again. But it turns out I should have been more worried about my other brothers doing that," I spat.

"Yeah, you should have. Shame you're such a fucking idiot." Maverick sneered.

"Would you just shut the fuck up?!" JJ growled at him. "Are you just set on self-destruct mode all the fucking time?"

"Something like that," Maverick hissed back.

I jerked against their grip on me, but they both shoved their weight down harder and a growl bit at my throat. "What are you gonna do? Tie me up again, continue fucking Rogue in front of me? Because it looks like she's not interested in you parading her around like a paid whore any longer, you motherfucker."

Maverick's fist cracked against the side of my head at those words and my skull smacked down on the floorboards.

He forced JJ off of me and suddenly my hands were free and I was facing the fury of my hellion brother as he came at me.

I relished the adrenaline surging into my veins as I lunged up to meet his rage, ready to rip him to pieces and leave his bloody corpse right here in this room. It was me against him, a fight that was long overdue. And I was finally ready to win and see him die.

CHAPTER FORTY TWO

The look of pain and betrayal in Fox's eyes was seared so deep within me that I was sure I'd never get this feeling out of me again. I felt like all the dark and hurt inside me had been lying dormant there, festering and growing into this unbearable weight and the way he'd looked at me had been the key to setting it free. To drowning me in it all over again and forcing me to face the reality of my damage and all the hurt I caused with my presence.

I'd done that to him. The boy I'd loved with all my heart had offered me his and I'd torn it from his chest and set the pieces ablaze.

Maverick laughed darkly while Fox laid into him, enjoying Fox's pain and Fox roared insults and accusations at him for stealing the one thing he'd ever really wanted for himself while JJ yelled right back that I'd never been his to claim in the first place.

They were fighting over me like a bunch of starving mutts with a bone, all the love they'd once felt for each other turned to poison by this divide. By me.

I'd heard what JJ had said to me when I'd pointed this out before and I'd heard Chase too. But now here it was, staring me in the face, the results of my destructive influence on the four men who had once been closer than brothers.

I closed my eyes as I tried to block out the sound of the hateful things they were saying and let myself fall back into our past, those precious days that I hadn't appreciated nearly enough at the time.

"There's a handhold here," Fox grunted as he heaved himself further up the crumbling cliff face and my heart raced with fear for the four stupid, stupid boys who I loved so freaking much as I lay flat on my stomach and looked down over the edge at them.

I didn't even know which one of them had decided that climbing the sheer cliff was a good idea with all of those jagged rocks below, but here I was, watching them do it while playing umpire to their dumb as fuck game.

When they'd headed down to the foot of the cliff to start their climb, I'd laughed at them, laying down on the grassy bluff up here as I sunned myself, expecting them to change their minds once they got down there.

But when I'd heard the four of them laughing and yelling at the base of the cliff, I'd rolled over and crawled to the edge to get a look down and found all of them starting the climb like it was just another fun adventure.

"Be careful," I groaned for the hundredth time. This was stupid. So fucking stupid, but they'd come so far now that it was safer for them to crest the top than it would have been for them to try and head back down.

"Whose dumb idea was this again?" Chase grunted, his dark curls sticking to his forehead as he climbed and the setting sun baked him.

"Rick's," JJ panted and I craned my neck to see him as he heaved himself a little higher, knocking some loose gravel tumbling down to the rocks below.

"Well I thought you'd all pussy out before I got half way up and I could just laugh at you assholes over my win," Maverick grumbled. "Who knew you were all this fucking stubborn."

"Maybe you shouldn't have raised the stakes then," Fox baited, his gaze shifting up to meet mine for a moment and making my breath hitch in my throat. He was so close that I was aching to reach down and offer him a hand up, but I was afraid to throw off his concentration at the same time.

"So who wins if we all make it to the top?" Rick asked and all four of them looked up at me like I held the answer to that.

"What's the prize?" I breathed, adrenaline making my fingers tremble with fear for them.

"Well, we said the one who climbed the highest could ask you for a ki-" Maverick's words cut off as his grip faltered and a yell of alarm escaped him as his handhold crumbled to nothing and he slipped down several feet, the loose rocks breaking apart as he fought to regain his hold.

I screamed in fright, lurching forward and reaching for him even though he was too far from me for it to make a difference. But it didn't matter anyway.

Fox had caught his hand and JJ gripped the back of his shirt while Chase held onto his arm in turn to lend more support.

"Holy fuck," I whispered as they all froze there for a moment, waiting to make sure the cliff was done trying to kill them. Then Rick broke a wild laugh, crowing like a rooster and throwing his head back while the others all followed suit.

Fucking, crazy, stupid, asshole boys.

They continued to climb for the top together and I scrambled back out of their way as they all reached it as one, hands coming up over the edge and clawing into the dirt as they heaved themselves up and onto the clifftop.

"Water," JJ gasped dramatically and I cursed him out while turning and running away from them towards our bags and the boys' bikes which we'd left in the shade of a towering rock.

I tore through the bags, grabbing the bottles of water from them and turned to sprint back to them.

But as I did, I paused, finding the four of them sitting shoulder to shoulder facing the sea, their laughter floating away on the breeze as the setting sun silhouetted them there together.

I dropped the water and fished my phone from my pocket, snapping a pic of that moment so that I could keep it forever.

They'd forgotten their competition and were just joking and teasing one another, elbows nudging and curses spilling from their lips.

They were happy. So freaking happy just there in each other's company. And I gave them a few moments like that without me, not wanting to interrupt their triumph while drinking in the feeling of their love for one another.

"Get your ass over here, Rogue," Fox called, turning his head to hunt for me and the others all started yelling at me to hurry back too.

I smiled, grabbing the water bottles and breaking into a run again as I approached them. The answer to all the bad in my world. The only good I'd ever had and would ever need.

I held onto that memory as I started backing away, trying to block out the sounds of those same boys screaming abuse at one another, of their fists striking each other and the anger and hatred that lay so thick within the room.

I'd done that to them.

I'd started it by attracting Axel's gaze despite my best attempts not to. I knew that part wasn't really my fault. That sick fuck had been a predator who more than deserved the death I gave him.

But if I'd just called the police when it had happened instead of calling them. If I'd just run and stayed quiet. Or even if I hadn't fought back so hard and my short, pathetically beautiful life had ended then, it would have been better than this.

At least then I would have died with love in my heart and a lifetime full of memories of me and my boys in the sun to guide me on into whatever came next. I could have just been this tragic story which darkened their memories but which they could have moved on from. Anything but this.

I'd become the thorn in their sides. The itch they couldn't scratch. The wedge which divided them and the catalyst to their destruction. The love they'd held for each other had turned toxic and it would only continue to fester the longer I was here.

Chase was gone and I knew in my heart that he wasn't coming back. That far too brief kiss he'd stolen from me the morning of the carnival had tasted of goodbye. I just hadn't recognised it at the time. And now I was standing here watching as the rest of my boys fought and spat venomous words at each other. Watching as they took joy in causing one another pain and feeling every twist of betrayal and heartache that had been inflicted upon each of them like it was a knife in my own gut.

And worse than that, I'd brought the demons of my life without them right up to their front door. Shawn was never going to stop this war. It could only be finished with blood and death, and I knew in my heart that all of Chase's suffering had only been a taste of what Shawn was capable of.

This was all my fault. And if I stayed here, it wasn't going to stop. They wouldn't stop fighting over me, using me to score points against one another and trying to win me for their own. This wasn't some fairy tale where I could just get what I wanted because I hungered for it enough. It was all well and good for me to insist time and time again that I wouldn't pick between them, but all that did was leave them in this pain and torment, this burning cycle of jealousy and envy and heartache every time I moved from one to another. It wasn't right and it wasn't fair.

But there was one thing I could do to end it.

I backed up, moving towards the door and none of them noticed me as I went, too caught up in their hatred and rage to even remember the one who had caused it all.

I pushed out of the door with my fingers trembling a little, but I wasn't going to back down. I knew that now. I got it. This was my fault, so it was on me to fix it. And I would, even if that might be the last thing I ever did.

I took one final, desperate look at them all, then the moment I was out the door, I turned and ran.

Maverick's men were all keeping out of sight like he'd commanded them to, so no one stopped me as I sprinted down the stairs, through the hotel and raced for the dock.

There were four boats tied up there, bobbing on the choppy waves as cool air whipped around me and I couldn't help but glance up at the dark sky and the thick clouds which were closing in over the stars.

There was a storm blowing in tonight. But that only meant I needed to move faster.

I hopped up onto the first boat, making quick work of starting her up and loosing the throttle just enough for it to tug against the mooring rope which was still tied to the jetty.

I jumped back down again, glancing towards the hotel to make sure they hadn't noticed my absence yet, but they were clearly still too caught up in their anger for that.

I untied the boat and it pulled away from the shore, moving at a slow but steady pace over the ocean and out of reach.

I watched it for several long seconds then repeated my work on the other boats, sending them away from the shore until only one remained for me to use.

I strode towards it, my jaw set with determination as I tried not to think about what I was leaving behind and focus on what I might be able to fix by doing so.

This had only ever been a fleeting dream anyway. The future I'd once relied on in this town had never really been destined for me. I knew my place in this world and it wasn't with the Harlequins. It hadn't been for a long damn time.

I strode towards the final boat, but fell still as a sharp bark pierced the night and I looked around to find Mutt racing down the jetty towards me.

My heart cleaved in two at the sight of my little buddy, and the tears which I'd been fighting to hold back burst free of my restraint as I dropped to my knees and he leapt into my arms.

He wagged his tail feverishly, licking the tears from my cheeks and jumping all over me as if to say he was coming too. But he couldn't. I wouldn't risk his safety where I was going, and I knew full well that it would be in jeopardy if I did. No matter how much I ached to keep this one, loyal companion by my side for what was to come, doing so would have been endlessly selfish and I refused to hurt the one creature in this world whose love had always been nothing but pure for me.

"I'm sorry, boy," I whispered, squeezing him tight and trying not to break as I stole a last moment in his company. "I wish I didn't have to go."

Mutt whimpered, nuzzling against me defiantly as if he was insisting on coming too, but I just shook my head.

"They're assholes, but you'll be safe here with them," I breathed. "I can't say the same for where I'm going."

Mutt growled softly, seeming to catch the tone of what I was telling him and he bounced in my lap, knocking my cell phone from my pocket so that it fell onto the boards beside me.

I stared down at it through the blur of tears in my eyes and I swallowed down the thick lump in my throat as I finalised this decision. I had to do it. And they had to understand that there was no coming back from this. I was done being the thing which tore them apart. So I was going to break them one final time and prove to them that they were better off without me. Because maybe then they'd be able to find a way to move on from the idea of me at last. Maybe then they'd remember why I was the girl who was always tossed aside. Maybe then they'd find their way back to each other and be able to claim the love they were owed. But that could only happen without me there to destroy their happily ever after and that meant I had to make sure they understood that they were far better off with me gone and they always had been.

Thunder rumbled in the distance, lightning forking through the clouds way out over the sea like even the sky knew that this was it. Our paths had always been leading here and now it was time for fate to run its course.

I looked back towards the hotel, unsure if I was hoping for one last glimpse of my boys or if I was glad they still hadn't realised I was missing before lifting my phone and opening the camera app.

I held the camera up to look at myself, taking a moment to wipe the tears from my cheeks and draw in a steadying breath. Then I caught hold of each and every emotion in me, all of my feelings over doing this and what it would mean for me and them and I just bundled it all away. I crushed it down inside me and fought it with an iron fist until finally, my face fell blank and I was left numb to it all.

If I was being totally honest, it was a relief. Everything that had happened since the day of the carnival had been eating away at me piece by piece up until this moment. I'd been cast adrift, aching for Chase, aching for Fox, not knowing what I could have done differently while feeling certain I'd done it all wrong.

But now that was gone. And as I set the camera recording, there wasn't so much as a flicker of that girl left in me. I was the girl I'd been before I woke up in that shallow grave. I was the empty vessel that could never be filled. I was the broken girl who no one ever wanted to keep in the end. And maybe that was for the best.

"Well," I began, my voice steady and gaze hard. "If you're watching this now, then you already know I'm gone. And don't worry, I won't be coming back. I got what I wanted from each of you and as much as I'm sure you won't want to believe it, it was this. Your destruction. Your pain." I forced the hint of a smile to my lips before I went on. "Ten long years ago, the four of you broke me. You took away the only good I'd ever had in my life and threw me to the wolves out there on the streets. So now I broke you back."

I went on, forcing the words past my tongue and ignoring the way they burned like acid as they spilled from my lips. I mocked them with my gaze and used the mask I'd perfected so long ago to sell them every single line of it. Because they had to believe this if they were going to accept it. They had to hate me if they were going to stand a chance at loving each other again. And I needed to be sure they wouldn't try to come for me. I'd made my choice and this was it. No come backs, no shining knights or even cunning thieves trying to rescue me. This was how our story ended and that was the way it had to be.

When I finished the recording, I placed my phone down beside me with the message ready to play when they discovered it.

I squeezed Mutt tight, my eyes burning and I apologised to him once more and he whimpered as he nuzzled into me like he understood exactly what was happening.

But I couldn't change my mind. Not even for him. So I placed him down on the jetty and jumped into the final boat, tossing the mooring line onto the deck as I moved to start the engine.

Mutt barked at me in a clear plea, his little eyes imploring me to come back and the knowledge that I never would burned through my heart like a blazing knife, leaving a scar which I knew wouldn't ever heal right.

But this wasn't about me.

I didn't matter.

I turned my eyes to the horizon as the thunder crashed through the heavens again, nearer this time with the lightning forking right behind it off to the south.

I let the throttle loose and a mournful howl coloured the air as Mutt raced to the very end of the jetty, his grief pouring from him as he watched me go and my own pain sharpening to the point of breaking me as I refused to turn back.

"I'm sorry," I whispered, my voice stolen by the wind as I left him behind alongside my heart and the only hopes I'd ever had of claiming some kind of true happiness for myself. "I love you," I added, my words for the four men who had stolen my heart before I even understood what that meant, the four keepers of my soul and the only things that had ever brightened my dark existence so that I could see up out of the gutter. They'd given me a taste of something that someone like me never should have tried to claim. And now I was giving them a chance to find happiness without me tainting everything around them.

The water spread out darkly before me and I fixed my gaze on the lights of Sunset Cove in the distance. I was almost there. This was almost over.

I was a dead girl walking, and it was time I returned to my grave.

CHAPTER FORTY THREE

"**S**top it you fucking idiots!" I dove onto Fox's back, trying to pull him off of Maverick as the bastard tried to lock his hands around his throat.

I rolled us hard so Fox landed on top of me and I locked my arms and legs around him as he started thrashing to get up. Maverick shoved to his feet, spitting a wad of blood from his mouth as he panted, advancing towards Fox once more.

"Let him go, Johnny James," he snarled. "This fight is long overdue."

"I'm tired of this bullshit!" I barked. "Rogue's had enough of it too, haven't you pretty girl?"

We all turned our heads, looking for her but the room was empty and Mutt was in the doorway, yapping at us like he was calling us every swear word in dog language he could think up.

"Rogue?" Maverick called, striding to the door and Mutt savaged his ankle. "Watch it, you little beast."

Mutt barked again, looking from Maverick to me and Fox and my arms and legs went slack around my brother.

Fox pushed to his feet and I followed, bruises throbbing against my skin as Fox stalked after Maverick to the door with tension in his posture. Mutt barked more furiously, backing away down the corridor, and growling when we didn't go after him.

"He wants us to follow him," I said in realisation, striding straight towards the little dog. "What's up, boy?" My pulse skipped unevenly at his strange behaviour. Where had Rogue gone off to?

"Is it Rogue? Is she okay?" Fox asked gruffly, appearing at my side half a heartbeat before Maverick appeared on my other.

Mutt turned into the stairwell and started running and I broke into a run too, my heart beating unevenly, sensing something was wrong. Maverick and Fox charged along beside me, the three of us sprinting full pelt down the stairs and through a corridor towards the exit.

Mutt barked more furiously as he sped outside and we tore after him through the compound and towards the jetty as a crash of thunder sounded in the sky.

My breaths came heavier as I spotted the boats way out in the water, moving away towards the horizon and Maverick spat swear words as we ran up the jetty to where Mutt was now pacing back and forth. He stared back at us, yapping angrily and the three of us came to a sudden halt in front of him, staring down at the phone before the dog. Rogue's phone.

We all stooped down to grab it, but my hand closed around it first, my gaze locking on the video waiting to play on the screen, Rogue's empty expression staring at me through the glass.

A sickness twisted my insides as an ominous prickle ran along my spine. I stood upright and Fox and Maverick's shoulders jammed tight against mine as they leaned in to look at the screen and with a horrible sense that my entire world was about to end, I pressed play.

"Well," Rogue began, her expression cold and hard. "If you're watching this now, then you already know I'm gone. And don't worry, I won't be coming back. I got what I wanted from each of you and as much as I'm sure you won't want to believe it, it was this. Your destruction. Your pain." A smile danced around her lips and ice slid deep into my veins, coating my insides with fear. *What is she talking about?* "Ten long years ago, the four of you broke me. You took away the only good I'd ever had in my life and threw me to the wolves out there on the streets. So now I broke you back."

"No," I refused what I was hearing, panic cleaving my chest apart. "She's lying."

"Shut up," Maverick snarled as Rogue continued.

"You think you know me, but you don't. The girl who's been sleeping in your house, painting kisses on your lips and fucking you until you were professing your pathetic love stories to me has been an act. She was created by the real me, and the real love of my life."

My lungs constricted as her next words fell upon me like an axe to my neck. "Shawn Mackenzie is everything I've ever wanted and all the things you could never be. He's the kind of monster that answers all of my darkest desires." Her gaze hooded as she thought of him and my throat filled with bile at the lustful look in her eyes. It wasn't true. It wasn't fucking true.

"Don't get me wrong, he plays rough." She ran her fingers over her throat where he'd left bruises on her before she'd come home. "But we had to make it believable, right? I wanted to show up in this town as the little broken girl you'd all imagined me to be for the last ten years. But I knew just falling into your beds wouldn't be enough to destroy you. So I played the game, seduced each of you in turn. A lifetime of friendships sure are easy to shatter," she said in an arctic tone that made my gut churn. "I was kinda surprised when I found out Maverick had turned on all of you, but it made it all the more fun to be honest. You became my weapon, Rick. You tortured Fox for me without me having to do a single thing - apart from take yours and JJ's cocks like a good girl and let you think you owned me." She smirked and I felt Fox shaking with rage beside me, but Maverick was unnaturally still. "Johnny James, you were the easiest. I thought you'd be the best place to start as fucking comes so naturally to you these days, but I was surprised to find out you're just the same pathetic, lovesick boy you were for me when we were kids."

The sting of her words burrowed deep as she shook her head at me like I was the biggest fool she'd ever played and that was exactly how I felt. "I thought you'd tell Fox though, I really thought it'd fall apart so much faster than it did, but it worked out even better when you didn't. Because you showed your true colours. Choosing one pussy over your boys? Tut, tut." She licked her lips like she was relishing each word that fell from her mouth. "And Fox, honey, you really need to get laid more often. Ten years pining over one girl? That's kinda pathetic, don't you think? I was never yours even back then, so thinking I was yours now was really fucking dumb. But it definitely made it all the more satisfying when you caught me and your best friend together. Do you know how many times I fucked him in your house hoping you'd come home? Nearly every morning when you went for a run, JJ was buried inside me, panting my name and fucking the girl you love. Brutal." She looked straight into the camera, her gaze clear and it cut my chest to ribbons. I couldn't even turn my head to check how Fox had taken that, too stunned, too fucking horrified to do anything but just watch.

"Then there was Chase. He was the one who made it more of a challenge. You really should have listened to his warnings, guys. He saw your ruin coming from a mile off. Shawn went a bit off-plan when he brought The Dollhouse down and kidnapped him, but that's what he's like. *Wild*," she said the word slow and seductively like she loved that about him. Like Shawn really was the man who owned her, who she desired with all her being. But my ears were ringing too loud and a part of me still wanted to refuse every word that fell from her lips.

The problem was, every time objections rose in me, I looked into her eyes and saw the stark truth in them. I couldn't see even a hint of a lie and that was the most terrifying thing of all.

"Chase got what was coming to him seeing as he almost fucked up my whole plan when he abandoned me on that ferry. You really should have left me to rot in jail, Rick." She gave the camera a mock pitying look. "But instead you took me home to fuck me like a queen and, baby, I may be in love with another man, but I have to admit I enjoyed that part a little too much. You and JJ really know how to fuck a girl right. But sadly that's where the fantasy ends. Because who could ever want more of either of you when you're so messed up inside?" Her lip curled back in disgust and every insecurity I'd ever had peeled open like ripe fruit. "Do you know what I enjoyed even more than all the fucking and all the fighting over me like starved animals while I ripped your little family apart though?" She leaned in closer to the camera as dread seeped through my being and turned my entire body cold. "Seeing how broken you all are, hearing every detail of your sad little tales over all the years we've been apart. I wished suffering on you a long, long time ago and to know you've all been here in hell this whole time is the sweetest gift you could ever give me in payment. Shawn may have fucked up Chase on the outside, but I fucked you all up on the inside. I was the demon sleeping in your beds, making you love a girl who died ten years ago. Karma's a kick in the balls, isn't she? And vengeance tastes so goddamn sweet." She smiled, shaking her head at us all, making feel so fucking small I wanted to disappear completely. "Excuse the Bond villain rant, I guess Shawn's rubbed off on me and ten years is one helluva long time to have been planning your destruction. I think I'm owed a moment to bask in the sun." She sighed contentedly as lightning flashed in the sky behind her. "Anyways, keep the mutt as a reminder of me, won't you? I'm going home to my man now. Where I belong." She wiggled her fingers at the camera in a goodbye then turned her hand and flipped us her middle one before cutting off the video.

Silence fell like death descending on the entire world and my arm lowered to my side with the phone gripped painfully in my hand.

The three of us stared out at the churning sea as the storm blew in and picked up vigour, the sky darkening to deepest, gravestone grey.

"She's lying," Fox rasped, breaking the silence at last, but there was no real conviction in those words. We'd all heard what she'd said, all seen the way her face had twisted with vengeance, how her eyes had flashed with victory. This was all a sick revenge plot, and we were the stupid fucking idiots who'd fallen for it.

Maverick suddenly fell to his knees and started punching the jetty boards, over and over and over until his knuckles were turning bloody. I fell on him, unable to just stand there and watch him fall apart as I wrestled him back against my chest and he snarled furiously through his teeth. I could feel his pain as keenly as my own, splitting apart some vital piece of my body as I tried to reason with everything I'd just heard and find a way to refuse it. But I couldn't see any reason for her to lie. And there was too much truth to her words that made it all too fucking real.

My gut yanked as I remembered she'd been trying to get our keys. I'd seen it for myself. I'd even given her back the ones I'd found in her trailer, trusting her not to open that crypt.

Oh fuck, fuck, fuck.

"Give me your phone," Fox demanded suddenly, falling down beside us and patting my pockets as he tried to find it. I pulled it out, shoving it into his palm as Maverick elbowed me away and buried his face in his bloody hands.

"Luther," Fox barked as he made a call. "You need to intercept Rogue, she's on her way to the Rosewood Manor alone – it doesn't fucking matter why, just stop her!" he boomed then hung up and looked to me with his hands shaking and his eyes wild.

"Tell me she didn't mean it." He grabbed my shirt in his fist, yanking me closer as I started to slip into a dark abyss of chaos and agony inside me. "Tell me this is all some fucking joke, some other way to torture me that you two are in on, anything but this being true."

I opened and closed my mouth, my throat burning and my heart so broken that I knew it would never recover from this.

"I can't," I choked out and hurt washed through Fox's expression as he hunted my eyes for a lie, but he didn't find any there.

He turned his head to the sky and roared his fury as the clouds split apart and rain started crashing down on us, the cold trickling over my body and encasing me whole. Mutt howled to the sky with him, a mournful noise leaving his throat like he understood that he'd been left behind too.

This isn't happening.

This isn't the end of our story.

But I knew in my soul that it was.

Rogue had played me like a fool, taken her revenge out on all of us like a wolf toying with lambs. Now she'd ripped us to pieces, leaving us bloody in her wake. And all I could think about was that I should have known. Because Rogue Easton could never really love the boys who'd destroyed her. We'd broken her and should never have expected forgiveness for that. And now we were finally paying the price of that betrayal and it was the worst kind of torture I'd ever known.

CHAPTER FORTY FOUR

I dumped the boat by the Harlequin House dock and jumped out onto the jetty just as the storm made it to me and the rain broke free of the clouds.

There was an ache in my chest which kept growing, sharpening, trying to force me to turn from this path and make another choice. Any other choice. But that was the problem. There wasn't one. Not one that could save them from themselves or the curse of wanting me. This was the only solution that would work, and I was fixed on this decision.

The kiss of the cold raindrops against my skin helped sharpen my focus as I forced that knot of tension deep down into my gut and locked it away with every other bad thought and feeling contained within my aching soul.

This wasn't about me. Never had been. Never should have been.

I strode up to the house as lightning broke across the sky overhead, letting myself in through the back door and glancing around at the dark building in relief as I realised Luther had clearly left.

I lingered for a moment in the kitchen, breathing in the memories of the time I'd spent here with the Harlequin boys and wondering if I'd ever had a chance to do this differently. But as I glanced up at the mirror in the hall, taking in my bruised lips and the emptiness in my eyes, I knew I couldn't have.

Shawn had been right about me in that regard. I was just a broken toy, fighting against my place in this world when everyone around me could see where I was destined to end up. So this was just me accepting that fate.

I stepped into the kitchen and pulled open one of the cupboards, pushing aside boxes of cereal before claiming the gun which was stashed there and jamming it into the back of my shorts. Then I turned away from the house full of memories, heading into the garage and snatching the keys for my Jeep from the hook before hurrying down the stairs.

The roof was down but I didn't care about that. I wanted to feel the rain on my flesh. I wanted to feel something other than the burn inside me which was fighting against all of my attempts to contain it.

I started up the engine and drove out of the garage without looking back.

The Harlequins guarding the gates stepped forward as if they had some idea to block my escape, so I just flattened my foot to the gas and smashed straight into the metal gates. The impact sent a spike of shock through my limbs but then I bounced over the fallen ironwork and tore away into the night with the yells of the Harlequins chasing me away.

I chose the most direct route across town while the rain picked up its intensity, pounding down on me and plastering my hair to my shoulders and my clothes to my flesh.

I focused on the feeling of it. Drowning all else out with the cold, wet sensation as I sped through the streets I'd once loved so dearly and headed for my end.

The blast of a horn forced me out of my endless turmoil and I glanced up to look in my mirror as a blue truck accelerated closer behind me, flashing their lights and blaring their horn in a clear demand for me to pull over.

My heart pounded as I just drove faster, ignoring the truck as its engine roared over the sound of the rain and I kept my gaze focused on my destination.

"Rogue!" Luther's voice bellowed over the snarl of the engines and crash of the rain and I glanced in my mirror again, seeing him behind the wheel, his features set into a determined snarl. "Pull the fucking car over before I have to make you!"

I didn't respond. There were no words that I could offer him anyway and my mind was made up, my destination drawing closer. I could end this. I had to end this.

I accelerated harder, taking the next bend so fast that my back wheels slid out on the wet tarmac. I righted the wheel with my heart in my throat as the blare of Luther's horn rang out over and over again.

But I was so close now. I couldn't stop. I just had to get there and the agony of this decision would be lifted from my shoulders. It would be too late to go back on it and I'd finally be able to do something good in my miserable life.

Luther yelled at me again but I only upped my speed, racing between the trees as I shot down the road. But as I took the next bend, Luther pulled out to overtake me, his truck's engine far more powerful than my own and for a brief moment, I looked at him as we drove neck and neck and the rain washed down on me.

The flare of headlights drew my attention to the road again as the blast of a horn alerted me to the truck coming the other way.

I screamed in alarm, jerking the wheel as Luther was forced towards me to avoid the collision. But my wheels had no traction on the saturated road and as Luther's truck clipped my back end, the world lurched out of my control.

The Jeep hit the verge and my stomach leapt up into my throat as the wheels lifted clean off the road. My knuckles turned white where I gripped the steering wheel and my foot slammed down on the brake despite some part of me knowing that it was already too late for that.

The world spun, the screech of brakes and crunch of glass and metal all I knew as the car flipped and I was tossed into the trees within it, fear capturing my heart in a vice and squeezing tightly. The airbags exploded in my face and I was pinned back against my chair for several long seconds before they deflated again and I found myself hanging upside down by my seatbelt.

I coughed out a curse as I unclipped myself and fell out of my seat, throwing my door open as I clambered out of the wreck and pushed myself upright, my body surprisingly intact after surviving that shit.

The blast of the truck's horn racing by sounded as the asshole kept on going down the road, leaving us here to rot and I silently wished a bloody death on him some time in the near future.

My head rang as I looked around for Luther's truck and I swallowed a lump in my throat as I spotted it wrapped around a tree a little way from me.

I stumbled over to it, drawing my gun hesitantly as fear crept along my spine and I found him slumped against the steering wheel with a trail of blood trickling down from his temple.

I leaned in close, pressing two fingers to his neck and sagging in relief as I located a pulse which was closely followed by a groan of pain escaping his lips.

His cell phone was clamped in a holder on the dash and I reached past him to grab it, holding it in front of his face and managing to unlock it with the face recognition. I quickly sent a message to his men, dropping a map pin where we were and telling them where to come help him before forwarding a photo of the wreck so they knew to hurry the fuck up.

But as I moved to drop the phone back into his lap, Luther stirred and caught my wrist, making me gasp as I tried to lurch back.

"Don't do this to them," Luther muttered. "Whatever the hell you think you're doing. Just don't."

I looked into his eyes, seeing all the pain of his past there and knowing that he feared me gifting it to his boys too. But he didn't understand. My leaving wasn't what was going to break them. It was me staying that would do that.

"I'm trying to save them," I breathed, but I was pretty sure he didn't even hear me as his eyes rolled back and his grip fell slack again.

I double checked his pulse to make sure he'd only passed out then turned and took off through the trees.

I scrambled back up to the road as the rain crashed over me and thunder broke across the heavens.

As soon as my feet hit the tarmac, I took off running, my destination so close now. The end of this almost on me.

But as I ran towards the looming gates, Luther's voice boomed out behind me, followed by a gunshot which carved a chunk out of the road a few feet to my left.

"Stop!" he bellowed and I skidded to a halt, turning to look back at him through the sheeting rain as he stood there in the road, one hand gripping his side while the other held the gun primed at me. "That's an order from your fucking boss."

I arched an eyebrow at his words, the Harlequin tattoo on the back of my thigh seeming to tighten like a leash around my soul. But I wasn't his puppet, and he wasn't going to be pulling my strings. I whipped my own gun from the back of my shorts and levelled it at him in return.

"You were right about me," I called to him over the storm. "You were right to get rid of me back then. I'm a curse just like you said. But now I'm going to fix it."

"I can't let you do that, wildcat," Luther warned, stumbling to one knee as I gripped the gun tighter.

"Don't make me pull the trigger," I said fiercely, my posture tightening. "Just let me go."

The gates behind me rattled open and though I didn't turn my head, I knew exactly who was closing in on me from behind. I could feel his presence like a cloak of darkness dropping over my shoulders.

"Well what do we have here?" Shawn called, his voice laced with excitement as he took in the scene and my fingers trembled slightly around the gun.

Luther's aim shifted to him and fear twisted through me as his upper lip peeled back in a warning.

"Back the fuck off, Shawn, or I'll be putting a bullet between your eyes," Luther warned.

"Well you're the ones who have shown up at my door in the middle of the night, waking the children and causing a ruckus. So I think I'm well within my rights to know what you're doing here, don't you, sugarpie?" His fingers brushed down my spine as he closed right in on me and a shiver of fear darted through me.

This was insane. I knew it. But I'd made my choice and I was going to stick to it.

"I'm home," I said roughly, forcing my tongue to bend around the words that were just for him. "Just like you wanted. So that you'll stop hurting everyone around me."

"Step away from her," Luther snarled, his arm shaking as he tried to hold his gun steady against the pain of his injuries.

"Nah. I don't think I will." The blast of a gunshot sounded right beside my ear and I screamed in alarm as my brain fought to catch up to what had happened.

Luther fell back with a sickening thump, the flare of headlights illuminating him from behind as he collapsed on the road with a snarl of agony as he slapped a hand over the wound to his stomach and Shawn chuckled darkly.

"Well, this is a nice surprise," he purred, reaching out to grasp my chin and make me look around at him at last.

His blue eyes found mine, the hunger in him clear to see as a wild smile filled his face and he drank in the sight of me, drawing every inch of my pain out of me so that he could view it in full.

"Look at you," he breathed, his fingers biting into my flesh. "All fucked up inside and ready to come begging for my forgiveness. Tell me, sweet cheeks, did it hurt real bad when you made the choice to come back to me?"

I held my silence as fear took me captive but something so much more intoxicating than that pushed its way into me as well and I gave into the madness of it as I swung my gun around and jammed it against his gut, wondering if I could end this even more simply than I'd planned.

But the cold kiss of his gun against my temple froze me solid as his smile grew.

"Stalemate," Shawn taunted, pressing himself forward so that my gun dug into his abs even harder. "But I like my chances better if we both pull the trigger."

"So now what?" I asked, my pulse hammering as I forced myself to hold the gaze of the man who'd tried to kill me not so long ago.

"Now you're gonna drop that thing or I'm gonna take my chances with us both firing."

I almost took him up on that. My finger tightening on the trigger with the desperate desire to just do it, let him take me from this place and bring him with me to end this shit once and for all. But I knew the devil before me, and I knew a gut shot wouldn't be the end of him. Which meant my death would serve no purpose. And the sad thing was that even now, knowing the life I was giving myself to, I still couldn't bring myself to choose death over it.

I released my weapon with a shuddering breath just as a bullet tore through the air and the approaching car roared towards us.

Shawn collided with me, taking me out before I could fully grasp what was happening and gunfire echoed through the sky as the Harlequins in the car and the Dead Dogs at the gates all opened fire on each other at once.

Shawn crowed with laughter while crushing me to the ground as the Harlequins' car skidded to a halt beside Luther who was pushing himself onto his hands knees and they threw a door open to haul him inside.

More shots were fired our way and Shawn leapt up, taking cover behind a tree and firing pot shots from behind it while Luther snarled my name, his teeth gritted against the pain of his wounds.

"Rogue! Get your ass in this car right now!" Luther demanded.

I pushed to my knees as I looked right back at him, seeing the determination flaring in his gaze as he moved to get back out of the car and make a grab for me despite the bleeding wound in his stomach.

But I couldn't allow that. I wouldn't. Because as soon as I was back in that house with those boys, the cycle would just start up again. I'd never be able to break it and I'd only end up breaking *them* which was more than my heart could allow.

So with a yell of refusal, I raised my gun at him and aimed a wide shot his way to warn him back. But Shawn had the same idea, lurching out of cover and firing his own gun, which hit Luther square in the chest, knocking him back into the car with a cry of pain and closing the final door on my old life. Fear cut into my soul. I could never head back there now. I'd just committed the cardinal sin and every Harlequin worth his salt would be out for my blood in retaliation for what I'd done by striking at their leader.

With a final scatter of gunfire, the Harlequins whirled the car around as they hunched around Luther's body in the backseat with grief filled screams, tearing away down the street and leaving silence in their wake. Horror crept up my spine as the reality sank in. Luther Harlequin was most likely dead. And I'd brought him here, which made me responsible. Why couldn't he have just let me go? Why couldn't he have fucking listened?

A hand closed over mine and the gun was tugged from my grip as I just stared after the taillights, watching my last shot at the life I'd always hungered for tear away from me and cement this decision irrevocably.

"Well, well, well, it looks like you really are ready to start repenting for your sins with me, aren't you, sugarpie?" Shawn purred in my ear as he held out a hand for me, waiting for me to take it and let him lead me inside.

I gave myself one single second to feel it. My love for the four boys who had been mine for as long as I could remember. The joy I felt in their arms, the safety I found in their embraces and the pleasure they gifted my body. All of it made me ache and burn with need until I was sure I would combust with the heat of it.

I loved them so hard it hurt. It had been hurting for ten long, lonely years and now I knew why. Because it was too much and the cost of it was too high. I'd stolen a taste of something which I could never afford to keep and now it was time for me to pay up. The Devil didn't care for my money though, no matter how much I could steal. He just wanted my soul in payment for theirs and though it was a battered, broken thing, I was willing to sacrifice it for them. And all I could hope was that it would be enough.

With a deep breath, I cast aside my love for them and let the rain wash it from my flesh. It was beyond time for me to accept my lot in life and this was it. I was the girl who didn't get to claim love or live a pretty dream, I was the one no one wanted but too many craved. I was the stain on this place of sunshine and lost dreams. And now I was the sacrifice required for their chance at peace.

I stepped through the gates and placed my hand into Shawn's, sucking in a breath as he dragged me against his chest with a wide smile claiming his chiselled features.

"Oh, sugarpie, I've missed you so," he murmured, his gaze dropping down to take in the press of my nipples against JJ's shirt which the rain was making cling to my skin.

"Promise me you'll stop the war like you said you would," I growled, knowing I had very few chips to play with but banking on this one piece to be worth enough.

"Cross my heart and hope to die," Shawn swore, painting a cross over the void in his chest which should have held a heart. "So long as you play nice with me. So what do you say? Are you ready to be a good girl for me?"

A shudder ran down my spine as I forced all of my emotions and heartache away and gave myself back to the emptiness I'd existed in for so long before coming back here. I could be that girl again. I would do it for them. So as that numbness crept over me and I accepted my lot in the world once and for all, I nodded.

"Yes," I breathed, ignoring the fears which clung to my skin with the passing of that word from my lips. "I'm yours."

CHAPTER FORTY FIVE

My oh my, what a day to fucking rejoice. My sugarpie was home and ripe for the breaking. She was all sharp tongue and backbone these days and I'd been getting hard just thinking about crushing her spirit. Mia had been a fun toy for a while, but Rogue Easton was the Buzz Lightyear of toys and I planned on inking my name onto her foot, so she knew exactly who she belonged to.

For now, I'd bide my time, play the long game as I started to wear at her walls, find paths beneath her flesh again. It was a fine art, one I'd honed and crafted over the years. I always sensed the broken ones and their weakness for love. They had a desperate desire to be needed, to have a constant place to rest their heads and be part of something. And I provided that all while inching them toward a state of insecurity, making sure the only compliments they ever believed were the ones that came from my lips and knowing that I could strip down their confidence with nothing but a single cutting word.

Mm, yeah, I was gonna like having Rogue on her knees again. I'd break her fully this time, give her my undivided attention. When I'd had her before, I'd been busy building up The Dead Dogs and fucking anything that moved when she wasn't around. But now? My cock was aching to be buried in the subservient pussy of my greatest challenge. She wasn't going to easily let me in again, but I knew how to play this. I'd be sweet and tender, mixed with nasty and cold. I'd make sure I was the hand that fed and the hand that took away. And when she realised I was the master of her universe, she'd come to heel.

Because I wasn't all about destruction, I liked feeding pretty broken girls sweet words too. I liked seeing their eyes light up when I gave them my attention and I especially liked when they begged to please me. I'd make her happy just as soon as she realised I was her god, and the faster she got to serving me, the faster she'd get to enjoying it.

I adjusted my hard dick in my jeans as I walked out across the Rosewood grounds with a stick of good ol' fashion dynamite in my hand and a celebratory cigar wedged between my lips.

I was wearing a couple of Kaiser's gold chain necklaces and a silk red shirt that did wonders for my skin tone, thank you kindly. His wardrobe was eclectic to say the least, and I found I rather liked wearing my exuberance on the outside as well as the in.

I walked to the graveyard at the edge of the property and flicked my cigar butt away across the headstones as I started whistling. It was a beautiful night for disarray, the storm still thick in the air, though the rain had eased to a light drizzle now which clung to my hair. Thunder grumbled in the distance as I made it to the huge stone crypt and smirked at its grey walls.

Now that Rogue was home, it was time to set some more balls of destruction in motion. I'd been holding off on cracking into this place because I'd wanted to be in the right mood, and now my spirits were at their highest and I was feeling all kinds of ready to see what secrets lay within its walls.

I lay the stick of dynamite on the ground by the door, taking out Chase Cohen's Zippo lighter and lighting up the dynamite fuse before backing the fuck up.

I sheltered behind a large headstone, ducking my head as the flame sizzled down to the stick and…*boom!*

"Woo-wee!" I hooted as the stone door was blasted to shit and rubble cascaded through the air.

I stood upright, taking my time as I swaggered into the dark space beyond the blasted door and used the lighter to see what was hiding in here.

There were bags of stuff stashed around the tomb, but my gaze hooked on a red ribbon poking out of a wooden box on top of the stone sarcophagus. I moved toward it, pinching it between my finger and thumb and gazing down into the box. The ribbon was attached to an old medallion with the symbol of the Castillo Cartel on it. My jaw went slack as memories stirred in my mind over that name and I gazed down at the other objects in the box with disbelief and utter fucking joy running through me.

Well my, my, fucking my. This is one helluva jackpot.

"You naughty, naughty kids," I purred, smirking triumphantly at my prize. "I've got you by the balls now."

I glanced back at the door, making sure none of my men were lurking on me out there, wanting to keep this little secret mine until I figured out what to do with it. This day was getting better and fucking better.

I was now the keeper of one very dirty truth. And it was mine to do what I pleased with. So help the motherfucking Harlequins, I almost felt sorry for them, because I was their goddamn apocalypse.

But oh, what a way they were gonna go out.

AUTHOR'S NOTE

Well, well, well, what do we have here? Looks like a reader cursing our names and wondering why you read our books again while priming yourself up for the next rollercoaster all at once.

Oh, sorry, I went a bit Shawn on you there.

Umm.

So what I meant to say was, heyyyy are you okay? I hope so. Because we get no satisfaction from gathering your tears into our jars of sustenance – although I will admit they do help fuel the next book, so maybe there's a silver lining to all of the betrayal, heartache and general carnage we gifted you in this book.

Sorry for Chase's eye.

Funny story about that – Caroline had this big secret plan for what she wanted to happen to him at the end of the last book and she refused to tell me what it was going to be, wanting me to give her the raw reaction so that we could decide if it was going too far or not. Then I was driving along one day, singing Disney songs with the kids as standard (Come challenge me to sing You're Welcome one time and then you'll see where my real talents lie btw) and it just occurred to me that Shawn would probably go in hard with someone he was torturing so I suggested to Caroline that he take an eye. WHICH TURNED OUT TO BE HER SECRET PLAN ALREADY!!!! Kapow. The sister mind meld strikes again. So of course at that point his fate was written, his eye was doomed and fucking Shawn won once more.

Then again, you did all say you wanted him to suffer hard following the end of Sinners' Playground, so some might say you reap what you sow. Anywho, he clearly still hasn't suffered enough and I guess he's out there somewhere now, living a new life as a dairy farmer, hand milking cows and goats until his fingers cramp. Let's hope he doesn't cry into the milk and make it all salty though.

Speaking of salty, I wonder how the rest of the Harlequin boys are feeling right about now? Hmmmmmm….

Guess you'll have to come stalk us for the next book to find that out. And don't worry, the wait won't be long, but if you want to be sure you're the first to hear about the release of book 4 then sign up for our newsletter here and join our reader group here.

And most importantly of all – we love you, we thank you for reading despite our somewhat evil tendencies and we can't wait to give you more of our words soooon.

Love Susanne & Caroline x

ALSO BY
CAROLINE PECKHAM
&
SUSANNE VALENTI

Brutal Boys of Everlake Prep
(Complete Reverse Harem Bully Romance Contemporary Series)
Kings of Quarantine
Kings of Lockdown
Kings of Anarchy
Queen of Quarantine
**

Dead Men Walking
(Reverse Harem Dark Romance Contemporary Series)
The Death Club
Society of Psychos
**

The Harlequin Crew
(Reverse Harem Mafia Romance Contemporary Series)
Sinners Playground
Dead Man's Isle
Carnival Hill
Paradise Lagoon

Harlequinn Crew Novellas
Devil's Pass
**

Dark Empire
(Dark Mafia Contemporary Standalones)

Beautiful Carnage

Beautiful Savage

**

The Ruthless Boys of the Zodiac

(Reverse Harem Paranormal Romance Series - Set in the world of Solaria)

Dark Fae

Savage Fae

Vicious Fae

Broken Fae

Warrior Fae

Zodiac Academy

(M/F Bully Romance Series- Set in the world of Solaria, five years after Dark

Fae)

The Awakening

Ruthless Fae

The Reckoning

Shadow Princess

Cursed Fates

Fated Thrones

Heartless Sky

The Awakening - As told by the Boys

Zodiac Academy Novellas

Origins of an Academy Bully

The Big A.S.S. Party

Darkmore Penitentiary

(Reverse Harem Paranormal Romance Series - Set in the world of Solaria,

ten years after Dark Fae)

Caged Wolf

Alpha Wolf

Feral Wolf

**

The Age of Vampires

(Complete M/F Paranormal Romance/Dystopian Series)

Eternal Reign

Eternal Shade

Eternal Curse

Eternal Vow

Eternal Night

Eternal Love

**

Cage of Lies

(M/F Dystopian Series)

Rebel Rising

**

Tainted Earth

(M/F Dystopian Series)

Afflicted

Altered

Adapted

Advanced

**

The Vampire Games

(Complete M/F Paranormal Romance Trilogy)

V Games

V Games: Fresh From The Grave

V Games: Dead Before Dawn

*

The Vampire Games: Season Two

(Complete M/F Paranormal Romance Trilogy)

Wolf Games

Wolf Games: Island of Shade

Wolf Games: Severed Fates

*

The Vampire Games: Season Three
Hunter Trials
*

The Vampire Games Novellas
A Game of Vampires
**

The Rise of Issac
(Complete YA Fantasy Series)
Creeping Shadow
Bleeding Snow
Turning Tide
Weeping Sky
Failing Light